IN THE CROSSHAIRS

If Paladin tried to climb they'd be all over him. So whatever was going to happen it was going to be low. Belly-grinding low.

"Come and get me, you bastards."

The Avengers couldn't line up for a shot unless they were diving straight toward him. He pushed the yoke forward, hugged the sandy hills, and raced past rocks and trees—not giving them a static target. If they wanted a shot at him they'd have to come down and play in the dirt, where the agile flying wing might have an advantage over the more cumbersome Avengers.

Paladin glanced backward. Four planes were falling fast after him. Two more were staying high, presumably acting as spotters and radioing his position back to their friends.

A stream of magnesium bullets blazed over his head and a smoky trail of a rocket appeared, detonating against a rocky outcropping just a few feet from his nose.

They wanted him all right. Bad enough to risk their necks getting as close to the ground as he was. Good. He looked back. A pair of the Avengers slowly dropped behind him; they almost had him lined up in their sights. . . .

Books published by The Ballantine Publishing Group are available at quantity discounts on bulk purchases for premium, educational, fund-raising, and special sales use. For details, please call 1-800-733-3000.

CRIMSON SKIES

**ERIC NYLUND,
MICHAEL B. LEE,
NANCY BERMAN,
AND ERIC S. TRAUTMANN**

BALLANTINE BOOKS • NEW YORK

A Del Rey® Book
Published by The Ballantine Publishing Group
Copyright © 2002 by Microsoft Corporation

www.delreydigital.com

ISBN 0-345-45874-5

Cover painting by Stephen Daniele

Manufactured in the United States of America

First Edition: October 2002

OPM   10   9   8   7   6   5   4   3   2   1

22438

Acknowledgments

PAST

Crimson Skies owes a tremendous debt to the pulp writers of yesterday—most notably: Lester Dent, Walter Gibson, R.T.M. Scott, and Robert J. Hogan.

PRESENT

The original creators of the *Crimson Skies* setting: Dave McCoy and Jordan Weisman; Vic Bonilla, Derek Carroll, Loren Coleman, Chris Hartford, John Howard, Tom Peters, and Michael A. Stackpole; and the current torchbearers: Brannon W. Boren, Geoff Skellams, Clay Griffith, Noah Dudley, and Brian Lowe; and Microsoft's Franchise Development Group (Nancy Figatner and Doug Zartman).

FUTURE

Finally, special thanks are due to the *Crimson Skies: High Road To Revenge*™ development team at Microsoft/Ironworks. Singled out for conspicuous gallantry are: Scot Bayless, Stephen Daniele, Jim Deal, Irvin Gee, John Hermanowski, Rob Olson, and Jack Turk.

Contents

Introduction: Where Were *You?*

I was standing on the fiftieth floor of the Chrysler Building—drinking champagne I could barely afford and dancing with a beautiful blonde—when the United States fell apart.

It was a quarter past midnight, and 1929 had just given way to 1930. The Chrysler Building's night watchman, Gus, was a pal, and he let my "companion" and me into the construction site. We rode the elevator to the fiftieth floor. (The other floors were still being built, and wouldn't be completed until later that year.) "See you later," Gus said with a wink, then rode the elevator back down to the lobby.

The night was perfect. The nation was filled with hope for the future. As a nation, we were digging ourselves out of the blues that the Great War (and subsequent influenza epidemics) had caused. Sure, we had our differences, but this was "one nation, indivisible." Ringing in the New Year, from within a crowning symbol of what American ingenuity could create, just felt . . . right.

At 12:22 A.M., the elevator reached the fiftieth floor and Gus stepped out, his face pale. I was about to protest—he'd told me the girl and I could hang around for a couple of hours, and things were just starting to get interesting. "Come on, Gus," I said. "What's the big idea?"

"Texas just . . . seceded," Gus croaked. "I heard it on the radio. They just up an' quit."

I bolted for the elevator, leaving the champagne, Gus, and the girl behind.

I had been working as a stringer for a number of newspapers all around New York City. I was still small potatoes in the journalism game, but I'd had a couple of big scoops now and then. The editor over at Sentinel Publications liked me; I'd done a nice piece on a corrupt city councilman for him.

I had to get to a typewriter, to a telephone, to anything so I could find out what happened. The Sentinel Publications building was six blocks away.

When I got there, the room was filled with veteran reporters. Normally, when a big story broke, the room would be choked with cigar smoke and bustling with the din of typewriters and raised voices.

Tonight, the room was silent, save for the voice of a shocked radio announcer: ". . . as of 12:01 A.M., January the first, nineteen hundred and thirty, the state of Texas has seceded from the United States of America."

There had been noises for weeks from Texas, threats of secession from the good ol' U.S. of A. The men in the room who had covered the story just dismissed the ultimatums as typical Texas bluster. No one really believed that an entire state—especially one the size of Texas—would *actually* declare independence from the United States. It was ridiculous. Ludicrous.

It had just happened.

If I had to name the biggest cause of the breakup, I'd have to say Freedom to Drink. The Federal initiative to ban alcohol had failed a few years back (thanks to a fresh outbreak of influenza, one that many blamed on our adventures in Europe during the Great War). Voters stayed away from the polls during the prior election, and a strong wave of states' rights platforms won out. Now, each state determined for itself if it was "wet" or "dry"—if liquor was legal or illegal.

One of the first stories I covered didn't get a lot of press up north, but was a big deal in the southern states: the Bluefield Incident.

It was 1924, and the "bootlegger brushfires" were just heating up. Kentucky and West Virginia actually ended up in a brief shooting war with Virginia and North Carolina. At stake was control of the Appalachians, the source of a large percentage of illegal alcohol that was smuggled north.

The Virginia National Guard captured a large Kentucky

convoy outside the town of Bluefield, only to discover that their prize was a Kentucky guard unit running alcohol out of the Appalachians toward the West Virginia border.

Though the courts maintained that the whole mess was in Kentucky's jurisdiction, the men involved were tried and jailed in Virginia on a number of charges—some legitimate, but most just trumped-up nonsense. Virginia refused Kentucky's request to transfer the men back to their home state, and later rejected a similar "suggestion" from Washington, D.C.

Only under the threat of U.S. Army intervention did Virginia finally release the prisoners to federal authorities, almost two years after their capture.

I can't say for certain, but I believe that the Feds moving in and dealing with the problem made secession inevitable. Texas was just the first to fall, and when it left the Union, others quickly followed suit. Soon, the Federal government lost ground; now, only the tiny nation of Columbia—Washington, D.C., with a small amount of Virginia and Maryland territory thrown in—is all that remains of the once-proud United States.

The new North American nations are an eclectic mix, from Pacifica and the Nation of Hollywood in the west, to the Empire State, the Maritime Provinces, and the Confederation of Dixie in the east. The Christian Communist nation, the People's Collective, dominates the central United States, along with its capitalist arch-rival along the Great Lakes, the Industrial States of America.

North America's love of airplanes—rooted in the exotic, adventurous mystique surrounding them—became a matter of necessity as trade between the new North American independent nations ground to a halt. The intercontinental railway system was no longer viable since the rails now crossed hostile national borders. The automobile gave way to gyrotaxis, aerobuses, and large cargo zeppelins that commanded the sky lines and made trade possible between friendly nations.

Shortly after zeppelin trade routes were established, the first "air pirates" captured the public eye. Generally small, disorganized bands of thrill-seekers and publicity hounds, these pirates began crime sprees that would inspire others to follow in their footsteps years later.

Which brings me to Nathan Zachary and his own gang of air pirates, the Fortune Hunters. Zachary is one of many air bandits, a man with a reputation for bravery, daring, and intelligence—a flamboyant Robin Hood for the modern aero-age.

He's a thief and a grifter, to be sure. He's a wanted man in many nations, both in North America and abroad. Still, Zachary's exploits have captured the public eye. He never steals from those who can't afford it, and he refuses to harm the innocent during his crimes.

They say a man is judged by the quality of his opponents. If this is true, then Nathan Zachary is at the top of his game; his opponents are formidable, indeed. *Spicy Air Tales* is pleased to present the following trio of tales, which showcases Nathan Zachary and his foes.

Perhaps one of the most dangerous enemies a pirate faces in the skies of North America is Paladin Blake—a dedicated pirate fighter, bent on ridding the skies of crime. Today, Blake is a wealthy captain of industry, respected across North America. But before he tangled with Nathan Zachary, before he became the continent's premier air security ace, he was a down-on-his-luck pilot, struggling to keep his business afloat.

Strap in, throttle up, and enjoy "Paladin Blake and the Case of the Phantom Prototype."

—NERO MACLEON
Editor in Chief, *Spicy Air Tales*
Manhattan, 1938

Paladin Blake and the Case of the Phantom Prototype

From the Files of Blake Aviation Security

by Eric Nylund

1: Bourbon and Red Ink

Paladin Blake took a bottle of bourbon from his desk
drawer. He grabbed two glasses from the watercooler, set
them on his blotter, and opened the bottle. This was the ritual
he performed after every assignment.

No ritual, though, would save Blake Aviation Security
from bankruptcy.

Sunlight and fresh air streamed through his office window.
Paladin watched the sun set behind the Santa Monica pier.
The view cost him a bundle in overhead. He lowered the
blinds.

With a steady hand, he poured the twelve-year-old bourbon
into the glasses. He set one by the photograph of his father.
"Here you go, you old bootlegger."

In the picture, his father sat on the wing of his plane, a
pistol in one hand. In the other hand, the elder Blake held a
bottle identical to the one on Paladin's desk.

"And here's to coming home alive."

This last assignment had been a peach. Only one of his
planes had been shot down. Pretty good, considering Blake
Aviation Security had put five pirates into the drink delivering silver bullion to the Kingdom of Hawai'i. The payoff
had been considerable.

For every success, however, there were two assignments
that lost money because of hospital bills, repairs, maintenance for his fleet of a dozen aircraft . . . and checks sent to
his pilots' widows. Paladin was pouring money into his company by the bucketful.

He pulled out the company ledger and sighed. Red ink tattooed its pages.

Paladin cradled his glass of bourbon, warming it until he could smell the smoky aroma. He clinked the glass to his father's. "Don't worry, Dad. No matter what it takes, I'll get every last one of them for you. Even if it means doing it alone."

He poured the two glasses back into the bottle, then put it away. The ritual was over.

Running Blake Aviation Security hadn't always been like this. Every day, though, the job grew harder. There were more pirates in the air, and, as improbable as it seemed, they were becoming bolder. From Maine to Hollywood to Alaska—the skies were heating to a boil.

Paladin stared at the bleeding ledger. There *had* to be a way to squeeze a profit from these numbers.

The intercom buzzed. "Mr. Blake?" his secretary asked. "There's a Mr. Justin here to see you."

"Tell him to make an appointment."

"Mr. Justin?" she repeated. ". . . representing the Lockheed Corporation?"

Paladin lost his place in the columns and rows. "You said 'Lockheed'?"

"Yes."

A corporation like Lockheed could mean, for once, a fat profit margin. The boost in prestige couldn't hurt Blake Aviation Security, either. It could lead to other corporate clients— real money. Maybe enough to finally get his company off the ground.

But he was getting ahead of himself. He didn't know what Lockheed wanted. "Send him in."

Paladin quickly slipped on his suspenders, tucked in his shirt, and ran his fingers through his hair. He stood and slammed the ledger shut.

The office door opened. A man paused in the doorway. He was seven feet tall if he was an inch, and he had to turn his wide shoulders to clear the door frame. Paladin had never seen a size sixty-four Italian-cut suit before—enough navy blue wool to make a tent. The color of his gray silk tie matched his pointed beard. Bushy brows arched over his blue eyes.

"Paladin Blake?" There was a richness to his voice, a slight Slavic accent. "I am Peter Justin." He extended a hand that engulfed Paladin's as they shook.

"What can I do for you, Mr. Justin?" Paladin gestured to a padded chair.

Justin gracefully sat. "Lockheed has business for you, Mr. Blake. Security business."

"Good," Paladin said. "Great." He slowly sank into his chair, then added, "But Lockheed has its own security. Why use us?"

"I am well aware of Lockheed's security resources, Mr. Blake. I am in charge of them." Justin reached into his coat and removed a sterling cigarette case, opened it, and offered one to Paladin.

"No, thanks," Paladin said.

Justin took a cigarette for himself. "Lockheed requires an outsider for this particular assignment, an outsider with an impeccable record and a reputation for discretion. In short, we need *you*."

"I see," Paladin said, not really seeing anything, but managing to sound nonchalant. "Tell me about it."

"A simple matter," Justin replied and rolled his unlit cigarette between his fingers. "Two months ago, parts for a new aircraft disappeared from our Pasadena facility. Last week, the blueprints disappeared from our vault—then reappeared. We are concerned that a prototype we recently constructed will vanish next. So we want you to fly this prototype."

Paladin held up his hand. "I'm no test pilot. I'm a good combat pilot, but you need—"

"There is no testing involved. The plane is quite airworthy, I assure you. All we require from you is to deliver the plane to our secure base in the Mojave Desert." He fished into his coat pocket again, this time retrieving a slender notebook and gold fountain pen.

"You see," Justin said, leaning forward, "we cannot afford to trust anyone at Pasadena. The mechanics, engineers, even our test pilots could have been responsible for the previous thefts. This completed prototype will be a tempting target."

"I didn't know Lockheed had an airfield in the Mojave Desert."

"Few do," Justin replied. "Which is another reason to employ someone with your reputation for discretion." He opened his notebook and scrawled on it. He tore off a sheet and pushed it across the desk. "The first half of our payment to Blake Aviation Security."

Paladin scrutinized the note. It was a Lockheed corporate check drawing on assets from the First Bank of Hollywood. There was a line of zeros neatly arranged after the first number in the amount box.

After a moment, Justin cleared his throat. "Mr. Blake? I trust the amount is adequate?"

Paladin's mouth was suddenly dry. "Yes. Adequate." He swallowed and got his bearings. "For this kind of money, though, I assume you expect trouble?"

"No, Mr. Blake. I expect this kind of money will buy Lockheed a decided lack of trouble."

Paladin looked again at the number on the check. It was too good to be true—especially for a quick run over the San Bernardino Mountains. Or maybe there was no catch. Maybe this is exactly what he needed: a juicy contract.

Even if there was a catch, Justin was playing his cards close to his vest. If Blake Aviation Security didn't take the job, Justin could find a dozen other outfits to take his money.

"I assure you, Mr. Justin, Blake Aviation Security can handle any trouble."

"Excellent." Justin stood and smoothed his suit. "I knew we could do business. Meet me at five o'clock at the Pasadena airfield."

"My team and I will be there."

Justin crinkled his bushy eyebrows. "You misunderstood me, Mr. Blake." He set his still-unlit cigarette in the ashtray. "You—and you alone—are required. At the last minute, you will replace our test pilot on tomorrow's scheduled flight. Additional planes will only draw unwanted attention."

Cloak-and-dagger operations weren't exactly Paladin's style. He preferred force to stealth—preferably the force of a heavily armed squadron of his best fighter pilots.

But what choice did he really have?

"Okay," Paladin said. "It's your show. I'll be there like you want. Alone."

"I shall make the arrangements." Justin shook Paladin's hand again, then turned and closed the door behind him so softly that Paladin didn't hear it click shut.

Paladin's eye fell upon the unlit cigarette Justin had left in the ashtray. It was one of those black European deals, expensive and hard to get since the collapse of the United States.

Big money or not, something didn't sit right. Lockheed wouldn't dole out this kind of cash unless they thought they'd get a good return on their investment. And why, if Justin couldn't trust his people, was he trusting Blake Aviation Security? Paladin knew his outfit was small potatoes.

He picked up the phone and dialed. It rang six times before someone answered.

"Dash? Get out of bed. I *know* you just got off a deadline. Look, I need a favor, some information. Find Jimmy the Rap and meet me at the Club Gorgeio, say ten o'clock? Good."

Paladin hung up, then buzzed his secretary. "Dust off my tuxedo. I've got business tonight."

Out of the corner of his eye, Paladin spied the picture of his father. It looked like the old bootlegger was laughing at him.

The Club Gorgeio was packed with wall-to-wall tuxedos, slinky sequined evening gowns, and buxom waitresses laden with trays of cocktails. A haze of smoke gave the air a velvet texture. The band played "Hop Off."

Paladin, Dashiell, and Jimmy the Rap sat at a secluded corner table. Paladin told them about his visit this afternoon.

"I dropped by the First Bank of Hollywood," Paladin said. "Got a friend to run the check's serial numbers. They verified Justin's signature. It's legit."

Dashiell tapped out a cigarette and lit up. "I don't like it, Paladin." He puffed once. "It doesn't add up."

Dashiell wore a La Blanca tuxedo, the same label as Paladin, only he managed to make it look like a million bucks. It hadn't a crease or a speck of dust on it. His hair was slicked back, and his pencil-thin mustache was perfectly trimmed.

At the opposite end of the fashion spectrum was Jimmy the Rap. Jimmy fidgeted, uncomfortable and out of place in his two-bit tweed suit and crumpled tie. He finished his second drink in a single gulp.

"Doesn't add up how?" Paladin asked.

Two years ago, Dashiell had been a stringer for *Air Action Weekly*—a starving writer working under a pseudonym, in desperate need of money until his "serious" projects paid off. Paladin put him to work checking the backgrounds of his clients and the competition, since Dashiell had a flair for research . . . and a nose for treachery. Later, when he hit it big with book deals and movie screenplays, suddenly everyone was his friend, from mobsters to studio executives to starlets.

His good fortune, though, was Paladin's, too. Just as Dashiell had used Paladin's real-life escapades for his fiction, Paladin now used Dashiell's connections and smarts as a writer to solve real mysteries.

"It doesn't add up," Dashiell said, "because Mr. Peter Justin, aka Piotr 'Neyasvy' Pushkarev, is an ace pilot."

"I never heard of him," Paladin replied.

"You wouldn't have." Dashiell tapped the ashes off his cigarette. "He was a hero of the Russian revolution. That is, a hero, if you were a White Russian. His family escaped to Alaska, but not before the Reds got some of them. He made a name for himself up there before Lockheed hired him . . . or so I've heard." Dashiell waved his cigarette in a flamboyant gesture. "You're a pilot, Paladin. Maybe you can tell me why someone like that would give up his prize aircraft?"

"He wouldn't," Paladin muttered.

Dashiell turned to Jimmy. "What about these stolen parts? What's the word on the street?"

Jimmy slid out of his chair and took a step toward the exit.

Paladin set a hand on Jimmy the Rap's shoulder, pushing him back into his seat.

The "Rap" part of Jimmy's name came from his pair of stints in prison. In both cases, he could have spilled his guts and walked away clean. The fact that he refused to rat out his former associates had earned him the reputation of being a man who kept his mouth shut—he was willing to take the rap.

It made him a valuable middleman to the shadier businessmen of Hollywood.

Jimmy walked a tightrope, though. One word from Dashiell to Jimmy's parole officer and he'd be off the streets until his hair was gray. One slipup with his employers, and he'd be off the streets permanently.

Paladin pressed a twenty into Jimmy's sweaty palm. "The parts?"

Jimmy's gaze darted around the room, then settled on Paladin. "These ain't no spark plugs that got taken. We're talking engine blocks, a spare fuselage, and some sorta aerobrake."

"So who bought them?" Dashiell asked.

Paladin slid his untouched scotch to Jimmy.

Jimmy downed it. "That's the strange thing," he said. "The guys with the brains to fence something that big—Icepick Marvin, the Weston Brothers—they've all taken vacations . . . real sudden-like."

"That doesn't make sense," Paladin said.

"Unfortunately, it does," Dashiell replied. "Someone big engineered these thefts from Lockheed. It stands to reason someone just as big wants to purchase the items. Someone big enough to make Jimmy's nastier associates think twice about getting involved."

"So what do you suggest?" Paladin asked.

"I'm going up to Santa Barbara for the weekend. You, my dear Paladin, are in way over your head. I suggest you tag along and take a vacation, too."

"I know I'm in over my head," Paladin whispered. "Way over. But if Blake Aviation Security is ever going to be more than a small-time operation, I've got to get in that deep." He stood.

"Thanks for the information and the advice, Dashiell. You'll have to excuse me, though. I've got a plane to fly in the morning."

2: A Wing and a Prayer

The sun wasn't up yet. Paladin fumbled in the dark until his hands found his bag and parachute in the aerotaxi's trunk.

The driver craned his head out the window. "You need a hand, buddy?"

"Got it," Paladin said. He slung his chute over his shoulder and paid the driver.

"Lots of flyboys showing up here lately," the driver said. "They all bring their chutes. Don't Lockheed have the bucks to spring for you guys?"

"Sure they do," Paladin said. "But when there's nothing between you and the ground except a mile of air, would you trust someone else to pack your silk?"

"Point taken," the driver said. He started to roll up his window.

"Wait." Paladin passed the driver a dollar tip. "When did a lot of pilots show up here?"

"A week ago." The taxi driver pocketed the dollar. "Maybe a dozen. All flyboys . . . either that or parachute salesmen."

"Thanks," Paladin replied. He marched to the security shack at the eastern gate.

Pilots with their own chutes meant independent operators. Why was Justin hiring more outsiders? Was he rotating his test pilots regularly because he didn't trust anyone? Paladin filed that under "miscellaneous curiosities." He'd ask later.

The guard inside the shack tracked Paladin's approach with an unwavering glare.

"John Smith to see Mr. Justin," Blake said, using the phony

name Justin had insisted on. He felt like a heel, just saying the name. John Smith—real original.

"You're expected." The guard made a check on his clipboard. He lifted the barricade and waved Paladin through. The guard then handed him a brass key. "Pilots' lockers are there." He pointed to the nearest hangar.

Paladin stole a glance at the clipboard. The only thing written on the page was his phony name.

"Got it," Paladin said, and started toward the hangar.

Through the slowly dissipating fog, Paladin saw a dozen other hangars, and in the distance, the gray outlines of two zeppelin aerodromes. A hundred planes were precisely parked on the tarmac: every make of bomber and fighter, even a fleet of autogyros. There were no people, though. Sure, it was five o'clock in the morning, but there should be mechanics or guards . . . *someone*. The place was a ghost town.

Paladin entered the hangar. On the other side of a row of gleaming P2 Warhawks was a building, presumably the pilots' locker room.

"Hello?"

Only an echo answered.

It wasn't too late to accept Dashiell's offer: a weekend of starlets and sailing in Santa Barbara. But that wouldn't bring in the cash he needed to save Blake Aviation Security.

No. This setup may be getting weirder by the second, but Paladin couldn't afford to lose the job. He chalked up his growing unease to preflight jitters.

Paladin walked into the changing room. There were showers and rows of large lockers with benches. He examined the brass key the guard had given him. Stamped on it was A303. He found locker A303 and opened it. Inside hung a flight suit and a fur-lined jacket; there were gloves, leather helmet, goggles, a steel lunch box, and a new parachute. The flight suit had a Lockheed logo embroidered on the back, and the name JOHNNY stitched on the right front pocket.

Paladin slipped into the suit, jacket, and gloves. They were a perfect fit.

"Mr. Blake?"

Peter Justin stood in the doorway—or rather, his body

filled the doorway. He wore a gray suit, green tie, and he looked crisp and fresh. "If you could don the helmet, as well— in case anyone spots us?"

Paladin put on the helmet and goggles.

"Our time is limited," Justin said, "so please follow me." He turned and strode away.

Paladin picked up his bag, the lunch pail, and his own parachute, kicked the locker shut, then trotted after the big Russian.

He caught up to Justin on the tarmac. "I admire your thoroughness," Paladin said. "No one here but the one guard at the gate. The prearranged equipment. Like clockwork. If I didn't know better, I'd say you had the fix in on the fog, too, just to keep everything under wraps."

"I also took the liberty of packing you a lunch," Justin said, without pause in his gigantic stride. "A thermos of coffee and two sandwiches, one jelly and peanut butter, and one liverwurst. I was unsure which you preferred." He pointed into the fog. "There she is."

Paladin squinted, and saw a plane's silhouette . . . at least the wing of a plane.

No. It was *all* wing. It reminded Paladin of the Ravenscroft Coyote—the mainstay of the Navajo and Lakota air militias. Unlike the Coyote, which sported a single "pusher" prop, this bird had engines mounted on the leading edge. The cockpit was a bubble in the center of the craft, and twin .30-caliber guns were mounted underneath. There were control flaps along the wing, but it lacked anything that resembled a rudder.

"You can't be serious," Paladin said. "It'll spin out of control."

"No, Mr. Blake, it will not. The controls are sensitive, but they function quite well. Rolls-Royce developed the concept, but they never pursued the design. We recently purchased their patent."

Paladin walked around the plane. Something else was wrong. He stepped back and figured it out. The proportions were out of kilter. The plane had huge engines, a tiny fuselage, and limited control surfaces. It was all power. Maneuvering wouldn't be difficult; it would be impossible.

"Has this thing even been *flown* before?"

Justin laughed. "Many times. It is safe." He crinkled his bushy brows together. "Assuming the pilot is sufficiently skilled. You are not having second thoughts, are you?"

Paladin had been having third, fourth, and fifth thoughts about this job since he met Peter Justin. "No," he said. "No second thoughts."

"My ground crew inspected her last night. I have personally double-checked their assessment."

Paladin climbed onto the wing and slid back the canopy. Inside, wires spilled out of empty sockets where some of the gauges had been ripped out. Sections of the floor were exposed, revealing the guns and the landing gear struts.

"Someone hasn't finished putting this thing together."

"It is a *working* prototype, Mr. Blake, not a finished product. Certain amenities have been overlooked. The plane, however, is eminently airworthy. Now—" He removed a map from his pocket. "—if you could give me your attention."

Paladin stowed his gear in the cockpit and climbed down.

Justin unfolded a map of southern Hollywood. "I have traced your route. You will cross the mountains here." He smoothed his thumb over a red line on the paper. "If you experience problems, you are to immediately land at the Palmdale airstrip, or at Palm Springs, should you end up farther east. As a last resort there is the dry lake bed." He circled a large region outlined in yellow. "If you experience any difficulties, call for help on the channel marked *B*. We will abandon the secrecy of this mission and send a squadron to retrieve you."

Paladin followed the route. It ended in the middle of nowhere. "And Lockheed's secure facility is here?"

"Yes. You will receive the balance of your fee upon landing. Is this acceptable?"

"Sure." Paladin frowned. "No, not quite acceptable. Can I ask you a personal question, Mr. Justin?"

Justin glanced at his watch. "A quick one."

"I've always made it a point to know my clients. I mean,

know who they *really* are. Your real name isn't Peter Justin—
it's Piotr Pushkarev. You fought in the Russian Revolution on
the side of the Whites and earned the nickname Neyasvy,
which, I'm told, means 'invincible.' When the battle spilled
into Alaska, you fought there, too. You're an ace pilot. A
hero."

Justin locked eyes with Paladin. He didn't smile to hide his
unease, nor was there even a raised eyebrow betraying shock.
"And your question?"

"Why the fake identity? You have every reason not to trust
anyone with your prototype. But why am I flying it? Why
aren't you?"

"Your information-gathering skills are indeed impressive,
Mr. Blake, but you are incorrect on one point. My name *is*
Peter Justin. I have had it legally changed. As for not trusting
anyone else—you are correct. I do not.

"I am forced by circumstances to trust you. You see, my
skills—" His gaze dropped to the ground. "It is not easy,
when one reaches a certain age. My reflexes, my eyesight . . .
they are not what they once were. I am still a patriot, and I still
serve in my own way, but I cannot risk that which I have been
hired to protect to prove that I am something I am not."

It took a big man to admit that. Would Paladin be as smart
when he started to lose his edge? He hoped so. There were no
old fighter pilots.

"I'm sorry," Paladin said. "I had to ask."

"If you knew my reputation and walked into this blindly, it
would mean you are a fool. I am glad to see you are not."
Justin glanced again at his watch. "Now, if there are no further questions, we must get you into the air."

Paladin climbed into the cockpit. The seat was rock hard,
and his long legs didn't fit. He managed to adjust it until he
was merely uncomfortable.

He fired up the engines. They coughed and sputtered and
caught. Despite Justin's assurances about the plane's condition, they sounded out of tune.

Justin circled behind the plane, climbed the wing, and
leaned into the cockpit. "You have already been cleared with

the tower. The runway is yours, Mr. Blake. Good flying." He gave Paladin a thumbs-up, then slid the canopy over his head. It closed with a solid click.

Paladin returned the thumbs-up and waited for Justin to climb off before easing the plane out onto the tarmac. Blue lights winked down the runway. The fog was still thick, restricting visibility to two hundred feet . . . not the best take-off conditions.

Paladin clicked on the transceiver and called in a radio check. The tower confirmed and told him he had the runway to himself.

He eased the throttle forward. The flying wing accelerated quickly. Paladin let her build speed for a moment, then pulled back. The plane soared into the air—teetered and almost flipped into a roll.

Justin wasn't kidding when he said the controls were sensitive. He'd have to be more careful.

Paladin held his angle and climbed. The altimeter said four hundred feet. He glanced down at the grid of Pasadena streets, the orange groves, and the foothills ahead. He judged his altitude to be over two thousand. The oil pressure gauge pulsed up and down. His rpm indicator read zero.

" 'Certain amenities have been overlooked,' huh?" Paladin muttered. He tapped the fuel gauge. It read full, but he wasn't sure if he believed it.

This wasn't going to work. No instruments he could trust and a plane only half-assembled? How was he going to spend Lockheed's money if he crashed? He should turn back now while he had the chance.

Paladin pushed the left rudder petal. The plane banked so sharply that the hull groaned and his harness cut into his shoulders.

This plane moved like nothing he had ever flown. He wasn't sure how it was maneuvering, but it was as agile as a dragonfly. He continued the turn, then rolled the flying wing, the maneuver crushing him into his seat.

That was almost fun. Maybe he could fly this thing, after all. Paladin pushed the throttle to three-quarters power. The wing jumped forward. He nosed her over the San Bernardino Mountains, admired the snow on Mount Baldy, then dropped altitude, and skimmed over the treetops.

This little flying wing was growing on him. The controls were twitchy, though; every nudge jinked the plane.

He crossed the summit, and the Mojave Desert stretched out beneath him, flat and gray, painted with yellow dust-storm streaks far in the distance. He aimed for the Saddleback Buttes. From there, according to Justin's flight plan, he'd head due east into the middle of nowhere.

So far, smooth sailing.

Paladin reached back for the lunch pail—and spotted planes on his six. A pack of Grumman Avengers.

He'd been an idiot. He'd been busy enjoying the ride, and had forgotten that this *wasn't* a ride. It was a job. A job he might have just botched.

He squinted. Five of them. No registration numbers. That meant pirates. But there were also no symbols, crests, or markings of any kind. He'd never seen a pirate *not* decorate his plane. So who were they?

He waggled the flying wing to indicate he was friendly.

They fired. Bullet holes stitched his port wing.

"So much for trying to be neighborly," Blake growled, nosing his plane into a dive.

Paladin skimmed along the slope of the mountain, then pulled up hard. He pushed the throttle to maximum, looped the plane, and then pushed her into a dive—emerging behind his attackers.

Before they could scatter, he lined up a shot and fired the prototype's guns.

Fire belched from his .30-caliber cannons. He peppered the tail of one of the Avengers, destroying the rudder.

Paladin whooped, pleased with his marksmanship.

Both his guns jammed.

"What the—?" He squeezed the trigger again. Nothing.

The loss of his plane's guns made the firefight far too one-sided for Paladin's liking. He grabbed the radio: "Mayday, Mayday. Lockheed special flight encountering pirates. Mayday, Mayday."

There was no response. Not even static.

All right, he thought. *I can't fight or get help. Maybe I can outrun them.*

Paladin peeled off and headed straight into the sun.

"Come on," he whispered to the plane. "Faster!"

The Avengers turned to match his new heading, but he was putting some distance between his bird and the attackers. Good. He had a chance.

Bullets riddled the back of the flying wing. A rocket whistled past him; a second impacted near the port engine. There was a shower of sparks and shrapnel. The motor sputtered and stalled.

Paladin knew when he was beat. He checked his parachute to make sure it was strapped on tight.

"I'm sorry, Justin," he murmured, "but it looks like I've just lost your plane."

Another volley of bullets tattooed the flying wing.

Paladin pulled on the canopy's release. With luck, he wouldn't be shot on the way down.

The canopy didn't budge. He pulled harder, with all his strength. No dice.

He was stuck inside.

3: In the Crosshairs

Paladin was a dead man if he didn't get out of this flying coffin. His plane spiraled out of control—sky and clouds and yellow earth whirled around the cockpit.

He yanked again on the canopy's latch, but it was wrenched tight. He needed a crowbar, a screwdriver . . . or a gun. He *did* have a gun, a Colt .45 automatic he had packed in his bag.

He twisted in the seat, quickly rummaging through the tangles of cables, wires, and fuel lines where he had set his bag. It wasn't there. He searched the floor and spotted the bag. It had fallen through the exposed sections of the unfinished cockpit. The bag's strap was snared on the strut of his landing gear, three feet beneath him. If he were a contortionist, he might be able to reach through and get it; otherwise, that three feet might as well be three miles.

There was no choice. He was trapped inside. He had to get the plane running.

He flipped the kill switch for the port engine, reset it, and pushed the starter. The engine coughed smoke and wept oil across the wing. He pushed the starter a second time, a third. Flames shot out of the casing as the motor roared to life.

Paladin laughed—half elated, half panicked.

He pushed the throttle to full and pulled back on the yoke. He had to gain some altitude.

The flying wing groaned and shuddered. Paladin closed his eyes and willed his craft to hold together, willed the plane to climb. He opened his eyes and saw his spiral descent had straightened.

Paladin sighed. That was a lucky break. The port engine, though, wouldn't run for long. He had to find a—

Bullets riveted across his starboard wing. Magnesium rounds sizzled into the metal . . . too close to the fuel tank for comfort.

His attackers were still on his tail.

Paladin quickly weighed his options. It was five against one. If his attackers didn't shoot his flying wing into confetti, then his engine would seize up. In either case, with the canopy jammed, he had a one-way express ticket straight down. There had to be a way out of this mess, a way to open the canopy.

There was. Maybe. Paladin stared at the smoldering bullet holes. He'd had some wild ideas before; this one qualified as downright nuts.

He eased up on the throttle and allowed the lead Avenger to catch up to him. He had to give them a better shot.

Bullets peppered the fuselage. Paladin jerked left. The line of bullet holes curved right—off the flying wing, completely missing him.

The yoke bucked under his hands, fighting his control. It was nearly impossible to hold the plane steady as shot up as it was, but Paladin had to if he was going to pull this off. He loosened his grip and forced himself to relax, preparing to react to the plane's erratic pitching and yawing.

He heard another burst from the Avenger's guns, felt staccato impacts as bullets stitched across the starboard wing. He jinked the plane to the right. Slugs ripped into the fuselage—just where he had hoped—across the canopy.

Shrapnel blasted into the cockpit. Paladin screamed as red-hot metal tore through his shoulder and blood spattered across the clear canopy dome.

He huddled over in pain and slammed the yoke forward. The flying wing dived. The ground was only a thousand feet away.

Paladin made a feeble attempt to pull back—then stopped, startled by what sounded like a locomotive slamming into the plane. The port engine seized. Pistons and rods ripped through the casing, and bolts zinged off the nose. Exploding scrap metal shredded half the wing.

The only flying possible with this plane now was the kind you did with a halo.

He glanced at the canopy latch. Between the Avenger's .30-caliber bullets and the engine detonating, it had made Swiss cheese out of the lever and track. Out of the corner of his eye he saw the ground rushing up, maybe six hundred feet left. He unbuckled his seat belt and pulled on the latch.

It moved, but not enough to open.

He swiveled in his seat, ripping through the tangle of wires and hydraulic lines around his feet. He kicked at the latch—once, twice. The canopy ripped open with a rush of wind. Paladin tumbled out of the cockpit.

There was a blur of blue skies, smears of cirrostratus, a flash of the desert floor rapidly approaching . . . so close he saw spiny Joshua trees and a jackrabbit bounding for cover.

Paladin wrapped his fingers around the rip cord and pulled—rope and silk unraveled and caught the air. His body snapped like a whip, and he howled in pain as his harness bit into his injured shoulder. He hit the ground. His legs crumpled; he rolled, tangling himself in rope and fabric, sticks and sand.

He lay there, dazed and wrapped in blood-flecked white silk. He wondered if he were still alive. There was grit and blood in his mouth. His shoulder felt like it was on fire and twisted out of joint. Every muscle in his legs and back ached, too.

He had to be alive. You couldn't feel this lousy if you were dead.

Paladin unbuckled his parachute and wriggled out from under the silk. The sun was a handbreadth above the horizon, but the desert was already hot. His head was ringing. Or was that just the crickets buzzing their high-pitched song? A dry wind kicked up and pelted his flight suit with sand.

He smelled smoke, turned, and saw the source: a serpentine column of flame and soot emanating from the flying wing's crash site.

"Sorry, Justin. I blew it."

It wasn't only Justin he had failed. He'd lose Blake Aviation Security over this fiasco. He should have radioed for help the second he saw those Avengers. He shouldn't have tried to outmaneuver them, shouldn't have allowed his plane—correction: *Lockheed*'s plane—to get shot out from under him. It was his fault.

Overhead, he heard the unmistakable drone of the Avengers' Feldman sixteen-valve engines. One of the Avengers trailed smoke. Paladin must have gotten more than a piece of his tail rudder.

They circled like buzzards. One peeled off—his wingman followed. Then another pair dived in graceful arcs . . . arcs that lined them up perfectly for strafing runs.

Paladin half ran, half limped for the nearest twiggy creosote bush. He crouched in the improbable cover of its shadow and watched as the Avengers leveled off at fifty feet and fired.

Bullets carved lines in the sand.

He flinched, fully expecting the rows of magnesium rounds to rip him apart. But they weren't shooting at him. Instead, they hit the wreckage of the flying wing.

The four Avengers circled, made another run, this time dropping bombs. The bombs detonated, sending a shower of silver sparks into the air. They made another low-altitude pass, then climbed, apparently satisfied with their destructive handiwork.

Paladin stood and shook the sand out of his helmet. It didn't make sense.

He understood the ambush. Justin's "airtight" security obviously wasn't. Someone at Lockheed had gotten wind of his plan and knew exactly where and when to nab the prototype. But they hadn't even tried to take it intact.

Paladin walked toward the wreckage. His knees wobbled but held.

The flying wing—the twisted bits of black steel that were left—no longer resembled an airplane. It looked like someone had taken a can opener to it. The stench of melting rubber and burning aviation fuel forced him back. There would be no salvaging the radio or his bag of gear. The cockpit was a charred crater. If he hadn't jumped when he did, there would have only been pieces of him left for the scorpions.

He examined his shoulder, gingerly peeling back the tattered flight suit. The wound was deep but cleanly cauterized about the edges. Nothing life threatening . . . but it hurt like hell.

Paladin clenched his fists, then uncoiled them and exhaled. He'd get even with those Avengers. But who were they?

They could be the same thieves stealing from Lockheed. They'd gone to a lot of trouble to get a few parts and the prototype's blueprints; yet, they had wasted a chance to get their hands on the real thing. Did destroying the prototype make their parts more valuable?

If they weren't the Lockheed thieves—if they were, for instance, Lockheed's corporate competition—then that would explain the lack of pirate insignia on the Avengers. It wouldn't explain, though, why they hadn't been eager to get a look at the flying wing. Destroying it set Lockheed back only a few months while they built a new one.

There were too many missing pieces to this puzzle.

Paladin scanned the skies and spotted the Avengers. They were flyspecks in the distance now, seemingly hovering on the northern horizon, dwindling into the distance.

With them dwindled his chances for filling in those missing pieces.

Paladin turned and walked south. There should be a road along the base of the San Bernardino Mountains. If not, he'd have to head for the pass. That was at least a day's walk.

He looked back, shielded his eyes. The Avengers were flecks of dust, one trailing a thread of smoke. They were still on a northern bearing.

North? What was north? Lockheed's secret facility was northeast. Palmdale was to the west. Palm Springs was east. Those Avengers should be heading back to civilization, not away from it. They had a range of six hundred miles, so they could be headed anywhere. Not the one Paladin had shot, though. It had a bad rudder and engine problems. He shouldn't be flying into the middle of the desert.

Paladin looked back at the mountains. That way was Pasadena, where he would have to explain to Justin how he had turned his ultrasecret prototype flying wing into a heap of scrap metal. Lockheed would take over the investigation into the ambush. It would be the end of Blake Aviation Security.

He turned north.

That way led to wherever those Avengers were headed. It was a walk into the middle of nowhere. It would be a heck of a lot more trouble than it was worth. He might die of thirst, blood loss, or a rattlesnake bite. But it could lead to some answers.

Paladin took a deep breath and then started marching deeper into the desert.

"I should have listened to Dashiell and gone to Santa Barbara."

It was almost dawn. A band of navy blue wavered on the horizon. Another half hour, and the sun would turn this ice locker back into an oven.

It had been a day since Paladin had walked onto Lockheed's Pasadena airfield and flew Justin's little plane. Twenty-four hours, most of them spent staggering under a sweltering sun, thinking every step of the way about what a long shot he was chasing.

He must have hit his head harder than he realized when he bailed out. No one in their right mind would have gone after those Avengers on foot.

Paladin stopped. He resisted the urge to lick his cracked lips. One day without water was bad enough. He had at least another day going back the way he came.

How far could that shot-up Avenger have gotten? Apparently farther than he could on foot. He scanned the sky like he had a thousand times before. He'd seen plenty of ravens and bats but not a single plane. This time was no different.

He turned and started back. He took only three steps before he halted dead in his tracks.

There was a faint drone. It revved up and down; it was an unmistakable noise. It was the sixteen-valve Feldman engine of a Grumman E-1 Avenger.

Paladin spun, trying to zero in on the source of the noise.

There. Just over the rocky hills to the north, the silhouette of a plane dived, soared, circled, and then disappeared.

He ran toward the closest slope. The predawn light warmed the ledges and outcroppings, turning them red and amber. As the sun peeked over the horizon, Paladin scrambled to the top and overlooked a canyon full of shadows.

Pale yellow lights traced a runway down the center of this canyon. There were a dozen tents, a fleet of twenty Avengers, and an old water tower that had been converted into a radio shack. On the opposite side of the ravine sat a moored zeppelin.

Paladin stared for a full minute. Someone had done a lot of planning and spent a fistful of cash to set this base up. He squinted and saw mechanics and pilots on the runway, moving briskly and pausing only to salute one another.

A military base? Paladin was willing to bet Blake Aviation's last dollar it didn't belong to Hollywood's militia. He remembered Jimmy the Rap's story about how all the fences in Hollywood were muscled out of town. Who else but another nation could do that?

Sunlight illuminated the side of the zeppelin. It was smooth, metallic gray, and it bore no insignia. It had gun turrets on each engine nacelle, a rack on the undercarriage for bombs and rockets, and two bays for launching aircraft. This thing was a war machine.

A crane next to the zeppelin moved; its neck extended and cables whined as it pulled something off the ground. A dozen men clustered about the object. Whatever it was, they were aligning it to fit into the port bay.

They were getting ready for action. A firefight? Or were they moving out?

Paladin waited and watched as the shadows evaporated from the canyon. His heart skipped a beat, then pounded in his throat. They weren't loading just any plane. It was the flying wing.

The same plane Paladin had crash-landed and seen incinerated.

4: Ghosts in the Sand

"What the hell is going on here?" Paladin muttered. He watched the crane lift the aircraft. The little flying wing had the same oversize engines, the same bubble canopy, and the same smooth rudderless design. To his eye it was identical to the plane he flew from the Lockheed facility in Pasadena . . . the same plane that had been shot out from under him in a sneak attack.

Maybe the Lockheed thieves had built their own plane from stolen parts. No, that didn't figure. Jimmy the Rap said they had taken some big-ticket items—but nothing near enough to construct an entire aircraft.

The sun broke free of the horizon. Paladin's shadow was a hundred feet long and spilled over the edge of the canyon.

He was being a dope. If he could see the mechanics and pilots on the airstrip, then they'd be able to see his silhouette up on the ridge.

He dropped, crawled to the edge, and peered over. No one seemed to have noticed. In fact, they looked too busy down there to notice anyone up here. Men dug up runway lights. Mechanics in coveralls worked on the engines of the Avengers. A dozen people loaded crates into the zeppelin.

They were breaking camp.

It was a stroke of luck for Paladin—rotten luck. He silently cursed himself for not thinking ahead. Sure, he'd found the thugs that had shot him down . . . only he hadn't figured out what to do when he caught up with them. If he left now to get help, there wouldn't even be footprints left in the sand when he returned.

Whatever he was going to do, he had to do it soon. He had to do it alone.

He needed an inconspicuous way to get a closer look. The canyon walls, however, were vertical. Quickly surveying the scene, he spotted a branching ravine with slopes that a determined person could slide down. Better yet, this side passage twisted out of sight from the main camp.

There was just one problem, though: The ravine wasn't empty. One man marched into the gully, while another wandered out and waved a greeting to his buddy.

If Paladin's luck changed, he might time it just right so no one saw him crashing the party. He moved along the ridge of the canyon, half crouching, until he came to the edge of the branching channel. He then understood what the attraction was in the ravine: in the shadow of a rocky ledge sat an outhouse.

Through the crescent-moon slit Paladin spied someone moving. He'd have to move fast.

Paladin stepped off the edge and slid down the gravel slope. A cloud of dust trailed behind him. He ran to the outhouse.

The man inside must have heard him. "Cool yer heels, buddy," he yelled through the door. "Wait yer turn!"

Paladin thought of himself as a fair person. If he knocked someone down, he waited for them to get to their feet before taking another swing. Not this time. He'd left all pretenses of chivalry a day's walk away—when five planes had shot him out of the sky.

He flung open the door and caught the mechanic with his pants down. Paladin threw a left hook and a right uppercut.

The mechanic grunted in pain and collapsed against the wall, unconscious.

Paladin cast a glance up the ravine. No one there. He dragged the unconscious mechanic from the outhouse, far enough out of sight in case anyone came looking.

He took the man's coveralls and cap, hog-tied him with his belt, then gagged him with his own dirty socks. The restraints wouldn't hold forever; Paladin hoped that they would hold long enough for him to find out what was going on here.

The mechanic's greasy blue coveralls were two sizes too big. Paladin stuffed it with his flight jacket and then tucked his hair under the cap. If anyone got too close to this lousy disguise, they'd see through it in a heartbeat.

He took a deep breath, steeled his nerve, and walked out of the ravine.

Men scurried about the airstrip—all of them moving faster than Paladin had seen ten minutes ago. They struck tents and lowered radio gear from the water tower. Two mechanics worked on each of the Avengers. Ground crews loaded belts of ammunition and slung rockets on hardpoints under the fighters' wings.

The Avenger pilots were clustered by the edge of the runway, chewing on cigars and shuffling nervously. They kept glancing at the sky like someone was about to drop a bomb on them.

Paladin tried to look like he had someplace important to get to, then marched across the field, passing as close as he dared to the pilots. He recognized the Neanderthal eyebrows of "Dogface" Dougan, the vivid flame tattoos that covered the arms of Lady Kali, and the thick glasses of "Crosseye" Malone—notorious mercenaries who would shoot down anything or anyone as long as there was enough money in it for them.

He averted his gaze before they saw him. These weren't the kind of people you stared at unless you wanted to start a fight.

These also weren't the kind of people especially noted for their brains.

So who was pulling the strings around here?

Paladin continued past the pilots, then paused and knelt, pretending to tie his shoelace. He needed time to think. Maybe time to figure out a way to steal one of those Avengers. If he could get to Lockheed's base before these goons disappeared, he might be able to return with—

A shadow fell across his face.

"You!"

Paladin got to his feet and slowly turned . . . ready to go down swinging if he'd been found out.

A middle-aged man in a linen suit and panama hat regarded Paladin with mild disgust. His skin was as pallid as his white jacket. He wore kid gloves and sported a monocle that magnified his right eye so it looked like it bulged out of its socket. There wasn't a grain of sand on him.

Standing next to the pale man was a woman. She wore a smart black-and-white striped skirt, black vest, and matching pillbox hat. She shaded herself with a lace parasol. Paladin had to force himself not to stare at her fall of black silken hair or into her deep blue eyes. She was movie-star material.

"Take this—" The pale man gestured to a steamer trunk sitting next to a flattened tent. "—to my stateroom. Immediately. And take care not to jostle it."

Paladin followed the man's gaze to the zeppelin. "Sure."

The pale man narrowed his eyes to slits. "What did you say?"

If this was a military operation, then Paladin had just given the wrong reply. He quickly corrected himself. "I mean, yes, sir." He saluted. "Right away, sir!"

The pale man turned and strode toward the pilots. The woman examined Paladin a moment; then she, too, left.

If he were going to remain inconspicuous, he'd have to follow that order. At least he had a clue what the guy in charge looked like.

The steamer trunk was made of soft leather, with brass-reinforced corners and three silver stars embossed on the lid. Paladin picked it up and balanced it on his good shoulder. He glanced back. The pale man seemed to be giving instructions to the pilots. They nodded and laughed.

Paladin trudged toward the war zeppelin. He fought the urge to duck as he neared the gun turrets mounted on the engine nacelles. Facing that much firepower was bad enough inside a cockpit racing by at two hundred miles per hour . . . but to stare it down face-to-face gave him the creeps.

He climbed the stairs to the gondola and got a glance at the bridge—dials, gauges, and a table overflowing with navigation charts he would have loved to look at. The bridge was also full of armed guards.

He continued down a hallway into what might once have been the dining section. Fifty-caliber machine guns were mounted where the best window tables would have been on a passenger liner. Crates of ammunition were neatly stacked alongside the guns. Paladin kept his head low and walked past crews cleaning and oiling the weapons. He entered another passage at the end of the galley.

There were bunk rooms and a storage room full of boxes and sacks. One door had a placard with three silver stars hung on the handle. Paladin knocked, waited, and then eased it open.

He slipped inside. No one was here. He dropped the trunk, then closed and locked the door behind him.

The room had a picture window with bulletproof steel shutters. There was a rolltop desk bolted to the floor, and two chaises longues upholstered with silver silk. Gilt-framed landscapes and portraits adorned the walls; they seemed vaguely familiar, like Paladin had seen them before in a museum. There was a case full of books: Nietzsche, nineteenth-century history texts, and the latest scientific journals.

Paladin had almost overlooked the most important feature of this parlor, a fully stocked wet bar. He rummaged through the bottles and found a seltzer dispenser. He filled three glasses and quaffed the fizzling liquid. He ate an entire can of Spanish peanuts, then a jar of maraschino cherries, drank the rest of the seltzer, and caught his breath.

He almost felt human again. He tried to stretch his wounded

shoulder, but it was too swollen and stiff. He touched it and winced. Not a good sign.

He'd been running on adrenaline ever since his crash. Now that he finally had a chance to slow down, he was struck with a sense of just how much danger he was in. If they found him, there'd be a little impromptu firing squad organized for his benefit. He had to get off his zeppelin and as far away from here as he could.

On the other hand, if he wanted to find out who was behind the Lockheed thefts, this might be his only opportunity.

Five minutes. He'd give himself that long to find something; then he'd scram and take his chances in the desert.

Paladin jimmied the lock on the steamer trunk. The scent of expensive perfume wafted from inside. There were skirts and blouses with French labels and a dozen pairs of high heels. Paladin was no fashion expert, but the stuff looked like it had cost a bundle. He dug deeper and found a hatbox. Inside was a nickel-plated .38 pistol . . . and a grenade.

He couldn't picture either the pale man or his lady friend packing this kind of heat. They both looked so genteel. Still, nothing about this case had been as simple as it appeared on the surface. Why should they be any different?

Paladin slipped the pistol and grenade in his pocket.

Next, he forced open the desk's rolltop cover. There was the usual stuff: stationery, envelopes, a gold fountain pen, and a pack of unopened cigarettes. There was also a key.

He took the key—it might come in handy if he found a locked door on his way out. He grabbed the smokes, too.

He started to roll down the desktop when a flash caught his attention. Sitting in a velvet box was a signet ring with a jade stone. Carved in relief was an eagle with talons extended around a star. He pocketed the ring, too.

Sure, it was stealing. Blake Aviation had always gone out of its way to conduct business on the up-and-up, but this was different. There was more at stake than his reputation or playing it fair . . . even more at stake, he realized, than Lockheed's prototype. Another nation was conducting secret military operations in Hollywood. That was an act of war.

Paladin suddenly didn't want to be here, clues or not. He moved toward the door, but his knees buckled and his stomach sank. He caught himself, sitting on one of the chaises.

Outside he heard thunder . . . only this thunder didn't fade. It was the roar of the zeppelin's engines. And it wasn't his legs that had given out; the zeppelin had suddenly lurched.

They were taking off.

5: No Graceful Exit

Paladin felt the acceleration in his gut—like he was moving up on an express elevator. He got to his feet and lurched to the window. The zeppelin had cleared the canyon walls; its shadow rippled along the desert crags below.

He gripped the steel shutters and rattled them. No luck. They were locked. Even if he found something with which to pry them off, he was already a hundred feet off the ground and climbing.

Unless he sprouted wings, he was stuck on this airbag.

And with his luck, the guard he had knocked out before sneaking aboard would be found soon. There'd be a quick radio call to the zeppelin, a search, and when they found Paladin, they'd shove him out the nearest exit. He'd take the longest step of his life.

He couldn't sit around and wait to be discovered. He had to find a place to hide.

Paladin left the parlor and locked the door behind him. Retracing his steps, he went back to the shooting gallery. The drone of the engines reverberated through the open windows. The dozen .50-caliber guns were loaded and ready for action. The men standing next to them looked just as ready, scanning the skies for trouble. No one noticed him.

Paladin swayed and steadied himself against an aluminum brace. Squares of light and shadow stretched and angled across the long room as the zeppelin turned north.

There was a door or two in the corridor between here and the bridge. Paladin tried to look casual as he strode to the opposite side of the galley. There had to be a place where he could—

Halfway across the room, he stopped dead.

The pale, authoritative man and his stunning escort stepped onto the galley. The gunners stood and saluted.

The pale man brushed the lapel of his linen suit and casually looked over the room. He wandered to the nearest window, ran his white-gloved fingers over the frame, and inspected their cleanliness. Satisfied, he removed his monocle and admired the expansive view of desert and cloudless horizons.

His female companion leaned over a machine gun, brushed her dark hair from her face, and examined its ammunition belt. She straightened her pillbox hat and then spoke to the soldier manning the weapon. He nodded and quickly left. She turned and scrutinized each gun along the left-hand side of the room, idly twirling her closed lace parasol . . . until she noticed Paladin. Her eyes locked with his, and she froze.

There was something familiar about the slight upturn of her nose, and eyes that could have been chiseled from icebergs. Sure, Paladin had just seen her on the runway, but he now realized that they had crossed paths somewhere else. He couldn't quite put his finger on when.

Her eyes widened and her mouth formed a tiny *o*.

While Paladin hadn't figured out where he knew her from, she had apparently remembered where she had seen *him* before. He dropped his eyes to the deck, did an about-face, and headed back the way he'd come, trying to appear as nonchalant as possible.

It took all his nerve not to look back or break into a run. Paladin was sure every guard on the zeppelin was after him. He'd never hear them coming over the roar of the engines.

He stopped at the door to the parlor and risked a quick glance over his shoulder. The pale man and woman were still there, but neither one was looking his way. Paladin exhaled and regained his composure.

One thing was for sure: he couldn't go back. The woman

had either recognized him and not said anything or she had written off his familiar resemblance as a coincidence. Paladin wished he remembered how he knew her, and if she might help him out of this jam. That was a long shot, though. She seemed awfully chummy with the pale man in charge.

He continued down the hall past a bunk room full of men engrossed in a game of poker, past a kitchen with glistening copper pots and the aroma of roasting turkey, past a storage closet crammed with crates—but nothing that looked like a good hiding place.

Paladin looked back down the hallway and spotted the pale man and woman walking toward their room. When they saw their opened steamer truck and ransacked rolltop desk, they'd quickly realize who was responsible.

He figured he had thirty seconds.

The hall ended in a double set of swing doors. Paladin pushed through.

He found himself in the launch bay, a cavernous room with the skeleton of the zeppelin's beam-and-girder superstructure exposed. Paladin saw a control room perched thirty feet overhead.

There was a fleet of Grumman Avengers, hanging like Christmas ornaments on tracks. At first glance, it looked like a standard launch bay in a military zep. When the zeppelin was high enough those planes could roll off their tracks, through the open bay doors in the floor, and the zeppelin would have an instant squadron to defend against pirates or, in this case, Hollywood's militia.

This launch system, though, was different from any Paladin had seen. The planes rotated on a universal joint. They pointed toward bays where mechanics checked engines and hydraulics, loaded rockets and belts of ammunition—all made easier because they could be worked on from any angle. It was a brainy setup.

Paladin stopped admiring the engineering and did a double take. The Lockheed prototype dangled directly over his head.

He stepped around it to get a better look. This close, he saw it was very different from the plane he had crashed yesterday. This one had a mirror polish on its steel skin; the engines were larger and smoothly melded into the frame; the bubble canopy was a recessed cyclopean eye. The plane looked slick and seamless, a far cry from the half-finished, temperamental craft he had flown out of Pasadena.

"So where the hell did this one come from?" he muttered to himself. Paladin had no time to figure it out. He was attracting curious looks from the guards and mechanics here.

He glanced to the prototype, to the three guards starting toward him, then took a gamble—maybe his only way to make a not-so-graceful exit.

Paladin steeled his nerve and took a deep breath. "Hey!" he yelled across the hangar to the guards. "We got a problem."

For once, his bad luck was a blessing. Alarm bells jangled throughout the hangar. The guards broke into a run, reaching for their pistols. The mechanics followed, brandishing wrenches, crowbars, and other makeshift weapons.

"Quick," Paladin said. "They need help on the bridge. Hurry!"

The men pushed their way through the double doors. No one looked twice at Paladin.

He spied a wrench on the floor, grabbed it, and jammed it through the door handles. That bought him maybe another fifteen seconds. He rolled a wheeled ladder under the flying wing.

A man in the control room banged on the window. He waved his arms to get Paladin's attention. When Paladin ignored him, the man got on the radio.

No turning back now, Paladin thought. *Everybody on this zep is gonna know I'm here.*

Paladin scrambled up the ladder and climbed into the prototype's cockpit. This definitely wasn't the same plane he'd flown. The seat was soft padded leather, almost obscenely comfortable in comparison to the Spartan interior of "his" prototype. The instrument panel was burnished brass and teak with a Rolls-Royce precision floating horizon, a Swiss Gersbeck altimeter, and a Rothschild Blackhawk rpm gauge and speedometer. There were also a few dials and switches that Paladin didn't recognize.

He found the manual docking release and pulled. There was a click, and the plane slowly began to roll forward on its track, toward the hole in the zeppelin's belly.

The prototype jerked to a halt. Paladin cracked his head on the instrument panel. The flying wing swung back and forth.

The guy in the control room had his hand on a lever and a smug look on his face.

Paladin could have killed the creep—if he had had the spare time. He squinted and found the cause of his problems: a spring-loaded clamp three feet from the rail's end—an emergency brake. There was no way the flying wing could roll off. No way for him to escape.

He heard banging and raised voices. Paladin turned and saw the double doors jostle and the jammed wrench begin to shake loose.

He drew the nickel-plated .38 pistol he had swiped from the steamer trunk . . . then realized he had more firepower. He pulled out the grenade he had found with the gun.

But one grenade wouldn't stop the army on the other side of those doors, unless—Paladin turned and examined the rail—he found a better use for the thing.

He set down his gun and pocketed the grenade. He clambered out of the cockpit and balanced on the teetering wing.

Paladin grasped the rail overhead. His wounded shoulder blossomed with fire, and he felt something inside tear. He gritted his teeth and pulled himself to the locking clamp, hand over hand. Hanging by his right arm, he retrieved the grenade, pulled the pin with his teeth, and then jammed it into the clamp.

He swung himself once, twice, dropped back onto the wing, and rolled into the cockpit—covering his head and bracing for the blast.

It sounded like a cannon going off in his ears. Metal fragments zinged off the canopy and the steel skin of the flying wing. He shook his head to clear his ringing ears and risked a glance at the damage. The spring-loaded clamp and rail had blown clean off.

Paladin's streak of bad luck still held, however. The clamp was gone, but the track had twisted into a slight upturn. The plane wouldn't roll off . . . not unless someone got out and gave it one heck of a push.

The double doors burst open. The three guards he had sent on a wild goose chase rushed in with their sidearms drawn. They weren't alone, either—the poker players in the bunk room were on their heels, as were a half-dozen gunners from the galley. Even the pale man was there, monocle gleaming and a Thompson submachine gun in hand.

And they were all looking for him.

Paladin crouched lower in the cockpit. His dogfighting instincts made him want to reach for the yoke and pull it back—dodge, try an Immelmann, and somehow shake these jokers off his six. But this was no dogfight.

Paladin glanced at the pistol in his hand and briefly considered a frontal assault. Maybe the element of surprise would buy him enough time to get clear, get out of the hangar; maybe find a parachute—

That would be crazy.

His eyes fell to the rubberized grip and trigger on the yoke.

No. Crazy would be trying to hold off an army with a peashooter, especially when he was sitting behind twin .30-caliber cannons. He could use the plane's guns. But he'd have to turn the thing around first.

He pressed the port and starboard starters. The engines turned over and roared to life, growling like metallic tigers. Paladin inched the port throttle forward. The differential in power to the engines started to spin the flying wing on the universal joint, rotating it to face the guards.

They raised their weapons; Paladin saw the blur of whirling props reflected in their wide eyes.

One of them fired. A bullet pinged off a propeller blade.

Paladin squeezed the trigger. The plane's nose was pointed too high for him to hit anyone, but that didn't stop him from unloading a few hundred rounds over their heads.

The men scattered like rats, hit the deck and crawled for cover.

It wasn't the smartest thing he'd ever done. As the plane turned, Paladin spotted barrels of aviation fuel and racks of high-explosive rockets. If he kept shooting, they'd all go out in a blaze of glory.

The pale man set down his Tommy gun and stood. He held up his white-gloved hands and shouted at Paladin.

A truce? Paladin couldn't hear what he was trying to say over the drone of his engines. He eased the port throttle back a bit to kill his spin. The flying wing rolled to a low spot on the track as the engines slowed.

In his peripheral vision he saw some of the guards flanking him.

"Want to play hardball, huh?" he said. "Well, I can play that game, too."

He gripped the trigger and readied himself. The slight rocking of the flying wing was going to make this a tricky shot.

Paladin froze. The plane was rocking like someone had given it a good push . . . and wasn't that exactly what he had said he needed? A good push to get out of this jam?

He revved the starboard engine, turning the plane back to its original facing.

He narrowed his eyes and pulled the trigger. The twin .30-caliber machine guns stitched the deck, sent a flurry of sparks flying, and riddled aviation fuel barrels with holes. Amber liquid gushed and ignited into a river of fire.

The pale man dived back into the hallway.

Paladin let the flying wing turn until its nose pointed toward the open bay doors in the zeppelin's undercarriage.

He pushed both throttles full open. The plane accelerated, gained momentum up the track, then launched off the twisted, upturned end with a wrenching squeal.

An explosion surrounded the cockpit with flame and smoke and thunder—and the flying wing plunged through the launch bay door, hurtling toward the earth.

6: The Big Fall

Icy wind tore through the open cockpit as the flying wing dropped from the belly of the zeppelin. Veils of smoke and steam parted before the windshield.

Paladin had misjudged how high the zep was. There were only a few hundred feet between him and the desert floor.

He instinctively pulled back on the yoke—then quickly stopped himself. That was wrong. Instead, he pushed the yoke forward and nosed the flying wing into a dive.

The problem was speed . . . or rather, a lack of it.

This was a mistake almost everyone made on their first free-fall launch. A pilot's training taught him to pull up in order to gain altitude—but no plane could fly without the speed to produce sufficient lift.

Sure, his engines were at full throttle, the rpm gauge was pegged, but technically the plane was still starting from a dead stop.

Paladin gripped the yoke with his sweaty hands. His gaze flicked to the altimeter as it rapidly ticked off the distance to the ground. Needles of wind blurred his vision as he spared a quick glance at the air speed gauge. Almost.

Below him were sandy waves, washed against outcroppings of red rock. Paladin could see dots of sage and creosote, and spiny yucca drawing so close that he could make out their columns of white flowers blooming. He was running out of room.

The plane's airspeed was a hair under what he needed. It had to be enough.

He pulled back on the control stick with all his strength,

ignoring his instincts which screamed that no plane, no matter *how* advanced, could pull out of a dive at this speed.

The airframe creaked and pinged from the increasing stress. Paladin was crushed into the padded seat, and blood drained from his head and hands. His peripheral vision swirled and dimmed as his body fought to compensate for the tremendous punishment inflicted upon it.

He pulled back harder, bracing with shuddering legs. There was only a pinpoint in the center of his vision now; the only thing visible was the ground rushing to meet him. The thunder of the engines Dopplered into a faint drone. The pulse in his neck strained and struggled to pump blood. He felt like he was drowning.

Paladin waited for the end. It would, at least, be quick—slamming face-first at a hundred miles per hour into the earth . . .

. . . only the end was taking its sweet time getting to him.

Paladin's pinpoint of vision swelled open: half of it was sand and sage; half of it was turquoise sky.

He shook his head, trying to recover from the near blackout. His hands had gone limp and rested gently on the controls.

There was a scrape and clatter along the undercarriage and a grinding buzz through the blades of the props.

With a start, he realized that the altimeter read a hair above zero. Paladin peered outside. The plane skimmed five feet above the ground—cruising at two hundred miles per hour. Prop wash kicked up a cloud of dust and sand as the prototype rocketed by, clear-cutting sagebrush and yucca as he flew past.

He eased the yoke back with a light, precise touch, then quickly nudged the controls to evade a rock that otherwise would have bisected the flying wing.

Paladin pulled back and climbed fifty feet. He exhaled, realizing that he'd been holding his breath.

"Thanks," he said, smoothing his hand along the brushed brass and teak instrument panel. "I owe you one."

Paladin wasn't quite ready to throw a victory party. He

looked over his shoulder. The zeppelin billowed black smoke, and fire puffed from her launch bay. She was still in one piece, more or less. Too bad—she must have been filled with expensive helium, not hydrogen. Otherwise she would have gone up like gasoline-doused tissue paper.

Aircraft buzzed around the wounded zep like flies. For an instant, Paladin wasn't so sure that he'd damaged the zep's launch bay.

"Nuts," he muttered.

He'd forgotten about the squadron of Grumman Avengers that had been parked on the airstrip—the same Avengers that had shot him down once already.

They, however, had not forgotten him. They dived.

The usual tactics didn't apply here. Normally whoever had the higher altitude in a dogfight had the advantage. But these Avengers had to dive low just to catch up to the flying wing. If Paladin tried to climb, they'd be all over him. So whatever was going to happen, it was going to be low. Belly-grinding low.

"Come and get me, you bastards."

The Avengers couldn't line up for a shot unless they were diving straight toward him. He pushed the yoke forward, hugged the sandy hills and raced past rocks and trees—not giving them a static target. If they wanted a shot at him, they'd have to come down and play in the dirt, where the agile flying wing might have an advantage over the more cumbersome Avengers.

Paladin glanced backward. Four planes were falling fast after him. Two more stayed high, presumably acting as spotters and radioing his position back to their friends.

A stream of magnesium bullets blazed over his head and the smoky trail of a rocket appeared, detonating against a rocky outcropping just a few feet from his nose.

They wanted him, all right. Bad enough to risk their necks getting as close to the ground as he was. Good.

He looked back. A pair of the Avengers slowly dropped behind him; they almost had him lined up in their sights.

"A little closer," he whispered. "Come on . . . just a little more."

Paladin firewalled the throttle and pulled back on the yoke, accelerating and rising ten feet before the Avenger on his six could blast him to confetti.

He rolled the plane upside down and killed his throttle.

The Avengers roared *under* him, a blur of props and metal; he caught a glimpse of Lady Kali and the flaming tattoos on her arms—so close he could almost reach out and touch them.

Paladin continued the roll and righted the flying wing, dropping neatly behind his would-be pursuers.

His finger tightened on the trigger, spraying gunfire at the nearest Avenger.

The Avenger on his port side tried to bank. Its wingtip grazed the sand, sending the plane into a deadly cartwheel. The Avenger disintegrated into flame and smoke.

Paladin blasted through the debris and kept firing. Bullets peppered the tail of the remaining Avenger.

Lady Kali pulled up, climbed a hundred feet, and kept going. She and the other Avengers banked and headed back toward the zep.

Paladin pulled back on the yoke. He'd finish what they started.

No. There were too many Avengers waiting up there . . . and he'd already pushed his luck past the breaking point.

He eased the flying wing to the relatively safe altitude of thirty feet and headed northwest.

"You're going home, little friend," Paladin told the plane. Lockheed's secret airfield was no more than fifty miles along his current heading.

He glanced once more over his shoulder. The zep still trailed smoke, though the oily black clouds had softened into pale gray wisps. She was gaining altitude, heading north. Maybe he hadn't crippled her, after all. He'd bet those machine guns he'd seen on the observation deck were still working, too. Paladin was glad he was putting distance between him and that monster.

This isn't over, Paladin thought. Not by a long shot. He'd find some way to even the score.

He banked the flying wing around a rocky hill, reveling in the craft's responsiveness and agility. Maneuvering the plane was like sliding across silk. Paladin heard the starboard engine throttle back and the port engine rev faster as he turned. When he leveled out, the engines returned to their normal synchronized purr. He marveled at the engineering.

Paladin poured on the speed, blasting over desert dunes and gravel rivers that fanned into alluvial patterns on a dried lake. This was the perfect location for a flight research facility. Just one big flat surface—all runway.

Upon the horizon, wavering in the rising heat, he spotted the rippling outline of a control tower.

This had to be the place, but Paladin didn't know which radio frequency to use.

He deployed the landing gear and circled once. There were a dozen aircraft lined up in neat rows, and three hangars . . . ringed by .50-caliber machine gun nests. *Looks like they take their privacy seriously around here,* Paladin thought. *Maybe "surprising" them isn't such a good thing.*

He glided down the runway, touched down, and taxied to a stop near the first hangar.

A dozen men ran out from the control tower: mechanics, gentlemen in dark suits, and even the Hollywood police in their pressed blue uniforms.

Paladin climbed out of the cockpit and slid off the wing. "Hello, boys." He waved at them. "No need to roll out the red carpet. Just doing my job."

The men exchanged confused looks; then one of the cops reached for Paladin's hand.

Paladin mirrored the gesture, thinking they'd shake.

Handcuffs snapped around his wrist.

"Mr. Blake," the officer said. "You're under arrest."

"We checked out your story, Mr. Blake."

The young Lockheed official sat on the edge of the table and leaned closer to Paladin. He was near enough for Paladin to get an eyeful of the large dimple in his prominent chin. The reek of the man's expensive cologne was overpowering.

"And your story doesn't check out."

Paladin sat with his hands still cuffed and resting on the tabletop. He would have punched this joker's lights out if he thought he could get away with it. But he couldn't.

They had locked him in a room with Mr. Expensive Cologne and an older gentleman—neither identifying themselves, but both radiating authority. For the last two hours, Mr. Cologne had asked the same questions about what had happened, and Paladin had told him the same story.

The older man wore a tweed suit with leather elbow patches. He nodded as Paladin explained about the pale man and the second prototype, but otherwise kept quiet and watched the show.

This room was on the second floor of the control tower. There was one window, covered by thick curtains. The cinder-block walls dampened the sound so much that Paladin thought his ears would bleed from the silence between their questions and his answers.

As far as he knew, they could be the only people still at this facility. He hadn't heard or seen anyone since the Hollywood police escorted him inside.

"What do you mean my story doesn't check out?" Paladin demanded. "There was an air base. And there had to be something left of that Avenger that crashed between here and there."

"No." Mr. Cologne got up, grabbed a pitcher of water, and poured himself a tall glass. He drank it without offering Paladin a drop. "You want to know what I think, though?"

How could a search team have missed that Avenger? Sure the desert was a big place, but from the air, the smoldering wreckage should be obvious. Even to a clown like Mr. Cologne.

"I don't care what you think," Paladin shot back.

"I think," Mr. Cologne continued as if he hadn't heard Paladin, "that you flew our plane to Hughes' Burbank airfield. They took photographs and had their people go over our new engines; then you concocted this fantastic cover story and flew the plane here. How much did they pay you, Mr. Blake?"

"*You* paid me," Paladin yelled. "Check your own account books, clown. Justin paid me before I even got in the plane."

"We have indeed confirmed that your bank account has grown rather substantially," the older man cut in. "There have been no large payments made to you from a Lockheed account, however. Only the standard test pilot fee: one hundred dollars."

"What?" Paladin was stunned. "What about the rest of my story? You think I faked this hole in my shoulder?" Paladin's face was flushed. He rose from his chair. "Or the sand in the cockpit? You think I faked the shrapnel scars across the plane's wings?"

"Yes, Mr. Blake, I think you would endure almost anything for the right amount of money." Mr. Cologne raised his eyebrows in obvious disgust. "We have a complete file on you."

Paladin wondered how much they really knew. If they had all the dirt on him, why did Justin hire him?

"What about the second prototype? Peter Justin sent me out in one plane, and I came back in another. How do you explain that?"

"Mr. Justin is presently on his way here to verify that the plane you brought is indeed not the one you were given," the older man said. "We will pick up that line of inquiry when he arrives."

Paladin eased back into his seat. At least Justin could back up part of his story.

He was about to tell them how much better the pale man's prototype flew, but decided to keep his mouth shut. So far, telling the entire truth had gotten him nowhere fast.

And where exactly was this question-and-answer party going? Lockheed was a big corporation. They apparently had the Hollywood police in their pocket, too—at least the cops that weren't in the pocket of Hughes Aviation—since they were here and looking the other way while Mr. Cologne conducted his interrogation.

There had been no mention of criminal charges, and due process appeared to be out the window. If things didn't go right, Paladin might just disappear. If the desert was big enough to hide a busted-up Avenger—or for that matter, an entire military base—how hard would it be to hide one inconvenient pilot?

The older man cleared his throat. "Please," he said to his companion, "give Mr. Blake a glass of water."

Mr. Cologne sighed, shook his head, but nonetheless poured a glass and set it down on the table.

Paladin grabbed it with both hands and drank it down.

"Do you smoke?" the older gentleman inquired.

Paladin's eyes fell to the items they had removed from his pockets and scattered on the table. There were the items he had "liberated" from the zeppelin: a brass key, a signet ring with a jade stone, and a pack of cigarettes he swiped from the pale man's parlor. Paladin licked his lips. It had been years since he'd had a smoke, but this might be as good a time as any to start again.

"Yeah," he whispered. "A smoke would be great."

Mr. Cologne tore the wrapper off the cigarettes. He tapped one out, handed it to Paladin, then flipped his lighter open.

The cigarette was wrapped in black paper—one of those expensive European brands that were nearly impossible to get in North America these days.

Paladin brought the cigarette close to the flame. He stared at it as it smoldered, and his mind raced as he struggled to come to grips with recent events.

Something sparked, a brief flicker of intuition. He rapidly pieced together the clues: the battle zeppelin, the unmarked Avengers, the pale man, and these cigarettes . . .

There were a few blank spots to fill in, but the entire two-day ordeal now made sense in a twisted sort of way.

Paladin looked up. "Give me twenty-four hours and two phone calls," he said, "and I guarantee I can answer all your questions."

7: Pointing the Finger

"**A**ll right, Mr. Blake," growled the young Lockheed rep, "you've got your two phone calls . . . and twenty-four hours to explain your part in this mess. I'd make sure one of the calls is to your lawyer."

"That's all I need," Paladin replied. "By this time tomorrow, I'll have it all sorted out." *At least,* he thought, *I'd better.*

If he didn't get to the bottom of this dizzy affair, Blake would end up taking the rap for the theft of the prototype.

He dialed. The line rang eight times before Dashiell picked up.

"Hello?" a sleepy voice asked.

"Dashiell? It's Paladin. I need a favor. Round up your buddy on the Hollywood PD. What's his name? Slaughouser? Then bail Jimmy the Rap out of whatever drunk tank he's in. Get them all out to Lockheed's Pasadena airfield by noon."

"That's three favors," Dashiell said, and yawned. "I suppose this is an emergency? A matter of life and death?"

"Yeah . . . *my* life and death."

There was silence on the other end, then, "Very well, then. I'll see what I can do."

"One more thing," Paladin said. "Get to my Santa Monica office. Bring that fancy detective kit with the fingerprint equipment. If we're lucky as hell, you'll find the break I need."

Paladin quickly outlined what he wanted it for.

"It's a hundred-to-one shot," Dashiell replied.

"Try anyway," Paladin told him. He hung up, then rang Tennyson.

Tennyson was his business partner. Paladin had met the

Englishman during the Great War, then hooked up with him again after Blake's brief stint with the Pinkertons. Tennyson had taught him how to fight and fly and kill and be a gentleman all at the same time.

"Has the cleaning woman come, Tennyson?" Paladin asked. "Yes? Well chase her out of my office. I need it intact and messy, just the way I left it."

Paladin heard the receiver drop, an exchange on the other end in heated Spanish, and then Tennyson picked up and reported: "She's gone."

"Good. Let Dashiell in when he gets there. He'll fill you in. Then get to Lockheed's Pasadena airfield with your tools . . . and be ready for anything."

"Consider it done," Tennyson replied.

Paladin set the phone back in the cradle and looked up.

Mr. Cologne and the older Lockheed official exchanged an incredulous glance; then the older man asked Paladin, "Will you require anything else?"

"I'll need you to fly my people here. I also need the personnel files of your security people at the Pasadena airfield."

The older man told his associate, "Ship the files Mr. Blake requires on the next flight out."

"I could also use a little lunch. Maybe a shower, too," Paladin said, scratching the stubble on his chin. "And a decent razor, so I can clean up."

Or, Paladin thought, *so I can cut my throat if this daffy scheme doesn't work.*

The transport plane landed at half past one that afternoon. There were no windows in the passenger section of the fuselage. Lockheed wasn't taking any chances of revealing the location of its secret testing facility.

Tennyson sauntered off the plane first, lightly stepping down the stairway as if he were the Duke of Kent in tails and black tie at the Queen's Reception. He was, in fact, wearing a set of freshly pressed white coveralls, a Hollywood Stars baseball cap, and mirrored aviator glasses. He carried a bulky tool chest in each hand.

When Tennyson saw Paladin, he set his tools down,

clasped Paladin's hand, and patted him on the back. "So good to see you, my friend." A smile split his white beard, then disappeared. "We had been told there was an accident, and that you were injured."

"That's the least of my problems," Paladin muttered, and absentmindedly massaged his bandaged shoulder.

Jimmy the Rap got off the plane next. His crumpled suit looked like it had been slept in, and he winced when he got a dose of desert sun.

Following Jimmy was a pudgy man in a navy blue suit and worn fedora that had *cop* written all over it. That had to be Detective Slaughouser.

Last to deplane was a giant of a man, the Russian fighter ace who had gotten Paladin into this mess: Peter Justin.

"Where's Dashiell?" Paladin asked.

"He did not come," Tennyson replied. "He said the only desert he would be going to would be Palm Springs. All the others were too dry, he told me. And I do not believe he was referring to the climate."

Paladin gritted his teeth. "That's it? He didn't say anything else?"

"He told me to give you this." Tennyson reached into the vest pocket of his coveralls, removed an envelope, and handed it to Paladin. "He said, 'Your long shot paid off,' and that you owe him a bottle of champagne."

Paladin cracked it open and frowned at its contents. "Hmph. It isn't as clear as I'd hoped," he whispered. "Still, we're lucky we got anything at all. It'll have to do."

"What will have to do?" Tennyson asked.

"A miracle . . . if I can pull it off," Paladin said. He stuffed the envelope into his pocket.

"Mr. Blake?" asked a voice embellished with a Slavic accent.

Paladin turned. Peter Justin—all seven feet and three hundred pounds of him—had somehow crept up behind him. Justin's pointed beard had been immaculately trimmed since Paladin had seen him last. He wore a light gray silk suit and a panama hat to shade his face. "It is most distressing news about the prototype," he said. "I very much would like to see the wreckage." He shot a suspicious glance at Tennyson and then looked back down at Paladin. "If there is anything I can do to help, please tell me."

Paladin took a step back. "Did you bring those Lockheed employment records?"

"Of course." Justin hefted an alligator-skin briefcase.

"Good." Paladin nodded toward the hangar. He raised his voice so everyone on the field heard him: "Then let's take a look at the plane."

He marched to the hangar. Across the dry lake bed, shimmering heat rose in waves so it looked like an oasis in the distance. A mirage . . . a reminder that maybe it wasn't the truth he was chasing, just smoke and mirrors.

No. His hunch had to be right.

Paladin stepped through the door adjacent to the gigantic hangar bay entrance. The temperature inside was twenty degrees cooler, and Paladin's sweat immediately chilled his skin to gooseflesh.

A trio of armed guards scrutinized him and reached for their sidearms. They relaxed, though, when they saw the older Lockheed official and Mr. Cologne.

The prototype was the only plane in the cavernous building. She was parked in the center, and a spotlight painted her steel with reflections and glare. Paladin could still see the scrapes and scorch marks from their close calls and felt sorry that he'd banged up the beautiful craft.

"First thing," Paladin said, trying to sound like he knew what he was doing, "I'll need my chief mechanic to look over the plane."

"Absolutely not," Mr. Cologne said, stepping between Paladin and the plane and raising his neatly manicured hands. "You've done enough damage. For all we know you're trying to steal more technical data and sell it to our competitors."

"If you think I already stole the prototype," Paladin replied, lowering his tone and meeting Mr. Cologne's stare, "and if I already had it to examine for an entire day, what could it possibly hurt for me to take one more look?"

Mr. Cologne considered, cupping his dimpled chin; then

he said, "Very well, but I insist one of our mechanics watch you."

"Good," Tennyson remarked. He started to lug his tools to the plane. "We could always use a little help."

Detective Slaughouser cleared his throat. "Is this something the Hollywood police needs to look at? I was told a plane here was stolen."

"Stolen and recovered," Mr. Cologne said. "We already have the thief. All that we require of you is to take him into custody."

Paladin crossed his arms so he'd be less likely to take a poke at Mr. Cologne, who was really starting to get under his skin. "There'll be a charge of espionage to add . . . maybe even a count or two of treason."

Detective Slaughouser raised his eyebrows and tipped up his fedora. "That so?"

"The suit here has it wrong, though," Paladin continued. "I'm not the thief." He turned to Mr. Cologne. "And what he thinks was stolen . . . wasn't."

Jimmy the Rap looked nervously about, as if he were suddenly claustrophobic in the immense empty hangar. "Don't no one go pointing a finger at me." He backed away from Paladin. "I was in lockup for the last two days. I didn't take nothing."

"Shut yer trap," Detective Slaughouser barked. He scratched his head, then asked, "So what's going on, Blake? I know you're on the up-and-up. Spell it out for me. But in English, huh?"

"I will. I'll even gift-wrap the thief for you, complete with the details on how they did it, and their motive. But I'll need to ask everyone a few questions first." Paladin glanced from Justin, to the older Lockheed official, to Detective Slaughouser, to Jimmy the Rap. "Then I'll reveal which one of us is the crook."

"This is outrageous," Mr. Cologne said.

"I must agree," Justin murmured.

"I ain't done nothing," Jimmy said, and edged toward the door.

Detective Slaughouser grabbed Jimmy by his wrinkled collar and marched him back.

"But one of us did steal the prototype," Paladin told them, "in a way.

"Mr. Justin," Paladin said, "take a careful look at this plane. Is it the one you sent me out in two days ago?"

Justin removed a set of spectacles from his coat pocket. He circled the sleek craft. "It is a close approximation of our prototype, but—" His forehead crinkled as he searched for the right word. "—more refined, as if a movie studio reproduced it from a picture perhaps."

"Not quite," Paladin said.

"The real prototype?" Justin inquired. "I have been told it was crashed."

"I was shot down. It's completely destroyed."

"A pity all that is left is this forgery," Justin said.

"Is it?" Paladin asked. "Jimmy, two nights ago, you told me about some parts that left the Lockheed facility in Pasadena? Parts belonging to a prototype?"

"How would I know about that stuff?" Jimmy squeaked.

Detective Slaughouser slapped Jimmy on the back of his head. "Because you're a fence for every jewel thief, burglar, and high roller in Los Angeles. Answer the man's question."

"Okay, some stuff walked out of Lockheed, sure. You hear things on the street. That ain't against the law. These were big-ticket items, too. A pair of engines, a fuselage, and some newfangled air brake."

"Impossible," Justin said. "Those items would have been missed."

Paladin asked Detective Slaughouser, "Do you think it's possible?"

"Naw, couldn't be done," Slaughouser replied. "Not the way Lockheed's got the airfield locked up. And not with the Hollywood police on the job. Besides, why risk moving the parts if it was a spy job? Why not just scram with the blueprints?"

Paladin turned to Mr. Cologne. "Can you think of a reason, other than espionage, that your prototype might be stolen?"

"Sabotage, for starters. That plane represents a year and a half of development and investments. It will cost a fortune to replace, if we can replace it at all."

Tennyson slammed the engine compartment shut and then returned, wiping the grease from his hands with a rag. "The plane is a jigsaw of sorts, Paladin. The fuselage, engines, and other components are missing any manufacturer's serial number. The remainder of the plane appears to be off-the-shelf materials: a Hydrodyne water pump, Delco wiring, Top-Flite tires."

"Good," Paladin said. "Very good."

"One more thing," Tennyson said in a low whisper so only Paladin could hear. "I don't know what the old girl has been through, but I wouldn't take her up in the air. She's got stress fractures up and down her frame. An engine block is cracked. It's a wonder you made it back to the ground in one piece, old boy."

"Excuse me," Mr. Cologne demanded. "What does this prove?"

Paladin ignored him. "One last question: Can I see those files you brought, Mr. Justin?"

Justin opened his briefcase and handed over a stack of manila file folders.

Paladin flipped through the paperwork until he found the one he wanted. He checked the fingerprint on record.

"Ah, there we are," he said with a smile. "You wanted answers? Well I've got some.

"Let's start with this prototype—" Paladin pointed to the plane in the center of the hangar. "—the *real* Lockheed prototype. The one that was stolen, piece by piece, from Pasadena, and then reassembled. Its fuselage, the engines, and air brake system all match the list of stolen goods our friend Jimmy provided. The parts that weren't swiped from Lockheed were replaced by the best fitting parts available."

"But that doesn't add up, Blake," Detective Slaughouser said. "If this thief could have gotten big items like the fuselage, they should have been able to grab 'em all."

"No," Paladin answered. "Our thief needed an alibi. They used the remaining parts to build a mock prototype. One that would have never passed the close scrutiny it would have received had she ever reached this test facility . . . but it was good enough to shoot down. And good enough to send me up in to play the patsy."

Justin reached into his coat.

"Not so fast," Detective Slaughouser said, and drew his pistol.

Justin slowly removed a silver case, opened it, and took out a cigarette.

Detective Slaughouser relaxed and lowered his revolver.

"It saddens me to hear this from you, Mr. Blake," Justin nonchalantly replied as he lit his cigarette. "I would have thought that you would take responsibility for your mistakes, rather than try to shift the blame with some implausible story."

"I have proof." Paladin removed the envelope from his pocket. He withdrew the card inside and showed everyone the half-smeared fingerprint. "I think you'll find this print, which we lifted off the plane, matches the print on Mr. Justin's personnel record."

He handed the card and Justin's file to the older Lockheed official. "I took the liberty of borrowing a friend's fingerprint kit and had Tennyson dust the plane."

Paladin held his breath, hoping that his bluff sounded only half as phony as he thought.

Justin shrugged. "If this plane has stolen Lockheed parts, then my fingerprints *should* be on it. I supervised every phase of the production of the prototype parts."

"True enough. However, your prints are on the other parts, too," Paladin said. "On parts that you should have never touched."

Justin examined the glowing tip of his cigarette. He straightened his arm. There was a click and a slim, silver .38 popped from the sleeve of his silk suit and into his massive hand.

Moving with deceptive agility for such a large man, Peter Justin stepped behind Mr. Cologne, locked him in a stranglehold, and pointed his gun at the Lockheed executive's neck.

"Drop your weapons," Justin growled. "Back away, or this man dies."

8: One Way Out

Paladin took a step toward Peter Justin. "Don't do it, Justin." His words echoed though the cavernous hangar. "There's nowhere to go."

Tennyson took a step closer, trying to flank the massive Russian. Paladin gave him a short shake of his head, and Tennyson froze in his tracks.

Justin twisted the neck of his captive and pushed the muzzle of his gun deep into his target's throat. "I disagree," Justin hissed. He backed away—using Mr. Cologne as a shield between himself and the trio of armed guards and Detective Slaughouser—moving closer to the prototype. "I will be flying away from this place."

"No way," Slaughouser said. The cop steadied his grip on his .38, trying to aim past the squirming hostage, hoping for a clear shot at Justin.

The older Lockheed official set his hand on Slaughouser's arm. "No, Detective. Let him go." Slaughouser muttered something Paladin didn't quite catch. He lowered his gun.

How much influence did Lockheed have with the Hollywood police? Paladin thought that Hughes was the big player in Hollywood. But a man like Slaughouser didn't back down in the middle of a standoff—not unless someone with a lot of clout was pulling his strings.

Paladin dismissed that thought and focused his attention on Justin.

"Why'd you do it?" Paladin asked. "Was it the money? How much did the pale man pay you?"

That stopped Justin more effectively than the threat of

Slaughouser's gun. He stood straighter, crinkled his bushy eyebrows, and looked like Paladin had just slapped him in the face. "I thought a man like you would understand, Blake. This was *never* about the money."

Justin's eyes were steel hard and stared through Paladin. Blake had seen the look before on the soldiers and fliers from the Great War—half shell-shocked and full of the reflections of dead friends.

Paladin hazarded a guess: "So that's it: you're a *patriot*. White Russian to the core, huh? Maybe you don't fly against the Reds anymore, but you're still fighting for Tsar and country."

Justin relaxed his grip on the young Lockheed official, who managed to finally gasp and inhale a full breath.

"Then you *do* understand," Justin whispered.

"Well *I* sure as hell don't," Slaughouser muttered.

"Alaska," Tennyson offered, and tugged thoughtfully at his white beard. "Our Mr. Justin is from Alaska . . . and before that from Russia, a soldier of their revolution."

"When the White Russians were ousted by the Reds," Paladin continued, "a bunch of them lit out for Alaska."

"Da," Justin growled. He tightened his grip on his captive and took a step back.

"The Reds and Whites are still going at it up there," Paladin said. "The Reds want the last of the aristocrats dead. If half the reports are true, the fighting up north is twice as bloody as the 'glorious revolution.' Innocent civilians are getting planted . . . all in the name of Mother Russia."

"The 'pale man,' as you called him," Justin replied, "promised me planes, guns, supplies, even a combat zeppelin in exchange for the prototype—" He glanced quickly over his shoulder to the flying wing, then back. "My people need these things or all will be dead within a month."

"There are other ways," the older Lockheed official said. "We can negotiate—"

"We will negotiate *nothing*," Justin spat. He dragged his captive backward to the prototype. "Capitalists and police," he sneered. "I trust you less than I trust the Communists." He nodded to Paladin, and added, "I must thank *you*, Mr. Blake, for returning the prototype. I shall bring it to the 'pale man.' Perhaps it will not be too late for my people."

"Don't do it," Paladin cautioned. "That plane's had it."

Justin smiled. "A few bullet holes will not stop me from flying this plane."

"It's not only the exterior damage," Tennyson told him. "Look for yourself. She's got stress fractures up and down her frame. The block is cracked. And the intakes are—"

Justin ignored Tennyson and sat on the wing's leading edge. He saddled back, pulling the young Lockheed official up on the wing with him as if he weighed no more than a rag doll. Mr. Cologne let out a strangled squeal. With more dexterity than a man Justin's size should have possessed, he eased into the cockpit, dragging Mr. Cologne with him.

"Stay calm, people. Let them go," the older Lockheed official said, glacially cool. He slicked back his neat white hair, then gestured at the guards to back off.

The three Lockheed guards lowered their weapons.

"No!" Paladin protested.

"There are alternatives to fisticuffs and gunplay, Mr. Blake," the older man admonished, "as our Mr. Justin is about to learn."

Justin closed the canopy. The prototype's engines roared to life and the aircraft eased forward.

Paladin backed away from the plane's twin .30-caliber machine guns.

The older Lockheed official signaled the guards to open the hangar doors.

For the first time in his life, Paladin almost wished one man could escape the law. Justin was a warrior, a patriot. Maybe he had done the only thing possible in his desperate situation. Maybe he'd done what Blake himself would do, if the situation had been reversed.

The flying wing rumbled onto the runway.

Paladin and the others ran outside. The sun was high, and heat shimmered off the dry lake bed.

The prototype accelerated down the runway, then arced into the air. It banked left, pulled up higher, climbed toward the glaring sun—

—and disintegrated into bits of spinning wing and confetti metal, a spray of fuel and fire and smoke.

Paladin's insides ran cold. That could have been him. Maybe it *should* have been him, and Justin, one of the last White Russian resistance fighters, should have walked away from this mess alive.

He turned to the older Lockheed official, whose gray eyes were squinting at the smoky scar in the sky. "You said there were other alternatives," Paladin growled. "Like what?"

"Like," the older man shrugged, "we can always build another plane."

Paladin clenched his fists and stepped toward the Lockheed rep.

Detective Slaughouser reached into his overcoat pocket and shook his head.

Paladin stopped in his tracks.

The older gentleman ignored Paladin's clenched teeth and hate-filled stare. He calmly asked, "Dinner, Mr. Blake?"

The Lockheed secret airfield, the wreckage of the prototype, and the sweltering desert sun were a hundred miles away and twelve hours in the past. Still, Paladin hadn't quite washed the sandy grit or the bad taste of the incident from his mouth.

Paladin straightened his tuxedo and sipped ice water. He avoided looking at the prime rib and the martini that had been ordered for him, nor did he look at the swing band or the dancing feather girls on the stage of Oscar's—a ritzy hole in the wall for Hollywood's movie moguls and power brokers. From the steely-eyed bouncers to the well-bribed maître d', the message was plain: No party crashers allowed.

The older Lockheed official sat across the table from him. He wore a light gray tuxedo that matched his eyes and hair. His name was Dunford. James Dunford.

Since they returned, Paladin and James were on a first-name basis. He was very grateful to Paladin for wrapping up his problems—the missing prototype and the elusive Peter Justin. He was even more grateful that Blake Aviation Security had a policy about keeping its mouth permanently shut about clients' cases.

"Unless there's some illegal activity the police should know of," Paladin added.

"I assure you, Paladin," Dunford said with a smile, "Lockheed engages only in legal activities and commerce."

Legal activities and commerce might, however, cover a lot of territory if the Hollywood police were looking the other way. Come to think of it, Detective Slaughouser hadn't said a word after the plane crash. Would a report get filed? Or would the incident—and the death of two Lockheed employees—be swept under the rug?

Paladin leaned closer to Dunford, wrinkling the white linen tablecloth. "You knew about the plane? Knew it would fall apart?"

"Of course," Dunford said calmly and cut into his porterhouse. "The frame was a special aluminum alloy designed for light weight but with reduced tensile properties. I am amazed it held together for your aerial combats, Mr. Blake." He chewed. "Remarkable."

Paladin had an urge to reach across the table and, if not strangle Dunford, at least blacken his eye. *Maybe* both, Blake thought. *He's just too damn smug for his own good.*

Paladin reined in his impulse, though. The theft of the prototype, the Russian connection, and Lockheed's apparent control of the police were all part of a much larger—and more sinister—picture. If he wanted to find out what was really going on, Paladin had to keep his cool and play along. It wasn't easy.

"I assume," Dunford said, "that you found our retainer sufficient?"

"Very," Paladin replied.

Sufficient didn't begin to cover it; Lockheed had paid him a considerable sum to retain Blake Aviation Security on a semipermanent basis for what Dunford called "special operations." The kind of money they dished out would keep his offices from here to the Empire State in black ink for the next two years.

Dunford set his fork and knife down and riveted Paladin with his eyes. "How did you know Mr. Justin was our thief?"

Paladin found himself unable to hold Dunford's stare. He looked instead at his martini; it was cool and clear and shimmering silver. It would be easy to sip—to drink the thing down. He inhaled the faint scent of gin . . . then reluctantly slid the glass toward the middle of the table.

"It was the cigarettes," Paladin finally said.

Dunford eased back, raised an eyebrow, and then retrieved his own package of cigarettes. He shook one out for himself, then offered one to Paladin.

"No thanks," Paladin said to the offered smokes. "I found a pack of European cigarettes on the pale man's zep. You know, the kind wrapped with the black papers? They're hard to get in North America these days. Especially in Hollywood."

"True." Dunford examined his plain white Lucky Strikes and then lit up. "So I can assume our Mr. Justin smoked the same European brand, yes? That *could* have been mere coincidence."

"Yes, it could have," Paladin conceded. "Hell, it may have even *been* a coincidence, but who else was in a position to steal the major components for the prototype from the Pasadena plant? Who was the only person to see me off in that mock prototype? Who arranged the flight schedule to ensure that my takeoff didn't lead to any inconvenient witnesses? All the pieces fit."

"That bit about the fingerprints," Dunford chuckled. "It was a dazzling display of deduction, Mr. Blake."

"Thanks," Paladin muttered.

In fact there had been no deduction. Tennyson hadn't found a single fingerprint on the prototype. He had, however, lifted one of Justin's prints from Paladin's desk in his Santa Monica office. That was the print Paladin had handed Justin—the print Blake had compared to his Lockheed employment record. It had been nothing more than flimflam.

As far as Paladin was concerned, though, no one at Lockheed ever had to know *that* little detail of the case.

Dunford wiped his mouth with a napkin and covered his

plate with it. "Very good. But now, on to new business, Mr. Blake . . . or rather, a continuation of our old business. Our retainer is conditional on Blake Aviation Security following through on this case."

"*What* case?" Paladin asked. "This whole mess is wrapped up. You've got your plane back . . . most of it, anyway."

"There is no need to feign naïveté, Mr. Blake," Dunford said, and grinned. "There will be a bonus upon completion of your investigation, of course, but I must insist that you continue. This 'pale man' must be found. *You* must find him."

Dunford paused to sip his martini. "When you locate him—and I do not doubt that you will—there shall be no need to immediately involve the authorities. The pale man's day of reckoning will come in a court of law, but Lockheed would like to have a word with him first."

"I see."

Dunford wasn't only buying Blake Aviation Security's service—he was also buying his silence. Why? What did Lockheed want with the pale man? Revenge?

The pale man had promised Justin planes and guns, men, and even a military zep. Where the hell was he getting that equipment? And why was he so willing to give it away? He was risking the wrath of Lockheed and bringing the entire nation of Hollywood to a boil, not to mention the lives that would be spent in bitter conflict in Alaska. That was a lot of heat for one plane, fancy prototype or not.

"Sure," Paladin said, finally. "I'll find him."

Paladin would find the pale man, all right, but for his own reasons. *And one thing is for damn sure,* he thought. *Before Lockheed or the Hollywood police ever get to talk to this mysterious "pale man," I'm going to have my own question-and-answer session first.*

When Paladin learned the truth, no one—not Lockheed, not the police, not the entire nation of Hollywood—would stand in his way of seeing justice done.

9: Chasing Shadows

Blake stepped under the police tape that sealed the threshold of Peter Justin's apartment. The place was in shambles. The Hollywood cops had given it a thorough going-over: a sofa was overturned, its stuffing ripped out and strewn about the small living room; yellowed photographs of Russian farmers and the spires of Saint Peter's Cathedral had been pulled off the walls; potted cacti that had once rested on the windowsill had been uprooted, their sandy soil scattered.

Fortunately, the police were done with the place. Not that they had found a clue. Paladin had reluctantly been given permission—after a few well-placed phone calls from Lockheed—to look the apartment over.

Late afternoon sunlight filtered through the panes of the window, casting four clean squares of illumination that seemed far too orderly when projected onto the chaos.

"Amateurs," Paladin muttered, and gingerly placed the prone cacti into their pots.

Peter Justin had run a clandestine operation past his own security at Lockheed for weeks, maybe even months. Did Detective Slaughouser and his crew think the wily Russian would be stupid enough to hide anything of value *here*? The cops were looking for obvious signs of criminal activity: stolen goods, wads of cash, incriminating photos, and the like.

The cops were way off target, though. Justin was too subtle—and too smart—to simply leave damning evidence lying around his apartment.

Peering out the second-story window, Paladin saw La Cienega Boulevard below, and the trolley station across the street. The place must get noisy in the morning with all the cars rolling in and out on the track. Justin made a bundle of cash as a Lockheed executive. So why live in this crummy neighborhood?

Paladin stepped into the bedroom, cringing at the pants, shirts, and sheets that looked like they had been through a tornado. There were slashes in the mattress, and handfuls of wadding had been scattered haphazardly around the room. Part of the wrought-iron headboard had been unscrewed.

He spied the gleam of gold in the corner and moved closer. A picture of the Virgin Mary, framed in gold-leafed scrollwork, had been overturned.

Nearby, a dozen jelly jars holding candles were toppled over, too, but were remarkably intact. Their wicks had been recently trimmed and soot marks on the glass had been wiped clean. One of the jars, however, had heavy dribbles of red wax on its side as though it had been tipped over while still lit.

It was nothing; still . . . it struck Paladin as oddly out of place.

Peter Justin, with his fastidious habits and immaculately tailored suits, would have kept this place as neat as a pin. So what was one candle doing with this dribbling of wax? Maybe because he had done something so fast that he had forgotten, or hadn't had time, to clean up?

Most likely, it was just meaningless wax.

Paladin started back toward the living room, stopped, and on a whim ran his hand over the back panel of the picture. Smooth wood grain. He brushed across the front. It was smooth, too—no, not quite. A tiny scar of slick candle wax marred the otherwise glassy surface, obscured from casual observation by the glitter of gold leaf and lacquer.

He tilted the picture in the light and saw a faint wax imprint: a circle with a stem. The circle had reversed numbers printed on it, L9879. The stem had a jagged side . . . the outline of a key.

Paladin reached into his pocket. This was a long shot, but he had lifted a signet ring and a key from the pale man's zeppelin. The key he had pilfered from the pirates, while similar in shape, had no numbers.

"If you want to live," a female voice behind Paladin an-nounced, "just keep your hand in your pocket."

Paladin froze when he heard the cold, metallic ratcheting of a pistol's hammer locking in place.

He slowly stood, and turned—keeping his hand in his pocket.

A woman stood in the bedroom doorway. She wore a Free Colorado Zephyrs baseball cap, a flight jacket zipped to her breastbone, and loose pants that were tucked into a pair of shiny, knee-high boots. Waves of red hair had been tucked into her cap. Her black-gloved hands steadily held a massive .45 revolver.

The skin above her open collar bore the swirls and traces of flames ... tattooed flames. Paladin knew her face in-stantly, a face that had been on several wanted posters in Hollywood, Texas, and Utah—Lady Kali, recently employed by the pale man.

"You have one hand free," she said. "Use it to open the left side of your coat. No sudden moves, please—" She smiled. "—since it would be a shame to shoot such a handsome specimen." Her smile slowly hardened into a line of clenched teeth, and Paladin saw that a few of those teeth had been filed to points.

Paladin opened his coat, revealing his holster, the butt of his .38 revolver, and his handcuffs.

"Use two fingers," she ordered him, "and place the gun and cuffs on the floor—then kick them here." Her eyes were dark, and they didn't waver from his for a second.

Paladin complied.

"Your wallet next. Toss it to me."

Did she recognize him? Then again, why should she? She may have gotten only a glance of his filthy face at the pale man's military outpost. And he had been wearing a dirty cover-all then, not his gray Brooks Brothers suit. He fished out his wallet and tossed it to her.

Lady Kali didn't try to catch it. She let it fall at her boots. "Turn around," she said.

Paladin wasn't about to rush a confirmed killer with a gun

pointed at his heart . . . but he wondered if he'd get it in the back and die facing Justin's little shrine to the Madonna.

"Blake?" she said. "Never heard of you. Let me see your face again."

Paladin exhaled and turned around. Every day he wished Blake Aviation Security was big enough to scare pirates out of the skies from here to the Empire State. This once, though, the tiny stature of his company was a blessing.

"You're no cop," she said, looking him up and down appraisingly. "No badge. No cheap suit. So what's with the bracelets? And what are you doing here?"

Paladin carefully removed his hand from his pocket. "Mind if I sit?" He nodded to the torn mattress.

"Go ahead," she replied, and she lowered her aim a notch from his heart to his stomach.

What was she doing in here? Could Lady Kali and Justin have been friends? That didn't figure; Justin wouldn't endanger his patriotic operation by fraternizing with the hired help. Nor would the pale man trust a mercenary with sensitive reconnaissance work. That left only one reason for the deadly aviatrix's presence: cash.

"I'm a private investigator," Paladin told her. "Did a little pavement pounding for Justin."

That wasn't too far from the truth. Lady Kali must have sensed that because she lowered her gun, then sighed, and stuck it in her belt. "Did he stiff you, too?" she asked.

"It was nice and professional for a while, wasn't it?" Paladin said. "But things apparently went to hell in the desert and everyone disappeared or suddenly developed amnesia . . . at least as far as my money is concerned. All I ended up with is a measly retainer and more bills than I can cover."

She chewed on her lower lip, thinking, then said, "Maybe we can help one another." She dug a packet of cigarettes from her leather jacket and offered one to Paladin. He took it, and she lit it for him. "You're the detective; where do *you* figure the pale man is?"

The question threw Paladin for a heartbeat. She didn't know?

"And what do I get paid for my services?" he inquired.

"Why, Blake," she said, and batted her eyes, "you get to

live." Her pointed smile returned. "And maybe if you tell me something I like, I can sweeten that deal."

Paladin eased back with all the nonchalance he could muster. "It's like this: Justin paid me to follow up on rumors that Lockheed was missing some expensive experimental equipment. After a while I figure *he's* the one that grabbed the stuff and just wants me to cover his tracks. I have no problem with that. All part of the business—if you get my meaning."

Lady Kali nodded and sat on the mattress, not too close, but not too far away from him either. Apparently she was more at ease with one of her own kind.

Paladin was momentarily distracted by her scent: lilacs mixed with aviation fuel. He shook his head to regain his composure, though he was sure that Lady Kali had seen his momentary lapse . . . and was amused by it.

"The last thing I heard from Justin was that there was a problem with the prototype. He flew off to Lockheed's base near Palm Springs." Paladin shrugged. "Later, I got word that he bought the farm in some air crash. The police came up here for a visit; the housekeeping is their handiwork, not mine, by the way. After they left, I let myself in to see what they missed. Next thing I know," he added, "a beautiful woman with a gun shows up."

Lady Kali drew on her cigarette and blew a perfect ring. "And?"

"And nothing. I've laid my cards on the table. Now it's your turn. Tell me what you know and I might be able to track down the pale man. If he was paying Justin, then maybe we can both collect."

Lady Kali shifted and stared at Paladin. Her jaw clenched; then she relaxed and draped an arm over the wrought-iron headboard. "Okay, Blake. I'll take a chance on a pretty face." Her eyes narrowed to smoldering slits. "Cross me, though, and it'll be your last mistake."

"I figured as much." Paladin looked away from her and pretended to examine the burning tip of his untouched cigarette.

"The pale man," she finally whispered, "he had something big planned. Not the Lockheed prototype—that was just one of his small-time operations leading up to something big . . . *really* big. This guy has three zeppelins, eight squadrons of planes, mechanics, and enough ammunition to start a small war. Only, he's cagey, walking on eggshells every step of the way. Doesn't make too much sense, does it?"

"Maybe. Maybe not. So what happened to these big plans?"

"What happened?" Her eyebrows shot up. "Someone took off with the prototype, and the pale man started grousing about a rat in his ranks. He ditched us when we touched down in Free Colorado. I barely had enough cash to get back here. It's a good thing Justin's dead or I would have killed him myself."

"I see," Paladin said. He could sense a pattern forming in this whole caper, but it didn't quite make sense yet.

"Here." Lady Kali flipped open the cylinder of Paladin's revolver and dumped the bullets into her palm. "If we're going to be partners, you might as well have this back." She handed the gun to Paladin.

"Thanks," Paladin said, and stuck it in his holster. "The cuffs, too, please?"

She twirled them once around her index finger. "What are you going to use them for?" Her smile—part seductive, part predatory—gave Paladin the chills.

"You'll see." He mirrored her leer and leaned closer—near enough to feel the heat from her face upon his.

"Mm. I can see you're taking this partnership seriously," she murmured, her hands moving toward his face, her eyes closing, her lips parting—

—until Paladin snatched the handcuffs from her.

With a catlike move, he snapped one shackle on her wrist. He slapped the other around the iron post of the bed frame. His free hand grabbed the gun from her belt.

Lady Kali let out a strangled scream and lunged for him. She was fast, with the reflexes of a seasoned combat pilot; Paladin barely avoided the brunt of her attack—but not before she landed a sharp blow on his shoulder.

Paladin aimed her gun at her chest. "I appreciate that a mercenary like you wants to get paid, but I want the pale man for my own reason, Lady Kali. A reason that pirate scum like you will never understand."

"What reason?" she spat, still struggling with her restraints.

Paladin backed into the corner near the Madonna icon. He carefully confirmed the backward number in the wax impression, L9879, and then scratched it off.

He kept the gun trained on Lady Kali as he edged out of the bedroom. "Justice," he said. "You better warm up to the concept. You're going to get a taste of Hollywood justice after I call the cops."

Paladin left the apartment building, ignoring Lady Kali's screamed obscenities as he crossed La Cienega Boulevard and entered the trolley terminal.

He took out the key he had lifted from the pale man's zeppelin. It looked like it matched the imprint in Justin's picture, though the serial number had since been filed off.

There was, Blake mused, a good reason for Justin to live in this crummy neighborhood after all. It was a perfect transfer point, a place where information could be anonymously exchanged at a moment's notice. No one down here paid any attention to the activities of others. People who noticed too much or were seen talking to the cops tended to meet sudden— and nasty—ends.

Justin could also watch all the comings and goings in the neighborhood, just in case someone tried to engineer a double cross.

Paladin strolled into the terminal lobby, his shoes clicking across the well-worn terra-cotta tiles. He took a left, passed the cafeteria, and found a wall of lockers. A nickel rented you a breadbox-size container. It was a nice hiding spot, if, for example, you had something you didn't want the cops to find . . . or you needed to move secrets between two parties.

He stopped at locker L9879.

Paladin took his pilfered key and smoothly slid it into the lock. It clicked open.

10: Pirate Try Outs

"**S**o what does it mean?" Paladin asked Dashiell. He leaned forward on the edge of the chaise longue, trying to not ruffle the silk fabric.

When Paladin had seen the contents of Justin's locker, he brought it all up to Dashiell's Hollywood Hills bungalow. It was private up here. Neither Lockheed, the police, nor anyone else would be getting through the gated community unannounced. Until Paladin knew more about what he had found, he wasn't taking any chances with anyone—not even the people who were supposed to be on the side of the angels.

"It means trouble," Dashiell said with an unlit cigarette dangling from his mouth. He was rapt with concentration, poring over the architectural diagrams that had been laid across his Persian rug.

The blueprints had been in the locker, along with a manila envelope containing three thousand dollars and a note scrolled with neat cursive that stated,

> *Need a dozen pilots. Must have their own aircraft. Must not be afraid to fight. Money, as usual, not an issue. Dalewick Airfield. Dusk. July 7.*

Today was July 7.

"What kind of trouble?" Paladin asked, and crossed his arms.

Dashiell stood, straightened his navy blue satin lounging robe, finally lit his cigarette, and took a long draw. "For a man who has been to so many exotic places, Paladin—" He exhaled silver smoke. "—I'm shocked you do not recognize it.

The long rectangular wings and the enormous central round gallery? The marble cornices and colonnades?"

Paladin stared at the building's cross section but saw only white lines and blue smudges.

"It's the old Capitol building," Dashiell told him. "In Washington, Nation of Columbia."

"Sure," he muttered. "I see it now."

It was more than just the white marbled rotunda Paladin was seeing. He saw the vague outlines of what Lady Kali had called the pale man's "big" plans. He wasn't sure what those plans were exactly, only that he was liking them less and less.

"The note," Dashiell said, "appears to be written by a woman of distinction and breeding. And from what you have told me, I can only surmise these 'pilots' she refers to are replacements for Lady Kali and her cohorts."

Paladin got up and paced. "Okay. That takes care of the contents of the late Peter Justin's locker, and the key and the black cigarettes I found on the pale man's zeppelin. But there's one last piece of the puzzle to fit. This." Paladin handed Dashiell the gold signet ring with a cabochon of jade he had "borrowed" from the pale man's desk. Carved in relief on the stone was an eagle with talons extended around a star.

Dashiell raised an eyebrow.

"You recognize it?"

"Yes," Dashiell remarked as he tried the ring on for size. It was too big. "I'd say getting caught with this number would buy you a rubber hose massage from the Hollywood police and three years' hard labor. You're quite lucky Slaughouser didn't see it." He returned the ring to Paladin. "We used a similar prop in a recent film. Had to cut that scene, though. The censors didn't—"

"The note said dusk," Paladin reminded him. "I've got three hours, maybe, to make it to that airfield and stop what's going on. Just tell me what the ring is."

Dashiell sighed. "Unionists, my dear Paladin. The rampant eagle clutching a star was the symbol of one of the splinter factions. The Brotherhood of America, I believe they called themselves. As far as I know, its members had all either been caught or killed. Perhaps those reports were in error."

Unionists. Since the breakup of the United States, a handful of anarchic splinter groups had appeared, all crying for the reunification under the old American banner. Paladin sympathized with their goals—until a handful of the more fanatical groups started lobbing bombs to achieve their ends. Today, the word *Unionist* was synonymous with "mad bomber" and "crank."

Paladin whispered, "I've never heard of Unionists with battle zeppelins, squadrons of planes, or buckets of cash to throw around. And why a blueprint of the old Capitol building? You'd think they'd revere it as the center of their America." He stared into thin air, trying to see the connection.

Dashiell got up, frowned, and ground his cigarette in a crystal ashtray. "I know that look. It's your nothing-is-going-to-stop-me-until-I-solve-this-even-if-it-kills-me look. So let's pretend this time that I've tried to talk you out of it, and you ignored me. That way, you can get to the airfield before the sun sets. Just do me a favor—" Dashiell dug into the magazine rack next to the chaise longue and withdrew a holstered .44. "—and take this. Since you lost your .45, you'll need a replacement . . . something other than that sissy .38 you insist on carrying. A gun like that could get you killed."

Despite his recent mishaps in the air, Paladin felt the weight of this case lift from his chest the moment the wheels of his plane parted from the runway.

"Lightning Girl," a modified Curtiss-Wright P2 Warhawk, was Paladin's current favorite. Tennyson had tinkered with the three stock Wright, R-1350 engines and coaxed out a quarter more horsepower than they had been rated for. She burned quarts of oil and guzzled fuel like a bonfire, but she was faster than anyone suspected a Warhawk could be . . . a surprise that had saved his skin on more than one occasion.

But speed wasn't why Paladin had named her "Lightning Girl."

Her standard guns had been replaced with four .60-caliber Smith & Wesson "Scorpion" cannons. Tennyson had engineered a double set of triggers on the stick, one over the other, for each pair of guns. Using two fingers, squeezing both triggers at the same time, all four guns could be fired simultaneously.

The blazing lead, streaks of tracers, and sheer mayhem that Lightning Girl could deliver was an awesome sight. So far, no one had seen her spit fire and lived to tell her secret.

Paladin nosed his plane up, banked east, and headed toward Riverside, and Dalewick Airfield.

A layer of nimbus clouds had settled around four thousand feet, a white-and-gray inverted landscape that glowed gold and orange as the sun set. Below, large boulders dotted the landscape; white and yellow washes of soil made meandering patterns broken by an occasional emerald patch of avocado grove. To the south were rolling hills, and farther, the San Bernardino Mountains, the highest peaks still capped with snow. Nice country.

Dalewick Airfield serviced the region's handful of seasonal crop dusters. Paladin had stopped over before. It was a smooth patch of dirt runway and a radio shack, as close to civilization as the middle of nowhere could be.

A speck hovered in the distance, then another, then three more. Hard to tell—but there must have been twenty aircraft circling like buzzards over Dalewick. And they weren't crop dusters. As Paladin got closer he saw these planes were painted in gaudy colors and sported a variety of emblems: fiery horses, crossed rifles, and falcon silhouettes.

There were six Grumman Avengers, a Ravenscroft Coyote, a pair of new M210 Ravens, and a few battered PR-1 Defenders.

Paladin flipped on his radio and tuned in the airfield's frequency.

"Dalewick come in. This is 3-Delta-475 requesting permission to land."

There was a hiss of static, then, "Denied 3-Delta-475. This is an invitation-only party. Better scram while you can, buster."

That definitely was no Hollywood-certified radio operator.

"Dalewick, this is 3-Delta-475. I was invited. Justin sent

me . . . before his last flight. I've already been paid to show up. You want me to leave? I'll just pocket the money. It's all the same to me."

The radio crackled with silence for three heartbeats. "Okay, 3-Delta-475, join in. We were odd anyway."

Odd? Now what does that mean? he wondered. Paladin didn't want to blow his cover, so he just kept his mouth shut.

"3-Delta-475, your partner is Foxtrot 41-niner. That's the red J2 Fury."

"Roger that, Dalewick."

Paladin would play along. *Partner* probably meant he had been assigned a wingman. Maybe for a test of skill?

Planes buzzed around, under, and over Lightning Girl as they all continued to circle the airfield. He spotted the red J2 Fury, which also bore a silver snake emblem coiled on each wing. Nice and subtle.

The Fury was circling directly across from Lightning Girl. Paladin eased back on the throttle so they could catch up.

The little red plane slowed, too, however, matching his speed and keeping a fixed position across from him.

"Helluva lousy wingman," Paladin muttered.

The radio crackled, "Okay, ladies and gentlemen. The show's on. Let's see what you're made of."

Gunfire erupted, and every plane veered from the circling formation. The red J2 banked and dived toward the underside of Paladin's bird.

A Defender on his wingtip shattered as a rocket exploded over the cockpit—Paladin reflexively banked hard to starboard.

So this recruitment of Justin's was apparently open to only a select few. That's what the ground controller meant by "partner." Not wingman. The J2 Fury was Paladin's *target* . . . and Lightning Girl was the Fury's.

Paladin inverted Lightning Girl, rolling upside down to get a better look. The nimble J2 Fury was attempting to come up under him, to align its deadly .70-caliber cannon, and make short work of him.

"Nice try," Paladin growled.

The Fury was lighter and faster than his Warhawk, even

with Tennyson's modifications. But the Fury was nose-heavy and could stall even at a moderate angle of attack unless the pilot knew exactly what he was doing.

Still inverted, Paladin poured on the speed and climbed into a loop. The Fury followed him—almost straight up.

He leveled out at three thousand feet; he had to. Ribbons of smoke poured from his port engine. Lightning Girl couldn't take much more.

Beneath him, however, the Fury sputtered black smoke, and her nose dipped. The pilot quickly recovered from the stall and leveled out. That was all the invitation Paladin needed.

The Fury's pilot must have realized his mistake. He dived.

Now it was Paladin's turn to pursue. He opened up the throttle, and the full weight of his Warhawk gave him a crucial speed advantage. Lightning Girl fell toward her prey like a meteor.

The Fury rolled to port, a mistake at stall speed. If he had continued a full-power dive, he might have gotten close to the ground and pulled out at the last moment. A Warhawk wouldn't be able to match such a maneuver.

Paladin didn't hesitate to exploit his enemy's error. The instant the Fury lined up in his sights, he opened fire with the outer pair of .60-caliber guns. Bullets streaked past the Fury's wingtip.

He let all four guns blaze. The noise was deafening— louder than the trio of engines at full speed. The Warhawk's frame shuddered, but Paladin held her steady in the dive, ruddered over, and let the torrent of bullets spray across the Fury. A moment later, amid a fountain of red paint chips, the Fury fell—her snake decorations obliterated by the dark, smoking pockmarks of bullet impacts, both wings chewed off.

Paladin rolled and pulled back on the stick, easing out of the dive. He cast a glance over his shoulder and glimpsed what was left of the Fury's fuselage spiraling toward the airfield.

He looked away. He wasn't squeamish by any means, but there were dogfights in every direction, whirling pieces of metal, clouds of smoke, and tracers whistling past his cockpit—he had to get out of here.

Paladin spied a clear piece of sky and nosed Lightning Girl in that direction. He sailed over Dalewick Airfield, not more than a hundred feet off the ground. The radio shack was on fire.

"Ladies and gentlemen," the radio announced. "Cease fire. That was an excellent demonstration of skill and daring. We regret that we have only a limited number of berths for your fighters, and that we had to resort to such a drastic selection method. But as they say: to the victors go the spoils."

Overhead, a shadow darkened the clouds, which parted as a massive zeppelin began its descent. Mounted within the observation deck were a dozen machine-gun nests and the gleaming noses of a hundred rockets.

"3-Delta-475, please climb to one thousand feet and proceed to dock. Welcome aboard *George Washington*."

11: Under a Banner of War

Paladin was exhausted. He couldn't let his guard down, though. If he nodded off, he'd wake up with his throat slit.

He sat in the dark, along with dozens of soldiers, pirates, and mercenaries, any one of whom would have gladly tossed him overboard if they discovered who he really was.

The thrum of the engines reverberated through the chamber—a section of the zeppelin's interior superstructure. Instead of a gasbag, there were crates, spare airplane parts, and three bleachers arranged before a small projection screen.

A beam of light pierced the darkness. The pale man stood in front of his audience, hands held in a steeple. He wore a linen suit, had slicked back his thinning hair, and sported a monocle. His white suit and pallor blended into the screen behind him so he appeared—to Paladin's sleep-deprived eyes, at least—to step out of the flat surface.

"Ladies and gentlemen," he said, "thank you for accepting our invitation. Now that we are close to our destination, I can brief you on the mission."

Paladin counted his lucky stars to have made it this far. It had been a full day since he had docked Lightning Girl with the *George Washington*.

When he got out of the cockpit, he kept his leather helmet and goggles on. Unlike Lady Kali, someone in this group might recognize him. If not one of the hired pirates, then one of *George Washington*'s crew. They wouldn't soon forget the man who had stolen their pilfered prototype from the heart of their secret base.

So far, no one had grabbed him or put a gun to his head. Yet.

Each pirate lined up, signed a contract (with the usual clauses stipulating nonpayment in the event of mutiny or cowardice), and got paid three hundred dollars in the national scrip of their choice. Another five hundred dollars plus bonuses were also promised, upon completion of the mission.

One clause in the contract caught Paladin's eye, however. It gave the pale man and his crew permission to reinforce his plane's hardpoints. Lightning Girl could already carry rocket racks and extra fuel tanks, so what gave? He didn't ask. The last thing he wanted was to draw attention to himself.

Along with the new pirates who had survived the "interview" process, there were another two dozen mercenaries on the zeppelin and a comparable number of soldiers in drab gray-green uniforms with shorn heads and black circle insignia.

He and the rest of the hired help had been fed pheasant, mashed potatoes, and pumpkin pie before being assigned to cramped berths. The others in the informal "barracks" played poker or told wild tales of their exploits to pass the time.

Paladin had curled up in his bunk and pretended to sleep. He tried to rest, but his heart wouldn't stop racing.

It probably wouldn't be too suspicious to keep to himself. Pirates and mercenaries weren't noted for their friendliness. That wasn't too much of a problem. But where were they?

The zep's engines had been running at full throttle for twenty hours. If they had caught a trade wind, they could be two or three thousand miles from Hollywood—anywhere from Panama to Hawai'i to Alaska.

"Our mission is clear," the pale man said, snapping Paladin back from the edge of his groggy recollections. "Our mission is destruction."

This brought murmurs of approval from the audience.

The pale man nodded. There was the ratcheting of a mechanism from the shadows and an aerial map of a city flashed upon the screen behind him. Two river tributaries ran down either side. On the left there was a grid of buildings, but the right side had only a few structures, acres of green lawn, and rows of trees.

"We have prevailing cloud cover today at four thousand feet. Two of the three zeppelins in our battle group will maintain position just above this altitude with their escort squadrons."

Another slide and three zeppelin silhouettes appeared in the corner.

Paladin spied a figure sitting in shadows next to the stage. She sat just close enough to the illuminated screen that he could make out her features: a fall of dark hair, full lips, a tiny dimple in her chin, and wide expressive eyes. Paladin instantly recognized her—the pale man's companion, the one he had seen during his raid on the pirate base.

"George Washington," the pale man continued, "will launch our two dozen fighters, half of which will proceed toward—" He nodded again, and a large arrow flashed upon the map from the zeppelins to the center of the city. "—this green belt. There, they will briefly engage the defending units, perhaps four to five squadrons, which will have been scrambled to counter our attack."

A voice shouted from the dark: "Two dozen planes against five squadrons? That's nuts."

"Hardly," he said, and peered into the shadows. The light reflecting from his monocle made the one eye seem huge. "I said 'briefly engage.' " He turned back to the map. "Napoleon called it the passive lure."

Another arrow appeared from the center of the map back to the zeppelins.

"You will let these defenders chase you to *George Washington*. Climb to four thousand two hundred feet. *Thomas Jefferson* and *Samuel Adams* will then enter the fray." He inhaled deeply and let out a sigh of contentment. "Between the machine-gun fire and our initial salvo of rockets, there will be little resistance left for our fighter escorts."

The pale man snapped his white-gloved fingers. "Phase two."

He pointed with his cane to a white rectangular building on the map. "Our heavier planes in reserve will then proceed unopposed to the primary target."

This structure looked familiar to Paladin.

"These planes have been fitted with two quarter-ton incendiary and two high-explosive bombs. When the primary target has been destroyed"—the pale man pointed to another building—"this will be your secondary target. And this"—he indicated a tiny square that cast an unusually long shadow— "is our tertiary target. Destroy them all, ladies and gentlemen, and your pay shall be doubled."

The motley crew in the auditorium broke out in applause.

Paladin, however, had a sinking sensation in his stomach. Not only for the defenders of this city—who were certain to get blasted into confetti by the three battle zeppelins—but because he finally recognized the targets.

It was that long shadow that gave it away. The tiny white square came to a point at the top. Paladin stretched out the shape to match the length of the shadow compared to the relative sizes of the other buildings' shadows. The structure had to be a hundred feet tall, maybe more. There was only one building like that in North America: the Washington Monument.

And the secondary target across the beltway park? That was the White House.

The primary target, east of the others, that was the Capitol

Building—just like he had seen it in the blueprints from Peter Justin's locker.

"Ready yourselves, pilots," the pale man said. "We will be arriving shortly."

The audience members started talking excitedly to one another as they pushed their way out of the auditorium. Paladin sat for a moment and stared numbly at the map until they were all gone.

"You see a flaw in this plan, perhaps?" a female voice from the dark asked.

The woman who had been near the stage, the one who had always been by the pale man's side, was seated a few feet away from Paladin on the bleachers.

His heart skipped a beat and then pounded in his throat. She, if anyone here, would recognize him. She had gotten close to Paladin before. Maybe she couldn't quite see him in the darkness.

"No. No flaw," he replied.

What stumped Paladin were the pale man's motives. No Unionist in his right mind would attack the Capitol Building of the old United States. Paladin couldn't ask him directly, but maybe his friend here might spill the beans.

"I don't see the analogy between this plan and Napoleon's passive lure," Paladin said in the calmest voice he could muster. "The French used cannon, cavalry, and infantry. We have none of that."

"An educated pirate?" she cooed. "*On aura tout vu.* I'm impressed, Mr.—?"

"Call me Dashiell," Paladin told her.

She moved closer. From the reflected light off the screen Paladin saw she wore a tight skirt that flared around her shapely calves, a tight blazer, and a ruffled white shirt. He also spied the sparkle of diamonds on her fingers.

"Well, Dashiell," she said, "the analogy *does* hold. Our zeppelins each carry over a hundred rockets. The exhaust backwash is ducted out the opposite side so we can launch dozens simultaneously. That is our artillery. The machine-gun nests next to them are the infantry. And you, and your fellow fliers, are the cavalry."

Paladin imagined the battle: rockets could do a boatload of damage from a considerable distance to a tight formation of planes. *If* they got closer, the machine guns would finish them off; add a dozen fighters and two more zeppelins bombarding the incoming wave of advancing planes . . . and there'd be nothing left of them but smoke.

"It'll work," Paladin admitted, "but why bother? I mean, bombing a few buildings hardly seems profitable. Unless profit isn't your motive?"

"Are you sure you're a pirate?" she asked. "Most pirates concern themselves only with money."

Paladin started to say he was a pirate—but he checked himself. He always tried to tell the truth, because frankly, he was lousy at lying. Most people picked up on it.

"I'm not a pirate," he whispered. "I'm a patriot. My family fought in the American Revolution and my grandfather lost both legs in the Civil War. My father died when the States fell apart. I guess my family always ends up fighting and dying when their country is in need."

That was not far from the truth. Paladin's father had died during the breakup of the States—but on a bootlegging run gone sour, not on some patriotic crusade.

Was telling her this the right approach? Were the pale man and his crew Unionists? Paladin had found a Unionist signet ring in the pale man's room, but that didn't mean he was a member of the Brotherhood of America. It could have been a trophy taken from an enemy, or for that matter, he could have picked it up in a pawnshop. Yet, would a man like Peter Justin have allied himself with anyone but a patriot? Paladin decided to take a gamble.

"I guess what I'm trying to say is that a real American has to operate outside the law when he lives in a country that itself is illegal."

"Eloquently put." She set her hand consolingly on his. "Would it help if I told you that you are in the right place at the right time to serve your country?"

Her touch gave him the chills. Paladin didn't move away, even though every instinct screamed that this woman was poison.

"How, exactly?" he asked.

She was silent a moment as she considered his question; then she said, "As we speak, representatives from every nation in North America are in the old capital making deals to strengthen their political ties and lower trade barriers."

"Isn't that a good thing?"

"Good?" She withdrew her hand. "I suppose it is good for the tiny nation-states. Good that they will become complacent with their diminished status. And good that their divisions will be all the more permanent, cemented by new treaties and agreements and guarantees of peaceful coexistence. But there is another way . . . not necessarily easier, but better for all in the long term."

"I think I see where this is going," Paladin murmured.

He had heard similar words years ago in Europe, and he had witnessed the brutal consequences.

"Then you understand," she said. "We disrupt the talks and encourage the nations to believe another state was responsible. One such operation was successful in Pacifica. Boeing and the Pacifica government have been led to believe that Hollywood spies stole a new plane. We had some . . . setbacks during a similar operation in Hollywood, but suspicions between nations will now grow.

"We drive them toward conflict," she continued, her eyes glittering. "The most aggressive we back with money and weapons and guidance. Only a strong nation, willing to risk everything—to do anything—will have the willpower to reunite our country and make it great again."

"Under a banner of war," Paladin said.

She gave his arm a squeeze. "Yes."

Paladin had a couple of other names for this deal: Nationalism. Fascism. Rotten through and through.

But as much as the morals of the pale man's scheme repelled him, the logic driving the plan was sound, and its eventual outcome was horrifyingly possible.

A klaxon blared, echoing throughout the chamber.

"We are preparing to launch phase one," the dark woman said. "You must go."

"Yeah, I better," Paladin said, and stood.

It looked like he was going to be a patriot after all. He had to stop the pale man—even if he had to die doing it.

12: One-Man Invasion

Blake held his breath, carefully maintaining his plane's position in the double-arrowhead formation of warplanes. Paladin's every instinct screamed at him to blast his way out of this mess . . . but that would be suicide.

Instead, he gritted his teeth and pointed Lightning Girl at the heart of Washington, capital of the nation of Columbia.

The pale man's officers had positioned their black Grumman Avengers on the tips of this double-V formation, herding the characteristically sloppy pirate pilots into a precise pattern of aircraft with no more than ten feet between any one of them.

It was a sight that the defenders of Columbia couldn't possibly miss—which was the point.

Paladin had been assigned a dual role on this mission of destruction. He was to fly Lightning Girl out and lure the defenders of the peace conference back to the Unionist zeppelins. After the zeps made confetti out of them, he had orders to turn back and bomb the Capitol Building.

Lightning Girl had been singled out for both parts of the mission because the pale man's mechanics had been wowed with her horsepower and devastating firepower. They also knew she'd be one big, flashy target that would be irresistible to the defending militia pilots. And she could take far more punishment than the majority of the lighter craft on his Warhawk's wingtips. The Unionists had offered Paladin a hazard bonus for the extra duty, and he had accepted— itching to do something . . . *anything* to stop this.

But how was he going to stop them? He was just one plane against dozens, each flown by an experienced killer.

He glanced over his shoulder. *George Washington* floated under a ceiling of iron-gray clouds at four thousand feet. The other two zeppelins, *Samuel Adams* and *Thomas Jefferson,* were concealed just above her, nestled within the cottony banks of clouds.

Paladin dialed through the radio frequencies, hoping to pick up some chatter, trying to remember what channel Columbia's militia used, but heard only static. He reset his radio.

"'Lightning Girl,'" a voice growled though his speaker. "Get your nose up!"

"Roger," Paladin replied, startled.

He had allowed his plane to drift a few feet above the formation. He quickly pushed the yoke forward, easing his crate back into place.

He scowled, wishing Lightning Girl weren't so sluggish. She had been loaded with two high explosive and two incendiary bombs, not to mention her full fuel tanks, yards of ammo belts, and rockets.

It was a good thing the pale man's officer had caught his slip. A minor collision would mean disaster for everyone . . . which, perhaps, was exactly what Paladin needed.

Not that he was ready to sacrifice his life. There had to be another way.

Paladin pulled back on the stick and keyed his microphone: "Black Ace One, this is 'Lightning Girl.' I have a sticky wing flap. I need to give myself a little maneuvering room to see if I can free it up."

"Break and return to base, 'Lightning Girl.' Wait for phase two; then proceed as ordered."

Paladin eased his plane up and poured on the juice, pulling in front of the formation.

This wasn't the first time he'd flown in a dicey situation. In the Great War he had to hit moving targets—trains and tanks, and columns of soldiers—but never a target like this. There would be no near-miss.

He glanced down at the double-V formation. Planes shifted gently, closing to fill the hole made by his absence. Good.

Paladin nudged Lightning Girl ahead, his eyes flickering between his instruments and the formation below.

There. That would be his best shot.

His radio crackled and whined. "'Lightning Girl,' I said return to base!" the pale man's watchdog snapped.

"I will," he replied. "But I have to leave you creeps a little going-away gift."

Paladin released his bombs.

He pulled up hard and firewalled the throttle. Lightning Girl climbed and inverted. Paladin watched as his bombs tumbled into the tightly stacked formation.

The first bomb shattered the canopy of a Kestrel, as another simultaneously slammed into—and through—the wing of a J2 Fury. There was an incendiary spark, which coalesced in a split second into a brilliant blue-white flash of light as the spark reached the glittering cloud of aviation fuel spewing from the Fury's severed wing tanks.

Like Fourth of July firecrackers, there was one flashbulb detonation after another, as Paladin's bombs found their marks. The planes slammed into each other, transforming the tight, precision formation into an insane tangle of smoke, whirling propeller blades, glittering shards of metal, and igniting fuel that mushroomed and roiled with screeching thunder.

Wings and tails and glass hailstones emerged from the cloud, fuselages spiraled out of control, and other twisted hunks of steel plummeted toward the earth. Paladin caught a glimpse of an opening parachute and a tangle of fluttering silk wrapped around a body.

Paladin didn't waste his time feeling sorry for any of them. They had wanted to start a war—now they'd damn well get a war.

He banked back toward the zeppelins.

It wasn't the acceleration that made his stomach sink; Lightning Girl had dumped her bombs to remove the advance squadron. Now how was he going to stop three fully loaded military zeps and their escorts?

Paladin eased the throttle back. He needed time to think.

The radio crackled: "Come in, Black Ace One: repeat your status and position."

It was now or never. The pale man's forces were confused and blind. Paladin quickly planned his approach and opened up the throttle. Whatever he was going to do, however he was going to stop them—he had to do it fast. Their confusion, and Paladin's window of opportunity, wouldn't last for long.

As he drew closer, he spotted the shiny bulk of *George Washington* . . . then saw the shadows of *Samuel Adams* and *Thomas Jefferson* as they descended from the clouds. They took positions in front of *Washington*—a triangular formation that would maximize their firepower if anyone was foolish enough to engage them.

Circling above the zeps were their escort squadrons—the fighters that would catch any strays the zep didn't get and the bombers that would turn Washington into rubble.

They were expecting Columbia's militia to be hot on the Warhawk's tail. They were expecting a fight. So he'd give them one.

Paladin pulled back on the yoke, executed a quarter roll, and accelerated toward *Jefferson*. He lined his plane up, aiming to pass slightly above the line of fire of the zeppelins' machine-gun nests and gleaming rocket tips.

He held his breath—waited until he was close enough to see people inside pointing and panicking and running from their positions, as the plane they thought was on their side barreled toward them—then opened fire with cannons and rockets.

Smoke trails snaked from Lightning Girl to the belly of the zeppelin. Fire blossomed inside the converted passenger's galley, followed by a staccato string of detonations, as the munitions inside exploded in a chain reaction. A hundred rockets launched to port and starboard, billowing thunderheads of smoke and flame and sprouting greasy blossoms of flak and fire.

Paladin snapped Lightning Girl upright and pulled back fast—arcing up and over the zeppelin, so close he felt the randomly firing machine-gun rounds zinging off his plane's fuselage, so close he thought he could feel the heat of the passing rockets.

He leaned over and strained to get a look at *Jefferson*. Her underside was ablaze, and flames and plumes of sooty smoke curled up the sides of the airship—flames that quickly dwindled and died.

"Damn," Paladin muttered. So much for the element of surprise. It figured, though. This wasn't some low-rent bunch of pirates; this splinter group of Unionists had the money and the resources to fill the zeppelin with helium. Had she been filled with cheaper hydrogen, she would have gone up like dynamite.

The pale man's moment of confusion, and Paladin's luck, had just run out. He glanced back. The sky was thick with swarming planes—all of them gunning for him. Bullet holes stitched across his starboard wing, and a trio of slugs ricocheted and pinged off the canopy, cracking it.

Jefferson was still aloft, and her engines were running at full speed. The zep, however, looked like a bite had been taken out of her. Where the galley had been, there was now a twisted, blackened mess of skeletal superstructure. The central gasbags were rapidly deflating, and jets of fire spouted from broken fuel lines.

Paladin had to make a break for it. If he gained altitude fast enough, he might be able to get away in the cloud cover.

But what about the peace conference? The pale man still had two zeps and enough planes to pull off his mission—maybe not so easily as intended, but it could still be done.

Paladin sighed and patted the instrument panel of Lightning Girl. "This may be the dumbest stunt we've pulled yet, friend." He pulled back on the yoke, rolled, and righted Lightning Girl—heading straight into the face of his enemies.

Two dozen fighters opened fire. They dived toward him. The sky was filled with a rain of tracers. Enough bullets impacted with Lightning Girl to make the plane's engine stutter.

The Warhawk's starboard engine smoked and coughed but kept going. Paladin squeezed both triggers and peppered a pack of Devastators directly in front of him—cracking the canopy of the lead plane. The planes veered aside at the last second, as the lead Devastator began to tumble. Scratch one pilot.

It was suddenly silent, save for the thrum of his plane's engines.

Paladin had broken though the pack of pirate escorts; however, it would take them only a second to turn and get on his tail. He refused to think about what would happen then; he had to stay focused on *Jefferson*.

He turned toward the line of engine nacelles on the wounded zeppelin's port side.

Blake knew he would never get another sweetheart shot like he had taken on *Jefferson*. *Adams* and *Washington* would cut him to shreds before he could blink. No . . . there was only one way to take out those zeps now—with another zeppelin.

Jefferson wasn't dead in the air; she kept pace with *Adams*. By destroying the bridge, Paladin had cut off only her head. Her engines were running at full speed—dumb and blind, but still running.

He was a quarter mile away from *Jefferson*'s port engine nacelles when he opened fire. It was a million-to-one shot at this range, but he'd need all the firepower he could squeeze off to make this work.

The Warhawk's guns sprayed destruction as she closed the distance to the zep. One motor sparked as Lightning Girl lined up on the proper trajectory and hit—then it exploded into sparks and bits of spinning metal. Paladin quickly aimed at the next engine and blasted away, then a third, before Lightning Girl zoomed past the dying airship.

A rocket blast shook Lightning Girl. Paladin looked over his shoulder and spied a pack of incoming Grumman Avengers. He rolled back and forth, then dived to gain speed.

They followed him like bloodhounds on the scent, a shower of lead shredding his tail.

"Come on, girl," Paladin urged his plane. "Hang on just a little longer."

Paladin pulled up, ignoring the shudder that ran through his airframe. If his luck could hold out for a few more seconds, then the party would really begin.

He spotted *Jefferson*. With three of the five engines on her port side shot to pieces, she slowly listed to one side, right toward *Samuel Adams*—

—and collided with the battle zep.

The starboard side of *Jefferson* impacted on *Adams'* stern. Their spinning props ripped into one another, tearing fabric and gasbags, wrenching blades and frames, pulling them into a tighter embrace. The zeps tangled and locked together.

Adams' nose crumpled and sagged. Many of *Jefferson's* gasbags had been torn open. They tilted and started to sink, locked in a deadly embrace.

Paladin lined up Lightning Girl, right over *George Washington,* and matched speed and direction. He double-checked his parachute harness, praying the chute he had packed wouldn't tangle.

He popped the canopy. Wind stung him with icy needles. He bid Lightning Girl a silent good-bye, then cut her engines.

The Warhawk sputtered and stalled, and Paladin jumped.

The thirty-foot fall wasn't bad—he broke a handful of his ribs on impact, rather than breaking his neck. Paladin bounced once—twice—toward the edge, then caught the slippery fabric before he went over.

He climbed back to the top. Beneath him, the zeppelin shifted and turned west.

He drew a knife from his boot and cut into the fabric, then grabbed onto the steel frame and pulled himself inside. "No you don't," he growled. "This time, there's no way in hell you're getting away."

13: The Lady and the Tiger

Paladin had one leg in the hole of the zep's fabric when he noticed Lightning Girl in his peripheral vision. His prized Warhawk, now without a pilot, arced wildly upward, wobbling, pitching, and yawing . . .

. . . before inverting, her engine stalling out. Seconds later, Blake's favorite airplane fell toward the nose of *George Washington.*

The Warhawk slammed into the zeppelin and ripped

through the hull as the plane's fuel tanks ignited in a stunning fireball.

The zeppelin shuddered, knocking Paladin off his precarious footing on a structural beam. He teetered, struggled to regain his balance—

—and fell, barely managing to grab hold of the beam with his left hand. His busted ribs exploded with pain.

He looked down. Below him was a seventy-foot fall, crisscrossed with a supporting skeletal framework that held *George Washington*'s bloated gasbags. If he lost his grip, he'd end up with a cracked skull. If he took his time climbing down, one of the gasbags could rupture. The flood of helium would probably suffocate him. Either that, or the force of the gasbag bursting would dash him against the deck or a steel crossbeam, knocking him unconscious or killing him outright.

He had to move—fast.

Paladin gritted his teeth against the pain in his chest and caught the beam with his other hand. He braced himself with his feet, then half climbed, half slid down, into the heart of the zeppelin's envelope.

From outside, he could hear the roar of cannon fire, the staccato echoes rattling through the zep. Bullet holes dotted the fabric skin, allowing thin, pale streams of sunlight into the dim interior. A flicker of shadow rippled past, blocking out the light passing through the punctures—a fighter plane, making a close pass to the zeppelin.

It looked like Columbia's defenders had finally wised up to the danger in their skies. Too bad their timing was lousy. Paladin was caught in the crossfire.

He stepped gingerly down onto the zep's gondola roof and made his way to the nearby hatch. The steel plates under his feet shook with the din of rocket and cannon fire, and the occasional metal fragment whizzed by, stray debris from the battle raging all around him. He took a deep breath—wincing as his tortured ribs protested the abuse—and opened the hatch, quickly climbing down . . .

. . . straight into Hell itself.

The fore end of the galley was engulfed in flame. Oily, choking smoke obscured Paladin's view, but he could see that the damage was extensive. Where there had once been a .50-caliber machine-gun nest, there was now a gaping, ugly hole, its razor-sharp edges blackened with soot. Smoldering metal twisted and blossomed inward, and burn scars and blood streaked the walls and floor.

Ammunition belts—spilled from a nearby ammo crate during the breach—were strewn across the deck, where the fire hungrily fed on them. Machine-gun rounds popped like firecrackers, sending slugs whistling past Paladin's head. Ricochets buzzed through the companionway like angry hornets. Five crews manned the remaining machine guns, grimly concentrating on defending the zep from the swarm of planes outside.

No one spared him a glance.

Paladin covered his head—more to keep from choking on the stench of smoke and cordite than to disguise himself— and ran aft. He moved quickly through the corridor, pushing past men clambering to assist the gun crews. Once clear, he made his way toward the passenger section . . . and the pale man's cabin.

The door to the cabin was locked. He drew his pistol and put his shoulder against the door. He shoved and cracked the frame. Paladin quickly entered, his gun sweeping the room, ready to shoot at the first sign of trouble.

Nothing.

The room was a mess: bookcases were overturned, every drawer in the rolltop desk had been opened and dumped, and a painting had been torn off the wall. The safe the painting had once concealed now stood open . . . and empty.

"So the rat's getting off this sinking ship," Paladin muttered. He started toward the door—and stopped when he heard a low moan from under the upended bookcases.

He carefully aimed his gun at the source of the sound, thumbed back the hammer, and kicked over the case.

A woman—the pale man's companion—lay there. She sat up unsteadily and rubbed her head, tousling her thick, lustrous black hair.

Paladin lowered his gun and knelt next to her. "You all right?"

"I was next to the bookcase," she said, still dazed. "There was an explosion." She pursed her lips, and her eyes came back into focus. "I always thought that 'seeing stars' was a figure of speech."

"It's not." Paladin helped her stand.

She teetered a moment, straightened her skirt, and smoothed out her wool blazer. Her gaze darted over his face, and she arched an eyebrow. "Ah, the intellectual pirate." She smiled and winced, gently touching the lump on her head. "I remember you."

He would have given anything to question her. She probably knew plenty about the pale man, but there was no time for that.

Paladin's father had been many things—a moonshiner, a bootlegger, and a con artist—but he had also been a country gentleman, and he had taught his sons how to treat ladies, even ladies who were accomplices to a crime. He'd have to get her off this floating deathtrap; he could hand her over to the cops later.

"I don't know how you're involved in this mess," he said, "but I've got a feeling you're just in the wrong place at the wrong time. At least, that's what I'm hoping. Don't prove me wrong."

He unbuckled his parachute harness and wriggled free. "This zep is going down. Your boss's plan has backfired. I want you to take this and get out of here."

She met Paladin's gaze. He didn't like what he saw in her eyes—hard reflections, like faceted ice, cold and calculating and unyielding.

"You know how to use one of these?" he asked, trying to ignore the disquiet her penetrating stare provoked.

"Yes." She took the chute, slipped into the harness, and secured the buckle. "But what about you?"

"I've got another way off this gasbag," he said.

Paladin shot the lock that kept the parlor's steel shutters closed. He rolled them up, and opened the large window. "Here."

He held out his hand and helped her sit on the edge of the sill. He reached down and pulled off her high heels. "You'll never make a landing on those," he told her. "Pull the cord only after you've cleared the zeppelin. Count to seven. Don't hold your breath."

The woman looked down and then back at Paladin, crinkling her brow with worry. "I don't—"

"No time for discussion, sister. Go!" He shoved her.

She gave a startled yelp and tumbled out.

Paladin watched as she plummeted, nervous and anxious until he saw the white bloom of hand-stitched silk pop into view.

"My good deed for the day," he muttered.

Paladin holstered his gun and left the parlor. He made his way down the corridor, past a dozen pilots and mercenaries bustling by. Steeling himself, he pushed open the double doors of the zeppelin's launch bay.

The cavernous room was nearly empty. A single Grumman Avenger remained in the bay, perched over the opening in the floor—ready for launch.

The pale man stood next to the plane, surrounded by three men in green uniforms. He wore his usual linen suit, but now, instead of its typical immaculate cleanliness, it was soot-streaked and sweat-stained. He held a briefcase in his right hand; Paladin noticed it was handcuffed to his wrist. He also wore a leather cap, goggles, and a parachute.

It looked like the pale man was taking the last plane off the *George Washington*. Blake smiled—time to hitch a ride.

Paladin started toward them.

"You!" the pale man shouted. "Help the others put out the fire on the gunnery deck. Move it!"

Paladin shrugged and waved, pretending he couldn't hear the pale man's orders. He moved closer.

When he was four steps away, the pale man opened his mouth as if he were going to say something. He paused, and looked back up at the Grumman Avenger, then back at Paladin. "*You . . .*" he growled.

Damn.

"Shoot him!" the pale man screamed, pointing at Paladin.

The guards reached for their guns.

Paladin had hoped for a ride in that Avenger, but it looked like there was only one way he was getting off the dying zeppelin in one piece. He lunged for the pale man, tackled him—

—together, they tumbled through the open launch bay doors.

The wind tore at Paladin, and made his eyes water. The pale man squirmed in his grasp, cursing and struggling to break Paladin's grip. Blake held on to him for all he was worth: one hand clutched the lapel of his suit; the other clamped on to his enemy's right wrist.

Spinning together, the pale man kicked at Paladin. The hastily aimed blows rained across Paladin's midsection: his leg, his hip, his stomach. Then a well-polished wingtip connected with Paladin's busted ribs.

He gasped, unable to inhale, as bands of red-hot pain clamped across his chest like a devilish vice.

Paladin lost his grip and flailed helplessly in a free fall.

He caught a glimpse of the ground, the sinuous, glimmering Potomac River, and the ivory sliver of the Washington Monument in the distance.

He spun dizzily, trying to slow his fall, the first hot spike of panic knifing through him like a bayonet. A scream welled up in his throat—

—until his fingertips brushed the handle of the pale man's briefcase.

Fighting back his mounting fear, he grabbed on tight, the length of his body snapping like the end of a whip.

The pale man yelled in pain as the briefcase—still handcuffed to his wrist—brutally jerked his arm, nearly dislocating it.

Paladin pinwheeled around his nemesis, the sky and ground spinning in his peripheral vision.

Paladin's panic began to subside, replaced by cold rage. With a growl, he reached for the pale man with his free hand. The pale man retaliated, hammering Blake with kicks and punches, trying to dislodge his attacker.

They were getting too close to the ground. Paladin spotted waves in the Potomac and saw tiny cars inching along the roads. Images of slamming into the unforgiving earth, of his body shattered on the unyielding stone and dirt below, filled Paladin's mind.

No. He had to focus on the pale man, forget the ground and his pain.

The pale man reached inside his jacket.

Paladin fumbled for his own holstered gun.

The ground rushed closer.

The pale man's gun cleared its holster first, the silvery muzzle swinging toward Paladin's head. There was a burst of smoke and fire as the pale man pulled the trigger, though the report was eerily muffled, swallowed by the rush of air.

The bullet whistled past Blake's head, missing him by a fraction of an inch.

For a moment, Blake was sure he was dead, that the pale man couldn't miss at such close range.

Lucky. He was damn lucky.

Blake's own gun was out. He fired, and the pale man jerked, blood exploding from a thigh wound.

Paladin shot the pale man again, this bullet taking him in the shoulder. The pale man went limp, the gun tumbling from his grasp.

Paladin climbed hand over hand, toward his unconscious foe. He looped his hand through the parachute harness.

He pulled the rip cord.

Silk ruffled and unfurled above him, crackling in the wind. Paladin saw the lines above him threaten to tangle.

Too low, Paladin thought. *The chute isn't going to open.*

Paladin's head snapped back as the lines yanked taut and the chute above him opened.

Seconds later, they bounced off the ground, locked together. Paladin let go, twisting to let the pale man take the brunt of the impact. The pale man's limp, unconscious form crashed to the earth with a bone-jarring impact.

Blake tumbled through blackberry brambles and over rocks before he skidded to a halt on the muddy banks of the Potomac.

Overhead, *George Washington* was in flames. Planes buzzed

around the dying airship. Rockets left smoky lace trails in the air, and tracer fire etched ghostly lines of light across the sky.

The zeppelin drifted over the mall, yawed slightly . . . and collided with the Washington Monument. The zep's steel frame sagged and crumpled to the ground with a terrible screech.

Paladin dragged himself to his feet, clutching his wounded ribs. He limped to the pale man, who was shrouded in white silk dotted with his own blood. Paladin felt for a pulse—and was almost disappointed when he felt a strong, regular rhythm.

"Gotcha," he whispered before collapsing to the ground, unconscious.

Light and fresh air streamed through Paladin's office window. The sunrise reflected off the distant water and sent waves of light dancing across his ceiling. He lowered the blinds.

"A job well done, Mr. Blake," Dunford remarked.

The Lockheed official straightened his white silk tie and adjusted the shoulders of his gray suit. He placed several manila folders on Paladin's desk, raising tiny clouds of dust—left over from Dashiell's fingerprinting of the room.

"Here we have a signed confession from Mr. Von Gilder, or as you called him, the 'pale man,' " Dunford continued. He set down another envelope. "Copies of his battle plans for Washington, Manhattan, and Dallas . . . for your personal files."

Dunford reached back into his alligator skin briefcase. "And, we recovered these stolen schematics for airplanes, machine guns, autogyros, and engines." He returned the documents to the briefcase, latching the lock with a sharp, metallic click.

"Yes, our Mr. Von Gilder was a very busy man. Once the extradition proceedings are concluded, I suspect there will be a speedy trial and execution in Chico." Dunford smiled.

"Maybe Aero-Tone News will cover it on a newsreel," Paladin said sarcastically.

Dunford met Blake's gaze. "We owe you a great deal, Mr. Blake."

"Oh?" Paladin limped back to his desk and sat down.

He was only half listening to Dunford. Yes, he had brought the pale man to justice. He had the broken ribs to prove it, too.

But something still felt wrong. Justin had strolled into this office a few days ago with what seemed like a simple delivery job, which had turned into a prelude to war on a terrifying scale. Nothing was ever what it first appeared to be in this case.

Maybe even the end wasn't what it seemed.

The dark-haired woman hadn't been found, lost in the chaos of police, firefighters, and militia forces that descended on the area. Something about her, something he couldn't put his finger on, still bothered him. There had been a moment of recognition when Paladin infiltrated the zeppelin to steal back the Lockheed prototype. But he couldn't place her. Fortunately, she didn't seem to remember him either.

It didn't matter. There was time enough to track her down later.

"As I said, we owe you great deal." Dunford handed him a slip of paper. "Consider this payment in full for your services, and a small down payment for our future dealings."

It was a cashier's check with more zeros than Paladin had ever seen before.

"You should rest now," Dunford said, and started toward the door. "But not too long, I trust. We have another business matter to discuss. Can we meet next Wednesday? Say, seven o'clock at Chasen's?"

Paladin nodded, still counting the numbers on the check. He finally tore his gaze away. "Of course. Let me see you out."

"No, no. Sit. Rest. I can see myself out." Dunford smiled kindly before quietly closing the door behind him.

This was it. Blake Aviation Security had enough cash not only to survive, but to expand and flourish. Paladin's ragtag operation had finally hit the big time.

There was just one last bit of unfinished business.

Paladin took the bottle of bourbon from his bottom desk

drawer. He grabbed two glasses, set them on his blotter, and then opened the bottle.

He poured the twelve-year-old bourbon into the glasses, then turned the photograph of his father to face him. "Here you go, you old bootlegger."

His father sat on the wing of his plane, pistol in one hand, a bottle—identical to the one on Paladin's desk—in the other. Again, it looked like the old bastard was laughing at Paladin, rather than toasting his good fortune.

Paladin set down his glass, perplexed.

Instead of his ritual toast with his father, he examined the pale man's battle plans, still laid across his desk.

They were identical to the briefing on the zeppelin. There were diagrams and blueprints of the various target buildings and tiny hand-scrawled notes in English, German, and French. It was a schematic for war, a chilling blueprint for death on a massive scale.

Next, he examined the pale man's confession.

Something nagged at him, but he couldn't quite put his finger on it.

It was all too easy, too neat. Nothing was ever this tightly wrapped up.

Paladin shook his head. He set the handwritten confession down. Maybe sometimes you got lucky and things *did* neatly wrap up—

Then he saw it. The two handwriting samples—the notations on the battle plans and the handwritten confession—caught his eye when he placed one next to the other.

The notes on the plans had neat loops. The *t*s were crossed and the *i*s were dotted with a perfectly straight and steady hand. The handwriting on the confession was slanted the opposite way and sloppy . . . as if the battle plans had been drawn by another man.

Or another woman?

Paladin remembered when he had stolen aboard the battle zeppelin in the desert—how the mysterious dark-haired woman had given orders to the gunners like she was in charge. He remembered how she had been seated in the shadows during the briefing before the attack on Columbia, and how the pale man looked to her from time to time . . . for what? Guidance? Approval? Orders?

And how maybe he had given his parachute to the one person he should have brought to justice.

No. It couldn't be.

Paladin cradled his glass of bourbon, warming it until he could smell the smoky aroma.

Paladin's dad was still laughing at him.

"Maybe she *was* the one behind it all," he told his father, "but we came home this time in one piece. And there will be a next time—don't worry."

He clinked his glass against his father's. "If it takes a hundred years, no matter what I have to do, I'll get every last of one of them for you."

He poured the two glasses back into the bottle, then put them away.

Paladin glanced at the check again.

Suddenly the money didn't matter; it was just a means to an end. Like the pale man, and maybe the dark-haired woman, he had his own personal war to start—a war against pirates and injustice.

It was a war he intended to win.

Intermission: Dark Clouds

If Paladin Blake represents law and order in the violent skies over North America, then Jonathan "Genghis" Kahn stands only for chaos and corruption.

Unlike many of his contemporaries, Kahn's family purchased him a medical deferment that kept him out of the Army during the Great War. Despite his "infirmity" he was enamored of flying and actually possessed natural skill.

After the war ended, Kahn made money peddling fake influenza cures. He later graduated to the "Drake scam," which provided him with a steady income. He told people that the heirs of Sir Francis Drake were going to sue the British Crown for all the gold Sir Francis had captured, and they would be paid ten dollars for every dollar they donated to the lawsuit. Kahn first flew from city to city himself, and later hired henchmen to harvest weekly contributions from families, threatening to cut them out of the deal if they didn't keep "donating funds to the legal effort."

Kahn invested his ill-gotten gains in the stock market, spreading his wealth around to industrialists and associates who subsequently fell for his other schemes. He bought extensively on margin, made fast trades, and even manipulated the press by leaking stories that spiked prices so that he could sell out at a fat profit. His stock market successes did not last, however; the stock market crash ruined him.

Destitute, Kahn cut a deal with the Purple Gang; he sold them all future profits from his Drake scam in return for a quick investment in a fleet of planes. The Purple Gang went for the idea, and the dreaded Red Skull Legion was born.

Shortly after forming the Legion, Kahn and his men flew

to Utah as an escort for a zeppelin that was supposedly full of
Mormon refugees from the Industrial States of America. The
cover story worked, and the pirates managed to slip past the
diligent Utah defense forces.

The zeppelin was actually a Trojan horse, filled with
hordes of armed pirates. Upon landing, the pirates seized the
airport while the Red Skull Legion made repeated strafing
attacks against the local militia. The landing party moved
quickly, damaging local defense stations and stealing the airship *Moroni*—later renamed *Machiavelli*. Next, Kahn had
the Red Skull planes repainted, giving them the colors of
Utah's militia. They quickly moved into the People's Collective and launched a series of brutal raids.

Again, Kahn's trickery was successful—the Collective
pinned the blame for the raids squarely on Utah. After a profitable period of raiding, Kahn returned to the I.S.A., while
Utah and the People's Collective faced a shooting war.

Since the Utah–Collective conflict, Kahn operates across
North America, relying on stealth, cunning, and trickery . . .
backed up by force.

Join us now for a tale of treachery and deceit, as Genghis
Kahn and the Red Skull Legion risk everything on . . . "The
Manchurian Gambit."

—NERO MACLEON
Manhattan, 1938

The Manchurian Gambit

A Tale of the Red Skull Legion

by Michael B. Lee

1: Raiders from the Sky

When it came down to it, the whole plan hinged on Harry Nesbitt being a fool. It was a calculated risk, Jonathan Kahn admitted to himself, but given Harry's reputation, it seemed like a chance worth taking.

Kahn eased back on the throttle as the Devastator leveled out at eight thousand feet, mellowing the snarl of the plane's Allison engine into a throaty growl. Sleek, black shapes closed in around him as the planes of the Red Skull Legion settled into a tight formation, heading north-northwest over the Black Hills of South Dakota. There was heavy winter overcast a thousand feet over their heads, an iron-gray ceiling stretching from horizon to horizon. The burly pirate frowned at the sky. It would be dark over Deadwood about a half hour sooner than he'd planned, but he refused to let it worry him. All it meant was a shorter wait. Nesbitt would have to strike soon or not at all.

One of the pirate fighters nudged closer to him than the rest. A twin to his own Devastator, the freshly painted grain-sheaf insignia of the People's Collective stood out boldly on the plane's gull wings and long fuselage. Henrietta Corbett had been his wingman for so long that she could cover him like his own shadow, always a single step behind him no matter how fierce the dogfights got. She tucked her plane in tight, just off his right wing; Kahn threw her a thumbs-up. Hetty stared back at him across the gulf of cold, thin air and shook her head apprehensively. Static hissed and popped over Kahn's headset, but her throaty voice came through clearly.

"I don't like this, boss. We shouldn't be depending on Nesbitt."

Kahn bit down on his stubby, unlit cigar. Hetty was tough as nails, as cold-hearted a fighter as they came, but he had to remind himself sometimes that she was still just a kid. "We aren't *depending* on him, we're *playing* him," he growled. "He knows that the Lakota are delivering their grain payment to Deadwood today, and he also knows that half the town's militia is grounded because they're short on engine parts. So once the Lakota escorts head back home—which would have happened about ten minutes ago—the only thing standing between Nesbitt and a cool fifty grand is a half-dozen militia planes and some flak guns."

"More like fifteen or twenty flak guns, with good crews," Hetty grumbled. "Nobody does business on the edge of the Lakota Badlands without being armed to the teeth."

"Details, details," Kahn said with a cold smile. "I suppose I omitted a few facts here and there when I arranged for Nesbitt to get his 'hot tip.' He won't know the full truth until the moment his planes start their attack."

"And you expect him to throw everything he's got at the flak guns."

"What I expect him to do is *panic*, but the end result is the same," Kahn replied. "He'll have assigned several planes to attack the town's radio tower and telegraph lines, but he'll divert them to the flak guns once he sees just how many there are. That gives Deadwood at least five or ten minutes to get off a call for help, and that, Hetty, is the opening we need."

"And if Nesbitt doesn't panic?"

Kahn shrugged. "Then he and his gang will be shot to pieces over Deadwood and the flak gunners will use up most of their ammo on someone other than *us*." He checked his watch. "It's an hour and a half until dark. If he's running on schedule, Nesbitt will have to attack within the next fifteen or twenty minutes. Settle down and keep an eye on the boys; I'm switching frequencies to listen for the signal."

Hetty's protest was cut off in midsyllable as Kahn turned the radio's dial, tuning in the frequency of the pirates' airship, the *Machiavelli*.

He'd known what Hetty was about to say. This heist *had* to

work. Without the money, the Red Skulls were finished. They had just enough fuel on the airship to get them back to the I.S.A. and half a load of ammo per plane. No spare parts, no spare armor—not much more than sardines and bread in the ship's galley, for that matter.

The Old Man had gotten him good this time.

Kahn shifted uneasily in the fighter's cold, metal seat. He'd known that sooner or later the con he'd pulled on the Purple Gang would come back to haunt him. He'd cost them eighty grand on the Drake deal when all was said and done, but by the time they'd wised up he had the Red Skull Legion, and they didn't have the guts to touch him. Everything went according to plan, or so it seemed.

What he *hadn't* planned on was the DeCarlo family suddenly stepping in and covering the Purple Gang's losses.

Owing money to the Purple Gang was not the same thing as owing Don Giovanni DeCarlo. He'd bought himself a little time by turning over nearly all the Legion's cash reserves, but the don's patience was notoriously short. If he didn't come up with eighty grand—plus interest, naturally—in *very* short order, the Red Skulls might as well not go back to Chicago. Ever.

He shook his head in bitter admiration. The Old Man must have pulled in a *lot* of markers with the don. But then, Samuel Kahn didn't believe in half-measures, especially where family was concerned.

Suddenly a loud voice called out over Kahn's headset: "Red Leader, this is Rover," it said, using the code name for the *Machiavelli*. "We're getting an urgent SOS from Deadwood airfield. The town is under attack by close to thirty bandits, and they're requesting assistance from any Collective airships in the area."

Nesbitt had taken the bait. Kahn grinned. "Message received, Rover. Continue as planned. Over and out." The radio hissed and screeched as he quickly switched back to the squadron frequency.

"Red Flight, this is Red Leader: the town's under attack. Let's go to work."

* * *

Fire etched the sky over Deadwood. Flak shells burst in ragged puffs of red and black, leaving angry smudges in the air. Streams of red and yellow tracers stitched through pillars of smoke rising from the burning town. Nesbitt's raiders had hit the town hard, but the Deadwood militia was giving as good as it got. Kahn watched a twin-engine Kestrel dive on a sandbagged gun emplacement and fire a volley of high-explosive rockets. The gun's ammo went up in an orange fireball, incinerating the crew, but as the bomber pulled out of its dive it came under fire from a concealed machine-gun nest. Tracers ate into the plane's left wing, and the Kestrel vanished in a sudden blot of flame as magnesium bullets tore into the bomber's fuel tank.

The Red Skulls were in a shallow dive, picking up speed as they hugged the low hills approaching the town from the east. Kahn looked for the black-and-gold planes of the Deadwood Air Militia and saw only three, surrounded by a swarm of motley-colored pirate fighters.

No one noticed them in the confusion. Kahn grinned like a wolf. "Red Flight, listen up. I want radio silence from here on out—I do the talking, and nobody else. Take out as many of Nesbitt's goons as you can in the first pass; then wait for my signal." Not waiting for an acknowledgment from the squadron, Kahn tuned his radio to the militia's regular frequency. Shouted curses and desperate warnings filled his ears as the Deadwood Air Militia members fought for their lives, and the Red Skulls, disguised as a People's Collective squadron, tore into the swirling dogfight.

Surprise was total. Kahn picked out the distinctive, twin-hulled profile of a Peacemaker 370 as it dived onto the tail of a Deadwood plane. The Deadwood fighter—a light, sleek M210 Raven—literally disintegrated under the savage fusillade of the Peacemaker's four .60-caliber guns. The pirate fighter leveled out, looking for another target, and Kahn closed to point-blank range before arming four of his rockets and letting them fly. Two high-explosive and two armor-piercing rockets thrust at the Peacemaker on lances of fire, three of them ripping into the plane's right wing and blowing it apart. The pirate fighter spun out of control, flames streaming from the shattered wing root, and crashed into one of the town's two-story buildings.

Kahn pulled the Devastator into a climbing left turn and surveyed the aerial battle. At least nine of the raiders had been shot down, and the shock of the Red Skulls' furious attack had panicked the rest. Nesbitt's fighters were breaking off, hugging the hills to the southwest as they ran for their airship. The barrage of antiaircraft fire had abated while the gunners on the ground tried to sort out their sudden change of fortune.

There wasn't any time to waste. Kahn keyed his radio. "Any militia pilots on this frequency, this is Comrade Major Smith of the Collective airship *Elijah*. We came as soon as we heard your distress call. Do you read, over?"

A woman's voice responded immediately. "This is Comrade Captain Angela Dane of the Deadwood Air Militia. You're just in time, Major . . . Another few minutes and we'd have been done for." The Collective pilot had a cool, steely voice, but she sounded relieved all the same.

The militia planes had formed up on one another, and Kahn came up alongside the lead fighter, a badly shot-up Defender. By the looks of things, Captain Dane had been in the thick of the battle from the start. "Glad to be here, Comrade," Kahn replied, waving at the militia pilot, "but we aren't out of the woods yet. We chased those bandits off for now, but I expect they'll be back. You and I both know what they're after, and they aren't going to quit until they get it."

From the cockpit of the ravaged Defender, Captain Dane glanced over at Kahn's fighter, her face unreadable. "Yes, sir, I have to agree," she replied grimly.

Kahn nodded, keeping his voice carefully neutral. "You and your squadron have put up a hell of a fight here, Captain, but Deadwood can't afford another raid. Half the town's been wrecked already—"

"Those pirate scum can burn the whole place to the ground." Dane swore with sudden vehemence. "We'll make them pay for every single building, and when they're gone, we'll just build again. But they aren't getting that grain payment, Major. I can promise you that."

Kahn gritted his teeth. "Comrade, your courage is an example to all of us," he said, trying to sound reasonable. "But we have to think of the civilians down there. How many have already suffered because of this raid? I don't know about you, but I certainly don't want that on my conscience."

When Dane didn't reply immediately he knew he'd struck a chord. Finally, she replied. "I'm open to suggestions, sir."

"You're a credit to the People's Collective, Comrade. First, I need to speak to your mayor. Can you escort us in to Deadwood Airfield?"

"Certainly, sir. Follow my lead." The beat-up plane started a slow right turn, and Kahn fell in behind Dane's struggling wingman.

The pirate leader switched frequencies. "Red Flight," he called, glancing at the formation circling just south of town. "They bought it. We're being escorted in."

Kahn switched back to the militia frequency and chewed thoughtfully on his cigar. Another thirty minutes, give or take, and their problems would be over. Providing that all went according to plan. If anything went wrong, he and his pilots were going to be caught on the ground in a town that shot pirates on sight.

The Devastator passed over the southern edge of the Deadwood Airfield. The tower was wrecked, but he could see that plenty of their antiaircraft batteries were ready for action. Kahn lowered his landing gear and tried not to consider how long it had been since anything he'd attempted had gone according to plan.

Comrade Captain Angela Dane had a stare that could drive nails. She wasn't more than five feet tall and built like a ballerina, but her blue eyes were hard and cold. Her short auburn hair and delicate features could do nothing to soften that bleak, forbidding gaze. Kahn hoped the captain wasn't going to be a problem.

Dane drove them into town in her Packard, weaving nimbly around piles of rubble and still-smoking bomb craters. Kahn sat beside her in the front seat. Three of his pilots, Amos Jones, John Scales, and Pete O'Neil were crowded in the back, trying not to look nervous. The rest of the squadron, led by Hetty, had been left at the airfield to refuel the planes—with orders to take over the field if things went disastrously wrong.

"Any other day and we'd have kicked their tails," Dane growled, slapping the steering wheel in frustration. "Four years Deadwood's been the transfer point for the Lakota grain payment, and no pirate's *ever* dared to hit us. But the one time we've got half our planes grounded—it's like they *knew* somehow."

Kahn studied the Captain's profile. "Maybe they did, Comrade," he said carefully. "A smart pirate would pay well for such information." He pulled a small flask from the inside of his flight suit, uncapped it, and took a small swig. Kahn offered it to Dane with a conspiratorial wink, and she accepted almost without thinking, knocking back a healthy gulp.

She handed back the flask, shaking her head. "Those were Harry Nesbitt's thugs," she said. "Vicious, yes, but not very smart."

Pete O'Neil let out a laugh. He was a short and wiry guy—dwarfed by the hulking figures of Amos and John—with slicked-back hair and rodent features. "Nesbitt's Nincompoops they ought to call them," he said in his sharp, New Jersey twang. "What morons—" O'Neil's eyes went wide as two large elbows dug into his ribs.

If Dane heard, she paid little attention. "I guess it's just lucky for us you got our distress call," she said, glancing at Kahn. "I didn't think there were any Collective airships within fifty miles of us."

"We just arrived in the area two days ago," Kahn said smoothly. "On an unannounced patrol. We heard you'd been having trouble with Lakota bandits lately, and hoped to catch 'em napping."

Dane nodded thoughtfully. "Lucky for us."

A minute later they pulled up outside the Deadwood General Store. Its windows had been blown out during the raid, but the building itself looked undamaged. A burly man wearing a shopkeeper's apron stood near the counter, talking to a handful of townspeople and trying to look after his store at the same time. He looked over as the pilots crunched across the broken glass. "That was as close a call as I ever want to see, Comrade," he called out to Dane. "Who's that with you there?"

"This is Comrade Major Smith and some of his men from the airship *Elijah*," Dane replied. "They heard our distress call and got here in the nick of time." She turned to Kahn. "Major Smith, this is our mayor, Ed Stovall."

Stovall smiled and reached for Kahn's hand. "Much obliged to you, Major," he said with undisguised relief. "I thought we were done for. What can I do for you?"

"Actually, I'm more interested in what I can do for *you*, Mayor," Kahn replied. "We're not out of the woods yet. Those pirates are after the grain payment, and they won't quit until they get it. Right now I expect they're loading up more bombs and rockets and getting ready for round two. Your town is going to get hit again unless we do something."

There were cries of dismay from the townspeople. Stovall raised both hands, asking for silence. "What do you suggest, Major?"

"I suggest taking the grain payment and loading it onto my airship, then running like hell for Tulsa," Kahn said. "Frankly, I don't know if we can outrun the bandits or not, but we can at least draw them away from the town."

"No way!" Dane interjected. "Sorry, Major, but that's a bad idea. We've still got more than a dozen working flak guns, plus your planes, and it's only half an hour before dark." She folded her arms defiantly. "We can hold out here."

Kahn turned to the Collective pilot. "I'm not saying we can't, Captain, but think of the damage the pirates will do to the town in the meantime." Frightened cries echoed off the store walls as the townspeople shouted their agreement.

"All right, all right!" Stovall cried, trying to restore order.

"Angie, he's got a point. Lord only knows how many people we've already lost today. I have to agree with Major Smith." Stovall dug in his pocket for a set of keys. "The bags are in the post office, Major. Take them and Godspeed. Angie, show the Major and his men how to get there."

Dane took the keys. Kahn put his hand on Stovall's shoulder. "You've made the right choice, Comrade," he said gravely, then looked to his men and nodded toward the door.

The Deadwood post office was less than a block away. Dane left the car engine running and led the fliers inside, her expression troubled. Kahn waited at the doorway, studying the sky. It was getting dark more quickly than he'd thought. If they didn't get off the ground very soon, they would be stuck there until dawn. It was going to be close, but it looked like they were going to pull it off.

One corner of the small building was taken up with a large steel cage, much like a jail cell. Inside were mailbags and the heavy, burlap sacks containing the grain payment. Dane unlocked the cage and pulled the door open, one hand resting idly on the pistol at her hip. "You're taking a hell of a risk, Major," she said as Kahn's men headed for the bags. "If everything you say is true."

"I know people like Nesbitt very well, Captain. Trust me, it's the only way."

Dane nodded thoughtfully, watching the fliers wrestle with the heavy bags. "Well, can you do me a favor when you get back to your ship?"

Kahn glanced at her curiously. "Of course."

The Captain's hard, blue eyes bored into his. "I've got a cousin serving on the *Elijah*. Teddy Dane. Can you send him my love?"

Kahn's mind raced, trying to conceal his surprise. Dane's cold gaze narrowed. Suddenly she slammed the cell door shut. Her pistol was in her hand.

"Put up your hands, pirate," she snarled.

2: In Enemy Hands

John Scales threw himself at the cell door with a shout, but the lock had clicked home and the iron bars wouldn't budge. The People's Collective fighter pilot, Dane, slid a few steps to the right so her back wasn't facing the cage. Her Colt .45 never wavered from Kahn's heart.

"Settle down," she snarled, her face red with rage. "Toss your guns out onto the floor . . . or your boss has had it."

Kahn was careful not to move. He caught the eye of Pete O'Neil, the Red Skulls' resident lock-pick and sneak thief; the wiry pirate had drawn his gun, out of sight behind the hulking forms of Scales and Amos Jones—a former circus strongman turned pirate. O'Neil gave Kahn a wink, signaling his readiness—and willingness—to start shooting.

"Do what she says, boys," Kahn ordered.

O'Neil's eyes widened in surprise, but after a moment he tossed his pistol through the bars. Scales and Jones followed suit, glancing worriedly from Dane to Kahn and back again. Kahn drew his own gun and set it with the rest.

He nodded to the Deadwood pilot. "That was a nice bluff, Captain. Simple but effective."

"I just needed to see the doubt in your eyes," she said quietly. The color was fading from her cheeks, but her eyes were cruel and cold. "The whole thing seemed a little too convenient: we just *happen* to get raided when only half our planes will fly, and then there just *happens* to be a Collective airship close enough to rush in and save the day. When you insisted on leaving with the payroll I knew something was wrong."

Kahn smiled. "I'll keep that in mind for next time."

"There won't be a next time." Dane took a step forward.

Her gun hand trembled with restrained fury. "This isn't like the I.S.A. or Hollywood, where the city folk worship you thugs. You're in the Badlands, now, and I'll have you and your crew swinging from a rope by dawn."

"My squadron is waiting for me, Captain," Kahn warned, "and they won't like the idea of my being hanged."

Dane shook her head. "Your pilots are parked at my air-field, and there's ten AA guns covering the strip. If they try to take off, we'll shoot 'em to pieces. It's the end of the line for you and your gang." She tossed Kahn the keys to the cage. "Now get in."

Kahn studied Dane carefully. There were bright spots of color at her cheeks and beads of perspiration glistening beneath her short-cropped hair. "Captain, I think you'd better sit down and catch your breath. You don't look so good."

The Collective pilot frowned. Her free hand went to her forehead and came away slicked with sweat. Suddenly she swayed on her feet. Her eyes went wide. "What—what did you do—?" Her thumb fumbled at the hammer of her pistol, trying to cock the weapon. Kahn rushed forward, grabbing the gun out of her hand moments before she collapsed. Her head hit the wooden floor with a muted thump and she lay motionless, barely breathing.

John and Amos stared gape-jawed at the unconscious pilot. Kahn tossed O'Neil the keys. "Get that door open and start moving those bags," Kahn said calmly, returning to the door-way to peer warily along the street.

Kahn's strongmen each had one of the heavy bags in hand by the time O'Neil got the door open. The thief scooped his pistol off the floor and joined Kahn, shaking his head bemusedly. "Talk about lucky breaks, huh, boss?"

"A wise prince makes his own luck, to paraphrase a certain Italian thinker," Kahn replied. "That whiskey I offered her earlier was laced with laudanum."

O'Neil's thin eyebrows rose. "But . . . you took a drink, too."

"No, I only pretended to, and Dane was too preoccupied to notice," Kahn corrected. "I wanted a little insurance in case she tried to cause trouble." He stared thoughtfully at Dane's prostrate form. "Unfortunately I was only partially success-ful. Once she wakes up she'll have the whole town up in arms."

The thief looked long and hard at the unconscious pilot and nodded. "I see what you mean." He holstered his pistol and pulled a small, thin-bladed knife from his sleeve. "You want I should take care of her?"

"Kill her, you mean?" Kahn said, faintly surprised. "Don't be ridiculous. You don't kill an unconscious foe, Pete, espe-cially a woman." He hefted Dane's pistol and took careful aim. "That's *my* job."

Just then Amos stuck his bald head back through the door-way. "Townspeople down the street, boss," he said. "They got guns and dogs."

Kahn let out an exasperated sigh and reluctantly stuck the pistol in his waistband. Squeezing past the strongman, he stuck his head outside and could see twenty or so men—armed with shotguns and rifles—leading a pack of leashed hounds down the street a couple blocks away. As he watched, they pushed open the door of a building to their right and rushed inside, weapons ready.

"Looking for downed pirates, I imagine," Kahn wondered aloud. "If it isn't one thing, it's another."

He turned to O'Neil. "We're going to have to take the good captain with us. If nothing else, she might make a useful hostage. Find something to tie her up with and stuff her in a mail sack. The boys can carry her out with the rest of the bags."

"Sure thing, boss," the thief said, and went to work.

Kahn left the doorway and went to lean against the Packard's rear fender, tossing his cigar stub into the street and pulling a fresh one from his leather jacket. It took two min-utes for John and Amos to get another set of bags into the car. He lit the cigar and puffed at it methodically. Two bags every two minutes. How many bags had there been in the cage? He couldn't remember. Kahn shook his head disapprovingly. He was getting sloppy.

The search party emerged from the building and moved to

a smaller building on the opposite side of the street. They weren't inside the smaller building more than a minute. Then they went to the next set and repeated the procedure. Only a block away, now. Kahn noted that the group moved with a certain amount of precision. They'd obviously practiced their routine many, many times. He wondered if they'd ever caught anyone before, and whether they'd just pass on a trial and proceed straight to the executions.

O'Neil stepped outside. "All taken care of, boss."

Kahn nodded. "Think you can drive this car, Pete?"

The thief grinned. "My mama has one just like it. I stole it for her last Christmas."

"Then get behind the wheel. We may be leaving in a hurry."

The search party worked its way down the street. John and Amos still weren't done. The townspeople were close enough now that the hounds could smell Kahn and his men; they lunged and barked, straining at their leashes until the searchers hauled them back to the job at hand.

"How many more?" Kahn asked Amos as the strongman loaded another bag into the car.

"Just a couple," the pirate answered, a little out of breath. "You know, we could've gone faster if we'd brought more guys."

"Remind me the next time we rob a payroll."

Amos grinned. "Right, boss."

The search party was dangerously close now. John and Amos got the last bags out in record time and hurried back for Dane. Kahn was just about to climb in the car when he saw the leader of the townspeople wave the party away from the next building on the street and start walking over to the Packard, shotgun at the ready.

Kahn took a few steps forward, away from the car. He smiled broadly around his cigar as the townspeople approached the post office. "Seen any pirates, Comrades?" he asked cheerfully.

The man in charge of the party evidently didn't have a sense of humor. He looked Kahn over sternly. "We saw two chutes during the fight," he said, spitting a stream of tobacco juice onto the ground. "They're holed up here somewhere, but the dogs'll get 'em right enough." The man cradled his shotgun in both arms and squinted warily at him. "Heard you're taking the grain payment back to Tulsa."

Kahn kept smiling, watching for his men out of the corner of his eye. "That's right," he said. "No sense getting Deadwood bombed again if we can help it."

The man frowned. "But how are the pirates supposed to know the money's gone? Seems to me they'll still think it's here, and hit us again anyway."

John and Amos emerged from the post office, carrying a large mail sack between them. Instantly the dogs lunged at it, barking furiously, and the men broke into shouts, leveling their guns.

The pirates froze. The man with the shotgun shouted down the rest and glared balefully at Kahn. "What you got in that bag, mister?"

Kahn summoned up his nerve. "Letters and packages, Comrade," he said carefully. "We figured as long as we were headed to Tulsa we might as well carry the post, too."

One of the townspeople, a short, round-bellied farmer, lowered his rifle and shook his head in disgust. "Dang it, I told Alice not to send her sister those jerky strips! We just about blew our mail to kingdom come."

The rest of the men laughed, pulling back the dogs. Kahn remembered to smile and waved at his men to finish loading the car. "Sorry about the scare, fellas," he said with a laugh. "I think that's the last of the bags, so if it's all the same to you we'll be getting out of your way." He went to the Packard's passenger door as John and Amos piled into the back. "Good luck with those pirates," he said, giving the men a salute.

"You, too!" one of the townspeople yelled back as the Packard sped away.

They got lost twice working through Deadwood's rubble-strewn streets. By the time Kahn and his men reached the airfield the sun was coloring the hilltops to the west. The AA guns were still fully manned, he noticed, as they sped down the access road leading to the hangars. They weren't out of the woods yet. All he needed was for Dane to wake up and raise an alarm and they were as good as dead.

The *Machiavelli* was waiting for them at the airfield's mooring tower, the People's Collective insignia prominent on her prow. Their airship had been lowered to the ground and was ready to take on cargo. Hetty stood nearby with a cluster of Red Skull crew, waiting nervously for Kahn's return. Not far away a group of Deadwood ground crewmen were unloading crates from the back of a flatbed truck.

Kahn told O'Neil to park practically in the zeppelin's shadow. Hetty ran over with the Red Skulls as Kahn emerged from the car. Her long face lit with a sly grin. "Our good comrades are loading us up with steak and potatoes in gratitude for saving the town," she said.

"Good, good," Kahn said absently, motioning hurriedly for the men to start hauling the bags onto the zeppelin.

Hetty's eyes narrowed. "Everything okay?"

"There've been a couple of ... complications," Kahn growled through clenched teeth.

The female pilot's grin froze. " 'Complications,' " she echoed. "I *knew* it." She peered into the car. "Where's that captain you left with?"

Just then one of the Deadwood crewmen trotted over to the car, carrying a clipboard. He looked around, his brow wrinkling. "Um, sir?" he asked Kahn, "I'm looking for Captain Dane. This is her car, isn't it?"

Kahn fought back a sigh. He turned to the man and summoned up a jovial smile. "She asked to be dropped off at the operations building," he said smoothly. "Needed to check on the condition of the squadron."

The man brightened. "Oh, no problem, then. I just need her to sign for these steaks. It won't take a minute." Before anyone could reply he turned on his heel and started jogging across the field toward the Ops shed.

Kahn watched the man go, shaking his head in quiet exasperation. "Hetty," he said quietly, "the next time we pull a heist we're just going to come roaring in and blow up everything in sight. Machine-gun everything that moves and bomb them again for good measure. Subtlety is for the birds." He turned to her. "Are the planes ready to fly?"

"Everybody but Emerson's," she said worriedly. "He took a round in the oil pan when we were running off Nesbitt's boys."

The pirate leader shook his head. "We'll have to leave it, then. Get him on the zep and get the planes in the air. Now."

"We can't just leave his bird behind!" Hetty sputtered.

Kahn grabbed her arm and pulled her close. "We've got fifty thousand in cash, Hetty," he hissed. "I'll give Don De-Carlo half to buy some more time and then I'll get Emerson a new plane, all right? Just get *moving*. It won't take that yard ape long to figure out Dane's not at the Ops shed."

"Then where is she?" Hetty asked, trying to keep up.

"I'll tell you later," he said, giving her a not-too-gentle push toward the grounded planes. Kahn turned back to the car to find O'Neil, Jones, and Scales holding a mailbag between them. The burlap was starting to shift sluggishly about.

"On the ship!" he said, motioning urgently at the cargo bay. He watched the pirates carry their load onto the zeppelin and made a silent promise to himself that if he survived the next few hours he would take great pleasure in tossing that mailbag from a very great height. Then he ran after Hetty toward the line of parked fighters waiting across the grassy airstrip.

The rest of the pilots were starting their engines when Kahn reached his plane. A few Deadwood mechanics were standing around, several looking a little bemused and wondering what the big hurry was. He motioned to one to pull away the Devastator's wheel chocks and climbed into the cockpit. As soon as the man was clear he jabbed the starter buttons and the twin Allison X-900 engines roared into life. Checking his gauges, Kahn pulled on his flight cap and rigged his throat mike. "Rover, this is Red Leader," he called. "As soon as you've loaded the mail, take off. Forget everything else. Things are about to get hot down here."

The airship acknowledged. One by one, the pirate fighters were rolling onto the strip, their engines revving for takeoff.

If no one sounded the alarm within the next few minutes, they had a chance.

Over the thunder of the revving engines came the high, keening wail of the alert siren.

3: Old Debts

The banshee cry of the alert siren made Kahn's blood run cold. The heist had very nearly paid off; another few minutes and the Red Skulls would have been home free. Now the Deadwood ground crew scattered, scrambling for cover, and all along the battered airstrip Kahn saw militia gun crews working furiously to bring their cannons to bear.

The pirate fighters had started their engines and were already rolling, taxiing to start their takeoff, but there was no way they'd survive the deadly gauntlet they'd be forced to run in order to make it into the air. At the far end of the field a rapid-fire gun cut loose, sending a crescent of red tracers fanning the air over the Red Skulls' cockpits. Kahn's hand tightened on the stick as he waited—with steadily mounting dread—for the shells to hammer into his plane, the "Whitney's Neglect."

A shadow passed overhead, an airplane low enough to send a blast of wind raging through Kahn's open cockpit. The ground shook, and the concussion of a huge explosion hammered at Kahn's chest. Craning his head around the seat's headrest, he saw one of the airfield's hangars ripped apart by a huge fireball. Motley-colored planes roared over the field at treetop height; as he watched, one fighter volleyed a salvo of rockets at the control tower.

Harry Nesbitt and his boys were back for round two, banking everything on a last-ditch strike just before sunset.

You're smarter—or more desperate—than I thought, Harry, Kahn thought to himself. Nesbitt had evidently counted on catching the town's fighters on the ground . . . and the gamble had paid off. Cannon and machine-gun fire tore into two of the Deadwood planes, blasting away pieces of armor and airframe until their fuel tanks exploded, hurling blazing debris high into the air.

Cody Emerson's Brigand was next. The pirate fighter, grounded by a punctured oil pan, suffered a near miss from a pair of bombs that flipped the aircraft over like a child's toy.

Nesbitt's boys had gone after the sitting ducks first. Kahn watched them scatter like crows, coming around for another pass, and knew who they'd be after next.

"Grab some sky, Red Skulls!" Kahn called over the radio. "If they catch us on the ground, we're dead!"

The first planes were already tearing down the grassy strip, fighting to get aloft. As one plane started rolling, the next turned into position and raced after it, with barely a yard between one plane's propeller and the other plane's tail.

Kahn cast a worried glance at the *Machiavelli*. The airship was still anchored to the mooring tower like a steer tied up for slaughter. He could see the ground crew staggering to their feet and running for the ship . . . but no one was carrying anything. Looking around quickly, he saw that Scales, Jones, and O'Neil were aboard their planes.

Kahn keyed his throat mike, fighting a surge of panic. "Tell me you got the money aboard the *Machiavelli*, Pete."

For a few seconds there was nothing but silence. "Hetty said you wanted us in the air, boss," the thief answered hesitantly, "so I told the grease monkeys to take care of it."

Kahn bit back a curse. With an angry scowl, he cut off O'Neil's frequency and switched over to the zeppelin's channel.

"*Machiavelli,* this is Kahn. Cast off immediately . . . but get a crew over to the car and unload the money."

Everything was happening too fast. He needed to move quickly, or the game was over.

He switched to the all-hands channel, and barked orders to the Legion pilots in the air, struggling to control the radio and manage his take-off.

"Everybody cover the airship!" he snarled into the radio as the Devastator's wheels left the ground. With barely enough airspeed to stay aloft, Kahn brought his fighter around in a tight left turn, pushing the heavy plane to its limits to lay his gun sights on Nesbitt's raiders.

The sky above Deadwood airfield was a churning cauldron of fire and smoke. Fighters spun and dived in twisting dogfights, slipping through curtains of tracer fire from the gun emplacements below. Across the field, a plane exploded in midair and tumbled to earth in a tangle of blazing metal—whether it was his or Nesbitt's, Kahn couldn't be sure.

Suddenly a drumbeat of light-caliber hits battered at his starboard wing and a red-painted Bell Valiant roared past, its port wingtip a scant two feet from his canopy. The raider had overestimated the Devastator's airspeed and overshot his mark.

Kahn brought his nose up and cut loose with everything he had. The Whitney's Neglect trembled as the plane's four .60-caliber cannons erupted in a long, roaring volley, riddling the Valiant from rudder to cockpit. Savaged by the armor-piercing shells, the light fighter flipped over and plummeted to the ground.

Kahn allowed himself a moment of satisfaction and smiled when the enemy plane smashed into the hard earth and exploded. He opened up the throttle and pulled into a high right turn, using a careful mix of rudder and aileron to keep the Devastator—yawing slightly from the damage to the wing—under control. He surveyed the aerial battlefield.

The freewheeling dogfight spread out in all directions as pilots fought to gain advantage over their opponents while avoiding the murderous AA fire around the airfield. Movement to the west caught his eye—two heavy fighters, a Kestrel and a three-engine P2 Warhawk in close formation, heading straight for the *Machiavelli*. Both planes were in a shallow dive, picking up speed by the moment, but they kept their course straight and wings level, plunging like arrows toward the airship. Kahn didn't need to see the long, shark-like shapes under their wings to know that they were setting up an aerial torpedo run.

The pirate leader cursed under his breath. He couldn't tell from overhead whether the airship had slipped her moorings or not, but she still sat motionless, a stationary target bigger than a barn. Even Nesbitt's amateurs couldn't miss. Kahn calculated the angles and figured he had less than ten seconds before it was too late.

Kahn dipped his right wing and dived, picking up speed as he raced head-on toward the two raiders. The enemy pilots both saw him at the same time, and staccato flashes licked out from their gun mounts, throwing a wild flurry of tracers across his path. Shells slammed into his nose and port wing, but he pressed on and placed his gun sight at a point well ahead of the enemy Warhawk. He squeezed the trigger, firing a series of short bursts. Hits burst in firecracker-like flashes across the Warhawk's nose and starboard wing, and suddenly the huge Wright R-1350 engine at the end of the wing erupted in flame. With one engine gone, the Fury's unbalanced thrust dragged the plane into a left turn, forcing it to break off its attack.

That just left the Kestrel. The enemy bomber roared past Kahn on his port side, and shells thudded into his fuselage. The Kestrel had a light machine gun mounted on a ring behind the pilot's position, and the tail gunner hammered at the Devastator with deadly accuracy. Kahn pulled his plane into a tight loop and rolled out onto the bomber's tail, unleashing a storm of gunfire that slashed into the heavy plane's wing and tail—

—to no avail. The raider pressed on, its armored hide weathering the Devastator's fire. Another machine-gun burst raked across the heavy fighter's nose; one round hit a metal strut on the fighter's canopy, sending splinters of Plexiglas into Kahn's face. He shook his head savagely, wiping a smear of blood on his sleeve, and fired another burst. The *Machiavelli* was looming ever larger in his field of vision—the raider could fire at any moment.

Kahn checked to see if he had any rockets left. There were only two, a high-explosive rocket and a flash rocket. He selected the HE and fired. The rocket roared off its rail and streaked toward its target, only to slide beneath the Kestrel's wing and explode harmlessly in front of the plane. The bomber drove on through the blast, but the flash of the explosion gave him an idea. He armed the flare, aimed just ahead of the enemy plane, and let it fly.

The Kestrel's pilot, intent on his target, never saw the flare until it burst right in front of him. Surprised and blinded by the actinic flash, he yanked the bomber into a steep climb—but not before releasing his load of torpedoes. A pair of the devastating weapons dropped from the Kestrel's wings and plunged toward the motionless airship. Kahn watched helplessly as the torpedoes fell in a long, almost leisurely arc—and hit the earth only scant yards from the airship. A curtain of fire and earth erupted from the half-dozen blasts, flinging wreckage high into the air—including pieces of Captain Dane's Packard.

When the fountain of dirt and debris settled, there was only a smoking crater to mark where the car—and the money—had been.

A cold wind raged through the open windows of the *Machiavelli's* observation gallery. Heavy winter clouds formed a sea of steel gray beneath the airship, lit by the glow of a silvery moon.

Jonathan Kahn rested his hands on the icy metal of the window frame and leaned out into nothingness. The stubby cigar in his teeth flared in the fierce wind and went out; he plucked it from his lips and considered it for a long moment, then tossed it to the waiting arms of the earth, five thousand feet below.

The door to the darkened gallery swung open and Henrietta Corbett slipped inside. She narrowed her brown eyes at the freezing wind and shivered despite the fleece-lined leather flying jacket she wore. "I should have known I'd find you down here," she said sourly, pulling her jacket's fleece collar up to cover her ears. "Things are bad enough without you trying to give yourself pneumonia."

Kahn folded his arms and leaned against the window frame looking out at the clouds below. "I thought a little sub-zero cold would get me a little privacy," he growled. "Life seems full of disappointments these days."

Hetty fished a cigarette out of her jacket pocket and a battered Austrian mountaineers' lighter. The tiny flare of light
threw her angular, rawboned features into sharp relief. She
blew out a long plume of smoke and studied him with eyes
that belied her eighteen years of age. "Deadeye Dugan says
we're headed back to the I.S.A."

Kahn shrugged. "What about it?"

"The minute you set foot in the country, Don DeCarlo is
going to know about it. What are you going to do when his
goons show up looking for the money?"

The pirate leader glowered at her. "Maybe if you gave me a
little peace, I could figure out some kind of plan."

"A *plan*?" Hetty said incredulously. "To do *what*, exactly?
We lost three guys over Deadwood, and with Emerson's bird
gone, that leaves us just eight planes, and they ain't got gas
enough to taxi, much less fly anywhere. Plus the zep's shot to
hell. There's so many holes in the hull the ship plays 'The
Star-Spangled Banner' when the wind's just right. A Manhattan cabbie in a busted autogyro could knock us right out of
the sky."

Kahn straightened to his full height and glared down at
his young wingman. "There's always options, kid," he said
coldly.

Hetty stood her ground. She took a long drag on her cigarette and gave him a rueful smile. "Yeah. That's what I'm
afraid of." The smile faded. "Are you thinking about cutting
your losses, boss?"

"What are you talking about?" Kahn said warily.

"I'm talking about you hopping into a car the minute we
get to Chicago and heading for greener pastures, leaving *us*
holding the bag. That's what you did after the Crash, when
you wound up owing all those investors. You did it when the
Drake scam hit the skids." She folded her arms and looked
him in the eye. "The question is, are you going to do it now?"

Kahn met her stare for a long moment, saying nothing,
then turned back to the open window. "How's our prisoner
doing?" he asked.

Hetty frowned. "What the hell does that have to do with
anything?"

"She's a People's Collective air ace, the commander of the Deadwood Air Militia," he said coolly. "When we get to Chicago we'll ransom her back for a hundred g's."

"That's nuts. There's no way those Commie farmers will pay that much for one pilot."

"Let me worry about that," Kahn said, staring out at the night. "How long till we get to the farm?"

For a second Hetty just stared at him, then finally let out a tired sigh. "Eight hours. Maybe less, if the wind shifts."

"Okay. I'm going to get some shut-eye, then. Wake me when we're there." He brushed past her and headed for the door. At the doorway he glanced back. "One other thing, Hetty."

Hetty half turned. Moonlight framed her long face, haloed with silvery strands of cigarette smoke. "Yeah, boss?"

"When we land, have Pete get the car ready."

The Red Skull Legion's base wasn't much to look at—which was precisely the point. A failed dairy farm that dried up just after the Crash, there was nothing left but a boarded-up farmhouse, a dilapidated barn, and a partially collapsed granary, set on twenty-five acres in the middle of an isolated valley.

But the fields were level enough to land aircraft on, and the granary was stronger than it looked, modified to act as a mooring tower. It held fuel tanks and a pump at its base. When the pirates took to the skies they didn't waste time and energy keeping the site under guard; they just threw tarps over the machine tools in the barn, padlocked the doors, and left. A chance passerby would see just one more failed farm—another casualty of the I.S.A.'s move to massive, corporate-controlled industrial agriculture—rotting away in the Illinois countryside.

The *Machiavelli* arrived at just after three in the morning, running silently down the sleeping valley on minimum power. The ground crew slid to the earth on ropes, and within minutes the ship was tied up at the granary tower. By the time the zeppelin was lowered to the ground, Kahn was ready to go.

"I still don't see the point in taking her with you," Hetty said, glaring at Angela Dane. The Collective pilot was awake, but her eyes were glassy as she still struggled to fight off the effects of the laudanum.

"I want her someplace where I can keep an eye on her, instead of letting her get into mischief in the cargo hold," Kahn said. He took Dane by the arm and led her down the gangway. "Is Pete getting the car?"

"He's supposed to be," Hetty answered darkly. Kahn was headed across the pasture in the direction of the old farmhouse. She followed doggedly in his footsteps. "Where do you plan on going at this hour of the morning?"

"Chicago. Where else? The longer I wait, the more chance DeCarlo has to find out I'm back." Kahn reached the house and pushed the front door open. Beyond the doorway it was dark as a tomb. "If you're going to trail after me like a puppy, why don't you make yourself useful and light a lamp or something?"

Hetty pushed past Kahn and stomped inside, biting back her anger. There was a kerosene lamp sitting on a table inside the front room, beside a book of matches. She lifted the glass bowl and deftly lit the wick. The room filled with pale orange light as Kahn and Dane stepped inside. She picked up the lamp and turned to face him, her expression defiant. "I think you've got some explaining to do—"

She froze, her eyes widening as she saw the man standing behind Kahn and Dane, hidden behind the farmhouse door.

"I couldn't agree more," the man said in a silky southern drawl. He pushed the door closed and pressed a large Colt revolver to the back of Kahn's head.

4: Under the Gun

The gunman stepped forward into the glow of the lamplight, pressing the barrel of his pistol against the back of Kahn's shaven head. He wore a leather flying jacket that had seen years of hard use and a pair of travel-stained brown jodhpurs tucked into battered pilot's boots. His tanned face showed a wrinkle or two around the eyes and mouth, and there were streaks of gray in his hair, but his rugged, square-jawed face was strikingly handsome. A pencil-thin mustache and a pearl earring in his right ear lent him an air of roguish charm, but when he smiled at Kahn there was a hard glint in his pale green eyes.

"When did you let yourself get so soft, Johnny-boy?" the man said in a deceptively lazy drawl. "If I'd been one of De-Carlo's thugs, you'd be dead right now."

Kahn reached into his jacket and pulled out a cigar, then leaned forward and lit it off of the lamp's flame. "If you'd been one of DeCarlo's boys, you would've wanted the money first," he countered, "and while we were talking, Hetty would have bounced this lamp off your forehead."

He turned and coolly appraised the grinning gunman. "Hello, Artemus. Still up to your old tricks, I see."

"You *know* this guy?" Hetty exclaimed.

"I should say he does," the man replied with a conspiratorial wink. The pistol flashed and twirled in his fingers, settling with a flourish into a leather holster. "I taught Johnny-boy here everything he knows. We go back a long, long ways, he and I."

"True enough," Kahn grudgingly agreed. "Hetty, allow me to introduce Artemus Hayes: pilot, gambler, con artist, and thief. A rogue for all seasons." He eyed Hayes warily. "The last I heard you'd conned an airship away from Hughes Aviation a few years back and run off to the South China Sea. So what are you doing sneaking around here in the I.S.A.?"

"Looking for you, of course," Hayes replied. He walked past Hetty and sat at the table. Hayes propped his feet on the tabletop and pulled a cigarette out of a silver case. A matching silver lighter flashed and clinked, and he blew a long streamer of smoke toward the ceiling. "I've been camped out at this old shack for most of the week waiting for you to show up. You're getting slow, Johnny-boy."

"How'd you know where to find us?" Hetty said, surprised.

Hayes laughed. "Honey, who do you think he got this place

from? He won the deed at a card game in Cincinnati back in '28, the one and only time he ever got the better of me at five-card draw."

There was a low groan from Dane, the captive People's Collective fighter pilot. Kahn glanced from her to Hayes and growled, "Did you come all this way to catch up on old times, or is there some point to this?"

The easygoing humor faded from Hayes' face. "Of course there's a point, Johnny-boy," he said quietly. "I'm in dire straits, old son, and I need to call in a favor. I reckon that you're just about the only man who can help me out of the fix I'm in."

Now it was Hetty's turn to laugh. "A favor! Since when are we the Sisters of Mercy—?" She stopped short at Kahn's raised hand.

Kahn stared hard at Hayes. "What sort of favor?"

"Well, there's something of a story behind it." He took a thoughtful drag on his cigarette. "How much do you know about what's going on in Manchuria?"

"Where?" Hetty asked.

"Northeast China," Kahn interjected. "The Japanese invaded a few months back, and are pushing deeper into the mainland. From what I've heard on the radio, they're almost to Nanking, the Chinese capital."

"It's a horror show," Hayes said flatly. "You can't imagine what's happening to people over there. I've seen it with my own eyes, and I still can't believe it." He rubbed a hand over his face, as if to wipe the memories away. "It's gotten so bad that the Nationalists and the Communists are actually working *together* against the Japanese, but they're still on the ropes. If they don't get help from somewhere, soon, they're finished.

"They managed to get an airship past the Japanese blockade a couple weeks ago and sent a delegation to the League of Nations with evidence of the atrocities in Manchuria."

Kahn pulled out a chair and sat down, his expression thoughtful. "But something went wrong, I take it. The Japanese seized the delegates?"

"They seized the senior delegate's *daughter*," Hayes replied. "They were stopped over in Manhattan, refueling before a final hop to Columbia. Snatched her right off the street after a Broadway show. They say that if her father speaks to the League, he'll never see her again."

"Makes sense. That's what *I'd* do," Kahn said, half to himself. "So where do you fit into all this?"

"The Chinese government hired me to get her out."

Kahn's eyes went wide. *"You?"*

"Hey! I've made a name for myself in Asia, thank you very much," Hayes replied indignantly. "Too much of a name, it turns out. The Japanese caught wind of what was going on and smuggled a bomb onto my zep in Hong Kong. Blew her and the whole crew to bits." He sat back and shook his head ruefully. "So I took the last of my cash, bribed my way onto a British merchant zep bound for Chicago, and here I am."

Kahn stared at him. "You want us to help you get the girl out."

"Not to put too fine a point on it, Johnny-boy, but yes, that's the idea."

Hetty slapped her palms on the tabletop and leaned in until she was nose to nose with Hayes. "You're out of your damn mind," she snorted. "You think we can just waltz into the Empire State anytime we please?"

He met her gaze evenly. "I don't know about *you*, honey," he said, "but I know *he* can . . . if he puts his mind to it."

She looked to Kahn. "Then *you* tell him we can't do it—"

Kahn silenced her with a look. "Where is the girl being kept?"

A sly smile spread across Hayes' face. "The Japanese Embassy, on Park Avenue," he said. "Right in the middle of Manhattan. I figured you'd enjoy the challenge."

"When we get her out, then what?" Kahn asked.

Hayes shrugged. "We fly her to the Chinese Embassy in Hawai'i. From everything I hear, it sounds like you could stand to get away from the mainland—and Chicago—for a while."

Kahn leaned back in his chair, his eyes narrowed in concentration. After a moment, he said, "Hetty, tell Dugan to take on all the fuel we've got left, and make what repairs he

can to the zep in the meantime. Then tell Pete he's got some
more painting to do. Looks like we're heading to the Empire
State."

Hayes beamed. "I knew I could count on you, Johnny-boy!
When do we leave?"

The pirate leader checked his watch. "In three hours."

Now it was Hayes' turn to look shocked. "Three hours?
Don't get me wrong, Johnny, but this is *Manhattan* we're
talking about. Are you sure you aren't being too hasty?"

Kahn shrugged, but there was a manic gleam in his eyes.
"The sooner we get the girl, the sooner you and I are even," he
said. "And I pay my debts. One way or another."

The aerotaxi dropped down out of a snowy sky and made a
perfect landing on the roof of the Park Avenue Plaza Hotel.
The autogyro's rotors kicked up swirling clouds of ice that
hung in the late-night air, causing the hotel's doorman to duck
and clutch at the collar of his overcoat as he rushed out and
opened the door for the taxi's passengers. Kahn and Hayes
stepped out into the wintry maelstrom, gloved hands pressed
to their fedoras, and headed for the edge of the roof.

Below them Park Avenue buzzed with activity, despite the
late hour. Revelers made their way back from Broadway, or
set out from hotels and stately apartment buildings to dance
the night away in jazz halls or speakeasies. Kahn rested a polished shoe on the roof's stone parapet and pulled out a cigar.
Wearing a dark oilskin overcoat and wool trousers, he was the
image of a captain of industry, surveying his Manhattan play-
ground. In fact, he had eyes only for the somber gray building
just across from the hotel.

"Built like the old Federal Reserve," he growled as he
studied the Japanese Embassy up close.

The embassy building was built to ward off a small army. It
was four stories tall, its walls made of massive granite slabs.
The windows on the ground floor were small and the close-
set frames made of bronze-colored iron, each pane barely
wide enough to fit a hand through. There were no fire escapes,
he noted.

He saw a service entrance on the right side of the building

and a grand main entrance that opened on a fountain bordered by a circular asphalt drive. A granite wall ten feet high, topped with decorative, but dangerous, iron spikes, surrounded the building and its grounds. The wrought-iron main gate was closed, and he could make out the outline of a guardhouse just past the gate.

Hayes hunched his shoulders against the cold. Like Kahn, he, too, had donned a business suit. "You still haven't told me how we're getting in there," he said nervously. "More important, you haven't told me how the hell we're going to get out again."

Kahn leaned forward slightly and surveyed the sidewalk below. "You sound like I've got a plan or something, Artemus. I've never even *seen* this building before."

"See, this is what I was talking about," Hayes said. "Why don't we get a room here at the Plaza and spend a couple days casing the joint? We don't want to go into this half-cocked."

The pirate leader eyed Hayes. "Where's all that bravado you had at the farmhouse? You're the one who came all the way from Hong Kong to get this girl out, and now you're getting cold feet? Besides, the *Machiavelli* can't keep circling La Guardia Airfield claiming engine problems for days on end. At sunup, the airfield will send a tug to bring her in, and then the jig's up." He shook his head. "We go tonight, or not at all." Kahn gave him a wolfish smile. "Relax, Artemus. I'll think of something. I always do. "

They made their way to the hotel's rooftop elevator, and down through the lobby. Once they were outside, they crossed the icy street and walked slowly down the sidewalk, alongside the embassy walls. As they passed the gate, Kahn noticed that there were two guards keeping warm inside the guardhouse, their bayonet-tipped rifles close at hand.

The embassy sat at the corner of Park Avenue and East Forty-eighth Street. Kahn led them around the corner, then across Forty-eighth and into a nearby alley. He pointed to a call box a few yards away. "That's the fire box for this corner. Go and pull the lever."

Hayes eyed him dubiously, but did as he was told. Kahn watched calmly as Artemus picked up the metal bar, broke the little glass pane, and pulled the alarm lever before scurrying back to the alley.

Kahn looked up at the embassy. "How long do you figure it'll take the fire department to get here?"

"On Park Avenue? Five minutes, tops," Hayes said. "But Johnny, there's no fire. When the firemen check out the place, they'll tip off the Japanese that something isn't jake."

The pirate glanced at Hayes with a slight smile. Kahn reached into his jacket and drew a bulky black pistol from his coat pocket. He carefully took aim, cocked the hammer . . . and fired.

The flare hissed across the street and punched through one of the embassy's second-floor windows. A red glow blazed behind the curtains as the magnesium ignited, followed by the familiar flickers of yellow-orange firelight.

"There's your fire," Kahn replied. "Now let's go be good little Manhattan rubberneckers for a bit."

They crossed the street again and waited at the corner. Shouts went up from the building's entrance, and soon the wail of sirens could be heard down Park Avenue. "Where do you think they're keeping the girl?" Kahn asked.

"It'd have to be someplace out of sight," Hayes answered. "There's too many people that move in and out of there. I'd guess she's in the basement."

Fire engines howled out of the darkness and pulled up in front of the embassy. Already fire and smoke were pouring from several upper-story windows. The guards pulled open the gates, waving to the firefighters. "That's our cue," Kahn said, and headed for the gate.

As they passed one of the fire engines, Kahn snagged a pair of firemen's helmets and passed one back to Hayes. In the dark, their oilskin coats looked very similar to the ones the firemen themselves wore. The Japanese guards waved them through with the rest, shouting frantically.

Pandemonium reigned inside the building. Kahn was surprised at the number of late-night workers still present, running and shouting through the grand foyer, clutching boxes or folders of important files.

Kahn and Hayes shoved through and moved to the ele-

vators that, mercifully, were empty. Hayes—scanning the
Japanese characters on the lift buttons—quickly sent the elevator down.

They stepped off the elevator and into a small stone room
that smelled of diesel oil and mildew. There was a table in one
corner, adjacent to a big steel door that was better suited to a
jail cell than an embassy.

There were four men in the room, talking back and forth in
frantic voices. Each wore a Japanese army uniform, Kahn
noted, and the most senior man carried an odd, slightly
curved sword at his hip. They saw Kahn and Hayes, and the
sword-carrying man shouted at them angrily.

Hayes shouted back in a long string of Japanese. The
guards' eyes went wide, and they bolted for the elevator. As
they disappeared from sight, Kahn turned to Hayes. "When
did you learn Japanese?"

"What do you think they speak in Asia? Italian?"

Hayes ran to the desk. There was a kind of logbook sitting
there, its pages crammed with dense lines of Japanese script.
"Okay . . . here! They brought in a woman and put her in
room 418. That's got to be her."

The iron door was locked. Kahn rifled the desk and found
the key ring in the top drawer. The doors in the hall beyond
were all marked in Japanese. Hayes took the lead, calling out
the numbers. "421 . . . 420 . . . 419 . . . here!"

The heavy wooden door was locked. None of the keys on
the ring fit. "The hell with it," Kahn said, and pulled a .45 automatic from his waistband and shot out the lock.

The room beyond was little better than a linen closet, with
no furniture other than a small chamber pot. A small figure
huddled in the far corner, wearing only a torn silk chemise.
Her arms and legs were covered with bruises, and when she
looked up at the two men her eyes seemed to stare right
through them. A bullet hole—from Kahn's shot through the
lock—was evident in the wall, just above the girl's head.

"Nice shooting, ace . . . She's in shock," Hayes said grimly.
"Can you carry her?"

Kahn bent and hefted her unresisting form over his shoulder. "Let's go!" he said.

The two men raced back down the hall. Kahn could see through the open doorway of the elevator room, only a few yards away. Suddenly, the call light on the elevator blinked. He heard the elevator open and a young Japanese officer in a dark blue uniform stepped out, followed by a group of rifle-toting guards.

The blue-uniformed man took in the room with a single glance—and saw Kahn and Hayes in the corridor beyond. His lean face twisted in anger, and his hand flew to the curved sword at his side. He drew the weapon in a fluid blur, light flashing off the blade. The soldier pointed the sword at Kahn and roared an order to the guards, who reached for their weapons.

Kahn didn't understand the officer's words, but the meaning was perfectly clear.

5: Caught in the Act

The soldiers swept around the Japanese officer like an angry tide, leveling their bayonet-tipped rifles. The metallic sound of rifle bolts cycling echoed menacingly in the narrow hallway.

Kahn, still carrying the girl over his left shoulder, roared like an angry bull and charged right at them, blasting away with the .45 in his right hand.

Three of the soldiers fell, knocked from their feet by the heavy slugs, and the rest opened fire, spending shots wildly. Bullets cracked and whined down the corridor as they ricocheted off the concrete walls in the elevator room. Two more of the soldiers fell, possibly struck by their own bullets; another shot flattened against the steel fireman's helmet Kahn wore and knocked it from his head.

Kahn fired twice more, and the remaining troops panicked, bolting for the relative safety of the elevator car and forcing their officer back along with them.

Kahn staggered into the room, followed closely by Hayes.

His head felt as if a mule had kicked it. There wasn't any other way out of the room, and it would take only a few moments before the troops got their courage back and tried again.

"Now what?" Hayes asked shakily. Blood flowed down his cheek from a cut above his eye.

A glint of metal on a dead guard caught Kahn's eye. He put away the pistol and crouched, plucking out a small, dark cylinder.

"Tell those goons to throw out their weapons and come out with their hands up or I'm throwing in a grenade," he said, hefting the small bomb in his hand.

Hayes blurted out an order in Japanese. Moments later, the remaining soldiers slid their rifles out onto the floor and emerged one at a time, their hands held high.

The Japanese officer came last, stalking into the room like an angry panther, sword in hand. He glared defiantly at Kahn. "You won't escape, Mr. Kahn," he said in flawless, unaccented English. "There are a dozen more men waiting in the lobby. Surrender now, and I promise you a quick death."

"I think I'll hold out for a better offer," the pirate replied dryly, motioning Hayes toward the elevator. They circled around the guards and stepped into the car. Hayes grabbed the car's operating lever.

As the doors closed, the officer fixed them with a malevolent stare. "We will meet again, 'Genghis' Kahn," he hissed.

Kahn glanced at Hayes. "He doesn't know me very well, does he?" The pirate pulled the pin on the grenade and tossed it into the officer's face as the elevator doors slid shut.

Hayes rolled his eyes. "Johnny, you big oaf, their grenades don't work like ours. The pin's just a safety—you have to knock the end against something to strike the fuse!"

"*Now* you tell me," Kahn replied sourly. "Don't just stand there . . . get this crate moving!"

"He said there's a dozen men waiting in the lobby," Hayes protested.

"Who said we're going to the lobby?" Kahn pushed Hayes aside and grabbed the lever. The car started to move. "We're heading for the roof."

"The roof?" Hayes echoed. "The roof is probably *on fire* right about now."

"If we're lucky," Kahn agreed. "Keep your fingers crossed."

The air grew steadily hotter as the elevator rose toward the roof. Smoke seeped through the ventilators. Hayes stared worriedly at Kahn, but the pirate simply shrugged.

It seemed like an eternity before the car lurched to a stop. The doors opened, letting in a furnacelike blast of air, and Kahn dashed out into a scene straight from Hell.

Flames writhed and roared from the embassy's fourth-floor windows and sent cyclones of heat and smoke curling up over the edges of the roof, washing back and forth like angry tides with every shift of the wind. Hayes snatched a handkerchief from his jacket and pressed it to his face; Kahn narrowed his eyes, coughed harshly, and tried to make out the embassy's taxipad.

"Find some way to jam those doors," he shouted to Hayes, and then staggered toward the center of the roof.

He couldn't find the taxipad in the smoke and the darkness, so he got as close to the center of the roof as he could and set the girl down. Kahn pulled the flare gun from his overcoat pocket and broke the pistol open to remove the spent shell inside. There were two spares in his left pocket; he quickly reloaded the gun.

Squinting through the dense smoke, he lifted the gun high and fired. A flare hissed up and vanished through the swirling haze; a moment later, there was a muffled report as the flare ignited.

Kahn pulled off the heavy overcoat. It was getting harder and harder to draw breath. Waves of heat beat at his face and hands. He wondered how long it would take for the Japanese officer to figure out where they'd gone, and whether he'd even bother to come after them; in another few minutes, the fire would probably do his dirty work for him.

The smoke was getting thicker. Hayes ran over and joined him, shaking his head. "No way to jam the doors," he said, his voice muffled by the handkerchief. "What do we do now, jump?"

"No," Kahn answered. "We fly."

As if on cue, a loud drone cut through the roaring of the flames and an autogyro appeared out of the smoke, flying low and slow over the building. The autogyro, emblazoned with the insignia of the New York Fire Department, swept past and pulled into a sharp turn. A moment later it was bouncing across the rooftop toward them, its brakes squealing as it slowed to a stop a few yards away.

The autogyro was stripped down and fitted out for rescue work. It consisted of little more than a frame, engine, rotor, and pusher prop, supporting a pilot and a passenger seat, plus a stretcher running lengthwise along each side of the vehicle. The fireman waved, and Kahn picked up the delegate's daughter and rushed her over to one of the stretcher mounts.

"Saw your flare and got here as fast as I could," the pilot yelled over the sound of the engine.

"You're a real lifesaver," Kahn replied. He finished strapping the girl down and pulled out his pistol. "Now get out of here."

The fireman's jaw dropped. "Are you *nuts*?" he exclaimed. "The fire—"

A bullet ricocheted off the autogyro's frame, then another. The fireman leapt from his seat, and Kahn looked back to see the officer he'd left in the basement leading more troops from the elevator onto the roof.

Hayes was less than ten yards away, pistol in hand, firing slowly and deliberately at the oncoming troops. Kahn leapt into the pilot's seat and fired a few wild shots of his own. "Artemus!" he shouted. "Let's go!"

The pilot looked back and caught Kahn's eye, then fired another careful shot in the direction of the enemy officer. Instantly the soldiers fired back in a ragged volley and Hayes cried out as he fell to his knees, one hand pressed to his gut.

"Hayes!" Kahn cried. He fired another shot at the oncoming troops, and the pistol's slide locked back, its clip empty. "Hang on!"

"No!" Hayes shouted, waving him away with a bloodslicked hand. "Get the hell out of here!" His soot-smeared face contorted in pain. "Just take the girl to Hawai'i, Kahn. Do that and you and I are square. *Go!*"

Another bullet zipped past Kahn's head, smashing into the autogyro. Sooner or later, he realized, they'd hit the engine . . . or something more vital.

Hayes crumpled onto his side, gamely raising his pistol and thumbing back the hammer as the Japanese troops drew nearer.

Cursing savagely, Kahn released the brake and turned the rescue bird around, then opened the throttle and didn't look back.

Kahn could just make out the zeppelins against the overcast sky, their silvery undersides lit from below by the lights of La Guardia Airfield. He picked out the *Machiavelli* easily—a prominent red cross had been hastily painted on her flank.

As far as the Empire State knew, the airship was on a mission of mercy, en route to deliver a load of medical supplies up north, into what was once Canada. Her gun mounts were covered with canvas tarps, disguising her true nature from distant observers, but the illusion wouldn't hold up to a daylight inspection.

Kahn adjusted a knob on the autogyro's radio and managed to raise the airship, warning them to get the "flycatcher" ready.

Kahn circled the huge airship twice before he saw the lights on the dorsal taxipad flicker to life. He brought the autogyro around, approaching the zeppelin from the bow and cutting the throttle until his airspeed was eighteen miles per hour—just above stall speed.

He coasted down two-thirds the length of the zeppelin—more than seven hundred feet—gradually losing altitude until his wheels nearly scraped the airship's skin.

The taxipad was a ten-feet-square wooden platform, the aft end of which was strung with a thickly woven cargo net. The trick to landing was to bring the wheels down right at the edge of the pad and lean hard on the brakes to kill as much momentum as possible before the autogyro hit the flycatcher.

The light craft touched the wooden platform, bounced slightly, and plunged into the net's embrace with a bone-rattling jar. The pirate cut the rear engine at once, and before he had unbuckled his restraints, the *Machiavelli*'s rigging crew was already swarming over the pad, lashing the auto-gyro down and preparing to lower the little bird down into the ship's small craft hangar. Kahn quickly gave instructions to carry the girl to the ship's infirmary, then left the riggers and made his way to the airship's bridge.

The *Machiavelli* had once been the flagship of the Utah Aerial Navy, and her layout and design had more in common with oceangoing warships than her cargo-hauling kin. Unlike civilian airships, her bridge was plated in steel armor and lo-cated inside the ship's hull, with Plexiglas view ports looking forward from the zeppelin's bow.

The bridge was bathed in the red glow of battle lanterns to preserve the crew's night vision. The men at the helm and trim controls were already wearing flak vests and helmets when Kahn stepped through the bridge's after hatchway. "Pour on the coal, Dugan!" he called out. "Turn us west and head for the nearest cloudbank. I want to be in the I.S.A. be-fore dawn."

"Deadeye" Dugan, the ship's captain, nodded curtly and barked orders to the bridge crew. Tall and gray-haired, the former I.S.A. airship commander had been cashiered when he was badly disfigured in a refueling mishap. The left side of his face was a mass of scar tissue, surrounding a glass eye that glittered like a piece of jade. "All engines ahead full," he called. "Helm, come to course two-seven-zero."

A map table dominated the center of the bridge, where a detailed map of New York was currently displayed. Holders lining three of the table's four sides were jammed with dozens of additional maps; Kahn rifled through them as Hetty ap-peared on the bridge.

"Thanks for letting me know you'd gotten back," she said, eyeing him carefully. "You look like you've been rolling around in a campfire. How did it go?"

"Well enough," Kahn muttered. "The girl's in the infirmary."

"Hayes is with her?"

"No," he replied. "He caught a bullet just as we were about to pull out."

Hetty's eyes went wide. "No kidding? Well, thank God for small blessings," she said. "This little 'favor' would have been the end of us. What do you want to do with the girl?"

"We're taking her to Hawai'i, same as before," Kahn said flatly. "Nothing's changed."

Hetty was dumbfounded. "Have you lost your marbles? Hayes is *dead*."

"But the debt remains," Khan replied, looking her in the eye. "And now this is the only way I can even the score."

"What the *hell* are you talking about?" Hetty cried. "You owe money to half the people on this continent! You owed the Purple Gang, and now you owe big money to Giovanni De-Carlo, but you've never lost any sleep over that!

"And what about what you owe *us*," she continued, gesturing angrily, "your *crew*, the ones who are going to go down in flames because of some damn fool favor you owe to a dead man?"

Anger clouded Kahn's face. He came around the map table slowly, his eyes locked on Hetty, who planted her hands on her hips and stood her ground, ready for a fight.

Before anything could happen, the voice of the watch officer cried out, "Aft lookouts report engine sounds to the northeast! Four, maybe six fighters, closing fast!"

Dugan crossed the bridge in three quick strides and got between Kahn and his wingman. "What do you want us to do, boss?" he asked pointedly.

The pirate leader paused, and took a deep breath. "Battle stations," he said quietly. "Uncover the guns. I'm going topside." Brushing past Hetty, he stormed out the after hatch and headed quickly down the main accessway as the alert klaxon sounded.

In addition to the *Machiavelli*'s four main cannon, the zeppelin mounted ten heavy machine guns for close-in defense—six .50-caliber guns in dorsal and ventral gondolas, and four .60-caliber guns in port and starboard blisters located amidships. The dorsal gondola was reached via an enclosed fifty-foot ladder covered by a submarine-style hatch. By the time Kahn threw open the hatch and climbed out into the wintry air the gunners were already at their weapons, loading in belts of armor-piercing ammo. The pirate leader leaned against the gondola's armored bulwark and peered into the gloom.

The heavy overcast above caught the lights of the city and reflected them back in a kind of diffuse twilight. Kahn could see clearly for maybe half a mile to port and starboard, and the waters of the Lower Bay gleamed black and silver three thousand feet below. After a moment, he could hear the sounds the lookouts described: fighter engines, loud, snarling radials out in the darkness maybe a mile behind them.

There was a set of earphones and a microphone on a hook by the hatch. Kahn fitted the set over his head, wincing at the feel of the icy Bakelite. "All hands, this is Kahn," he called over the ship's intercom. "Everyone hold their fire. This is most likely just a routine patrol, and they won't approach too closely. If we play it quiet, we can still slip away—"

He heard the engine sounds swell, and one of the gunners gave a shout. Kahn looked back to see four shapes materialize out of the gloom, flying in close formation. They swept down the starboard side of the airship, seemingly close enough to touch the zep's hull. The thunder of their high-performance engines beat against his face and chest.

They looked similar to PR-1 Defenders, but with a shortened fuselage and small, wing-mounted rudders. Their engine cowlings were painted black, and the rest of the airframes were white. Large, red circles on their wingtips stood out like bright drops of blood. Just as quickly as they appeared, they were gone, leaving the airship behind as though it were standing still.

"Damn!" exclaimed the gunner nearest Kahn. "What the hell were those things?"

"Japanese fighters," Kahn answered, unable to fully believe it himself. "Here. In the Empire State. Crawford and his Broadway Bomber lapdogs must be slipping."

Somewhere ahead, the fighters split up and doubled back; the snarling sound of their engines reverberated in the darkness all around the airship. Suddenly a voice cried out over the intercom: "Bandits, nine o'clock high!"

Kahn whirled in time to see two of the fighters diving on them to port. Yellow flashes winked from their cowlings and wings, and tracer fire clawed at the airship's side. He could hear the bullets punching through the layered fabric of the hull like hail on a paper roof. "Open fire!" Kahn yelled into the mike, and the *Machiavelli* erupted in noise and light, sending arcs of tracers after the enemy planes.

"Two more bandits at six o'clock!" one of the spotters called out. The pair of fighters bored in like arrows, closing to point-blank range. The gunner nearest Kahn swung his weapon aft and opened up, sending a short burst of fire lancing at the left-most plane. Hot brass casings, smoking in the cold air, rattled and rolled along the decking at their feet.

Flame streaked from the fighters' wings. The aft end of the zeppelin was outlined in strobe flashes of angry orange as the flak rockets exploded in a string of dull thunderclaps. "Number six engine out!" a tense voice exclaimed over the headset. "We've got holes in the ventral rudder and damage to the hangar bay. Looks like two of the rockets penetrated somewhere aft but didn't go off."

Lucky us, Kahn thought as the fighters dived beneath the airship and disappeared from sight. He pounded his fist against the bulwark in frustration; they didn't dare launch their own fighters to protect the ship. While the enemy planes could return to a well-lit landing strip, recovering planes aboard an airship in the dark was an invitation to disaster.

He looked toward the bow to see how close they were to the relative safety of a cloudbank—and saw danger instead. He yelled into the microphone: "Bandits, bandits, twelve o'clock high!"

The two planes struck from the darkness like thunderbolts, machine guns blazing. He watched the tracers march along the upper hull toward him. The gunners behind him opened fire as he dived to the deck, shells whizzing back and forth over his head like angry hornets. The fighters roared overhead and were gone before his knees touched steel. When he looked up again the gunner closest to him lay motionless on the deck, wreathed in a spreading pool of blood.

"Searchlights to starboard!" one of the remaining gunners

cried, pointing with a gloved hand. Kahn raised his head over the bulwark. White beams slashed through the darkness at their altitude, nearly two miles away.

He could just make out the sleek shapes of not one, but *two* Empire State patrol zeppelins, heading their way. As he watched, there was a bloom of yellow-white fire from the lead ship's port quarter. Seconds later came a sound like ripping canvas as a five-inch shell raced across their bow.

Wisps of mist trailed through the air, obscuring the Empire State warships. Suddenly the air turned clammy, and then the zeppelin plunged into a tunnel of fog as the *Machiavelli* found sanctuary within the depths of a cloudbank. The gunners let out loud sighs of relief. Kahn pulled off the headset and opened the hatch, disappearing below.

His thoughts raced as he ran to the bridge. Japanese fighter planes were bad enough, but Empire State zeppelins meant serious trouble. He'd never expected the Japanese to yell for help from the Empire State, much less have the whole Navy sent out after him. While there was no love lost between the Empire State and the I.S.A.—especially pirates from the I.S.A.—the military response was far too strong for a simple kidnapping. Something didn't fit.

Kahn made his way to the bridge. Shards of Plexiglas littered the deck from where a round had punched through one of the forward view ports. The door to the radio room, just right of the hatchway, was open. The radioman had tuned onto one of the New York radio stations, and the muffled, scratchy sound of a news program traveled out into the room.

"Good evening people of the Empire State and all the ships at sea," the news announcer said. "A fierce battle is raging over our heads tonight as our fair city has come under attack by none other than the infamous 'Genghis' Kahn and his ruthless band of cutthroats, the Red Skull Legion.

"According to reports from city hall, the treacherous pirate has struck the Japanese Embassy on Park Avenue and left the venerable old building in flames. Dozens are feared dead tonight, but worst of all, it has been revealed that the object of this dastardly raid was none other than Miss Chiang

Liu-mei, daughter of President Chiang Kai-shek—the em-
battled leader of the Republic of China.

"The motive for the kidnapping is unknown, but President
La Guardia has put the Navy on full alert, sending every
available airship in the sky to track down and apprehend the
pirates. A reward of no less than ten thousand dollars has
been offered leading to the capture of Kahn and his gang. Our
prayers go out to Chiang Liu-mei, and to the brave men and
women determined to bring these villains to justice."

Kahn felt a finger of ice crawl up his spine. He saw Hetty
step from the radio room, her face pale. Her hands were trem-
bling. She met his gaze, scowling in fear and anger.

"What in the hell have you gotten us into?"

6: Old Friends

The pale moon was a vague silver glow above the rapidly
moving clouds, limning the edges of the rolling hills in
frosty light. *Machiavelli* cruised high over the sleeping
countryside, her silvery hull just brushing the undersides of
the wintry overcast as she navigated by compass and the
sharp eyes of her shivering lookouts. The airship's flanks
were ragged with holes, and her two aftmost engines were
silent—the starboard motor a burnt-out shell and the port
motor shut down to keep the ship's thrust in balance.

After the fierce air battle over the People's Collective
and the skirmish with Japanese fighters above New York,
the zep was nearly crippled, fighting a headwind over the
Empire State as she struggled to make it across the border before dawn.

Jonathan Kahn stepped aside to let a pair of the ship's riggers make their way down the narrow passageway. Their
faces were taut and weary, smudged with smoke stains and
grease from long hours spent struggling to keep the zeppelin
in the air. The lead rigger stood a little straighter as he passed
Kahn, and gave the boss a tired smile as the men headed aft to

head off another crisis. The pirate leader waited until they were out of sight before rubbing fiercely at his aching eyes. He checked his watch. It was just after three in the morning.

The last time a lookout had seen searchlights was nearly an hour ago, some four miles to the east. The Empire State Navy apparently believed Kahn would head back to the I.S.A., the Red Skulls' home ground, and had thrown every ship they could into his path. Up until now events had occurred too quickly for La Guardia's forces to organize a coordinated search, but now the *Machiavelli* was struggling to make half her rated speed, and time was no longer on her side.

Kahn pictured the Empire State patrol zeppelins gliding through the night like sharks, peering through the darkness with searchlights and flares, drawing ever nearer to his stricken ship. They'd been lucky to lose their pursuers in the clouds over New York City, where a sane pilot couldn't risk groping blindly through the overcast with all the traffic filling the skies. The same didn't hold true out here, near the border, and Kahn couldn't shake the feeling that his luck was about to run out.

Kahn took a deep breath and tried to push the worries out of his mind. As long as he could still think, he could always find a way out. The pirate leader reached into his jacket and pulled out a cigar as he paced a little farther down the passage and pushed open the door to the zeppelin's sick bay.

The cold air in the small room smelled of smoke, blood, and death. Five of the sick bay's eight beds were occupied, and two more men sat dejectedly on the room's operating table, clutching bandaged limbs. One of the men stretched out in the beds moaned fitfully in a morphine-induced sleep. A short, broad-shouldered man with a grizzled crew cut stood in the center of the room and watched the moaning man worriedly, wiping his hands on a bloodstained apron. "Doc" Adams turned as Kahn entered the sick bay and nodded a tired greeting.

"How bad is it?" Kahn asked around his cigar. He had his lighter in his hands, but looking over the wounded men, he resisted the urge and put it and the cigar away.

"All told? Two dead, eight injured," Adams said with a

sigh. He gestured at the beds. "I did the best I could for the worst cases, but about all I'm really good for is simple first aid. Murphy took three rounds in the gut; I'm not sure he'll last the night." The former horse doctor looked guiltily at Kahn. "I've been giving him morphine pretty steadily, and it's used up almost a third of our stocks. I know how expensive the stuff is—"

"Don't worry about that," Kahn said quietly. "Make him as comfortable as you can. We'll worry about the rest later." His eyes settled on the room's eighth bed, hidden from the rest of the room by a curtained screen. "What about our guest?"

Adams shrugged. "I gave her some laudanum, so she's sleeping now. Somebody roughed her up pretty good—a lot of bruises, maybe a cracked rib. Looks like she hasn't been fed much, either. You can look in her eyes and tell she's been through Hell."

Kahn frowned. The Japanese wanted to keep the girl's father from addressing the League of Nations, so what purpose did torturing her serve? The mere threat of harming the girl should have been sufficient.

Kahn shook his head, trying to clear the cobwebs from his sleep-deprived brain. Clearly there was more going on than Hayes, his old partner in crime, had led him to believe. Now that Hayes was dead, Kahn found himself fumbling in the dark, unsure of how to proceed—but certain that there was no turning back now.

"Has she said anything, Doc? Anything at all?"

"Not a word," Adams said. "Boss, she's in deep shock. I wouldn't expect anything out of her for a good long while." He spread his hands in a gesture of helplessness. "I don't know what else to do. All I know are horses and airplane engines."

"Yeah. Okay." Kahn did his best to keep the desperation out of his voice. "You're doing okay, Doc. Stay here and keep an eye on everybody, and if she wakes up, let me know."

Kahn stalked out into the passageway and headed aft, deeper into the shadowy interior of the ship. He could still smell smoke from the fire that had broken out in the hangar bay. The Red Skulls were in deep trouble, far worse than they'd ever been before. His hands curled into fists, but there was nothing and no one he could strike at that would drive out the frustration that he felt. If there was one thing his father had taught him, it was that a man survived by controlling the events that surrounded him. Kahn wasn't in control anymore, and he knew it.

He lit his cigar and started pacing again, trying to think. Kahn's thoughts kept going back to his recent conversations with Hetty. The girl was worried; she was no dummy, and could see the signs as well as he could. She was afraid he was going to bail out on them.

The more he thought about it, the more he saw that skipping out would be the smartest play, given the way the cards were stacked against him.

Kahn kept walking, turning the problem over and over in his head. Without consciously intending to, he found himself wandering through the cargo deck. One of the cargo lockers was padlocked shut. There was no guard. Kahn considered the door for a moment, puffing thoughtfully on his cigar, and then reached a decision. He pulled out a set of keys and undid the padlock. The cargo locker was windowless and black as a cave. Kahn figured Dane was probably asleep. Standing in the doorway, he reached for the light switch and realized with a start that it was still turned on. She'd put out the light. That was when something came flying out of the darkness and smashed against his head.

Everything went white. Kahn fell to his knees. He felt a lithe figure try to force its way past him, and he grabbed blindly with both hands. His left hand closed on a small foot, and he jerked backward, hard. Dane fell to the deck with a loud grunt, and he knew he'd knocked the wind out of her. The pirate boss forced himself to his feet, holding the trapped foot as high as he could and blinking furiously at the stars that danced in front of his eyes.

Dane thrashed and writhed in his grip like a snared tiger, kicking furiously with her free leg. Kahn's head began to throb with a dull, pounding ache, but the passageway came back into focus. He let go of Dane, who quickly sprang to her feet, ready to kill or be killed. Kahn looked over her diminutive form and scowled. "Save it, sister. You've got the brass, but not the muscle. And even if you did, there's nowhere to run." He looked down and saw pieces of porcelain scattered around the deck. Kahn picked up a shard, wincing at the pain in his head. "You hit me with a chamber pot?" he said, examining the fragment in the light.

"It seemed appropriate," Dane replied. She hadn't relaxed in the least, her small hands balled into fists. "And if you don't cut me loose, you can expect a hell of a lot worse than that."

Kahn pulled his gun. "Of course, I could just shoot you and save myself the trouble."

Surprisingly, Dane gave him a humorless smile. "If you were going to kill me, you'd have done it a long time ago, pirate."

The pirate boss tossed the shard aside. "Touché," he said, and put the pistol away. "You're proving to be a headache in more ways than one, Captain Dane. In fact, I do have certain uses for you. Do you have any medical skill? A number of my men are seriously hurt, and need a doctor's attention."

Dane's lip curled in a sneer. "If I did, do you think I'd actually waste it on thugs like you and your men?"

"Where is your sense of humanity, Captain?"

The Collective pilot let out a derisive snort. "That's rich, coming from a man like you."

"Fair enough," Kahn conceded. "Then I'll settle for using you as a hostage if need be, or ransoming you back if the Collective will still have you." He picked out a piece of ceramic on the deck and methodically ground it under his boot. "If not, I'm sure we can find someone in Hawai'i willing to take you off our hands."

Dane's eyes narrowed appraisingly. "So you rescued the girl, then? You're the last person in the world I would peg for a knight in shining armor, Kahn."

"I'm not," Kahn replied darkly. "A long time ago, Artemus Hayes took me under his wing and taught me a great number of things . . . including how to fly a plane. He also saved my life." The pirate shrugged. "I owe him. And I don't like being indebted to anyone. It's as simple as that.

"Unfortunately this little errand has become a great deal more complicated than I'd bargained for. It's nearly dawn, and if we aren't across the border into the I.S.A. by then, things are going to get unpleasant." Kahn gestured down the forward passageway. "Let's go."

"You're not going to lock me up again?" Dane asked.

"I don't have enough healthy crewmen to keep an eye on you, Captain, and I don't want you left alone to get into any more mischief."

The Collective Captain raised her chin defiantly. "Watch me all you want, Kahn. I'll still find a way to escape."

"Feel free, Comrade," the pirate said with a wolfish grin. "Assuming we can clear up the debris on the hangar deck to launch any planes, there's a big enough reward on our heads that you'd get shot down or captured by the first militia you ran across, and I doubt they'd be inclined to believe your story. After all, the Red Skulls have earned something of a reputation for . . . misdirection. For the time being, you're much better off with our company than without it."

Dane paled. Her mouth worked, but no sounds came out. The look on her face was the best thing that had happened to Kahn in quite some time.

Dawn found the *Machiavelli* still a hundred miles short of the border, but the Red Skulls' luck still held. Snowstorms blanketed the Empire State's western border, cutting visibility to less than fifty feet and muffling the sound of the zeppelin's engines. On the downside, the airship's electrical heat failed shortly after daybreak, leaving the crew huddled and shivering in their flight gear for four long hours until it could be repaired.

Dugan and Kahn watched layers of ice build on the zeppelin's hull and deemed it an acceptable risk, given the alternatives. They crossed the border at a little after nine, but the crew knew better than to think they were home free.

All the radio stations were buzzing with the news of the Manhattan raid. According to the reports, La Guardia was ready to send his zeppelins into the I.S.A. if that's what it took, touching off a heated exchange of threats between Chicago and New York. Kahn wasn't fool enough to think that the I.S.A. was staring down the Empire State for his sake; if anything, they probably wanted the credit for his capture as much as La Guardia did.

Kahn kept the *Machiavelli* in the air, since the Red Skulls' hidden base was now a likely ambush site. Instead, he kept the airship headed west, well away from established commercial shipping lanes, and crossed over into the People's Collective the following night. As Kahn had hoped, the search for the Red Skulls hadn't yet spread into the socialist nation; according to the news, the authorities seemed certain that Kahn would go to ground somewhere in his home territory.

The Red Skulls needed a sanctuary, to be sure, but Kahn had another destination in mind.

Bright sunlight slanted through the zeppelin's bridge view ports, causing Kahn to squint against the glare. Beside him, "Deadeye" Dugan looked up from the bridge's map table and called out to the helm. "We're thirty seconds from the initial turn. On my mark, come to course three-three-five."

Ahead of them, the Rocky Mountains loomed in a jagged, forbidding wall of snowcapped rock. Kahn had run the treacherous route to Sky Haven dozens of times, but he still had trouble picking out the narrow defile that marked the beginning of the path.

Dugan held up a stopwatch. "Ready . . . Ready . . . Mark! Port engines back one third, new course three-three-five."

The huge zeppelin seemed to pivot in place, her bow swinging to port and seemingly pointing straight at a sheer rock face. Finally, just past the point of no return, Kahn saw the cleft, barely wide enough to let the airship through. The *Machiavelli* nosed into a tight, twisting defile that would eventually lead them to Sky Haven, pirate hide-out and unofficial capital of Free Colorado.

Hetty Corbett turned away from the map table and joined Kahn, eyeing Dane warily. The Collective pilot stood off to one side, well away from the telltale maps, watching her surroundings intently. Kahn's wingman folded her arms and spoke in a quiet voice. "We're just about out of gas, boss, and Dugan's worried that we might lose the number three engine before much longer. We need parts and supplies *bad*, and Sky Haven doesn't run on credit."

"Relax," Kahn said wearily. He hadn't slept more than a couple of hours at a time since leaving Manhattan, but with the Rocky Mountains finally around him he could afford to relax, and fatigue threatened to suck him under like a riptide. "We'll sell the autogyro I stole in New York for some seed money, and then I'll scam the rest. The worst part's over, kid."

Hetty looked sidelong at Kahn. "You think so? What about the reward? Ten grand is ten times what's been put on our heads in the past. I'd turn in my own mother for that kind of dough."

"You'd turn in your mother for a cup of coffee," Kahn shot back. "Don't get me wrong—I'm not fool enough to believe that there's any honor among thieves. But no one's nuts enough to sell us out. Sky Haven's neutral territory, and the locals want it to stay that way. A war between pirates is the last thing anybody here wants."

"It's not the locals I'm worried about," Hetty grumbled.

The officer of the watch pressed a hand to his headphones. "Bow lookouts report engine sounds ahead. Six fighters, sounds like heavies."

Kahn nodded. "There's our escort. Let's get on the horn and pay our respects before we get used for target practice." He headed across the bridge to the radio room with Hetty in tow.

Loud, snarling engines swept past the *Machiavelli* to port and starboard, heralding the arrival of the patrol. Kahn reached over to the radio and set the dial to Sky Haven's frequency and picked up a microphone. "Sky Haven Flight, this is Genghis Kahn and the Red Skulls," he said. "You're a sight for sore eyes."

The flight leader answered immediately. "The feeling's mutual, Kahn," he said, in a voice as cold as stone. "Me and the boys have been counting the days until we'd cross paths with you again."

Kahn's grin faded. Hetty's eyes went wide. "Oh, no," she said.

The voice belonged to Harry Nesbitt, the man they'd cheated at Deadwood.

7: The Welcome Mat

"**B**attle stations?" Hetty asked nervously. The bridge rattled again from the buzz-saw roar of engines as Nesbitt's heavy fighters came around for another pass, close enough to rattle the compartment's thick Plexiglas windows.

Kahn shook his head. "The second we go for our guns, he's going to start shooting; then we're as good as dead."

The Red Skulls were in no shape for a fight. Almost a third of the zeppelin's crew was walking wounded from the battle over Manhattan, and the ship was dangerously low on fuel and ammunition. Kahn leaned out through the radio room's doorway. "Dugan, have we got the hangar deck clear?"

The zeppelin's scarred captain was bent intently over the bridge's map table tracing a line with his finger and taking careful note of the sweeping second hand of the stopwatch he held. The airship was in the middle of a treacherous course through the Rockies to Sky Haven. Nesbitt and his men were the least of Kahn's worries at the moment; the sheer rock walls and hidden pirate gun emplacements were of more immediate concern.

"Deck's clear," Dugan called out, "but we can't launch. We don't have the altitude, and the wind's coming in from amidships. You'd hit the floor of the defile before you got enough airspeed to stay aloft."

"We're dead," Hetty said bleakly.

"Not yet," Kahn muttered. "He hasn't started shooting."

Kahn reached in his jacket for a cigar, but came up empty. The pirate boss ground his teeth and tried to make his tired brain function. He keyed the radio. "Not bad, Nesbitt. You caught us with our pants down. How'd you get so smart all of a sudden? You weren't this sharp over Deadwood, that's for sure."

Hetty's eyes went wide. The radioman's jaw dropped. Nesbitt's furious voice screeched through the radio's static. "You damn near ruined me, Kahn! I had to take a contract with Sky Haven just to stay in the air, but I knew that sooner or later you'd show up here, and I'd be waiting to collect!"

A sly grin spread across Kahn's face. "You aren't going to blow us away on Sky Haven's dime, Nesbitt. Not if you want to hang your hat here ever again. Karl Regen and his gang don't care for pirates shooting each other up over their heads, much less having one of their patrol pilots carrying on a personal vendetta."

"You listen to me, Kahn. You're going to fly that shot-up gasbag of yours to Sky Haven, and when you dock, you're going to turn over the money—*my* money—that you stole at Deadwood, or by God, I'll have your scalp for it!"

Kahn laughed. "Blow it out your ear, Nesbitt. You can't make me give you the time of day . . . let alone the money."

"You think I can't?" Nesbitt's voice grew shrill with anger. "Guess again, genius. I'm challenging you and your crew, right here and now. We're going to fly the Cut, winner take all. Unless you want to back down, and show everybody what a coward you are!"

The pirate leader affected an exasperated sigh, though Hetty watched him grin from ear to ear. "Have it your way, Harry. We'll do the Cut tomorrow at dawn."

Nesbitt made no reply. Kahn chuckled, handing the microphone back to the radioman. "No, no Bre'r Fox!" he muttered, grinning. "Don't throw me in that there brier patch . . ."

"Have you lost your mind?" Hetty exclaimed. "We're down to seven planes, no gas, and no bullets. How the hell do you expect us to fly the Cut?"

"I don't," Kahn replied, pushing past Hetty and stepping back out onto the bridge. Nesbitt's fighters roared past a final time, and ahead, the tightly hemmed mountains were falling away to the left and right, revealing the crowded plateau where the buildings of Sky Haven catered to their aerial clientele.

"C'mon, kiddo, this is *me* we're talking about here. Karl Regen owes me some favors. He has to agree to any duels flown around the town, and if I say so, he'll keep Nesbitt twisting in the wind until we can get fixed up. Then we'll slip out of town late at night and worry about Nesbitt some other day, preferably when he least expects it." The pirate boss breathed a sigh of relief. "It looked a little dicey there for a second, but don't worry. I've got it covered."

"What the hell do you mean you're approving the duel?" The thin mountain air didn't let Kahn put the full force of his voice behind the shout, but he leaned across Karl Regen's dark wood desk and glared down at the would-be "master of Sky Haven" with all the bluster he could summon.

Karl Regen was a tall, handsome man with a square jaw, straight silver-blond hair, and emotionless blue eyes. He spread his hands in a gesture of helplessness common to politicians the world over. "What do you want me to say, Kahn? I can't go doing you favors like this. It'll kill my credibility."

"That's baloney. What's he paying you, Karl? Name it, and I'll double it."

Regen sighed. "Kahn, be reasonable. Nesbitt's been bragging about this all over town. People will talk if I try to string him along. And he's got as legitimate a right to challenge someone as you or I." He shrugged. "Listen, if you don't want to take Nesbitt up on it, you can leave. He can't follow you."

"And have every pirate in North America think 'Genghis' Kahn backed down from a man like Harry Nesbitt? Not likely," Kahn growled. He leveled a finger at Regen. "Put the word out. The Red Skull Legion will be flying tomorrow at dawn." With that, he jerked his head at Hetty, who stood by the door, and the two pirates stormed out into the cold Colorado sunshine.

"So much for having things covered," Hetty grumbled, folding her arms.

"It's the whole flap about the Empire State and 'kidnapping' Chiang Liu-mei," Kahn said, seething with frustration. "Regen doesn't want any part of an international scandal, never mind that we were *rescuing* the girl from a Japanese cell. He wants us out of town, one way or another."

Hetty looked over at her boss, her long face somber. "We can't fly the Cut, boss," she said quietly. "We're at the end of our rope."

"We'll empty the zep's fuel tanks, and strip the ammo from her guns," Kahn said. "We won't be able to arm everybody, but at least the heavies should have something to shoot with."

"For *what*? Just so we can go up there and get killed tomorrow?" Hetty stopped in her tracks, fists planted on her hips. "Nesbitt's going to have more planes than us, and he'll be armed for bear. The word at the airfield is that he took out a loan from 'Fingers' Malone to make sure he'd have everything he needs when the time comes tomorrow."

"What do you want me to do, Hetty? Quit?" Kahn rounded on her, there in the middle of the snowy lane. "First you're nagging me about walking out on the crew; now you're on my back because I'm trying to hold everything together! What do you want?"

Hetty glared at him, her brown eyes blazing. She walked up until they were nose to nose. "What I want," she said quietly, "is for you to stop thinking about yourself for half a second and consider what is best for your crew. You know, all the little people that do the bleeding when one of your plans goes south."

For a moment, Kahn couldn't find the words to reply. "What is this, a mutiny?"

Hetty managed a choked laugh. "Good Lord," she said, shaking her head. "Does it always have to be all or nothing with you?"

"That's what life is all about, kid," Kahn said. "All or nothing. Take it or leave it."

"Yeah, well, what's to take, at this point?" Hetty stared hard at Kahn. "We're broke. Our birds are shot to hell. Half of North America is after us, and we're running on fumes. What the hell do we have to look forward to tomorrow except more of the same?"

"Well, what do you suggest?"

Hetty shrugged. "We're in Sky Haven. There are plenty of captains who could use experienced crews. If there was ever a point where we could pack it in and start over, this is it."

"You want to quit?" Kahn said, his voice hollow.

"What I want is for you to think about your crew for a change. That's all I'm saying. It's one thing to think you can beat the devil at his own game, and another thing entirely to wager our lives, too."

Kahn shook his head. "Hetty, have I ever let you down? *Ever?*"

His wingman gave him a sad smile. "Me? No. Maybe you should ask Murphy that, instead. He's the one who took three rounds in the gut because you owed Hayes a favor."

Before Kahn could answer she pushed past him and continued down the narrow lane.

The hangar deck still smelled of oil and smoke. The bulkhead walls were streaked with soot from the fire started by Japanese flak rockets, and a heavy crate sat in one corner of the cavernous compartment, filled with charred and twisted debris. One of the Red Skulls' remaining planes, Amos Jones' Sanderson "Vampire"—newly acquired a few months back during a raid in the Republic of Texas—was seared and blackened along its port side, out of action until someone could afford the parts to repair its notoriously finicky engines.

The hangar bay was packed with people. Kahn had called the entire crew to assemble there, even the seriously wounded. They sat in chairs brought down from the wardroom, holding themselves gingerly while they waited to hear what Kahn had to say. Everyone except Murphy; he died a few hours after the *Machiavelli* made port at Sky Haven.

Kahn eyed his crew and wished for the power to look inside their heads. To a man, they all looked exhausted, but none seemed fearful or angry—except Hetty, who stood near the back, her arms folded tightly. She looked as though her world was coming to an end. *Despite the fact that she is the one who pushed me to this point in the first place,* Kahn thought. He'd never figure out dames as long as he lived.

The burly pirate leader stepped forward without preamble, and immediately the deck went quiet. He found himself wishing for a cigar. *A last smoke for a condemned man, maybe,* Kahn thought. He took a deep breath.

"Anybody here who's been with me for any length of time knows I don't like making speeches . . . unless I'm about to put one over on somebody." Several members of the crew laughed weakly. "Well, this isn't a con. These aren't ordinary times. For the last few days we've been going at things hard and fast, and there hasn't been much opportunity to sit and take stock. It's high time we did.

"You guys aren't blind, and you aren't stupid. You can pretty much look around and see what kind of shape we're in. Frankly, we're broke. There's no money for gas or bullets, much less repairs. And now I've gotten a ten-thousand-dollar bounty on all our heads. Why? Because of another debt that I personally owed to someone else.

"Now, Harry Nesbitt, whom I'm sure you all remember from Deadwood"—a few more stifled chuckles arose from the crowd—"has got us dead to rights. He's called us out. Tomorrow at dawn the Red Skulls are flying the Cut, winner take all. And I mean *all*—if Nesbitt wins, he gets the *Machiavelli* and everything in her."

Now heads turned. Not everyone had heard the news, and looks of shock were appearing among the crew. It didn't take a genius to calculate the odds in a duel with Nesbitt's gang.

Kahn's eyes swept the room. "You people know me, or at least you *ought* to. I think we can still beat Nesbitt. There isn't a pirate crew in North America we can't outfly or outfight. But odds are we're going to pay a price for it this time. If we go up tomorrow, at least half our birds won't even have ammo, and maybe not even enough gas to fly the Cut, much less beat Nesbitt. We stand to lose a hell of a lot, no matter what happens."

He took another breath, dreading what he was about to say. "A pirate crew isn't a democracy. I don't make decisions by committee. But the fact of the matter is that nobody is forcing you to go up there with me at dawn. This ain't the army, and you didn't sign any contract. It's not like I can pay you any-time soon. So far, you've followed along and trusted me to make things right. Now I'm telling you that there's no reason to think that the Red Skulls have a future past tomorrow.

"There's eight different gangs in Sky Haven right now, and they'd give their eyeteeth to have you working for them." Kahn stepped up to an empty crate of machine parts and placed an empty jar on it. "You're a good crew, the best there is. I can't make you any guarantees for the future, and you've got a right to make your own decisions." He nodded at the jar. "Every one of you wears the emblem of the Red Skulls. You can take those wings off and leave them in the jar. You can walk away right now and start over. It's your choice."

For a few minutes no one spoke. No one breathed. Then, slowly, "Deadeye" Dugan, the zeppelin's captain, rose to his feet and stepped purposefully up to the jar.

Kahn's heart sank. Other members of the crew started to stand.

It looked like the Red Skull Legion was finished.

8: Death at Dawn

"Deadeye" Dugan strode through the crowd, his jaw set and his shoulders straight. Almost a dozen Red Skulls stood behind him, some of them fingering the red-and-brass Red Skull insignia pinned to their flight jacket collars.

Kahn studied the men and women packed into the hangar bay, and didn't like what he saw. The men on their feet looked guilty as blazes . . . and once the first set of wings fell into the glass jar he'd set before them, things would quickly gain momentum; within minutes the Red Skull Legion would com-pletely fall apart.

Despite his rising frustration, Kahn couldn't bring himself to blame the crew for wanting to cut and run. He had given them the choice to jump ship, and now he would have to live with the consequences.

Dugan stepped up to the jar. He reached up—not to his collar, but to the mass of scar tissue that twisted the left side of his face. His hand came away with something that gleamed dully in the overhead lights and clinked like a marble as it rattled against the sides of the jar.

The old captain's green glass eye came to rest against the side of the jar, glaring balefully at the ceiling. Dugan turned to face the rest of the crew, the left side of his mouth pulled back in a snarl.

"You want to come up here and throw away your wings, go right ahead," he growled. "That," he said, pointing to the jar, "is so you'll know that I'm watching. I'll remember, and if it takes the rest of my days . . . I'll make sure you *pay for it*."

Several of the men on their feet shuffled uncomfortably, and more than one blanched. None would meet the captain's grim stare. Dugan leveled an accusing finger at one of them.

"You," he snarled. "Jimmy Collins. You've been a Red Skull for two years. What were you doing when Kahn took you on?"

Blake ran a hand nervously through his curly red hair. "I was . . . you know . . . sellin' apples in Chicago."

"You were a starving little runt who robbed drunks and played lookout for rumrunners," Dugan barked. "And that's where you'd be now if it wasn't for the boss." The captain's one good eye swept the crowd. "Amos Jones: you were headed for the hangman down in New Orleans. Pete O'Neil: you wouldn't have a finger to call your own if the boss hadn't covered your debts in Atlantic City. And then there's me," he said. "I'd been given my walking papers after twenty years' service. Kahn didn't give a damn what I looked like, only how well I handled a ship. If it hadn't been for him, I'd be at the bottom of a bottle right now, or pushing up daisies in potter's field.

"Now I'll be the first one to say Kahn's no saint," Dugan said, nodding at his boss. "But there isn't one of you in this room who doesn't owe everything you've got to him. He made you part of the Red Skulls, and now you're known from Hollywood to the Empire State. The nations of North America sure don't like you, but they *do* fear you. All because of those wings you're wearing."

Dugan folded his arms. "So . . . which of you weak-kneed sob sisters wants to cut and run just because things have gotten tough?"

"Tough?" One of the men found his courage. "C'mon, Dugan, we've all got ten grand sitting on our heads. What do you want us to do?"

"I want you to act like the kind of man the boss pegged you for when he gave you those wings," Dugan snapped. "Ruthless. Aggressive. One of the deadliest SOBs in the sky. Somebody you'd want at your back when things get rough."

The Red Skulls looked uneasily at one another. The men who'd lined up behind Dugan seemed to shrink in upon themselves. Jimmy Collins stuck his hands in his pockets. "Well, *I'm* not gonna touch that jar now that you put your damn *eye* in there, you crazy old goat."

The rest of the crew laughed, and the tension broke. Within moments there was no one left standing but Dugan and Kahn.

The pirate boss did a poor job of concealing his relief. *It doesn't mean a thing,* he told himself. *This is just a scam like all the rest. One day, when things get too bad, I'll just chuck it all and run away.* But the vise squeezing his heart slowly relaxed, and it felt like he could breathe again. He stepped forward, clapping Dugan on the shoulder. "That was the biggest load of hogwash I've heard in my whole life," he told the crowd. "I think you missed your calling, Dugan: you should have been a politician . . . or a used autogyro salesman."

Dugan shook his head. "Not me, sir. I prefer to lie and steal the old-fashioned way: at gunpoint."

More laughter rang off the hangar walls. Kahn raised his voice over the din. "All right, Red Skulls, the party's over. You had your chance, and now you're in it for the duration. I want every drop of fuel and every round of ammo we've got left packed into the birds. We'll transfer them to the airfield and then hit the saloons. Drinks are on me." A ragged cheer went up from the crew as they climbed wearily to their feet. Within minutes a pair of grease monkeys were banging away at

Jones' fire-damaged Vampire. The Red Skulls were back in business.

Kahn moved through the bustling crowd, already trying to figure the angles for the next day's showdown. Suddenly he found himself face-to-face with Hetty. His wingman looked up from the clipboard in her hands. "The hangar monkeys say it's a fifty-fifty chance they can get Jones' bird ready by tomorrow, which leaves us with only seven planes.

"If we drain the zep's fuel tanks," she continued, "we can top off the fighters. We can take the fifty-cal and sixty-cal ammo from the gun positions to give some of our heavies something to shoot with. That's the good news." Hetty lowered her voice. "The word at the airfield is that Nesbitt's put out an open call to pilots to 'join' his crew in time for tomorrow's duel. He's promising them anything they want off the *Machiavelli* after they've beaten us. There could be a whole hell of a lot of planes on his side come dawn."

The pirate boss regarded his wingman with some surprise. "Sounds like you've been doing some legwork," he said bemusedly. "I thought you were ready to call it quits."

Hetty's eyes went wide. "Where the hell did you get that kind of idea?" Her eyes flashed angrily. "If you weren't my boss, I'd knock your teeth in!" She tucked her clipboard under her arm, spun on her heel, and stalked out of the hangar bay.

Kahn watched her go, trying to figure out exactly what had just happened. *Dames,* he thought to himself. *Go figure.*

Something Hetty had said stuck out in his mind. "Hey!" he called out. His wingman stopped at the hangar's entryway. "Did you just say that Nesbitt's doing a cattle call for pilots tomorrow?"

Hetty rolled her eyes. "I hadn't planned on making a public announcement about it, but yeah. Why?"

"Perfect!" Kahn said with a feral grin. "That's just the angle we need!"

She looked at him like he'd lost his mind.

As far as Kahn was concerned, that was the first normal thing she'd done in days.

* * *

"You're out of your mind," Angela Dane said flatly. "I wouldn't help you if you put a gun to my head."

"An interesting figure of speech, under the circumstances," Kahn replied. He reached in his flight jacket for one of the cigars he'd purchased in town. Sky Haven's airfield was still shrouded in darkness, though the rutted field bustled with activity. Dawn was less than a half hour away, and he stood with Dane and a cluster of the *Machiavelli*'s engineering crew by the nose of his plane.

"Comrade Captain," Kahn said, "has it occurred to you that if Nesbitt wins this little contest, *you* will be turned over to him, along with everything else the Red Skulls possess?"

The pirate leader bit off the end of the cigar, grimacing at the taste; it had been months since he'd had a hand-rolled Cuban. "Nesbitt lost a lot of men to you and your townsfolk. I doubt he'll be as . . . congenial as I have been. Besides," he said with a shrug, "if we win, you can legitimately say you were instrumental in putting a notorious aerial pirate out of business. Surely that has to count for something."

The People's Collective fighter pilot glared defiantly at Kahn, but he knew that he had her hooked. He nodded at the leader of the engineering crew. "You know what to do, Tony," Kahn said. "When Regen starts his speech, you make your move." He tossed a tired smile at Dane. "Good luck, Captain. See you at the finish line."

Tony and his men led the reluctant Dane off into the darkness. Kahn walked around the wing of his Devastator heavy fighter and started his preflight inspection. He was halfway through when Hetty found him. "They're buzzing like bees over there," she said, nodding in the direction where Nesbitt's planes waited. "Looks like he's got eighteen planes."

Kahn nodded, still looking over his plane. "How many of those are Nesbitt's new friends?"

"Almost half."

"Perfect," he replied. "We couldn't ask for much better."

Hetty shook her head worriedly. "I hope you know what you're doing."

"I know *exactly* what I'm doing, kid. I'm just not sure it will work."

Within ten minutes, the sky over the field had turned pale gray, hinting at the sunrise to come. Kahn climbed into his cockpit, wincing at the feel of the cold metal seat, and surveyed the dark silhouettes of Nesbitt's aerial fleet. The pirates' assembled planes stretched nearly half the length of the airstrip, parked wingtip to wingtip.

Karl Regen and a few other town leaders had gathered at the airfield's control tower, along with a surprisingly large number of spectators. Many would be making bets on who would win, or who would enter the Cut but not make it to the other side. No one knew how many people had died flying the canyon route since the challenge became popular.

They just knew that the number of fatalities in the Cut was very, very high.

The first faint streaks of color were staining the sky as Kahn pulled on his flying cap and plugged in his radio. Across the field a set of speakers hissed and popped, and Regen's voice carried across the still morning air.

"When I give the command, you will start your engines," he declared. "Once both sides have taken off, you will circle the field until the green flare is fired; then you can make your way to the Cut. The rules of the challenge are clear: the first pilot from either side to complete the course and land back at the field wins the duel. No firing is allowed until you have entered the canyon . . . so make sure we don't *see* you cheat, boys"—rough laughter rumbled from the crowd—"and once inside, anything goes. Start your engines!"

Kahn pressed the starter, and the Devastator's powerful engine roared to life. He looked down the length of the Red Skulls' parked planes and fervently hoped Tony had done his job.

"Okay, Red Skulls, you know the plan," he barked into the radio. "Stick to your wingman and go after Nesbitt's old-timers first. The rest are amateurs."

Kahn released his brakes, and the fighter rolled forward across the bumpy ground. Within minutes, friend and foe alike were racing down the strip, wingtip to wingtip. Kahn

searched the field and caught a glimpse of Nesbitt's Peacemaker 370. He threw a mocking salute at his adversary and
then sent his fighter hurtling into the sky.

The fighters took to the air like crows, circling tightly
over the airfield. The air itself quivered from the combined
thunder of twenty-four high-performance planes. Already the
pilots were pushing their planes to the limit, making the tight-
est turns they could in anticipation of the start flare. They
didn't have long to wait. The last plane was scarcely off the
ground when a streak of green shot into the sky and the pirates raced for the mountains to the east.

Nesbitt's recruits were already pulling into the lead. Four
light fighters, a mix of Bloodhawks and Valiants, pulled
ahead of the pack, their engines wide open. The rest of Nesbitt's planes were strung along in their wake, ready to provide
cover in case the Red Skulls went after them. They were the
barrier Kahn and his pilots had to break through.

They reached the nearby mountains in moments, and
ahead loomed the knife-edged cleft that marked the start of
the run. Nesbitt's light planes reached the Cut first, a decided
advantage, but Kahn's birds were close behind. The pirate
leader rolled his Devastator onto its port wing and hurtled
into the narrow, twisting canyon. "Let's get 'em, boys!"

The walls of the Cut were barely twenty yards across,
forcing Nesbitt's planes into a tight mass of darting, swooping
shapes. There was no way past, but on the other hand, they
were almost impossible to miss. Kahn checked his meager
store of rockets and selected half of them. "Flash rockets!" he
called, and let two of them fly amid a storm of tracer fire.

The rockets streaked into the middle of Nesbitt's group and
exploded, throwing stark shadows against the close-set rock
walls. The pirates scattered, climbing and diving like spar-
rows, but two weren't so lucky. A Brigand banked right into
the path of a black-painted Raven, sending both of them tumbling to the canyon floor in a tangle of twisted metal.

Another of Nesbitt's planes, a Defender, veered sluggishly
to port, its ailerons and rudder damaged by the torrent of fire
from the Red Skulls. Just ahead the canyon twisted to the
right, and the pirate fought to bring the nose of the Defender

around. Just short of the turn, the Defender's wing clipped the side of the canyon and the plane exploded in an orange flash.

Kahn whipped his plane through the turn. Ahead, four of Nesbitt's men were pulling into high, tight loops, ready to come down on the Red Skulls' tail. "Hold 'em off," Kahn called back to his pilots. "We've made the hole. O'Neil, Young, and Walker, you're up."

Three of the Red Skulls' planes—O'Neil's Valiant plus Young's and Walker's Bloodhawks—surged ahead like thoroughbreds, leaving the heavier planes behind. Nesbitt still had ten planes waiting ahead, a deadly gauntlet for the light planes to run. "Hetty, we've got to cover their tails," Kahn called to his wingman. "You with me?"

"Right on your tail, boss," she said confidently.

Four of Nesbitt's planes completed their loops, and Kahn's remaining heavies rose to meet them. They came together in a twisting, slashing dogfight that was quickly left behind. Nesbitt could afford to tie up all the Red Skulls' planes and still have plenty left to concentrate on winning the race.

Kahn's three light fighters were well ahead, closing fast on six enemy fighters. Nesbitt's four nimble recruits still led the pack, well ahead of the rest of the combatants.

O'Neil's Valiant led the Red Skulls' charge, plunging through the enemy formation. They passed Nesbitt's heavy planes nearly close enough to touch, but their guns stayed silent; their meager ammo loads had to be conserved for the front runners yet ahead. Nesbitt's men, however, had no such compunctions. They unleashed a torrent of cannon fire at the nimble fighters, and there was little room to dodge. A moment later, there was a bright flash, and a streamer of black smoke poured from the engine cowling of Hiram Young's Bloodhawk. The fighter lost speed immediately.

Kahn cursed and lined up one of the enemy planes in his sights. He sent his last two rockets streaking at the enemy Brigand and ripped apart its left wing. The pilot jumped clear as the plane spun out of control. *If there was anyone in the fighter's rear turret,* Kahn noted, smiling, *he didn't make it out. Good riddance.*

Hetty lined up behind the Brigand's wingman, a Vampire, and let off a long burst that tore into the heavy fighter's tail. Telltale smoke trailed from the magnesium rounds burning steadily through its skin, but the plane stayed in the air, jinking sharply out of the line of fire. Kahn watched as the enemy pilot dropped his flaps—which killed the Vampire's airspeed, and allowed the Vampire to drop into position behind them. Short bursts flashed past Kahn's canopy.

"Do you want me to take him?" Hetty called.

"No! Keep covering Walker and O'Neil!"

They swept around a hairpin turn to the left, then immediately right. The tight turns strung out the heavy planes even further, letting the lighter birds pull a little ahead. "I'm closing on the lead planes!" O'Neil called over the radio.

"Concentrate on the Bloodhawks," Kahn ordered. Just ahead, one of Nesbitt's recruits struggled to stay out of Kahn's line of fire. The pirate leader peppered the enemy Warhawk with short bursts that stitched across its starboard wing and tail. The inexperienced pilot was so preoccupied with Kahn he failed to notice Hetty, who fired two armor-piercing rockets into his tail. The plane exploded in a deadly blossom of crimson and orange fire, and metal shrapnel ricocheted wildly in the narrow canyon.

Rounds hammered into Kahn's plane, walking the length of his fuselage. The sound of the Devastator's engine turned ragged. Cursing, Kahn saw that his oil pressure was dropping. If he didn't slow down, the Devastator's engine would seize.

There was another tight turn to the right, and now they were through the midpoint of the course, heading back toward the airfield. "Got one!" O'Neil called out. "Boss, you better get up here! Nesbitt's goons are zeroing in on Walker!"

Kahn opened the throttle and watched the engine temperature rise. Nesbitt and three others were closing in on Forest Walker's Bloodhawk. "Hetty, you got any more rockets?"

"Way ahead of you, boss!" Two streaks of fire and smoke arced out and slammed into the wing of an enemy Devastator, sending it spinning to the canyon floor.

Harry Nesbitt settled onto Walker's tail and cut loose with

everything he had. The light fighter blew apart under the withering fusillade of shells.

Kahn grimaced. "Pete, Walker's gone. You're all that's left."

"Yeah?" O'Neil replied. "Well, this one's for Walker, then."

There was a flash up ahead. The last enemy Bloodhawk exploded. Only the two Valiants remained, but were now far ahead of everyone else.

Kahn's oil temp gauge was well into the red. He could feel the heavy plane losing power fast. "Hetty, I'm almost finished myself," he called out. "You've got to cover Pete. I'll take care of the Vampire."

"Roger, but I'm low on ammo."

Kahn looked back at the enemy Vampire, now closing in again for a sure shot. Abruptly he cut his throttle and popped his flaps; relatively speaking, the Devastator practically stopped in place. The Vampire flashed past, and Kahn cut loose, holding the trigger down in a single, long burst. Bits of shredded armor fell from the enemy fighter's fuselage, and then its canopy exploded. Two of the Devastator's four guns jammed, but the enemy plane rolled over onto its back and plunged to the canyon floor.

Suddenly the canyon walls parted like a curtain. They'd made the Cut, and emerged south of the city. Another of Nesbitt's planes was plummeting to the earth, victim of Hetty's deadly accuracy, but Nesbitt and his wingman were closing steadily on O'Neil. Already tracer bursts were reaching for the speeding Valiant. "Keep 'em off me for another ten seconds, and I can catch the rats!" O'Neil yelled.

"Hang on!" Hetty cried.

Kahn watched one of the Valiants peel off and come back at O'Neil. The two fighters raced head-to-head, firing as they came. Hits flashed along both plane's hulls, but still they charged at one another, neither willing to give way. At the last second, the enemy plane exploded as O'Neil's magnesium rounds found its fuel tank.

O'Neil whooped exultantly. "Got him, boss!"

That was when Kahn saw the rocket. A single streak of

white flashed from beneath the wing of Nesbitt's plane. No doubt he'd saved the shot until the last, just in case.

The rocket ran true, exploding between the Valiant's twin engines. Kahn saw a shape leap from the plane's cockpit just before the fighter exploded, scattering wreckage across the snowy plateau.

Moments later, Nesbitt's wingman fell from the sky, trailing black smoke. "I'm out of ammo!" Hetty cried.

The lone remaining Valiant lowered its gear and made a clean landing at Sky Haven's airstrip.

9: The Shell Game

Harry Nesbitt's Peacemaker 370 rounded Sky Haven in lazy circles, like a buzzard waiting for the inevitable. Kahn eased back on the throttle of his damaged fighter, hoping to take some of the strain off its engine. There was little point in prosecuting a dogfight; the race had been run, winner take all. As far as Nesbitt was concerned, shooting up Kahn's plane would only be damaging his newly acquired property.

Hetty circled back to cover him as he lined up for his landing. Other planes had begun to emerge from the treacherous course; of the seven planes the Red Skull Legion had started the course with, only five emerged, most of them heavily damaged.

Kahn lowered the gear on his Devastator and cut his engine. The heavy fighter glided down onto the rutted, snowy landing strip. He touched the brakes lightly and coasted to a stop just a few yards away from the winning plane. A crowd had already gathered around the Valiant. Karl Regen caught Kahn's eye and shrugged. *No hard feelings,* his expression said. The Red Skulls' leader responded with a wintry smile.

Nesbitt's Peacemaker landed next. It streaked in and bounced across the frozen ground. The twin-hulled fighter taxied in and stopped next to the Valiant. Spectators ducked and clutched their hats as the Peacemaker's powerful engines kicked up dirt and snow. Kahn pulled off his flying cap and rubbed wearily at his shaven head. *Time to face the music,* he thought grimly, and pulled himself from the Devastator's cockpit.

The crowd of onlookers parted as Kahn approached. Nesbitt climbed out of his cockpit and hopped onto the Peacemaker's wing, his hands planted on his hips and his face twisted into a vicious sneer. "You didn't think I had it in me, did you, Kahn?" he crowed. "How's it feel to get taken for a ride, mastermind?"

Kahn cocked his head and squinted up at Nesbitt. "I'm not sure I understand, Harry," he said mildly as he reached for a cigar.

Regen stepped from the crowd between the two men and nervously cleared his throat. "The rules of the challenge didn't say anything about how many planes each side could bring to the duel, or where they came from," he said, loud enough for everyone to hear. "Nesbitt didn't have to play fair any more than *you* did, Kahn. All that mattered was being the first side to get a pilot through the course and back on the ground."

"Winner take all!" Nesbitt cheered. Several people in the crowd added their voices to his.

Kahn looked from Nesbitt to Regen, and back again. "What makes you think I'm disputing any of this?" he said innocently. "You're absolutely right." He struck a match with his thumbnail. "I must say, Harry, you're taking this remarkably well." Kahn puffed thoughtfully at his cigar and cast his cold gaze at his opponent.

Nesbitt's exultant face froze, then started to melt. His expression went from glee to amazement, then unease. "What the hell are you getting at?"

The Red Skulls' leader walked around Nesbitt's Peacemaker and stood at the Valiant's port wing. He extended his hand with a smile. "Congratulations on a fine bit of flying, Captain."

Comrade Angela Dane, late of the People's Collective Air Militia, pulled the pilot's cap from her head and ignored Kahn's offer of assistance, leaping gracefully to the ground.

Her small mouth curled in distaste as Regen and the other on-lookers crowded around her and Kahn.

Regen's eyes widened. "Are you telling me she's one of *yours*?"

"Let's just say I was flying against Nesbitt and leave it at that," Dane said sullenly.

"We persuaded the owner of the Valiant to ... *lend* his plane to us at the last minute," Kahn interjected, "in return for a share of the winnings after the race."

Kahn looked back at Nesbitt. "I can't lay claim to the idea, of course. Harry was the inspiration behind it all."

Nesbitt spat out a curse, his voice rising to a shriek. He leapt from the Peacemaker's wing and charged at Kahn, clawing at the holstered pistol at his hip. "You son of a b—"

Nesbitt's tirade—and his pistol draw—were cut short as Kahn launched a powerful blow at the enraged pirate's solar plexus. Nesbitt sucked air, and crashed into the waiting arms of a cluster of burly men in coveralls.

Kahn nodded to Tony and his gang of engineers, then turned his gaze back on Nesbitt. "No one likes a sore loser, Harry," he said, "and as our mutual friend Karl here said, this had nothing to do with playing fair." The burly pirate stepped closer. "About all you've got left to lose now is your life. Are you sure you want to keep rolling the dice with me?"

Nesbitt slumped in the engineers' arms, eyes downcast. Kahn regarded him coldly. "Tell you what," he growled. "Just to show you there's no hard feelings, I'll let you keep your plane. You've got at least half a tank of fuel left. See how far that'll take you."

On cue, Tony and his boys flung Nesbitt back the way he'd come, and the pirate collapsed in an untidy heap in the snow. He glared at Kahn and the rest, but said nothing. His eyes burning with hate, he climbed to his feet and turned his back on the crowd, heading for his plane—which was already being stripped of rockets and ammo belts by Tony's mechanics.

Kahn turned his attention to Regen. He stepped close to Sky Haven's boss, looming head and shoulders over the man.

"Spread the word, Karl. I'll be sending some men over to my new zeppelin within the hour. I don't expect there'll be any more trouble. Do you?"

Just then Kahn's surviving planes roared low overhead, the rumble of their engines sweeping across the plateau like a peal of thunder. Regen went pale. Kahn grinned like a wolf, savoring the sense of power.

It was good to be calling the shots again.

"We would'a made out like bandits if you guys hadn't gone and shot down everything Nesbitt had," Pete O'Neil groused. One hand strayed to the bandage at his forehead. His Valiant had taken a rocket just shy of the finish line, and he'd been lucky to make it out alive.

The *Machiavelli* had been moved to a mooring tower close to Nesbitt's former airship, a converted merchant zeppelin called *Wanderer*. Kahn watched from the *Machiavelli*'s bridge as his crew moved crates from one ship to the next. Nesbitt's airship couldn't hold a candle to Kahn's heavily modified combat zeppelin, but her spare parts and supplies would go a long way toward putting the *Machiavelli* back in fighting trim.

"As I recall, you accounted for one of those kills yourself, Pete, so I don't think you've got much room to complain," Kahn replied.

He turned back toward the map table, where Dugan, Corbett, and O'Neil were going over the long list of plunder taken from Nesbitt's gang. "We'll sell off anything we can't use, and see about picking up some replacements for the planes we've lost."

He clapped O'Neil on his shoulder. "Don't worry. I'll let you lease one for a reasonable fee. I might even be persuaded to lend a fighter to our hero of the People's Collective." Kahn eyed Dane, who stood near one of the starboard view ports, apparently lost in thought. "What do you say, Comrade? The Red Skulls could use a good pilot."

The pirates laughed. Dane threw Kahn a look of pure murder. "Don't do me any favors, Kahn," she said. "I'd sooner die than turn pirate."

Kahn grinned savagely. "Such misplaced conviction. What makes you think you're any different from the rest of us?"

The color drained from Dane's face. "Are you kidding? *My* pilots don't rob and kill innocent people! We protect and serve a law-abiding government and try to keep the peace! You're just a bunch of bloodthirsty thugs!"

"Really?" The pirate leader started to pace, folding his arms and frowning thoughtfully. "So when the People's Air Militia are sent to raid airship convoys across the I.S.A. border, that's keeping the peace?"

"We do no such thing!"

"Comrade, please! You're not that naïve. The I.S.A. flies 'training missions' near your border to give new pilots a chance to shoot at live targets from time to time . . . and *your* government retaliates by hitting their supply convoys. Do you suppose that the innocent people in the crossfire are somehow magically bulletproof?" He pointed an accusing finger. "Your hands are no cleaner than ours in the long run, Captain. You and your superiors simply choose to obfuscate the facts behind the anonymous facade of government. You do what you want and justify it as 'national interest.' "

"You're just twisting the facts to suit you," Dane said disgustedly. "Save your breath, Kahn. It won't work. Sure, I've killed my share of men. But it was always in the observance of law."

"Law?" Kahn said the word with a sneer. "Laws are nothing but a set of excuses to keep the strong from preying on the weak, as nature intended. It's the sheep dictating terms to the wolves."

"No, it's about giving everyone an equal chance at prosperity. Government by the people and *for* the people. That's what America was about."

"Look how well *that* worked out," Kahn said with a snort.

"Hey, newlyweds! Knock it off!" Hetty cried. "Do you hear that?"

Kahn and Dane paused. From outside came a distant, rising wail.

Dugan cocked his head and frowned. "That's an air raid siren."

"So who the hell would *attack* Sky Haven?" Kahn said incredulously. "Even Paladin Blake isn't that stupid."

He crossed the bridge in four long steps and stuck his head into the radio room. The radio operator looked up, one hand pressing a headset to his ear. "What's going on?" the pirate leader asked.

The radioman shook his head. "There's a lot of chatter coming from Regen's tower controller. Sounds like one of the regular patrols picked up a Mayday, just outside the east approach." The operator paused, listening intently. "Yeah. It was Nesbitt. He'd just made it out of the mountains and ran into some kind of trouble. The patrol decided to go bail him out." His expression turned grim. "Now they're getting their slats kicked in."

Kahn looked back at Dugan and Hetty, then to Dane. "Could it be a Collective raid?"

Dane shook her head. "No way."

Dugan straightened. "You don't think La Guardia—?"

"The tower is asking the same thing," the radioman called out. "The Flight Leader says he's spotted unknown fighters—white with red circles on their wings."

Hetty's eyes widened. "The *Japanese*! They followed us all the way here?"

"They will follow you to the ends of the earth and beyond," a woman's voice said from the bridge hatchway. "And they will kill whoever gets in their way."

Chiang Liu-mei stood at the hatchway, leaning against its rim for support. Her fine-boned features looked incongruous against the oil-stained coverall she wore. The young woman stared hard at Kahn, her green eyes reflecting the torment she'd suffered at the hands of her captors.

"So long as I remain in your hands, 'Genghis' Kahn, you and your crew are in gravest danger."

"The man you saw at the Embassy was Major Saburo Murasaki," Chiang said, cradling a steaming cup of tea in her long-fingered hands. She sat at the edge of a leather couch in *Machiavelli's* wardroom, back straight and shoulders squared. Her English was precise, with a faint British accent.

"He is an officer in the Imperial Japanese Navy, and a highly decorated fighter pilot. Until recently he served in Manchuria as an agent for Naval Intelligence, gathering information on the Kuomintang and my father's attempts to stop the Japanese invasion."

It had taken quite a bit of explaining to convince Chiang Kai-shek's daughter that she wasn't the Red Skulls' prisoner, as the rest of the world seemed to assume. She dimly remembered the events leading up to her rescue, but had never heard of Artemus Hayes, much less believed that her father's government had any idea where she was being held. Ironically it was Angela Dane who managed to convince her that Kahn was telling the truth; the two young women had developed an immediate rapport that won Chiang's trust.

"So this Murasaki learned of your mission and pursued you to the Empire State, where he kidnapped you?" Kahn asked, puffing thoughtfully on his cigar and leaning back into a leather-covered armchair.

"That's right," she said. "And he is no doubt leading the pursuit now. The Japanese government gave him wide latitude to act in the occupied territories, and I expect he has the same authority here, as well." Chiang looked down at her cup. "He is absolutely relentless. And the cruelest, coldest man I have ever known."

"Really? Well, we'll see about that," Kahn said mildly. "He certainly seems intelligent and aggressive. Clearly, he reasoned we would attempt to return you to your government, and it was only logical to assume we would at least stop at Sky Haven while en route." His eyes narrowed. "He also has a zeppelin and a complement of fighters.

"But I don't imagine he's going to come in here after us," he continued. "Scrapping with an isolated patrol is one thing; poking blindly through Sky Haven's east approach is tantamount to suicide. I think he's trying to flush us out and then intercept us on the other side of the mountains." The pirate leader smiled. "But I doubt he's got a Deadeye Dugan commanding his zeppelin. We can slip out of Sky Haven tonight and be halfway across Hollywood by morning, while Murasaki is still trying to find a passage through the Rockies.

We'll have you at the Chinese Embassy on Hawai'i before he knows what's happening."

Chiang's head came up. "Chinese Embassy? No—we must go to the British Embassy. Surely this Mr. Hayes told you?"

Kahn frowned. "He told us you were on your way to Columbia to protest Japanese atrocities in Manchuria."

"What? No, no, that is wrong," Chiang said. "What is the point in protest? Our enemies have been committing horrible acts against my people for years, and the world has done nothing. We have no time to waste in empty protest. China is in a fight for its very existence." Now Chiang's voice strengthened, and her dark eyes flashed. "They think we can be terrorized into surrendering to their Imperialist demands, but they have misjudged us. We will fight!"

Kahn straightened in his chair. "Why *were* you in New York?"

"To meet with the British," she said. "To finalize a deal for weapons and equipment for the Kuomintang. They were negotiating with President La Guardia to use the Empire State as the transfer point between our two nations. The deal had been struck. I was sent to Manhattan as my father's representative to make payment for the first shipment. That was why Murasaki kidnapped me."

Kahn's mind whirled. "How much money are we talking about, Miss Chiang?"

"Half a million dollars," she said. "In gold. And Murasaki will stop at nothing to get it."

10: Serpents in Paradise

"You're a fraud, Kahn."

The pirate looked over his shoulder. Angela Dane stood with her arms folded and a smug grin on her elfin face. The boss of the Red Skull Legion quirked an eyebrow. "If I had a nickel for every time I heard *that* one, I'd never have to steal again," he said with a snort. "What, precisely, am I being accused of now?"

The bridge of the *Machiavelli* was bathed in the crimson glow of battle lanterns as the pirate zeppelin made her way south by west across the Nation of Hollywood. The night before, they had slipped out of Sky Haven under a heavy overcast and worked their way through a little-known canyon route that allowed them to reach the Utah border by midnight.

The next day found them holed up in a canyon in Arixo, a hundred miles from nowhere, where they were able to put some of their newly acquired spare parts to good use. Now with a freshly repaired hull and six working engines, the airship was high and quiet, keeping close to the clouds as the Red Skulls crept carefully through Hollywood's air defenses. Lookouts strained to peer through the moonless night, and the officer of the watch kept one hand pressed to the headphones he wore, listening intently for any reports.

The Red Skulls rarely found themselves so far west, and not even the well-traveled Dugan knew what to expect. There were rumors that Howard Hughes had secretly installed a network of huge listening devices in the Hollywood Hills that could track zeppelin movements hundreds of miles away. Conversely, another source had it that the Hollywood Knights, the nation's premier fighter squadron, had been destroyed in a pirate attack several months past. It was all taken with a healthy pinch of salt, but the crew remained vigilant nevertheless. Kahn had stood watch with the bridge crew ever since crossing the Hollywood border.

"You didn't rescue Chiang Liu-mei from the Japanese because of a personal debt to Hayes—you did it because she's sitting on half a million bucks in gold." She stared intently into his eyes, as if she could read his thoughts. "What I want to know is how you figured out she had the gold to begin with."

Kahn chuckled, a low rumble from deep within his broad chest. "My reputation for omniscience grows," he said, half to himself. "Comrade, I didn't have any idea about Miss Chiang's secret mission. She's here on this ship because I made a promise to Artemus Hayes, and that's it. Why is that so hard for everyone to understand?"

"Because you're a liar and a thief," Dane stated. "People like you don't put much stock in personal honor."

Kahn studied Dane carefully. "A comment based upon your vast knowledge of human nature, I suppose," he said. "Well here's a curious little anecdote for you: I keep my promises. Always. If I give you my word, it's iron."

"Yet you'll cheat old folks out of their life savings peddling fake influenza cures," she shot back.

"Of course. I don't give my word to just anyone . . . and, if folks are dumb enough to fall for my pitch, they deserve to be fleeced like sheep," Kahn answered. "Get down off your high horse, sister. You're afraid to accept that I might have a shred of integrity. In fact, you can't bear to think that we're even a little bit alike. That's hardly a *Christian* attitude . . . Comrade."

He expected her to fly off the handle, but Dane surprised him. Instead, she coolly met his stare. "So why did you make the promise to Hayes in the first place. It obviously wasn't out of any sense of compassion." Her eyes narrowed thoughtfully. "Was it guilt? I bet that's it. Once upon a time you were in over your head and Hayes bailed you out. He even saved your life. You'd screwed up, and he felt sorry for you, and it's eaten at you ever since."

Kahn's expression darkened. He stepped closer, looming angrily over the diminutive pilot. "A little knowledge is a dangerous thing, Comrade," he said quietly. "You'd do well to remember that."

Before she could reply, he gritted his teeth, collecting himself, and turned to Dugan. "Deadeye, why don't you take the good Comrade here to the galley and scare up some coffee? You could stand to have a break . . . and so could I."

Dugan took one look at Kahn and hustled Dane off the bridge without another word. The pirate captain stared after them long after they'd gone.

"When am I ever going to learn to stop arguing with women?" he muttered, shaking his head.

* * *

The Hawai'ian island shone like an emerald against the sapphire blue of the Pacific, ringed with white sand beaches that glowed in the warm afternoon sun. Massive, purple-black thunderheads were gathering behind the dark bulk of Mauna Kea, the island's restive volcano, sending warm, wet gusts of wind down its slopes and through the bustling streets of Hilo.

The new capital of the kingdom of Hawai'i had grown rapidly along the shore of Hilo Bay, with modern stone buildings set among stately wood and bamboo structures. As the taxi wound through a maze of twisting, crowded streets, Kahn watched native Polynesians in colorful local garb brushing shoulders with suit-and-tie Englishmen, Frenchmen, and North Americans. It was as if Manhattan or Washington had been dropped into the middle of the Garden of Eden. Before long, Kahn's thoughts turned to what manner of serpents such a paradise would harbor.

The taxi was shown through the gate at the British Embassy, a tall stone building just a few blocks away from King Jonah Kuhio Kalaniana'ole's newly completed palace. By the time the car pulled around to the building's grand entrance, a gentleman in a somber gray suit was waiting for them at the steps, as though they had been expected. He flashed a dazzling smile as Chiang Liu-mei emerged from the car, welcoming her to the island with all the respect accorded to visiting dignitaries. She accepted the courtesies graciously, and Kahn could see the relief in her eyes as she found herself back in the embrace of civilization. The gentleman ushered Chiang, Kahn, and Dane inside; Hetty remained with the ship under vociferous protest, but Kahn insisted on meeting the British with Dane alone.

They were taken across a marble foyer and up a grand, sweeping staircase built in the best traditions of British imperialism, and led through a pair of polished teak doors into a richly appointed office. The embassy official crossed the large room and paused at a set of French doors that opened onto a sunlit balcony. "Miss Chiang Liu-mei and associates," the official announced to the men waiting there.

A wicker table and chairs had been arranged on the balcony, with a view that overlooked the bay. Two men in tailored suits rose to their feet. The first was a tall, dapper gentleman of middle years with a thick mane of iron-gray hair and blue eyes that shone from a tanned, weathered face.

"Miss Chiang," he said warmly, taking her hand. "What a pleasure it is to meet you. I am Sir Trevor Carlyle, His Majesty's ambassador to the islands." Carlyle gestured to his companion, a gentleman not much younger than the ambassador, who gave the impression of a mild-mannered scholar—save for his cold, appraising stare. "This is William Downing, with the Foreign Service. He's been instrumental in working out the details of our arrangement with your father."

"How do you do?" Chiang said, smiling politely. She turned to Kahn. "Let me introduce—"

"Jonathan Kahn," Carlyle said with a smile, reaching for his hand. "Your reputation precedes you, Mr. Kahn."

The pirate took the diplomat's hand. "Am I to take that as a compliment or an indictment, Ambassador?" he replied.

"I'd say bringing Miss Chiang here safely makes the answer self-evident," Carlyle answered smoothly, refusing to take the bait. "We were just enjoying our afternoon tea. Do join us, please."

The ambassador nodded toward the table's three empty chairs, and Downing stepped around to pull one out for Chiang. Kahn took one of the proffered seats, and Dane did likewise. The Collective pilot had grown increasingly restless since they had arrived, and now it looked like she was working up the nerve to speak.

Carlyle was quick to take control of the conversation, however, entreating Chiang to relate the details of her capture and imprisonment at the hands of the Japanese. The young woman went on to describe what she remembered of her rescue, and her subsequent journey to Hilo.

After nearly an hour she set her teacup down and folded her hands in her lap. "I do hope you'll forgive my frankness, Sir Trevor, but now I must ask if your country's offer to my people still stands. I learned just before my capture that the Japanese army had surrounded Nanking, and I fear that the situation for China is very grave indeed."

The ambassador leaned forward and rested a paternal hand on Chiang's arm. "You may be assured, young lady, that His Majesty's government stands behind the Chinese people in their time of peril. But," he added, "there is the matter of your country's payment. Was it not to be delivered to you in the Empire State weeks ago?"

Chiang nodded. "That is correct. I was sent ahead to sign the necessary documents while the gold itself followed in a well-defended airship traveling along a highly secret route. It was hoped that the Japanese would believe the gold was with me, in the event their agents worked up the courage to openly interfere with our mission." The young lady smiled ruefully. "Compared to the arms payment, I was considered expendable.

"Unfortunately, something went wrong," she continued. "The airship made its last report over Taiwan, and then was to assume radio silence until reaching the coast of Hawai'i. We have heard nothing more after that."

Kahn digested the news. "The Japanese couldn't have intercepted the shipment—otherwise they wouldn't have bothered capturing *you*."

"Your airship might have run into bad weather," Downing said quietly. "There's been a typhoon brewing east of the Philippines for the last two weeks. They could have been lost in the storm."

"Or possibly they were attacked, but managed to escape pursuit," Chiang countered. "There were a few prearranged locations along the route where the airship was to take refuge—in the event they couldn't continue to New York—then call for assistance. The captain was ordered to take no chances that might risk the loss of the gold."

She paused, considering her options, and then continued: "There is one such location in the Marshall Islands, approximately halfway between here and Taiwan. If the airship survived, that is where we will find it."

"Except that we don't have any zeppelins immediately available to undertake a rescue," Downing said.

"Really?" Kahn asked, genuinely surprised. "I would have thought your forces here would be better equipped."

"Our 'friend,' the good King Jonah, frowns on the presence of armed British troops on his islands," Downing said. "An armed zeppelin would be . . . a political difficulty for us."

"Even if we had a zeppelin," Carlyle added, "if that typhoon starts to move our way, as the reports indicate it might, we'd be sending the expedition into the teeth of the storm."

"However," the ambassador continued, "we may have another—albeit unconventional—option. I'm certain Mr. Kahn and his resourceful crew can recover the gold with little bother."

"He *could*. However . . . he won't," Kahn said. "Never mind the fact that I'm short on crew and my ship is damaged—that area is probably thick with pirates *and* Japanese patrols. Plus there's the typhoon. No way," he said, rising to his feet. "I've got better things to do. Like paying off Don DeCarlo and waiting for the reward on my head to blow over."

"Ah, yes, the ten-thousand-dollar reward," Carlyle said. "I can see how that would make your professional life rather difficult. We might be willing to help with that."

This gave Kahn pause. "You can call off the reward?" he asked cautiously.

"I don't see why not," the ambassador said confidently. "Who do you think posted it in the first place?"

"*You* put the reward out on us?" Kahn replied, thunderstruck.

"Of course," Downing said. "We had been watching the Japanese Embassy from the moment we knew that Miss Chiang had been captured. We were planning a rescue attempt of our own, but you beat us to the punch. The only theory we could come up with was that you'd somehow found out about the arms deal and kidnapped Miss Chiang to demand a ransom."

Kahn leaned forward, looming over Downing and Carlyle. "But now, of course, you know the truth—and will cancel the bounty on my head."

Carlyle's smile turned cold. He sat back in his chair and sipped at his tea. "The moment you return with the gold, the price on your head will be a thing of the past, I can assure you. Downing here and some of his men will accompany you to the island and assist in recovering the shipment."

"I must go, as well," Chiang said in a tone that brooked no argument. "So that I can confirm the transfer of the gold from my country to yours."

Carlyle started to protest, but saw the look in Chiang's eye. "Very well," he said with an elegant shrug. "I admire your courage in the face of danger, Miss Chiang." He set his teacup down and stood. "It's good to see such an example of cooperation between our governments . . . and, of course, concerned 'private citizens' such as yourself, Mr. Kahn. You'll no doubt want to leave without delay, so Mr. Downing will escort you downstairs and secure a cab."

"Hey! Not so fast!" Dane shot to her feet. The words she'd been working up to came out in a rush. "Mr. Ambassador, my name is Angela Dane. I'm a captain in the air militia of the People's Collective, and I'm Kahn's hostage. I request asylum . . . until I can be returned to my government and country."

Carlyle looked from Dane to Kahn. "Indeed?" His eyebrows arched. "I'm shocked. Certainly His Majesty's government is sympathetic to your plight. We would be pleased to extend to you our hospitality in this difficult time. As soon as this present crisis with China is resolved."

Dane's hopeful expression froze. "You wouldn't—"

The ambassador tried to look apologetic, but the effort didn't quite reach his eyes. "I must. National interests, you know. Don't worry. The trip will be over before you know it."

Thunder rolled ominously down the slopes of dark Mauna Kea.

11: Into the Storm

"**I**f you ask me, I say we throw the lot of 'em into the sea," Hetty growled, glaring at Chiang Liu-mei and her British entourage.

The view ports of the *Machiavelli*'s observation deck were open, letting in the briny smell of the ocean as the zeppelin hugged the rocky coastline of an island barely ten miles across. If the island had a name, it wasn't on the detailed map Dugan had acquired in Hilo; once the airship was safely away from the Kingdom of Hawai'i, Chiang tapped a well-manicured nail over a brown dot in the Marshall Islands and left it at that.

Since then, the daughter of Chiang Kai-shek had been withdrawn and increasingly anxious, no doubt fearful of what Kahn and his crew would find once they reached their destination. The future of her country rested in large part on the gold that—hopefully—awaited them there. She paced the airship's observation deck, her shoulders uncharacteristically hunched, as if the suspense were a physical weight that threatened to crush her.

If Chiang had grown silent in the face of her concerns, the six men sent along by the British ambassador to take charge of the gold were all too eager to share their ideas about the expedition. Ostensibly, they were associates of William Downing, but Kahn thought the men were the youngest, fittest bureaucrats he'd ever met. He figured they were hand-picked soldiers or spies, members of their country's vaunted Secret Service. Despite the fact that they knew next to nothing about airship operations, their leader—a dashing fellow named Rupert Gordon, offered an endless stream of "suggestions" about every conceivable aspect of the "operation."

Kahn eyed the British team, clustered aft along the starboard ports, each member clutching a set of powerful binoculars. "Don't tempt me, kid," he growled. "We've got enough problems as it is."

We, indeed, Kahn thought ruefully. *Thanks a bundle, Artemus.*

Kahn thought back to the time, many years ago, when Artemus Hayes had saved his hide. A high-stakes poker game the pair was running went sour in New York City. Kahn had misjudged their mark, a Texas oil tycoon, and never dreamed the man would catch them dealing from the bottom of the deck. The memory of terror and helplessness when the tycoon threw the cards in the air and stuck a gun in his face still haunted him. Hayes, of course, never let him live it down.

Kahn eyed the dense jungle growth surrounding the island's twin peaks. The Chinese zeppelin carrying the arms payment had never reached the Empire State; either it had fallen prey to pirates, Japanese patrols, or the increasingly hostile weather. If the airship had been too damaged to complete the journey, there had been several waypoints planned where the zeppelin could lay up and call for help. The island was one such waypoint, and the likeliest place the Chinese airship would be hiding.

"Why didn't Hayes tell you who she was, or why she was in Manhattan in the first place?" Hetty asked, as if reading his thoughts. Perhaps she was—they'd been wingmen as long as Kahn had been terrorizing the skies over North America.

The pirate leader shrugged. "He probably didn't know. Mercenaries aren't usually kept well informed by their employers. Or maybe he was afraid I'd balk, knowing who Chiang Liu-mei really was, and planned on letting me in on the full picture only after I'd rescued her. Instead he caught a bullet, and here we are."

"What *I* want to know," said a small, hard-eyed woman to Kahn's left, "is why no one has heard any word from this gold-laden airship." Captain Dane rested her hands on the edge of an open view port and leaned out into the warm tropical breeze. "It's been, what, almost three weeks since the zep disappeared?" she continued. "You'd think they'd have gotten a message to someone by now."

"That concerns me, too," Kahn said. "Even if their radio was damaged, they've had plenty of time to make repairs."

"So something else happened once they got here," Hetty said thoughtfully. "You don't think the Japanese caught up with them, do you?"

Kahn shook his head. "I doubt they would have followed us across the continent if they already had the gold. There are, however, other possibilities."

"Such as?" said a cultured, British voice. Rupert Gordon spoke the question with a friendly smile, but something about his manner turned it into a demand. Kahn wasn't certain if it was Rupert's imperious tone that irritated him, or the fact that the Englishman had managed to cross the length of the observation deck without the pirate leader noticing him.

"Pirates, Mr. Gordon," Kahn replied curtly. "According to the newsreels, these islands are a favorite hiding place for pirate bands. It's possible that the Chinese might have stumbled onto one."

Gordon sniffed dismissively. "Attacking relatively unarmed merchant zeppelins is one thing, Mr. Kahn, but a military airship is another matter entirely. I doubt the Chinese would have much to fear from some South Seas rabble. In fact," he continued, "I and my men are coming to the conclusion that the zeppelin was likely lost at sea." He nodded toward the island. "I rather think a thousand-foot-long airship would be hard to miss, don't you think? Yet there's no sign of her."

Hetty looked pointedly at Kahn, then at Gordon, then cast a sidelong glance at the open view port. Before he could reply, however, Dane interjected. "There!" she said, pointing with an outstretched hand.

Kahn wasn't sure what she saw at first, but then he noticed the black stain, a subtle dark shading against the green jungle canopy. Gordon shouldered past Hetty and stared out at the island. "What is it?"

"The Chinese zeppelin," Kahn answered. "Or what's left

of her." He pointed to the black outline against the slope of one of the island peaks. "She crashed against the hillside there, and someone set fire to her later, hoping the jungle would conceal the evidence. Looks like South Seas rabble isn't so harmless after all."

They found the crew in a mass grave, not far from the zeppelin's charred and twisted skeleton. Kahn had landed the *Machiavelli* at the closest beach and led a landing party up to the site. He'd entertained little hope of finding the gold amid the wreckage, and he was right. What he *hadn't* expected to find was a freshly cut trail, leading to a lagoon on the other side of the island.

The pirates had hacked out a crude airstrip at the edge of the lagoon, and sometime in the past had built bamboo huts to house machine shops and living quarters. "Not all that different from our setup in the I.S.A.," Kahn observed, crouching with the landing party in the dense undergrowth alongside the landing strip. There was a mix of fighters parked haphazardly on the packed ground, some with their engine cowlings open but covered with tarps after the pirates had found something better to do. Judging by the sounds emanating from one of the larger huts they were in the middle of a raucous party.

The landing party formed a rough crescent around Kahn, clutching shotguns and pistols and watching closely for any sign of movement amid the huts. Kahn had brought Dane, Corbett, O'Neil, Scales, and Jones, plus Gordon and his men. He counted ten planes on the strip. If the pirates had any ground crew, there could be anywhere between fifteen and twenty men between them and the gold, possibly more. He cradled a Tommy gun in his arms and rubbed his chin thoughtfully.

"Looks like they haven't been here too long," Dane mused. "The jungle's had enough time to start reclaiming the strip, so no one's been using it in the last few weeks, at least."

"They've probably got little bases like this scattered all through these islands, and just shift from one to the other," Kahn suggested. "I bet the Chinese pulled in, and were in the middle of making repairs when the pirates showed up. They jumped the zep more out of self-preservation than greed, probably. Once it crashed, they settled in here at the base, and eventually put together a salvage party."

"And hit the mother lode," O'Neil whispered, shaking his head in wonder. "Why can't stuff like that happen to *us* once in a while?"

Gordon frowned. "I don't understand why they're still here, then."

"Their boss has probably been trying to figure out how he's going to turn all that gold into something he can actually use," Kahn replied. "He needs a fence to turn the gold into cold cash. Judging by the celebration, it sounds like he's finally got that part of the problem licked."

"Do you think the gold's still here?" Gordon asked.

"Absolutely," the pirate leader replied. He pointed to a well-made hut, separate from the rest. Two men stood outside, holding shotguns. "Those boys wouldn't be missing out on the fun without a damn good reason."

"Right. Right," Gordon said, putting it all together. "The only problem is that they most likely outnumber us."

Kahn surveyed the landing strip carefully. His eyes settled on a concealed ring of sandbags, partially covered by the tarp. He nodded to himself. "Sit tight," he told the Englishman, and crawled over to O'Neil and Jones. Kahn whispered instructions to the two men, and they set off silently through the undergrowth. He returned moments later. "Okay. Get ready," he said, checking his weapon.

The pirates quickly followed suit, readying for action. Dane shared apprehensive looks with Gordon. She looked at Kahn. "What do you want us to do?"

"Just follow my lead," he answered. "When I give the signal, we're going for the gold. Shoot whoever gets in your way."

Dane snorted. "With what? My finger?"

Kahn stared at her for a moment. "Under other circumstances, I'd say rely on your razor tongue," he said, "but—" He reached into his jacket and pulled out a pistol, a battered but serviceable Colt. "Here," he said, handing her the gun.

She took the weapon—and immediately checked to make sure it was actually loaded. It was. Dane looked at Kahn strangely. "I take it you've got some master plan to sneak in there and get the gold, with no one the wiser?"

Kahn smiled. "Not at all, Comrade. I learned my lesson at Deadwood." He turned to Hetty. "What was it I said to you?"

She grinned. "Stealth is for the birds."

As if on cue, O'Neil and Scales broke from cover. They sprinted across the strip and dived into the sandbag emplacement. Moments later Scales threw aside the tarp, revealing a .60-caliber machine gun mounted on a tripod. He swung the heavy gun around and cut loose with a roaring burst. Armor-piercing rounds scythed through the hut where the pirates were holding their celebrations.

"Now!" Kahn cried, leaping to his feet. The rest of the landing party fell in behind him, howling like banshees as they rushed the camp. The guards standing watch over the gold froze momentarily, but recovered quickly and brought their weapons to bear. Kahn fired a sustained burst from the Tommy gun. Both guards collapsed.

Kahn and his people stumbled to a halt in front of the hut. Scales' machine gun fired another burst, then went silent. There were no cries, no answering shots. The building where the pirates were celebrating had been torn to pieces by the heavy .60-caliber rounds. The ambush had been sudden, deadly, and ruthlessly effective.

There was a padlock on the hut's door. A quick burst from the Tommy gun took care of the problem. Kahn kicked the door open, still wary, but the one-room structure was empty, save for six chests. Each was roughly the same size as a foot-locker. One chest had been thrown open by a machine-gun round to reveal a gleaming mass of golden coins.

Kahn looked around at the awed faces of his crew and couldn't resist a triumphant grin. "We've *got* to do this more often."

The gold slowed the return trip considerably. Even with a freshly cut trail it took them nearly four hours to cover the five miles back to *Machiavelli*'s landing site. Kahn noticed along the way that the wind was picking up, and clouds were scudding across the sky. By the time they reached the edge of the beach there was an angry, black overcast looming overhead. The typhoon, it appeared, was headed in their direction.

"Step on it!" Kahn yelled to the landing party. "Let's get this stuff on board!" There was supposed to be a ground crew waiting for them, but the beach was deserted. Evidently they had gone back inside the zeppelin to avoid the coming storm. "We're not out of the woods yet!"

The team surged across the sands, and shots rang out from the tree line only fifteen yards away. Bullets kicked up sand all around them, and a loud voice ordered them to halt. "Put down your weapons!" came a shout, in accented English.

The pirates froze as a wave of brown-uniformed Japanese soldiers emerged from their hiding places, rifles leveled. Behind them came the proud figure of Saburo Murasaki, naked sword in hand.

But that wasn't the sight that made Kahn's blood run cold. It was the man who walked beside Murasaki, idly clutching a pistol of his own and grinning like the devil.

Artemus Hayes shook his head sadly. "Told you you're getting slow, partner," he said over the rising wind. "Now it looks like the end of the line."

12: Owning Up

Kahn let the Tommy gun fall from his hands as the soldiers closed in. One by one, the rest of the landing party followed suit. The Japanese soldiers charged across the sand and formed a firing line barely six feet away. Lightning flickered against the purple-black clouds overhead.

The pirate leader glared at Murasaki and Hayes. "Long time no see, *partner*," Kahn snarled at Hayes. "You're looking pretty good for a dead man."

Hayes gave Kahn a roguish grin. A gust of wind plucked at his jodhpurs and ruffled his salt-and-pepper hair. "People see what they want to see, Johnny-boy. I thought I taught you that years ago."

"I saw the Japanese shoot at you, and I saw the blood on your hand when you told me to leave you behind."

"You saw them shoot, but you didn't actually see me get hit, did you?" Hayes said, clearly proud of himself. "The blood came from that scalp cut I got when you pulled that damn-fool stunt in the Embassy basement." He shook his head ruefully. "You just about ruined the whole plan right then and there . . . but then, you always were a loose cannon."

Murasaki took a step forward. "Back away from the gold!" he ordered. His men advanced purposefully, bayonets at the ready.

Kahn and the landing party fell back. His crew looked calm; they'd all been on the wrong end of a gun many times. Dane glared defiantly at the Japanese, but backed away with her arms held high. Rupert Gordon and his men—the "bureaucrats" sent by the British Embassy to recover the gold— backed away warily, like cornered wolves. Pete O'Neil stumbled and fell; one of the soldiers grabbed him by the scruff of the neck and hauled the flailing pilot to his feet, then sent him stumbling along with the rest.

"How long have you been a patsy for the Japanese?" Kahn asked Hayes. He struggled to control his anger. Now that he thought about it, the clues had been there, but he'd missed them in the confusion.

"A long time, old son," the mustachioed smuggler replied. "Pretty much from the minute I left Hollywood. Murasaki-*sama* found me in Hong Kong, where I'd gotten into some difficulties with the local authorities. He bailed me out, and we've been business associates ever since."

"You mean he blackmailed you into spying on the Chinese—or whatever other dirty work he could think of," Kahn said coldly. "What I can't figure is why he'd involve a moth-eaten old dog like you in something this important." The pirate's eyes narrowed appraisingly. "Wait. Let me guess. He used you to intercept the gold shipment in the first place . . .

only you screwed it up. The Japanese didn't put a bomb on your zep—you got it shot down tangling with the Chinese."

Hayes' grin faded. "Murasaki-*sama* didn't want to risk antagonizing the Brits by sending a Japanese airship, so he decided on a pirate attack instead." He shrugged. "The Chinese put up a hell of a fight. I had to break off, and lost my ship just off the coast of Hong Kong."

Kahn nodded thoughtfully. "You must've thought Murasaki was going to skin you alive after you'd botched the job. But then the Chinese airship failed to show up in Manhattan, and neither one of you knew why. So you grabbed Chiang Liu-mei, hoping to shake loose some answers."

Deep, distant thunder rumbled to the west, and a warm, damp wind gusted through the trees. Murasaki suddenly barked a string of orders in Japanese, and half the troops shouldered their rifles. Most ran back to the tree line and pulled away crudely made camouflage screens to reveal two medium-size autogyros. The troops pulled them from cover and began preparing them for takeoff while the rest began wrestling with the crates of gold coin.

Murasaki paced around the crates, glaring officiously at his men. Hayes gave the officer a sidelong look. "He was sure Liu-mei would break," the smuggler said with a sigh. "But I knew better." Then he looked at Kahn and winked. "And that's where you came in, Johnny-boy. I figured that if she were loose, she'd run right for the gold."

Kahn felt his cheeks burn. "And you needed a sucker to come along and 'rescue' her," he said, angrily biting out each word.

"Oh, don't be so hard on yourself, Johnny," Hayes said with a cruel smile. "You were the perfect choice. I knew you'd go to Hell and back if it squared things between us, and that's exactly what you did." The smuggler let out a laugh. "I've gotta admit, though, you sure threw us some curve balls here and there. I had no idea you'd move so quick getting to the Empire State. You didn't give me any chance to warn Murasaki that we were coming. I had to send those soldiers we ran into in the basement to go find him so we wouldn't get killed on the way out!"

"And you had to make it look good enough that you could fake being shot in the confusion." Kahn gritted his teeth. "Not, bad, Hayes. Not bad at all. But how did you manage to follow us from Hawai'i?"

Hayes laughed. "Hell, Johnny-boy, we've been tracking you since you left Manhattan! That was all Murasaki's baby, though. When his fighters tangled with you on the way out of New York, they hit you with a couple of experimental rockets the boys in Tokyo came up with."

Hayes paused, clearly savoring his control of the situation . . . and Kahn's anger. "They work kind of like the beeper units we use for beeper-seeker rockets," he continued, "only they use the metal skeleton of a zeppelin like a big antenna to transmit a low-power radio signal in timed bursts. We were tracking you even when you were on the other side of the *Rockies*, Johnny-boy. You were out of your league from the get-go."

There was a cough and a rattle from across the beach, and the first autogyro's engine sputtered to life. Murasaki noted this and smiled grimly. He turned to Hayes. "There is no time left. The weather is worsening. Finish things here and then get under way." The officer then faced Kahn and gave a deep, mocking bow. "I told you we would meet again, Mr. Kahn," he said. "But now we part forever. You were an excellent tool, and it is a pity my country will not be able to make use of you again."

He gave the pirate leader a brief, mocking smile, then turned and ran for the waiting autogyro. The troops handling the gold redoubled their efforts to haul the cargo over to the second machine.

Kahn shook his head. "You know he's never going to give you a cut of that gold," he said to Hayes. "You're just another pawn to him."

"Gold? Who said I was getting any of the gold?" Hayes smiled. He jerked a thumb at the *Machiavelli*. "That's my prize right there, and I've got enough troops on board to make sure the crew behaves. If they get me to Hong Kong without any trouble, I might even let them go."

"I'm not stupid, Hayes," Kahn snarled. "Your boss isn't

going to be happy with any witnesses to what happened here. You're going to kill them—just like you're about to kill us."

Hayes paused. There was a bright flash of lightning, and then, distantly, a hammer-blow of thunder. "You catch on quick, old son," he said, almost sadly. "It's not personal, you understand. None of this was. Not that it matters much, I suppose."

Murasaki's autogyro roared down the beach and hopped into the air, wavering momentarily in the crosswind. Dane suddenly stepped forward, hands thrust into the pockets of her flying jacket. "Hey! Hold on! I'm not with these guys and you know it! Can't we come to some kind of arrangement?"

Hayes looked her over. "You know, normally I wouldn't be able to resist that kind of invitation," he said with a sly wink. "But Murasaki was very specific. Sorry, doll . . . but this just ain't your lucky day."

Dane's face fell. "Yeah," she said with a sigh. "That's what I was afraid of." She started to turn away—then pulled Kahn's pistol from her pocket and fired wildly into the cluster of Japanese guards. Men screamed and fell. Hayes threw himself to the ground, firing a couple of wild shots of his own.

"Run!" Kahn bellowed.

Everyone scrambled, kicking up plumes of sand. "Kahn!" O'Neil yelled, and threw a small, dark object at his boss. Kahn plucked it out of the air. It was a grenade, lifted from the pocket of the guard who'd grabbed the wiry little thief when he made his phony stumble.

Kahn pulled the pin—and at the last second remembered to strike its base against the heel of his boot. The fuse sputtered, and he threw it. The grenade sailed over the heads of the troops and rolled under the remaining autogyro, almost twenty yards away. The troops carrying the gold scattered, and the little bomb went off with a flash and a sharp *bang*, blowing out the autogyro's tires and windows.

The pirate leader turned and sprinted after his men. Rifle shots rang out behind him, and a bullet hissed past his head. He plunged into the gloomy depths of the jungle and put as many trees as he could between himself and the surviving troops.

People seemed to materialize out of the shadows around him as he ran. "What do we do now?" Hetty asked, gasping for breath.

"For now, just keep running!" Kahn said, hardly slowing down. "If we get deep enough in here, they won't bother to follow us. They're running out of time to get under way before the storm hits . . . and they know it. They won't waste time chasing us."

O'Neil's voice came from the shadows to Kahn's left. "If you hadn't completely blown that grenade toss, we wouldn't have to run at all. I swear, you hardly dinged the paint on that bird!"

"I put it right where I wanted it, smart aleck," the pirate leader replied. "That autogyro can't taxi without wheels, so the gold isn't going back to Murasaki's airship. They're going to have to load it onto the *Machiavelli* . . . and fast."

"A fair lot of good that does us, old chap," came Gordon's cultured voice. The man didn't sound the least out of breath. "Either way, it's still going to wind up in Japan."

"Not if I have anything to say about it," Kahn snarled.

"And how do you propose to catch them? Fly?"

"As a matter of fact, yes," the pirate replied.

They got back to the pirate base in record time. Kahn suspected that the storm brewing overhead encouraged them to pick up the pace. Each flash of lightning felt like another tick of a bomb timer . . . and everyone knew that time was running out.

All ten of the pirates' planes were airworthy, and two of them were two-seaters, so no one had to be left behind. The British agents, it turned out, were competent—if not especially combatworthy—pilots.

Once airborne, the ad hoc squadron conferred about what direction the two zeppelins must have taken. The consensus was south by southwest, figuring that they would try to skirt the edge of the typhoon and head for Hong Kong. They opened the throttle and sped through the steadily darkening sky, knowing full well that they were gambling their lives on being right.

"Even if we catch them, then what?" Corbett asked him once they were on their way. "We don't have any rockets, and even if we could knock down the Japanese zep, what about the *Machiavelli*?"

"We're going to have to take her back, of course," Kahn said.

"*How?* You don't think they'll just open the hangar and let us in, do you?"

"Something like that, kid."

13: Interesting Times

Kahn struggled to control his aircraft in mounting turbulence. He caught sight of the two airships, making fifty knots into a headwind at eleven thousand feet. The *Machiavelli* trailed about a mile behind the smaller Japanese zeppelin—and small, white shapes kept close formation around her flanks. "Tally ho!" Kahn growled over the radio. "Looks like the Japanese have got four—no, *six*—fighters escorting our ship."

"Flying escort? In *this*?" Hetty exclaimed. "They're either gutsy as hell or out of their minds!"

"I hope it's the latter," Kahn said. "Let's see if we can bounce these guys and take them down fast; then I'll get aboard the ship."

"You hope," Hetty said, her voice strained with worry. "Of all the schemes you've come up with, this one's got to be the worst."

"Thanks for the vote of confidence," he replied. "But it's all or nothing. We've only got about thirty minutes of decent light left, and that's it. It's do or die."

"Yeah. What else is new?" Hetty managed a throaty laugh. "What the hell. Let's get 'em, Red Skulls!"

The ten planes swooped down on their prey, engines roaring, and at the last moment the white enemy fighters scattered like startled birds. Kahn cursed under his breath. The

Japanese planes were fast, pulling tight turns and loops he knew that his captured Devastator couldn't match. "So much for the element of surprise, gang," he called out. "Let's see how well they mix it up!"

Kahn caught sight of an enemy plane in a tight, diving turn to port, and rolled in after him. The pilot saw him at once and began to pull his lighter plane into ever-tighter turns. Kahn cursed and fought with the Devastator's controls, but watched helplessly as the enemy plane slipped inexorably away. Startled shouts filled his earphones as the enemy planes turned the tables on their attackers.

Not only were the enemy fighters swift and maneuverable, but their pilots also knew them inside out. Kahn watched as the Japanese plane pulled far enough into the turn that now it was dangerously close to ending up on *his* tail. He rolled out of the turn and pulled into a climb, hoping the enemy couldn't follow. Moments later, bullets hammered into his wing and tail.

"Hetty, where the hell are you?" Kahn yelled.

"Hang on," she replied. Hetty's voice was strained as she fought the g's punishing her aircraft. "I can't get a bead on him!"

More hits struck along the Devastator's fuselage. Kahn thanked gods he never believed in that at least the enemy planes had to trade firepower for maneuverability. Still, he could see a half-dozen telltale wisps of smoke seeping from magnesium rounds buried in his tail and wings. He couldn't keep taking hits like this for long.

"Hetty, on 'three,' I'm going to roll right and fly level, like I'm shaken up," Kahn said. "Get in behind him and finish him off!"

"Roger!"

"One . . . two . . . three!"

Kahn rolled out to the right and leveled off. Tracers immediately filled the air around him, and hits struck all along his right wing. Then an orange flash lit up the sky behind the Devastator. "Got him!" Hetty cried. "They've got armor like tissue paper!"

"Great . . . but there's still five more of 'em out here, and we're running out of time," Kahn said. "Break off and help the others. I'm making my run on *Machiavelli*. It's now or never."

"Roger, boss," Hetty said gravely. "Good luck."

Kahn pulled the Devastator into a right turn, noting that the starboard aileron and elevator were shot to hell. He settled quickly onto the airship's stern and cut his throttle to ninety knots. So far, none of the enemy planes had noticed him.

The Devastator overtook the airship. Kahn slipped around the zeppelin's giant aft stabilizer; then he cut his speed to sixty knots and dropped closer to the airship's gray hull. Fortunately the zeppelin's guns were silent—evidently Hayes didn't have enough men to guard his crew and man the ship's weapons.

The fighter pulled along the length of the huge airship. Kahn cut his speed further, to just over fifty knots. *She's a thousand feet long and over a hundred and thirty feet across,* he thought. *Like hitting the broadside of a barn.*

He reached down and slipped a length of rope around the control stick. The rope—one end secured to the seat—held the stick relatively steady. It would keep the plane straight and level . . . but not for long.

Kahn pulled open the canopy and undid his seat harness. Roaring air slapped at his face and neck. He pulled himself to his feet and stepped out of the cockpit onto the port wing.

As he exited the cockpit, Kahn could see the red ember glow of the magnesium rounds eating through the armor plate at his feet, less than six inches from the wing tank. A tracer whipped past his head, and Kahn saw an enemy fighter boring in on his tail.

The Japanese pilot was good, maybe one of the best in the sky over the *Machiavelli*. He roared in on the zeppelin and streaked down the length of her hull, nearly close enough to touch. Kahn watched the guns blaze from the engine cowling and wings, and bright red flashes of light—more magnesium rounds—slashed across the intervening distance.

One bullet punched a neat hole in the rudder, and another drilled through the canopy, right beside his hand.

Then the enemy plane seemed to fly through a fan of

greenish sparks, as cannon fire raked along its starboard side. The enemy plane exploded, less than two hundred feet away, and Kahn caught a glimpse of a PR-1 Defender flying through the cloud of debris as he launched himself into space.

The wind flung him like a chip of wood as he dived from the wing, hurtling toward the zeppelin below him. The thick layers of armor fabric gave a little, but the impact still took his breath away and sent him tumbling end-for-end along the length of the ship. His shoulder slammed into something hard and unyielding, and he flung out his hands, desperately scrabbling for something to halt his tumble. His right hand closed on the armored lip of the dorsal gondola, and he held on for all he was worth, pulling his battered body over the lip and onto the steel deck.

He was only dimly aware of the Devastator exploding moments later as the magnesium rounds found their way into the fuel tank.

Kahn crept through the zeppelin's central passageway, biting back the pain in his shoulder. It didn't appear to be broken, but he was definitely injured, and the mobility in his arm was restricted.

There was no one about. Evidently Hayes had a skeleton crew on the bridge and everyone else under guard. Kahn worked his way to the hangar deck. If he could get the hangar doors open and the docking hook deployed, he'd have reinforcements fairly quickly. Provided anyone survived the dogfight.

He reached the hatch to the hangar bay. The metal door was slightly open, and he could hear worried voices inside.

Kahn peered through the hatchway. The hangar deck was one of the largest spaces on the ship, with two large hangar doors at either end—one for receiving planes, and the other for launching them. The planes themselves were parked in between the two. At the far end of the hangar, close to the receiving door and in the shadow of the huge crate of debris left over from the battle in the Empire State, three guards stood an uneasy watch over the Chinese gold.

The pirate leader shook his head. *Can this get any worse?*

He reached inside his coat for his pistol. Then he remembered he'd given it to Dane and never got it back.

All he could hope for was to live long enough to be embarrassed about it later.

Kahn pushed the hatch open wide enough to slip through and ducked inside. There was plenty of cover as he moved among the parked planes and over to the portside bulkhead, where most of the tools were kept. He quietly picked up a large wrench, stuck it in his pocket, and then carefully grabbed a heavy, five-gallon drum.

He crept aft, using the planes once more to conceal his approach, then dashed the final few feet to the other side of the large crate of parts. The troops paid little attention to their surroundings, speaking to one another in low, apprehensive tones. They never saw him come around the corner and bring the drum down on the first soldier's head.

The drum flew out of Kahn's hands—and doused the other two men with five gallons of motor oil. They staggered and sputtered, the rifles slipping from their hands, and Kahn pulled out the wrench and dispatched them with a few quick, deliberate blows.

There was an emergency release latch for the hangar door on the aft bulkhead. Kahn tossed the wrench aside and limped over to the latch. He paused to catch his breath—

—and was spun around by the impact of a bullet. A pain like a red-hot poker jabbed through his arm.

Kahn let out a yell and clapped his left hand over the wound. Echoes from the gunshot rang in the cavernous space.

"Get away from that latch, Johnny-boy."

Artemus Hayes stepped from the shadows of the parked planes and walked over to the downed guards, stepping carefully through the oil. He checked them quickly and shook his head. "Murasaki ain't gonna be happy about this," he said. He looked at Kahn. "I gotta tell you, Johnny, I knew you'd show up. I didn't know how, but I just *knew* you would. And here you are. Now step away from that latch."

"Or what?" Kahn said, wincing in pain. "You'll shoot me again?"

"I surely will," he said evenly. "And the next one is going

to be between the eyes." He watched Kahn for a moment and then smiled. "You know, we could make an arrangement, you and I."

"How's that?"

"Nobody but me knows you're alive right now. And we've got the gold right here . . . thanks to you." He indicated the crates with a nod. "We can wait till it gets dark, then slip away from Murasaki. Head south. Hell, maybe buy an island and live like kings. You sure wouldn't have to worry about De-Carlo anymore." He winked. "Just like old times, eh, Johnny-boy? What do you say?"

Kahn took a deep breath. "I've got people still outside. What about them?"

Hayes laughed. "Don't worry about them. If the Japanese don't get them, the storm will. Then we're home free."

The pirate considered for a moment, then nodded. "Yeah, that's what I thought you'd say. No dice, Hayes. No way in Hell."

Hayes frowned. "I do believe you're getting soft, old son."

Kahn grinned. "Think so?"

He dived for the latch.

The move caught Hayes by surprise. Kahn grabbed the handle and pulled down for all he was worth.

Behind them, the hangar doors fell open, letting in the howling wind. For a brief second, the wind filled the hangar deck. Invisible hands yanked at Hayes, and his feet slid out from under him in the oil. He hit the deck—and slid over the edge.

Kahn could hear Hayes' screams even over the raging wind. He walked carefully to the edge of the hangar door. The con man clung to the lip of the door with one white-knuckled hand. Hayes looked up at Kahn, his eyes pleading. He knew that look of helplessness well.

The burly pirate reached down and grabbed Hayes' wrist with his good hand, then hauled upward. The con man scrambled back onto the deck and struggled shakily to his feet.

"Now, finally, we're even," Kahn said gravely.

Hayes looked up at him and grinned. "Absolutely, Johnny-boy. No question." He took a deep, grateful breath. "It's lucky for me you *have* gone soft—"

That was as far as he got before Kahn shoved him off the deck. Hayes plummeted into the ocean far below.

Kahn refused to let Gordon take the gold off his ship until Ambassador Carlyle revoked the ten-thousand-dollar reward, and he stood over Carlyle's shoulder until the necessary telegram had been drafted and sent.

Rain fell in sheets along the Hilo docks. Kahn and Dane watched Chiang Liu-mei take her farewell. She was hustled down the long gangway from the zeppelin and escorted into a Rolls-Royce by Chinese diplomats. She'd expressed the deepest gratitude of her father's government to Kahn and his crew, then wasted no time in getting off the *Machiavelli* and back to the Chinese Embassy. In her wake went Gordon's men, lugging the heavy crates that were now His Majesty's property.

"It sure took you long enough to get that damn landing hook down," Dane groused, watching the British agents proceed slowly down the gangway.

"I had a bullet in my arm," Kahn said with a snort. "I'd love to see *you* try it sometime, sister." He wore his right arm in a sling; Doc Adams said the bullet went right through the meat and would heal up just fine in a couple of months. Until then he was going to have a hell of a time lighting his cigars.

The Japanese fighters had put up a fierce fight, but in the end, sheer numbers turned the tide. The Red Skulls and their British companions were circling the zeppelin and growing increasingly worried by the time Kahn had managed to run out the landing hook and start recovering planes. Once they were aboard, Gordon and his men proved remarkably talented at eliminating the remaining Japanese guards.

By the time the Red Skulls and their British allies had seized the *Machiavelli*, Murasaki had known something was wrong aboard the pirate airship, but it was too late; darkness had fallen like a curtain. After making sure none of Hayes' men were stowed away, Kahn ordered the Japanese tracker-beepers found.

Hetty found them, far back in the stern of the zeppelin, and Kahn tossed them into the sea. Then they turned away, losing the Japanese airship in the darkness. Not even the ruthless Japanese agent could risk an engagement at night, and in the teeth of a Pacific storm.

Two days later, after a circuitous route east, the Red Skull Legion made it safely back to Hilo.

Dane looked up at Kahn. "So, what now?"

"We head back home and settle up with DeCarlo," Kahn said. "I figure the Japanese will forget about me after a while, but the Don won't rest until he gets his money."

Dane nodded. She watched the crates being loaded into a waiting truck, surrounded by armed guards. "It's got to be tough, watching all that gold slip through your fingers."

Kahn watched the truck pull away from the dock and shrugged. "I try to be philosophical about such things. Easy come, easy go."

She watched the pirate intently. "I'm surprised you didn't try to switch the gold out with something equally heavy. Like that crate of spare parts."

The pirate looked at her and smiled. "My, my, Comrade . . . you're starting to think like a pirate. Of course, when would I have had such an opportunity? Gordon always had at least one man watching the crates from the moment they came aboard."

"Maybe. But somehow, if you'd wanted to, I'm sure you would have thought of something."

Kahn chuckled. "Don't go believing everything you hear about me, Comrade. I'm not as clever as the pulp novels would have you believe."

A taxi pulled onto the docks, picking its way carefully through the rain. Kahn nodded at the car. "That would be your ride, Comrade. Here is where you and I part ways."

Dane's eyes went wide. "But . . . I don't understand . . ."

"You saved my life," the pirate said solemnly. "That was

your Defender who shot down the Japanese fighter over the zeppelin, right?"

"Well, yes, it was . . . but—"

"Then, I hate to say it, but I'm in your debt." He gestured toward the car. "Think of this as a down payment."

She looked at the car, then back at him. "I'll never understand you, Kahn. Never in a million years."

"The feeling's mutual, Comrade. Now get out of here, before I change my mind."

Dane started to say something more, then thought better of it. She set off, moving hurriedly down the gangway. Then, at the bottom, she turned. "Hey! Wait a minute! You can't just leave me here in Hawai'i! How the hell do you expect me to get home?"

Kahn grinned. "Oh. Good point." He dug in his pocket and fished out a coin. "Here's something for cab fare," he said, and sent it tumbling at her with a flick of his thumb.

By the time she caught it, he was already gone, shutting the hatch behind him. The *Machiavelli*'s engines coughed into life. Dane opened her palm—then looked back at the airship.

"You sneaky son of a bitch," she muttered. Dane laughed and tossed the coin—solid gold, and stamped with a Chinese mint marking—high into the air.

Intermission: Rogues and Thieves

With the collapse of the United States and the subsequent rise of aerial commerce, crime eventually took to the skies. Squadrons of pirates prey on cargo airships, stealing cargoes and sometimes even the huge ships themselves. Privateers hunt the shipping lanes under the authority of Letters of *Marque* that define the split between the raiders and the governments they defy.

Pirates are by no means a homogenous lot, no matter what the Tinseltown cliffhangers would have one believe. Like their militia counterparts, pirates are highly individualistic—from opportunistic predators who prey on the weak (such as "Genghis" Kahn) to mysterious adventurers like the beautiful aviatrix known only as "The Black Swan."

Which brings us to our final tale, and its hero.

The infamous Fortune Hunters—and their enigmatic leader, Nathan Zachary—have built a reputation among the criminal fraternity, specializing in daring, high-risk raids that maximize profits . . . and minimize civilian casualties.

Formed in the early days of the breakup of the United States, Zachary insists that his crew steal only from those wealthy enough to afford the loss, earning the Fortune Hunters somewhat undeserved reputations as modern-day Robin Hoods. (They've mastered stealing from the rich; they just haven't gotten around to giving to the poor quite yet.)

In addition, the Fortune Hunters are not given to the savagery that typifies much of modern piracy; the group's "Articles of Piracy" states that no Fortune Hunter will harm or kill the innocent . . . a tenet that has led many brave (and foolish) pirates to underestimate Zachary's resolve.

For the first half of the 1930s, the Fortune Hunters were regarded as little more than flamboyant and daring but ultimately minor thieves. Zachary's raids rarely equaled the colorful exploits of the mysterious aviatrix, The Black Swan, and lacked the lurid appeal of the machinations of ruthless schemers like "Genghis" Kahn.

The Fortune Hunters' operations have grown increasingly bold, however—and more deadly. Zachary's recent conflicts across North America—including several dogfights with Paladin Blake, no less—have shown the rest of the pirate underworld that this intrepid band of rogues is anything but soft.

Now, follow Nathan Zachary as he enters a dangerous confidence game in the seedy underbelly of New Orleans. The stakes are high, and one slip means Zachary will be singing the "Bayou Blues."

—NERO MACLEON
Manhattan, 1938

Bayou Blues

A Nathan Zachary Adventure

by Nancy Berman
and
Eric S. Trautmann

Prologue: The Alley Cat

A distant fork of lightning punctured the night sky, the flash illuminating the iron-gray storm clouds that gathered in the distance. A thick mist blanketed the streets, an unpleasant drizzle that swallowed the glow from the street lamps.

On an ordinary night, the threatening weather would have chased pedestrians off the streets and into the warm, cheerful speakeasies that lined the boulevard. Tonight was anything but ordinary.

Streams of people flowed along the streets, some clad in garish costumes, others wearing very little despite the weather. The echoes of wild music, laughter, and happy yells crashed along Bourbon Street. The mob of revelers shouted and sang, heedless of the ominous thunderheads that drew closer by the minute. The jubilant crowd—mostly well-heeled tourists—cheered at the first distant peal of thunder, defiant in the face of the storm.

The swirl of activity was electric, and it cut like a searchlight through the gathering rain. Another flash of lightning—closer this time—heralded the clear ringing of the city's bells. The crowd howled with delight.

It was midnight, and Mardi Gras had begun.

A bedraggled man, stoop-shouldered and filthy, staggered through the swirling crowd. His threadbare coat, tattered cloth cap, and matted beard were wine-stained and filthy. As he took a long pull from a dirty bottle clutched in his fist, his gaze swept the milling crowds.

He spied a trio of men in gray raincoats and suits, half a block behind him. They pushed through the knots of people that clogged the street. Their heads swiveled methodically back and forth as they searched the crowd.

The bum muttered a curse under his breath.

He shambled on his way, swept along Bourbon Street by the pull of the crowd. Cheap wine sloshed from the open bottle. No one paid any attention to him.

Since Louisiana had declared independence almost a decade ago, the local economy was in a shambles; only help from the French government—in exchange for the unwelcome presence of a Foreign Legion garrison—and a roaring trade in stolen guns and illegal whiskey kept money trickling in. A lone, down-on-his-luck derelict was such a common sight in New Orleans that it was hardly worth noticing, especially in the middle of Mardi Gras.

The man reached the edge of the crowd. He paused, took another pull from the wine bottle, and then shuffled into a nearby alley—just another vagrant looking for a dry place to bed down for the night.

He crouched in the shadows behind a stack of discarded crates, pulled his dark coat tightly around him, and waited.

Minutes later, silhouetted in the mouth of the alley, the gray-suited trio stepped into view. Though they were only a few feet away, it was impossible to hear what they were saying over the barrage of Mardi Gras noise. The tallest of the three—probably the leader—gestured angrily back at the crowd. The motion brushed aside the man's coat and revealed a revolver tucked into his waistband.

The two men nodded, then moved back onto the street. The leader stopped to light a cigarette. He carelessly flicked the wooden match back into the alley. The match landed—miraculously still lit—on one of the crates that shielded the bum from the gunman's view.

The bum grimaced. If he moved, he'd be spotted for sure.

As the match flame guttered and faded, the gunman faced back into the alley. His eyes narrowed with suspicion as he noticed the stacks of rubbish that clotted the alley. He stepped toward the crates, and his hand slipped into his coat.

The vagrant's grip tightened on the neck of the wine bottle.

It was a poor defense against a gun—but maybe, in the dark, with the element of surprise—

There was a blur of movement from behind the crate. The startled gunman crouched and drew his revolver in a single fluid motion. The gun's muzzle swept the alley as he searched for his target.

An alley cat, wet and miserable, leapt onto the pile of crates and hissed at the man in the gray topcoat.

The gunman chuckled. He shook his head, holstered his gun, and walked back onto Bourbon Street.

The bum slumped with relief.

The alley cat peered down on him from her perch atop the crates. She hissed at him, her yellow eyes baleful and imperious.

"I know how you feel," he muttered.

He waited another minute, then stood and moved farther down the darkened alley. His drunken staggering had vanished, replaced by a sure, steady gait. The sounds of the Mardi Gras celebration were muffled now. The mounting rain sounded like marching feet on the cracked pavement.

The vagrant wound through the twisting maze of back alleys. With the relative safety of the tourist areas behind him, his motions became stealthy and cautious. The few people he passed on the street were hard-eyed and ready for trouble, and most of them were armed—dangerous people in a tough neighborhood.

He stopped in front of a small dilapidated building. Its once-vibrant green paint was peeling and faded. A weathered wooden sign above the door was the only decoration: a faded yellow-white drawing of an anchor.

He paused and looked back over his shoulder. Satisfied that there were no unwanted observers, he pushed open the door and stepped inside.

Even in the dim light, it was obvious that White's Anchor had seen better days. The air had that peculiar New Orleans smell of rot, cigarette smoke, and musty damp blowing off the lake. The few pictures on the pale redbrick walls might have been considered good nautical art once, but now they just looked cheap and old. A single wooden ceiling fan spun

in lethargic circles on the mold-speckled ceiling. A handful
of men in dark blue peacoats sat at the bar and nursed their
drinks in silence. The ones who bothered to look up glared at
the vagrant, then returned to their glasses.

A firm hand clapped him on the shoulder. "This ain't the
charity ward, Mac," a deep voice intoned. "Payin' customers
only. Go sleep it off somewhere's else."

The bum turned and faced the speaker—the Anchor's bartender. He was a large man, pushing six feet tall. He had the
crooked nose and scarred knuckles of a back-alley brawler.
Black eyes glowered at the vagrant from beneath bushy brows.
The large white apron tied around his ample waist made him
look more like a butcher than a barkeep. "I mean it, pally," he
growled. He cracked his knuckles impressively.

Without missing a beat, the bum produced a neat stack of
franc notes. "I *am* a paying customer."

The startled bartender looked the bedraggled man up and
down. Finally, he sighed and dropped his hand from the
grimy shoulder and wiped it on his apron. "All right, but don'
give me no trouble, okay?"

"No. No trouble." He paused, then asked, "You got a
phone?"

"Yeah, in th' back," the bartender grumbled as he returned
to his place behind the bar. "So what'll it be?"

The bum slid half the stack of franc notes across the bar
top. The paper stood about an inch high. "Five minutes of privacy on that phone."

The bartender's eyes again registered surprise, but he
merely shrugged, collected the bills, then jerked his thumb to
the phone booth nestled in the back of the taproom. "Make it
quick," he said.

The vagrant moved to the booth and closed the door behind him. He dialed a number from memory and waited.
When the call was answered, he spoke in a low, urgent
voice—almost a whisper.

"It's me. We're in play." A pause. "Yeah, it's all set . . . for
just after Mardi Gras. Any sooner and I can't be sure they'll
trust me."

Another pause, longer this time.

"What can I tell you? They're suspicious. . . . I had to shake a trio of his goons tonight. . . . No, they didn't pinch me. Look, I gotta get back. Just make sure everything's in place."

He hung up the phone, exited the booth, and walked back to the bar. He placed the rest of the francs in his pocket on the sticky bar top.

"What's this for?" the bartender asked.

"Peace of mind. I wasn't here, right?"

"Never saw you before in my life," the bartender agreed as he slid the stack of bills off the counter with practiced ease and returned to washing beer glasses.

The bum slipped out of the bar and back onto the street, where he resumed his drunken shuffling.

Soon, he had disappeared into the fog.

1: My First Impression of You

The door crashed open, shattering the midmorning calm with a sound like a gunshot. Nathan Zachary's hand dropped to the pistol in his jacket. His eyes checked the room for threats, although his tanned and handsome face gave no indication of any concern.

New Orleans was just settling down after the hubbub of Mardi Gras. The tourists who had survived the annual event had gone home; the bodies of those who hadn't were tucked away, sleeping peacefully in the local morgues. Zachary had no intention of joining them.

He didn't have any enemies in New Orleans—not serious ones, anyway. Still, he was a wanted man, and wanted men didn't last long in his business without being ready for trouble.

The kid who'd just burst into the bar was definitely trouble.

He was an interesting contrast to Zachary, who stood out in a dive like The Flyin' Horses bar. Though his attire—a battered flight jacket, a khaki work shirt, matching pants, and polished high leather boots—were common enough among air pirates, he somehow made them look like a million bucks.

Like Zachary, the kid was tall and rangy, about eighteen or nineteen years old. His blue eyes, rimmed with red, burned in his tanned, angular face. Sandy hair, slicked back, offset the kid's leading-man features. He wore a pearl-handled Colt revolver on his hip.

The kid was a pilot, Zachary noted. The back of his leather jacket was festooned with tiny, embroidered kill markers—a tradition with some Texan sky bandits. He wore a small squadron insignia, a comical picture of a mock-angry crawfish on a field of green and purple, which marked him as a member of the "Rajin' Cajuns."

The lanky young man took a seat at the bar and kept his eyes on the street. He slapped a handful of coins on the cracked and stained bar top; the barman wordlessly poured a shot of cheap bourbon. The kid downed the shot in one motion, then gestured for a refill.

The sound of raised voices from the kitchen startled the young man. He spun around, and his hand dipped for his revolver. Nathan's grip tightened on his own gun, just in case. The kid looked edgy enough to start shooting at any moment.

Zachary almost laughed in relief when the source of the young pilot's agitation burst in through the swinging kitchen doors. *It figures,* he thought. *It had to be a dame.*

She was young—seventeen or eighteen, Nathan guessed. The girl was a stunning brunette with legs for days. With a wry grin, Zachary sat back, nursed his chicory-laced coffee, and watched the little drama unfold.

The brunette flung herself into the young pilot's arms, and they shared a passionate kiss. The kid ushered her back to a little table in the corner, directly across the room from Zachary. They sat huddled together for a few minutes, their conversation hushed.

She was a real looker, who—judging by her clothes— came from money. She had knockout southern beauty: soft waves of dark hair framing a heart-shaped face, skin like creamy magnolia petals, and wide dark eyes framed with thick lashes.

With her stylish, expensive clothes, she was an odd match for the young man's battered leather and khaki outfit. No question, this had all the earmarks of a forbidden romance, which meant that—New Orleans being New Orleans—sooner or later there would be violence and bloodshed.

The capital of French Louisiana was no stranger to violence and bloodshed. Some called it the murder capital of the old United States. Despite the city's fearsome reputation, New Orleans was, in Nathan's estimation, if not a classy town, at least a colorful one. The city was a bit like a tawdry, fading grande dame whose lip rouge was a bit smeared and whose finery was a little tarnished . . . which suited Nathan just fine. But she had the patina, the sense of history, of a European city—something the metallic towers of the Empire State and the blinding lights of Hollywood lacked.

New Orleans was a proud city, and it showed in the way the locals talked about her, with pride that verged on obsession. Nothing tasted as good or looked as beautiful or boasted such a storied past as everything in New Orleans—just ask a local. Even though Nathan Zachary was fluent in French, he could decipher what the locals were saying only half the time. Their accent was a strange mishmash that sounded like a cross between stereotypic southern and nasal Bronx; one moment they were asking "where y'at" and the next, pointing out the location of the "catlick" church on the corner.

Zachary's ruminations ended abruptly when the young man cursed and pounded his fist on the table. "What? What the hell are you sayin'?"

The brunette burst into tears and flung her head down on her right arm while the young man held her left hand up to the light, staring at her ring finger. Zachary was impressed; the ice on the girl's finger could keep a pirate in champagne and caviar for a long time.

At the sound of her tears, the young man was immediately contrite. "Aw, jeez, sweetie. I'm sorry. C'mon, Emmy, please don't cry." When he tried to comfort the girl she sobbed even harder. Zachary looked away. He was starting to feel like a Peeping Tom.

He saw the sleek black Packard 1508 Touring Sedan pull up before the young couple did. The car doors opened, and two men got out. They were obviously bodyguards, the thick-chested, no-neck types, dressed in gray trench coats and fedoras. They carried weapons openly as they scanned the street. They weren't coming into The Flyin' Horses for a social drink.

One of them, a short fireplug of a man with red, close-cropped hair, opened the right side passenger door for a tall, well-dressed Creole man in his early forties, who emerged with arrogant grace. He was wearing a dark charcoal gray suit, beautifully cut and expensive, over which he sported a camel-colored vicuña coat.

Before Zachary could warn the lovestruck couple, the door crashed open and the trio entered. The young man jumped to his feet and drew his pistol. The gunmen crouched and produced guns of their own. The girl screamed.

The fireplug flicked off his pistol's safety. "Drop the gun, boy," he growled. "Or, as God is my witness, you're a dead man."

Zachary quietly slipped his own pistol from its holster, hidden beneath the table. The whole scene looked like something on a Tinseltown movie lot, complete with cheap hoods, a hotheaded kid, and a damsel in distress—except the guns were real.

The man in the expensive suit made an elaborate show of handing his fedora to Fireplug. "Now, now, Benny," he said, "no need to get so dramatic." He smoothed the sides of his perfectly cut hair, although nothing on the slightly graying temples was out of place.

"Emmeline, *ma chérie.* I had no idea that you knew about places like this." Disdain was etched on his face. "Y'all come home now. A nice long bath should wash the stench of this rat hole away."

"Deschaines, you can't treat her like she's property." The young pilot was still pointing his gun at the well-dressed man.

"Listen up, Tug, ol' son. I can treat my *fiancée* any way I damn well please. And right now it would please me a whole helluva lot if she just got in the car and came home." He held out a leather-gloved hand to the girl, who was shaking like a leaf.

"Emmy isn't going anywhere with you, you son of a—"

"Emmy and Tuggy! The city's answer to Romeo and Juliet, eh?" The two bodyguards snorted like bulldogs at their master's joke.

"Get the hell outta here, Deschaines. Like I said—" He thumbed back the Colt's hammer. "—she isn't going anywhere with you."

The girl spoke up in a soft accented voice. "Tommy, please. Don't do this. They'll kill you." She rose reluctantly from the banquette, her shoulders sagging in despair. "I'll go with you, Bertrand."

Tommy's head snapped back, as if he'd just been slapped.

A thin, arrogant smile tugged at the corners of Bertrand Deschaines' cruel mouth. "That's a good girl. You see, Tommy? Emmeline knows who the better man is."

The girl stepped toward Bertrand, but pointedly ignored his outstretched hand. For a moment, the arrogance fled from Deschaines' face, and was replaced with anger. He roughly pulled the girl closer to him.

Nathan watched as Tommy's eyes narrowed and the Colt tracked Deschaines. The damn-fool kid was about to turn the bar into a shooting gallery. Zachary was on his feet in an instant. He crossed the bar in two quick strides and locked the kid's arm in a vise grip.

Everyone froze, startled by Zachary's sudden, unexpected actions.

"Pardon me, gentlemen," he said, his voice calm. "Am I interrupting?"

He whispered into the kid's ear: "Put the gun away, son."

The young pilot bristled. "You with them?"

"If I were, you'd be dead now," Nathan replied. "Just relax."

Zachary stepped forward and placed himself directly in front of the kid. He gestured at Deschaines' gunman—

Benny—with his own pistol. "You, too, pal. It's too nice a morning for a gunfight."

A faint smile crossed Bertrand's face. He nodded to the two thugs who frowned but tucked their weapons away.

"Why don't you take the young lady out of here before someone gets hurt," Zachary said. Tommy started forward, ready for a fight, but Zachary barred the kid's path.

Deschaines clasped his fingers firmly around the girl's shoulder and guided her toward the door. He paused, and called back over his shoulder: "Maybe you can teach the boy some manners, Mr. . . . ?" He trailed off, the question implicit.

"Nathan Zachary."

One aristocratic eyebrow arched in surprise before Deschaines could recover his mask of nonchalance. "Mr. Zachary. Your reputation precedes you."

Zachary sighed. For years, his pirate gang—the Fortune Hunters—had been a small-time outfit. In the last year, they'd had a string of good luck . . . which meant his face had been plastered in the papers. *The price of fame,* he thought. *So much for anonymity.*

"What brings you to New Orleans, Mr. Zachary?" Bertrand inquired. "Not here on 'business,' I hope."

"Plane trouble, actually. My bird's laid up at Pontchartrain Aerodrome for repairs, so I thought I'd cool my heels here for a bit." He shot a pointed glare at the gun that Deschaines' man, Benny, still had trained on them. "It's supposed to be quiet here after Mardi Gras, after all."

Deschaines gave a humorless chuckle. "Put it away, Benny. It's time to leave." He nodded at Nathan. "It's been a . . . pleasure making your acquaintance. Another time, perhaps." With that, Deschaines exited the bar and ushered the girl into the backseat of the black car.

Zachary's handsome face hardened as he kept his gaze on the departing foursome, their image distorted by the bar's grimy window. Benny was the last to leave. He glared at Nathan and added, "Another time for sure, 'pal.' "

Satisfied that the danger had passed, he looked back over

his shoulder. The kid was a mess, drenched in sweat and shaking from the rush of adrenaline and anger. "Go in the back and splash some cold water on your face, kid. Then we'll talk."

Tommy began another splutter of protest—he was starting to sound like the faulty prop on an old Warhawk—but Zachary cut him off. "Just do it."

The young pilot crashed through the kitchen doors in fury.

It was a good thing the kid left the taproom when he did. Zachary watched as Deschaines got into the backseat behind the driver and turned to face the girl. It was obvious he was furious even before he slapped her hard across her face. She crumpled against the passenger window, her pale complexion marred by tears and a reddening handprint. For a moment, Zachary could see her look of utter defeat and misery—and then the Packard peeled away from the curb.

Zachary's own anger flared. If anyone needed a lesson in manners, it was Bertrand Deschaines.

2: Boy Meets Girl

"**D**amn it, Zachary," Tommy growled. "You should've let me send that bastard outta here in a box."

Tommy looked angry enough to take the bar apart with his bare hands. He paced back and forth like a caged animal, his fists clenched. Finally, he snarled and kicked a chair across the floor. It crashed into the bar and broke apart.

Nathan sized up the kid, from his battered flight jacket to his cheap boots. There was no way Tommy could pay for damages if he busted up the bar. Nathan suppressed a wry grin—he'd wrecked more than his share of speakeasies in his time, too. And, like the kid, it was usually because of a woman.

"Calm down, kid. Let me buy you a cup of coffee." Zachary steered the young pilot to the table and firmly sat him down. "Stay put . . . and take it easy on the furniture."

Zachary waved over the bartender and passed him a few franc notes. Within moments, the bartender returned with a plate of the ubiquitous beignets and two steaming cups of coffee.

Nathan took a sip of the coffee and grimaced. It was hot and dark, just the way he liked it. Unfortunately, the locals insisted on putting chicory in it, which made it slightly less drinkable than the sludge in his plane's oil pan. On the other hand, the kid had downed enough rotgut for one day, so coffee—even bad coffee—was an improvement.

"Go ahead, kid," Zachary said. "Looks like you could use some food." He pushed the plate of pastries across the table.

Suspicion clouded Tommy's face. "What's your story? Why would a big-time pirate want to buy breakfast for some stranger?"

Nathan shrugged. "Good question. In your place, I probably wouldn't trust me, either. But, since I just kept you from getting shot, I'd say I'm probably as trustworthy as anyone else in this town."

He pointed at the insignia on Tommy's shoulder. "So what if my motives aren't completely pure? I know the Cajuns—or rather, I've had some dealings with your boss—and maybe there's some money to be made by cooperating. Helping you out would get me in solid with him."

He paused, then leaned back his chair and grinned. "Mostly, though, I got in the middle of that mess because you were disturbing my breakfast."

The younger man chuckled and attacked the pastry like he hadn't eaten in a week.

After a few minutes Tommy came up for air, wiped the powdered sugar off his face, and reached across the table.

"I'm Tommy Boates, but everyone calls me Tug. Everyone except for Emmy." His blue eyes got that glazed-over look that said he had it pretty bad for the girl. Zachary knew that look—he'd seen it in the mirror a couple of times himself, although not recently, thank God. The kid had a good grip, nice steady hand. He was probably a pretty fair pilot . . . if he kept that hair-trigger temper of his under control.

"You're from Texas, right?" Zachary asked.

"Yessir. How'd you know?" That flat twang was unmistakable.

"Oh, I've traveled around a bit. How did you end up here?"

"Well, I ran into some trouble a while back." Tommy flushed and looked around the room as if he expected a posse to come through the door at any moment waving a wanted poster at him.

"No need to spell it out, kid. You're not the only one who's got trouble on his heels."

"Look, Mr. Zachary . . ."

"Nathan."

"Okay, Nathan. See, I had to leave Texas kinda suddenlike. I hitched a ride on the first plane outta there, an' I ended up here. I kicked around for a day or two but I didn't have anywhere to go. Deschaines an' his cronies have tied up all the legal flying gigs in this town. I didn't have my own wings, an' I couldn't get into the militia because of the trouble back home, so things were lookin' pretty bad."

"Why not sign on with the Foreign Legion? The garrison here always needs pilots, and they don't ask . . . uncomfortable questions."

"I almost did, but things between the locals an' the Legion are pretty tense. Seemed like a good way to get shot down. I was considerin' goin' back to Austin an' facin' the music when I met up with 'Wild Card' Thibodeaux. He took me into the Rajin' Cajuns, gave me a plane an' a place to hang my hat."

"*Louis* Thibodeaux? When did he join the Cajuns?"

Nathan had met Thibodeaux a while back—the cagey half-Creole was running a sweet gambling operation along the Mississippi (and was cheating the players blind, naturally). He was gregarious and charming, and as crooked as they came. Nathan liked him . . . despite the fact that Thibodeaux had conned him out of a bundle.

"Huh?" Tommy looked puzzled. "Thibodeaux runs the whole outfit."

Zachary studied his coffee intently for a moment and tried to keep a straight face. The Rajin' Cajuns were a pretty well-known pirate gang in these parts, going back some two hundred years when ships sailed on water instead of air. The last Zachary had heard, the head of the gang was a man named Gaspard—a wily old con man who'd bragged that his roots went clear back to Jean Laffite. Of course, every two-bit grifter in French Louisiana made the same claim . . . but Gaspard was colorful, so his antics were tolerated.

Under Gaspard's leadership, the Cajuns were airborne bandits who, in the old days, were likely to hand a lady a rose with a flourish as they took the diamonds off her neck. Despite their generally lawless activities in the past several years, they had actually done a lot to help the poor folks in the bayou who had gotten crushed under the wheels of the French Louisiana government—so the locals protected them when the law tried to shut the Cajuns down.

And now, Gaspard was out of the picture—and Wild Card Thibodeaux was the new top dog? Perfect.

"The Cajuns have been real good to me," Tommy continued. "Louis gave me my own plane—a Fury—an' let me fix her up so she really purrs."

Zachary smiled. Listening to Tommy talk about his plane, he could tell the kid loved to fly, but there was something guarded even in his rapturous description. "It's just that, well, my daddy raised me to respect the law, an' the Cajuns are sorta on the other side of it, if you know what I mean. I just don't feel real comfortable havin' to look over my shoulder for militia an' such when I'm flyin'."

Zachary had been on the wrong side of the law for most of his career. He nodded. "Enough said. So, what's the story with you and that rich guy?"

Tommy's blue eyes flashed. "Bertrand Deschaines," he said, his voice flat. "I'm tellin' you, Nathan, you should have let me finish that son of a bitch off—"

"Throttle back a second, kid," Nathan said. "From where I was sitting, it looked like *you* were the one who was going to get his ticket punched."

Tommy glowered, but before he could protest, Nathan cut him off, his voice kind. "Nothing to be ashamed of, Tommy. I've been outgunned myself on occasion—I just try not to make a habit of it. So, who's the girl?"

Tommy relaxed a bit. "Emmeline-Marie Fonteneau. Emmy. She's . . . she's . . ." The young pilot paused, his face red.

"She's special," Zachary said. "Happens to the best of us, kid. And I take it Bertrand is the competition?"

"No, sir!" Tommy's fist pounded the table. "I love Emmy, an' she loves me. The problem is her guardian, Henri Deschaines.

"See, Emmy lost her folks when she was real young. Her daddy was partners with old man Deschaines. So here she was, an orphan child with no relatives—an' a pile of dough she inherited. Old man Deschaines, he becomes her guardian. Makes sure she's treated real good, like a princess, best of everything."

"Sounds like a decent enough thing to do," Nathan said.

"No way. Henri Deschaines only cares about money, an' Emmy's folks died rich. Henri wants the money, so he's forcing Emmy to marry Bertrand—to keep her trust money under his thumb."

Zachary's interest was piqued at the mention of "trust money." He had a soft spot for damsels in distress— especially beautiful ones who were swimming in dough. Although the adored Miss Emmy was a little shy and retiring for his taste, there was no denying that she was a looker. He imagined it wouldn't be too hard to wake up every morning knowing that you were married to that kind of beauty—and that kind of money.

Tommy continued. "See, Emmy, she doesn't care about the money. She'd up an' leave it all if she could. An' me, I don't wanna marry her because of the money. Hell, a man's supposed to support a woman, not the other way around, right?"

Nathan nodded and hoped he looked convincing. He could think of a couple of ladies who were more than welcome to support him. The kid's sincerity made him feel old and a little sad. *"Kid,"* he wanted to say, *"you hang on to that dream as long as you can. You'll find out that sometimes, in the real world, things just don't work out like they do in fairy tales."*

"So, what are you going to do?" Zachary interjected. "You can't just run off with her. Bertrand strikes me as the kind of fellow who doesn't like it when people take things that belong to him. You run off with Emmy, his guys will gun you down like a dog."

Tommy shrugged. "Yep, I figured that out pretty quick, so I'm gonna have to beat these creeps at their own game. That's why I was meetin' Emmy today—to tell her my plan."

He paused, a mischievous grin creasing his handsome face. "See, Henri Deschaines is a respected 'pillar of the community'—but he's as dirty as yesterday's dishwater. He runs all sorts of gambling outfits an' bettin' parlors. Plus, he sponsors damn near all the air racin' in Louisiana, all of it illegal, an' all of it with cash prizes. The next race is the day after tomorrow, an' the payoff is a cool twenty grand."

Zachary gave a low whistle. "That's quite a prize. And you figure on collecting it?"

"Well, the way I see it, I spend more time out there flyin' the bayou than they do. My plane is better an' faster than most of the local racers' rigs. I can probably beat anyone Deschaines throws at me. I win the race, get the twenty grand, an' then Emmy an' me get the hell outta town. Maybe Hollywood or Pacifica, someplace like that."

"That's a pretty big *if*, Tommy. Is your plane in shape for that kind of race?"

The young Texan's face fell. "That's the problem. I can win the race, but I gotta make a coupl'a repairs to my bird . . . an' the parts ain't cheap. Thibodeaux ain't eager to spend the Cajuns' money on 'some damn-fool' race. I don't mean no disrespect, but—" A sly look crossed Tommy's face as he launched into an approximation of the local dialect. "—'Tommee, *mon garçon,* how far you zink ze twenty grand will go? Emmy's not some little bayou girl gonna be happy wid ze life of a poor man.' "

Zachary smiled at the Texan's imitation of his leader. "He does have a point, Tommy. I'm sure Emmy loves you but if she's been raised on chateaubriand and champagne, she may not be ready for beans and beer."

Tommy looked defiant. "She says she doesn't care where we live as long as we're together."

Zachary took another sip of his bitter coffee and considered the situation, looking for all the angles. The smart play was to leave this dime-store Romeo and Juliet act to play out on its own. On the other hand, there was money to be made here: an inheritance, a corrupt local businessman, and illegal cash racing all added up to a nice, juicy score.

The ace sighed. There was no point in kidding himself—there was more to this caper than money. He despised bullies, and there was no question that *père et fils* Deschaines were a matched set. The pit of his stomach went cold as he remembered the miserable look on Emmy's face after Bertrand slapped her.

Finally, he stood up and clapped Tommy on the shoulder. "Come on, kid. Let's go see your boss. I have a feeling we can work something out."

3: The Fox Den

"Almost there, Nathan," Tug called out. He eased the battered J2 Fury into a leisurely port bank. The thick green canopy of the Louisiana bayou stretched below the speeding fighter, shrouded in a yellow-gray haze.

"It's about time," Nathan muttered. He sat in the plane's "rumble seat"—the copilot position directly behind the pilot. His typical calm expression had been replaced with a dark frown. His hands clutched Tug's seat back in a white-knuckle grip. Nathan Zachary had never been a good passenger.

His expression darkened further as Tug rolled the plane out of its turn and dropped her nose. The Fury plummeted like a rock, then leveled off as Tug expertly trimmed out of the dive. Zachary's fingers tightened reflexively when the plane's fuselage scraped the tops of the taller trees.

"Kid, any lower and we'll be walking," Nathan shouted. His voice barely carried over the roar of the Fury's powerful fourteen-cylinder Wright R-1800-C engine. In the bar, Tug had said his plane "purred." *Some purr,* Zachary thought. *I've fired machine guns that made less noise.*

"If you think we're too low now," Tug replied, "you're gonna *hate* this."

Tug ruddered to starboard and aimed for a hole in the tree canopy. Nathan swore in surprise as the Fury dived through the gap in the foliage. Trees and vines flashed past as Tug shed more altitude.

As the Fury sped along the natural corridor formed by the trees, Zachary realized that much of the "tree cover" was actually overlapping layers of camouflage netting. It wouldn't be hard to spot the pirates' hideout from the air—it would be damn near impossible.

Moments later, Tug lined the plane up with a small dirt landing strip. He cranked the landing gear into position, then more or less bounced the Fury down the end of the landing strip. As the plane taxied to one side of the landing strip, Tug killed the engine. He stripped off his leather flight helmet and gloves, then turned to his white-faced passenger with a grin. "That wasn't so bad, now was it?"

Nathan managed a grin of his own. "Not bad . . . for a rookie."

Tug chuckled, rolled the canopy back, and climbed onto the wing. "Time to see the boss."

"Looks like the welcoming committee is already on its way." Nathan pointed at a cluster of men walking toward the plane. "And they don't look too happy."

There were five of them, all pirates judging by their attire. Zachary had lived and worked among air pirates for the better part of a decade. Some were like him—thrill-seekers interested in a life free of compromise. Others were just in it for the cash. Many were violent thugs, one step away from the electric chair.

This bunch fell firmly into the latter category: hard-looking men, dressed in stained dungarees tucked into high boots. Most wore work shirts, open to the waist. An assortment of powerful rifles and pistols were all trained on the Fury's cockpit.

"Hey, what's the big idea?" Tug called out. "It's me, Tug."

"Yeah, I know," one of the pirates replied, and then pointed at Zachary. "But who's *he*?"

The pirate was a big man, built like a carnival strongman. His shaven head was covered with a green-and-purple bandanna, and a large gold hoop hung from his left ear. An obscene tattoo decorated the massive expanse of his chest.

"Look, he's a friend," Tug protested. "There's no call for—"

"Shut up, Tug," the pistol-toting pirate cut in. "Let the chump speak for himself." He called up to Zachary. "Step on down from there and no funny stuff."

Zachary stood slowly and showed his empty hands. He joined Tug on the ground. He crossed his arms and looked the bald pirate square in the eyes. "I'm a friend of Tommy's," he said, his voice even and calm. "My name is—"

"Nathan Zachary." A new voice spoke up from behind the pirates. The voice was accented, that strange mix of southern and French that was so common in these parts. The bald pirate moved aside as the speaker stepped forward.

Louis Thibodeaux was tall, lean, and dark. His wine-red silk shirt was clean, as were his jodhpurs and high leather boots. A Bowie knife and pistol hung from his wide belt. His autocratic features were softened by a neat, pencil-thin mustache. Thibodeaux looked every inch the pirate—except for the somewhat threadbare beret he wore.

Thibodeaux faced Zachary, his arms crossed. "Nathan, *mon ami,*" he said. "It's been a while. You look—" He paused and looked around at the assembled gunmen. "—outgunned." His henchmen chortled.

"Good to see you, Louis," Nathan replied. "You've moved up in the world. Still wearing that stupid hat, I see."

Thibodeaux snorted with amusement. "Ah, *oui.* And you? I see you makin' 'eadlines all over the place lately. And yet, 'ere you stand, in the middle of the bayou, wit'out your Fortune Hunters. Wearin' a scarf, no less."

Nathan grinned.

"I don' see why you're smilin', *mon ami,*" Thibodeaux continued. His own smile was frozen on his face, but his eyes had become hard and cold. "I hate to be in'ospitable, but you crashed this party wit'out an invitation. If this is about that money I won off you, you lost to me fair and square—"

"I wouldn't call the way you deal cards 'fair and square,' Louis," Nathan said, "but no, I'm not here about old business."

"So?"

"New business. Let's talk somewhere more private."

Thibodeaux frowned, then shrugged. "All right, Zachary. Follow me back to the command shack."

The Cajun sent the other pirates back to their posts and walked toward the small collection of tin shacks in the center of the compound. Nathan and Tug followed.

Zachary nonchalantly looked around, sizing up the Cajuns' operation. It was a hell of a setup, he had to admit. Aside from the camouflage netting, several of the trees contained hidden antiaircraft emplacements. There were enough shacks to house as many as twenty pirates, and half that many were visible, working on a small fleet of fighter planes.

Fuel drums were stacked neatly in the southwest corner of the compound, near a larger wood and sheet-steel structure. Judging by the noises from inside the building, Nathan guessed it was a tool shop.

On the opposite side of the central compound was a big building, maybe the size of a warehouse, but much lower to the ground. He was about to ask what the building was used for, when the stagnant swamp air shifted slightly. One whiff answered his question—the Cajuns had their own distillery.

Thibodeaux opened the door to the central shack and stepped inside. Nathan followed him into the dark, cluttered room. Paintings and jewelry were stacked on shelves and piled in corners, undoubtedly loot captured during pirate raids. A half-dozen bottles of bootleg bourbon—the Cajuns' own brand—competed with a shortwave radio for space on top of a battered old card table. A scuffed and worn wooden desk—covered with papers, charts, and maps—dominated the center of the small room.

Thibodeaux took a seat behind the desk and gestured for Nathan to sit in a rusty folding chair. He poured bourbon into a pair of smudged glasses and pushed one across the desk to Nathan. "So, *mon ami,* what's this new business?"

"Tug wants to fly in Deschaines' air race. I think you should let him."

Louis smirked. "I never figured you'd be a soft touch for a 'ard-luck story, Zachary."

"Depends on the story."

Thibodeaux's smile vanished, and he leaned forward. "This isn't new business, Zachary. . . . It's *personal* business. Tug's personal business, to be precise. As long as 'e flies with the Cajuns, 'e flies when and where *I* tell him to—and I say 'is personal business is not my concern."

"So what's the harm in letting the kid fly in the race?" Nathan asked. "I saw him handle that Fury, and he's good. If a Cajun wins the race, that'll only enhance your reputation, Louis. That's good for business. So's the cash prize."

Thibodeaux made a slashing gesture with his left hand. "Don' con me. You never make a move wit'out considerin' all the angles. What do you care about my reputation?"

"Fair enough," Nathan conceded. He set his untouched bourbon on the desk and leaned closer. "This Deschaines clown has to finance these races with cash, right?"

"*Oui*. Twenty thousand francs."

"If we get Tug inside the race, we can case his operation and figure out how to steal the cash."

Thibodeaux laughed. "*C'est impossible*. M'sieur Deschaines, 'e draws a lot of water in these parts. I already have troubles wit' Prime Minister DuPre." He gave Nathan a conspiratorial wink. "Apparently, I'm a 'scourge of th' skies.' Why would I wan' to go makin' trouble in my own backyard?"

"That's the best part, Louis. If we play this right, he'll think *I'm* the one who stole the money. You get away clean."

Louis considered for a moment, then grinned. "And all you need is for me to front the money to fix up Tug's plane?"

"That's all."

"No deal."

"What?" Nathan exclaimed. "Why not?"

"Maybe you wan' to recruit Tug into the Fortune Hunters. Why should *I* pay for this?"

"Louis," Nathan said with an air of wounded pride, "you really should learn to trust people."

Zachary reached into his jacket and produced a deck of cards, still wrapped in paper. "Tell you what," he said. "Let's settle this . . . fair and square."

He tore open the package and removed the cards. He quickly fanned the deck and stripped out the jokers. "Here's my proposition, Louis," Nathan said. "Whoever draws the high card wins the bet. Simple as that."

Thibodeaux nodded. "What are the stakes?"

"If I win, you let Tug fly in the race. I'll even front the money to fix his bird *and* cover his entry fee. If *you* win . . . you get my Devastator."

Louis arched an eyebrow. "So? Devastators are a dime a dozen."

"Not like mine. She's got a nitro boost system—fast enough to leave Paladin Blake eating my exhaust."

Thibodeaux considered, then shrugged. "*Oui.* I accept," he said. "Not that I don' trust you, *mon ami,* but I'd prefer to use *my* cards."

He removed a battered deck from a drawer and set them on the desk. Nathan's expert eye spotted trouble right away: the cards were marked—and Thibodeaux had expertly palmed away the top card.

"I've got a better idea," Nathan said. He reached over and scooped up Louis' marked deck. His nimble hands shuffled it in with his own. He gave the oversize deck a one-handed cut.

The last time Nathan had gambled with Thibodeaux, the wily Cajun had won several times. Louis was a hell of a card-sharp, with a mechanic's grip that was almost invisible—even to a cheat as accomplished as Nathan. Thibodeaux could slip the palmed card to the top of the deck at will, given half a chance.

Louis' eyes never left Nathan's hands as the cards danced back and forth. Zachary spied one of the marked cards from Thibodeaux's deck—an ace—and curled the fingers of his left hand slightly, in preparation for a card steal he'd learned on Tortuga. If he could just jostle the cards just right, he could control the ace to the top of the deck—

"Ah, Nathan," Louis admonished, "you've gotten rusty. You need more practice. Next time, use the cards to cover your left 'and a bit more."

Zachary chuckled. "My apologies."

"Why don' we save some time, *mon ami,*" Thibodeaux said, "and just cut to the card, nice and simple? The way you 'andle those cards, *c'est horrible.* It pains me to watch you abuse them."

"Sure, Louis," Nathan said. He placed the cards down on the cluttered desk and gestured at the Cajuns' leader to go first. Louis would have to make his move now.

Louis cut the deck into two piles. It looked like Thibodeaux had simply drawn the top card from the second pile and placed it facedown on the desk, but Nathan had no doubt that Thibodeaux had simply produced the palmed card.

Nathan cut the deck again and drew a card.

Thibodeaux looked at Nathan as he turned his card faceup and announced, "*La reine du pique,* the queen of spades."

Nathan met Thibodeaux's gaze and smiled as he flipped his own card over. "The king of hearts. You lose."

Thibodeaux's eyes went wide. " 'ow the 'ell did you—?"

Nathan shrugged. "What can I tell you, my friend? Most people know better than to gamble with a Gypsy."

Louis laughed. "Well played, Zachary. I still win, 'owever."

Nathan's eyes narrowed. Thibodeaux was a cheat, but not a welsher. "How do you figure?"

"Simple. You pay to fix up Tug's plane—which means I come out ahead—but 'e can' win the race. You still lose."

The Cajun drained his bourbon in a single gulp. "The race is fixed, *mon ami.* The only winner is gonna be Henri Deschaines."

4: Les Faucons du Marai

The air was filled with the echoing thunder of dozens of fighter engines, loud enough that Nathan's ears rang. The din from the engines was not unusual for an air race; the crash of cannon and rocket fire was.

Nathan fought the urge to duck as a quartet of fighters roared overhead, low enough that he was buffeted by the prop wash. The planes were deep blue and devoid of insignia—except for the wings, which featured a meticulously painted pattern of silver and gold hawk feathers.

Zachary instantly recognized the fighters' distinctive bat-like profile—the Whittly & Douglass M210 Raven. Tough and agile, the Raven was built to be a dogfighter and zeppelin-buster. The Raven's six guns—a quartet of .40 cals and a pair of .60s thrown in for good measure—could tear a target apart. In sufficiently skilled hands, the Raven was an implement of mayhem and destruction.

The throaty roar of the Ravens' engines mingled with the coughing grumble of a fifth plane, a battered old PR-1 Defender. The Defender dived from the cloud cover and fell into position behind the Ravens.

As the Defender opened fire, the Ravens broke formation in perfect unison, banking in pairs. With pinpoint precision, the Ravens looped and rolled.

The Defender's dive had been too steep and too fast—it overshot the Ravens. In seconds, they had returned to their wing-to-wing formation directly behind the Defender. The lead Raven opened fire. Tracers carved a line through the sky.

The Defender was a designed-by-committee bona fide piece of junk; Nathan's wingman, Jack, had once joked that piloting a Defender was like flying a tractor: "It's damn hard, damn ugly, and damn sure gonna make the pilot look stupid."

Nathan scowled, and his hands flexed in frustration—he ached to be in the cockpit of his own Devastator, preferably with the lead Raven in his gun sights. In his years of combat flying, Nathan had seldom seen such a one-sided battle.

In seconds, the Defender's tail disintegrated in a hail of bullets. Smoke blossomed from the engine cowling as gunfire walked along the Defender's fuselage.

The Defender pilot dropped his landing gear—the sign of surrender. The Ravens broke off, still in perfect formation.

The Defender pulled into a sluggish, wobbling climb. Nathan had seen enough air combat to know the plane was doomed—and that her pilot was desperate to climb high enough for a relatively safe bailout.

Tug nudged Nathan. "Here they come again," he said.

The blue Ravens moved in for the kill.

The Defender pilot saw them, too. A bare few hundred feet from the ground, the Defender's canopy popped open and the pilot dived from the cockpit. Seconds later a pair of rockets slammed into the crippled Defender.

Smoke wreathed the Defender, just before it blew apart. Fire and steel careened into the bayou. Nathan caught a glimpse of white silk as the pilot's chute popped open, low to the tree line. Too low, in fact. The pilot would be lucky to get out of the landing with a busted leg . . . or a broken neck.

"Good Lord," Nathan muttered. He tapped Thibodeaux on the shoulder. "What the hell kind of race is this?"

Louis shrugged. "The illegal kind, *mon ami*. And this is just the qualifyin' run."

"Yeah, the qualifyin' run *I* should be in," Tug groused.

Zachary, Thibodeaux, Tug, and a half-dozen of the Rajin' Cajuns walked along a muddy footpath. Twisted, vine-strangled trees lined the path, making it hard to see anything save swamp and the sky directly overhead.

"We're here," Tug said.

Just ahead on the path was a crude gate, built from a couple of old sawhorses. The gate was flanked by machine-gun nests, each manned by a pair of gunners. Behind them, a dozen hard-faced men with pistols and rifles stood post. Their eyes never wavered as Nathan and the Cajuns approached.

A small canvas awning stood just beyond the gate. A hand-lettered sign tacked to the awning read ADMISSION: TWO FRANCS. NO FOREIGN CURRENCY. NO REFUNDS.

A slender man in wire-rim glasses stepped forward. "Two francs. Each." He held out his hand. When it was his turn in the line, Nathan drew out a pair of wrinkled one-franc notes and handed them to the man. Wire-rims inspected each bill carefully, then nodded. "Let 'em in. Check your weapons—" He jerked his thumb at the canvas awning. "—over there."

Two of the burly gunmen moved the gate aside and waved them toward the makeshift awning. One by one, Wire-rims disarmed the pirates.

He smirked when he saw Zachary's pistol—a cheap French automatic he'd picked up after landing at the Pontchartrain Aerodrome.

"Nice gun," Wire-rims quipped. A sarcastic smile tugged at the corners of his thin lips. Nathan couldn't argue with the creep's assessment of the pistol—it *was* garbage. The fact that Wire-rims was right didn't change anything, though; Zachary still wanted to wipe the smirk off the man's mug with a left cross.

Once the pirates' weapons had been collected, Wire-rims pointed farther along the mud path. "Seats are that way. Betting booths just beyond the bleachers." With that, Wire-rims turned back to counting the francs and placing them in a steel lockbox.

Just ahead, Nathan saw that much of the foliage had been cleared away. A few hundred yards ahead, a skeletal structure of wood and metal was visible—the bleacher seating for race spectators. There was enough seating for nearly a thousand people in a pinch, though today fewer than a hundred people were seated in the stands.

Thibodeaux nudged Nathan and pointed at a small concrete structure, partially sunk into the wet earth. "That, *mon ami,*" Louis said, "is where Deschaines keeps the prize money."

The building was uncomfortably similar to the enemy bunkers Zachary had seen in Europe during the Great War. A massive steel door dominated the front of the structure.

Nathan gave a low whistle. "It looks like a bank vault."

"It is," Louis replied. "Deschaines is the boss man of the national bank. Henri 'ad one of the vaults brought all the way out here." He winked and added, "Blamed the loss of the vault on 'air pirates', if you can imagine."

"Swell," Nathan groused. "A simple grab job was too much to hope for, I guess."

"Not unless you've got a key to the vault," Thibodeaux replied. "And not unless you're ready to tangle wit' them."

He nodded at a cluster of men that stood in front of the bunker. The hulking figures wore blue uniforms, despite the muggy heat. Nathan could see the thin sunlight glint off the gold-colored badges on their chests.

Cops. A lot of cops.

New Orleans had always been a tough town, rife with crime. That was, in Nathan's view, part of the city's charm— particularly when compared to the industrial fascism of Chicago or the stuffy, teetotaling elitism of Manhattan. In New Orleans, there was always someone with a hand out; bribery and graft were just part of doing business. It was effortless . . . almost casual. It made Nathan feel right at home.

After the fall of the United States—and French Louisiana's aborted conflicts with her neighbors—the corruption that permeated virtually every level of the government had worsened. Even the locals, who generally accepted shakedowns and protection rackets, had tired of the brazen criminal activity perpetrated by the city's supposed protectors.

Prime Minister DuPre had been elected to office with promises of rooting out the criminals hiding within the system. Several crusading journalists had assisted DuPre's campaign and kept the corruption scandals in the public eye. Bribery and graft hadn't gone away—not by a long shot—but most cops on the take at least made an effort to be subtle about it.

Which is what made the presence of uniformed police so unusual—and worrisome.

"So Deschaines has the cops in his pocket," Nathan said. "This just gets better and better."

"*Oui*. Rumor 'as it 'e's runnin' some kind of blackmail scheme on the chief of police and the mayor. Which means . . ." Thibodeaux trailed off.

". . . which means," Nathan finished, "if we cause trouble here, he'll have every cop in town on our trail."

They made their way to the bleacher seating. The bleachers were a ramshackle, rusty affair that looked ready to collapse at any moment. Thibodeaux led the way to the upper rows. From this elevated position, Nathan got his first good look at the racecourse.

The course was marked with low-flying hot air balloons, tethered at the race checkpoints. Nathan guessed that the route the racers had to fly was around five or six miles—short laps, compared with the races Nathan had seen elsewhere.

The fliers also had to pass through a number of obstacles. Nathan drew a small pair of field glasses from his jacket and studied the course. He watched a yellow-and-red Brigand dive through the nearest obstacle—the rotting wooden frame of an old barn that had long ago lost its battle with the swamp. The Brigand squeaked through with mere inches to spare.

Nathan focused the field glasses on the next obstacle: a large wood-and-metal hoop that stood almost two stories high. The hoop had spokes that radiated from a central hub.

Something about the obstacle nagged at him—it looked familiar, but he'd never seen anything like it in an air race. He frowned and examined the rest of the obstacles on the racecourse. Several appeared to be constructed out of all sorts of ordinary materials; large, circular wooden frames suspended between a pair of balloons seemed to be the most common of the dozen or so obstacles.

Among the makeshift obstacles were several structures that appeared to be more or less permanent. The rusting edifices were clogged with vines and mud. He squinted for a better look.

Then—like a black-and-white drawing of two faces resolving themselves into a vase—he saw it.

One of the distant obstacles appeared at first to be a roughly cone-shaped building, low to the ground. The front of the building was open, barely wide enough for two planes to pass through. Just inside the building, Nathan could see a central support pillar—the conical roof actually spun on a central rod.

The building was constructed around an old, and very large, merry-go-round. The carnival horses had been replaced with sheets of metal and wood, moving barriers that spun and bobbed erratically.

The racecourse had been built like a Frankenstein monster from a cast-off and dilapidated carnival. Nathan spotted the remains of an old roller coaster, a Ferris wheel, and a second merry-go-round.

Louis grinned. "Deschaines 'as an interestin' sense of 'umor, *non*?"

Nathan nodded. The scene disquieted him despite Louis' levity. The races were bloody, violent, deadly affairs—all built on the corpse of a carnival. It just felt . . . *wrong*. Perverse, somehow.

Something didn't figure, though. Since no one in their right mind would build a carnival out here in the middle of nowhere, Deschaines would've been forced to build it—or move it—out here.

"So, who builds a carnival in a swamp?" he wondered aloud. "This must have cost Deschaines a bundle."

"Non." Louis shook his head. "Mos' likely it cost the *bank* a bundle. That's 'ow Henri makes a lot of 'is money. He charges the locals extra interest on loans and mortgages and skims the diff'rence."

Nathan nodded. Now it made sense. "So he used the bank and foreclosed on the carnival owner."

"Oui," Louis said. "Then 'e forgave a few small debts to have locals move the 'ole mess out here."

"Smart."

"Jus' like these qualifyin' runs."

"How do you mean?"

"Deschaines opens up the course to local pilots—and most of them owe the bank back mortgage payments," Louis explained. "If they qualify, they can enter the race wit'out payin' the entrance fee. Otherwise, you just cough up the cash up front and you're in."

Nathan nodded. It was a smart setup. Deschaines could monitor the racers during the qualifying runs, fix the odds, and make a bundle when his ringers inevitably won the race. He'd have to lose a race now and then, just to keep the locals interested, but if Deschaines played it smart, Nathan reasoned, then he could clean up on the big day.

He turned his attention back to the racecourse, as the Ravens screamed back into view. The lead Raven broke off

and opened fire on a cherry-red Brigand. The Brigand turned
to evade . . . and banked right into a hail of rockets from the
other Ravens.

"Who are those guys?" Nathan asked.

"Deschaines' personal pilots . . . sky mercs, most of 'em,"
Tug said. "Call themselves *Les Fauçons du Marai*—the
Hawks of the Swamp."

"They're good."

"They're not so tough," Tug grumbled.

Nathan ignored Tug's bravado and studied their flying.

The Fortune Hunters had encountered all sorts of opponents in the skies over North America: aviation security hired
guns, rival pirates, and local militias. The only outfit Nathan had ever fought against that could hold a candle to Deschaines' pilots was the Flying Witch Squadron.

The Flying Witch Squadron was a crew of air mercs that
operated along the eastern seaboard. Nathan had tangled with
them over Dixie during an attempt to heist a cargo zep. The
Witches had earned Zachary's grudging respect; they were a
crafty bunch and the Fortune Hunters barely managed to
boost the airship and escape.

Unlike the Flying Witch Squadron—which was cunning,
sneaky, and unpredictable in combat—Deschaines' mercenaries were killers, plain and simple.

Finally, the blue-and-silver Ravens circled the landing
strip and touched down, one after the other. The other local
fliers who made it through the qualifying run—perhaps a
half-dozen planes all told—followed.

"Let's go check out the competition," Nathan said.

"It's your funeral, *mon ami,*" Thibodeaux said. "Lead on."

The pirates made their way to the landing field. As Nathan
approached the lead Raven, her pilot clambered down from
the cockpit.

"You again?" the pilot said. "I'm starting to see as much of
you in person as I do in the newsreels, Zachary."

Nathan gave the pilot an insincere smile. "Hello, Bertrand.
Nice bird."

Bertrand Deschaines stripped off his leather helmet and

goggles. The rest of Deschaines' squadron joined Bertrand. Among them, Nathan recognized the thugs who had almost gunned Tug down in The Flyin' Horses. The whole crew looked ready for a fight.

Bertrand glanced around at Nathan's companions and smirked. "Out slumming, Zachary? I thought the Fortune Hunters had a reputation for class . . . yet here you are, associating with common thugs." He shot a pointed look at Tug. "*Very* common thugs."

Nathan calmly surveyed Deschaines' men. "Dime-a-dozen thugs, from the looks of it," he snorted. "Seriously, Bertrand, your daddy can afford better than these clowns."

Behind Bertrand, one of the thugs bristled and balled his fists. Nathan recognized him—the red-haired fireplug from the encounter in the bar. "Who you calling 'dime-a-dozen,' you cheap little punk?"

Nathan met the man's gaze and held his ground. "Run along, little man," he said. "I'm talking to the organ grinder, not the monkey."

The Cajuns chuckled, and Fireplug's face reddened.

Without warning, the smaller man swung a vicious uppercut. His fist crunched into Nathan's jaw. Zachary saw stars.

He rolled to his left and narrowly avoided a brutal kick to the head. He grabbed the smaller man's leg and twisted it roughly. Fireplug hit the ground.

Nathan sprang to his feet, dragged Fireplug up by the collar of his flight jacket.

They traded body blows, neither man giving ground. Zachary winced as a hard left slammed into his kidney. He countered with a quick jab to Fireplug's ribs.

The stocky man stumbled backward, stunned by the blow. His partners caught him before he fell again.

Nathan glared at Bertrand and wiped a trickle of blood from his lip. "You should teach that little puppy some manners, Bertrand," he said, "before I swat him with a rolled-up newspaper."

"I'll keep that in mind," Bertrand said. He nodded at his

men—who drew pistols. Nathan cursed; the "no weapons" policy at the gate apparently didn't apply to Deschaines' own racers.

Deschaines turned to Fireplug. "Benny," he said, his voice thick with anger, "kill that bastard."

"With pleasure."

Before he could fire, Thibodeaux cleared his throat. "Perhaps you should reconsider, Monsieur Deschaines."

Zachary looked at Louis—who brandished a small pistol, aimed directly at Bertrand. The rest of the Cajuns produced a variety of concealed weapons, like magicians conjuring rabbits. Louis gave Zachary a mischievous wink.

Nathan grinned back. "I'm not sure I want to know where you hid that thing," he muttered.

He faced Bertrand. "It's your move, Deschaines."

Bertrand's face darkened with anger. For a moment, Zachary was convinced he'd misread Deschaines; he had thought Bertrand a coward at heart . . . but the man looked mad enough to start a shoot-out, regardless of the consequences.

Before Bertrand could order his men to fire, a rasping, gravel-laden voice spoke up from behind them. "What the hell is going on here? You men put those damn things away, right now."

5: R.S.V.P. . . . Or Else

"**Y**ou heard me. Put those guns away this *instant*."

Bertrand's expression shifted from anger to embarrassment. "Yes, Papa," he said. The gunmen holstered their pistols.

Henri Deschaines was tall—a full head taller than Nathan—and gaunt. He wore an immaculate white linen suit and matching panama hat. A cornflower blue tie—silk, naturally—matched the handkerchief that neatly adorned his breast pocket. A gold watch chain decorated his vest, and he clutched a sturdy, well-polished mahogany cane in his right hand.

He marched directly between Bertrand and Nathan and glared at both young men. His face was painfully thin, almost cadaverous. His body was frail, and he walked with a limp, but a fearsome vitality shone from his eyes, as if Henri Deschaines could stave off the ravages of age purely through the force of his will.

"Bertrand," he croaked in his strange, rasping voice, "what is the meaning of this?"

"Papa . . . I'm sorry, sir," Bertrand stammered, "it's just that these . . . men were trying to start trouble."

Henri shot the Cajuns an angry look. His gaze fixed on Tug. "Boates. I might have known. "

"Look here, Deschaines—you can't—"

"I can. And I just did, as a matter of fact. Now shut up."

Bertrand's gunmen chuckled, and Tug's face went red.

Henri turned to scowl at his men. "I fail to see what you all find so amusing."

The gunmen paled and fell silent.

"All of you better get this through your heads." He gripped the cane tightly and leaned forward, glaring at each of his son's hired guns in turn. "There's too much at stake for this foolishness. If there are scores to be settled, do it *in the race*. Do I make myself clear?"

Henri faced Nathan and his companions. "The same goes for the rest of you. If you don't have the sand to enter the race, go sit in the cheap seats with the rest of the rubes."

Tug stepped forward. "I'll race," he growled through clenched teeth. "An' I reckon we'll see who's man enough, won't we, Bertrand?"

"Tug, you could be *twice* the man you are," Bertrand spat, "and you'd still be half the man I am."

Henri's expression softened into amusement at his son's words. "Now, now, *mon fils*," he said, his voice patronizing. "You're being quite unfair to young Boates."

He looked Tug up and down and added, "It's not as if the

little ruffian has enough money to actually *enter* the race. Isn't that right, boy?"

Before Tug could respond, Henri clapped his son on the back. "A pity, too. We could settle this business about Emmeline once and for all but Boates here didn't even try to qualify for the race."

The elder Deschaines gave Tug a sardonic smile. "Makes me wonder what all the fuss is about, Mr. Boates," he said. "If you were serious about winning young Emmeline's hand, I'm surprised you weren't here for the qualifying run." He placed a condescending hand on Tug's shoulder. "I'm beginning to doubt your sincerity, boy."

Tug shrugged the hand from his shoulder.

"Then let him in the race, Papa," Bertrand said. "Let him in, and we'll finish it." Bertrand's men nodded in agreement.

Henri cocked his head, as if considering the idea, then waved his hand dismissively. "I can't fault your generosity, son," he chuckled, "but that would be *against the rules*. Can't be breaking the rules, now, can we?"

He looked Tug square in the eye and added, "Either you make it through the qualifying race, or you pay the entry fee. No exceptions."

Nathan stepped forward. From his jacket he drew a bundle of franc notes, wrapped in a paper band, and tossed them on the ground in front of Henri.

"I'll cover Tug's entry fee," he announced.

Henri Deschaines' eyes widened with surprise. He glanced down at the money on the damp ground, then stepped past it and peered curiously at Nathan. He was easily a foot taller than the pirate, and was accustomed to using his height and appearance to intimidate people—but Zachary met his gaze, his face impassive.

"And who might you be?" Deschaines asked.

"Nathan Zachary."

A thin smile crossed Deschaines' sunken features. "Ah, yes, Mr. Zachary, the illustrious 'Fortune Hunter.' My son mentioned that you'd been of some . . . assistance when dear Emmeline had wandered into town."

"I guess you could say that." Nathan shrugged. "Mostly, I just kept Tug from kicking your son's teeth in."

Henri chuckled. "Well, I'm sure my son appreciated the 'help.' " He nodded at Thibodeaux and the Cajuns. "I had no idea you'd joined up with the local undesirables."

"I haven't."

"Then, may I ask, what is your interest in this matter, sir?"

"Simple," Nathan replied. "I'm interested in *money* . . . and I know a sure thing when I see it."

Henri gave Nathan a curious look. "I've been known to indulge in a wager now and again, sir," he countered, "but I'm damned if I can figure how Boates is a 'sure thing.' "

Zachary shrugged. "I've seen your boys in action. They're adequate . . . for backwater bush pilots."

Henri flushed with anger, but quickly regained his composure. "I think you underestimate them, Mr. Zachary. My men are the best that money can buy."

"Your men are straight from Central Casting, Mr. Deschaines." Nathan pointed at the stocky gunman, Benny. "If a guy like *that* is one of your best, then backing Tug is money in the bank."

Benny stepped forward, his hand resting on the butt of his pistol. "You just keep on riding me, Zachary," he hissed, "and I swear to God I'll plug you where you stand."

Henri considered for a moment, then waved Benny back. "Benny raises a good point, Mr. Zachary," he said. "You seem to run your mouth rather recklessly."

Nathan ignored the rebuke. "We're not talking about me. We're talking about Tug. Is he in, or not?"

"Very well, sir. I'm happy to take your money." He nodded at Benny. "Collect Boates' entry fee, Benny."

Benny gritted his teeth, then bent over to pick up the packet of bills. It was caked with mud.

"It's all there: two thousand francs," Nathan said. "*You'd* better count it though, Mr. Deschaines." He smirked down at Benny. "Leave the job to a mutt like Benny, and you could lose your shirt."

Benny scowled up at Nathan, hatred on his face.

"I can see you do indeed like to gamble, Mr. Zachary," Henri said with a trace of amusement.

"I may bet, Mr. Deschaines . . . but I never gamble. Like I said, I'm interested in money. People who gamble eventually lose."

Henri nodded. *"Vraiment."*

Deschaines leaned close to Bertrand, and there was a whispered exchange, but Nathan couldn't make out what the father and son were discussing. Whatever it was, Bertrand didn't look happy about it.

Finally, Henri turned back to face Nathan. "I would be honored to host you for supper, Mr. Zachary," he said. "Why don't you join me at my home this evening? Say, seven o'clock? Perhaps there's some business we can discuss."

"Seven o'clock," Nathan agreed. "I'll be there."

Thibodeaux nudged Nathan. " 'ave you lost your mind?" he whispered.

"Relax. It's just dinner," Nathan replied, sotto voce. "I'll check the place out before I go in, and if it looks like a trap, I'll scram. No problem."

"Oh, Mr. Zachary?" Henri's rasp cut short the pirates' whispered exchange. "Where are my manners? My estate can be very difficult to find, especially after dark."

"I'll manage."

"Nonsense." Henri gave Nathan a cold smile. "Bertrand and Benny will make sure you don't get lost. Follow them, please."

Benny balled his meaty fist. "That's right, Zachary," he quipped. "I wouldn't want you to wind up missing . . . or worse."

6: Southern Hospitality

"**G**et movin', big shot." Benny gave Nathan a shove toward the waiting Packard. "The boss don't like to be kept waiting."

Zachary rolled his shoulders, stiff from the hour-long autogyro flight out of the swamps. "You need to work on your patter, Benny. It's getting a little stale."

"You just keep on crackin' wise, pirate," Benny shot back. "We'll see who laughs last."

Nathan looked around the private landing field. It was small but tidy and well maintained. He was impressed; between the standard hangar fees and the de rigueur protection money the local hoods undoubtedly charged, Deschaines probably dropped a bundle just to keep this place clean and secure.

To the northeast Zachary could see the sweeping beams of the searchlights that ringed Pontchartrain Aerodrome. In the distance, the ghostly silhouettes of low-flying aircraft drifted beneath the ever-present cloud cover.

Benny pushed Nathan into the Packard's backseat and slid in next to him. A second gunman took the front passenger seat.

Benny drew a revolver from his overcoat and pointed it at Nathan's ribs. "Just in case you get any funny ideas, comedian."

Zachary ignored Benny and leaned back against the leather seat. The Packard sped through the outskirts of New Orleans, then out of town—into the backwater. The cityscape had given way to woodsy swampland filled with droopy willows and kudzu.

The sunlight began to fade as the Packard turned off the road. Dirt and rock crunched beneath the car's tires as the driver guided the Packard down a narrow lane. The path led deeper into the thick, dank swampland. Zachary caught a glimpse of a gator as it splashed through the stagnant water. The Packard rounded a curve, then headed down a straight piece of road that afforded a panoramic view of the property.

For a wealthy man, Deschaines has a terrible eye for real estate, Nathan thought.

At the end of the road stood a large white plantation house. It displayed a picture-perfect antebellum facade, complete with wrought-iron railings, high French windows, and a spacious verandah.

The car rolled to a stop in front of the house, and Henri Deschaines stepped out to greet them. He had dressed for company—a clean white suit, an expensive silk handkerchief, and a cane, this time with a gold pommel. Deschaines' welcoming smile did little to soften his gaunt, skeletal features.

Zachary stepped out of the car and extended his hand to Deschaines.

Deschaines ignored the hand and nodded at the gunmen.

Benny grabbed Nathan's extended arm and shoved him against the hood of the Packard. The other gunmen took up positions nearby as Benny patted down Nathan's coat and pants.

Nathan looked over his shoulder at Deschaines. "You don't get a lot of repeat guests, do you?"

"Most 'guests' aren't in any condition to come back," Benny whispered in Nathan's ear. "Especially the visitors with smart mouths."

"I hope you'll pardon my lack of traditional southern hospitality, Mr. Zachary," Deschaines said. "I need to assure myself that you haven't had any unfortunate lapses in judgment."

"He's clean," Benny announced. He eased Nathan off the hood of the car. "Too bad."

Nathan straightened his collar and gave Benny a sour look. "I didn't bother to pack anything, Mr. Deschaines. I assumed Bertrand and his sidekick here would be able to protect me."

Deschaines gave a short laugh—a rasping croak. "One can never be too careful; that's my motto. In any event, welcome to my home, Mr. Zachary."

He extended a thin hand and Nathan shook it. He managed to hide his revulsion at Deschaines' clammy, cold grip.

Benny opened the door for them and Deschaines gestured for Zachary to enter. Based on Deschaines' fancy clothes and apparent wealth, Nathan expected the interior of the house to be ostentatious. He stepped into the foyer—

—and stifled a gasp of surprise.

The stark white room was almost completely bare. The few pieces of furniture—a settee, a pair of chairs—were draped in white cloth, like shrouds. The whole place felt cold and empty.

Deschaines ignored Nathan's puzzlement and strode through the foyer. "I do appreciate you coming so far out of your way for a visit, Mr. Zachary," he said. "I must apologize for the long trip. I prefer the quiet and solitude out here to the tiresome bustle of the city."

He paused, his thin smile devoid of warmth or humor. "Out here," he added, "there's no one to disturb us."

The veiled threat was obvious. Nathan had no doubt that those who "disturbed" Henri Deschaines ended up as gator food.

Deschaines looked around and sighed. "With the upcoming nuptials, I suppose I should do something to dress up the place. We wouldn't want Miss Emmeline getting married in anything less than splendor, would we, son?"

Nathan realized that Deschaines wasn't talking to him. The old man was looking past his guest to the base of a winding staircase. At the foot of the stairs stood Bertrand, dressed for dinner. Emmeline was at his side, wearing a striking peach-colored dress that fitted her like a silken skin. Nathan's mouth tightened involuntarily at the sight of her on Bertrand's arm. The two of them even *near* each other was just plain wrong, in every possible way.

"No, we wouldn't, Papa," the younger Deschaines said. He gritted his teeth and glared back at Zachary.

"Now, now, Bertrand. Mr. Zachary is our guest." He smirked. "*Ma cherie,* I believe you and Mr. Zachary have already met? Ah, but never mind—it was hardly a proper introduction. Sir, allow me to present my ward, Mademoiselle Emmeline-Marie Fonteneau. My dear, this is Nathan Zachary—the colorful fellow who's been in all the papers lately."

Zachary gave Bertrand a sly look, then kissed the girl's outstretched hand. Bertrand clenched his fists but said nothing.

Emmeline withdrew her hand graciously and used her momentary freedom to step away from Bertrand and take Henri's arm. "Please, Uncle Henri, can we go in to dinner now?" Her voice was soft but brittle—Nathan could see the girl was nervous as hell. He couldn't blame her—living in an empty house in the middle of a swamp would unnerve anyone.

Henri wrapped his thin arm around hers and patted her hand with his bony fingers. "Propriety would suggest some conversation before dinner, but I think you may be right. It might be best if we gave the boys something to do with their hands right away."

The dining room was spacious, with more of the high French windows that provided a view of the mansion's gardens—or what would be the gardens if they had been tended. The landscaping consisted mostly of the omnipresent kudzu.

The men waited while Bertrand seated Emmeline to Henri's right; then Benny helped Deschaines ease the high-backed chair up to the table. Nathan nodded with approval; the old man may not spend a lot on furniture, but he'd definitely laid out more than a few francs for the table setting. It was all expensive and in perfect taste, including a crystal decanter filled with a rich amber liquid that Zachary hoped was bourbon.

The waiters were by now familiar; they were the hired guns Zachary had met in The Flyin' Horses. The taller one was muscular and well built, and without his gray topcoat, the revolver in his belt was clearly visible. Benny took up his position behind Henri Deschaines' chair like a praetorian guard.

Sure enough, the amber liquid was bourbon—smoky, warm, and incredibly smooth. It was a taste Zachary would have recognized blindfolded: fourteen-year-old Black Knight, the really good stuff.

Nathan attempted some idle chatter, but with Emmeline's nervousness and Bertrand's hostility, the mood settled into one of sullen discomfort. Henri quietly sipped his bourbon and watched. Despite the food—a fabulous crab dish, spicy and hot—the atmosphere was charged with tension. Finally, Henri spoke into one of the lapses in conversation. "So, Mr. Zachary, your reputation has preceded you, of course."

Deschaines had not eaten much of the meal so far, apparently content with the Black Knight. "So, I have to ask myself, why would a well-known—dare I say it? *infamous*—pirate take such a keen interest in my affairs?"

Nathan shrugged. "Like I said, I take an interest wherever there's money to be made."

Deschaines chuckled—a raspy croak that sounded painful and unhealthy. "Money? Not on the scale that should interest such a notorious Fortune Hunter." He smiled, pleased at his play on words. The old man gave a convincing performance as an affable host, but his eyes held no warmth.

Nathan gave a noncommittal shrug and swallowed another gulp of the exquisite bourbon. "I suppose I must see opportunities that you don't." He flicked his eyes toward Emmeline and was rewarded with a flush of anger from Bernard. Benny started to move toward Zachary, but stopped at Henri's raised hand.

"Touché, Mr. Zachary. Indeed opportunities are sometimes found in the least likely places. Sometimes, in fact, right under one's nose. But you should be careful not to poke that nose where it isn't wanted, or it could get cut off."

"I once read about a scientist with a golden nose—he lost his own in a duel."

"If I may offer unsolicited fashion advice, I don't believe it would suit you."

"You never know. I may just start a trend."

The arrival of dessert—cherries jubilee—stilled the conversation yet again. Henri barely touched his food. He shifted slightly in his chair, as if he were in severe pain.

"Uncle Henri, are you all right? Do you need to go for a little walk?" Despite the circumstances, Emmeline appeared to be genuinely concerned for her guardian's well-being. No wonder Tug was so crazy about her.

"Perhaps I do," he admitted. He struggled to his feet, but waved off Bertrand's assistance. "Mr. Zachary, join me in the library."

When they reached the foyer, Emmeline stopped. "If you don't mind, gentlemen, I believe I will retire for the evening.

Mr. Zachary, it was a pleasure to see you again." She extended her hand; as he bent over to kiss it, he felt a slight pressure from her fingers. A small slip of paper slipped into his
palm. She looked him in the eye and added, "I do hope we see
you here again."

Nathan surreptitiously slipped the note into his pocket
and followed Henri, Bertrand, and their retainers into the library. The room was warm and cozy, and a fire burned in the
fireplace. The warmth from the fire seemed excessive—it
wasn't a particularly cold evening. Still, the air was damp
and Zachary figured that had to be hard on the old man's
joints. No one had mentioned anything, but from the way
Deschaines looked—and the rasping quality of his voice—
it was pretty clear that his health had been poor for quite
some time.

Once they were seated, Benny poured another round of
bourbon, then took up his accustomed watchdog position behind the old man. Henri sipped the drink, then faced Nathan.
His air of congeniality dropped away. In its place was the
stern, harsh man who had thundered at his men during the
scuffle at the racecourse.

"I don't know what your angle is, Mr. Zachary, but I'm
sure you have one. Men like you always do, and you couldn't
have achieved the reputation you currently enjoy without more
than a passing ability to deceive. Mind you, I respect a man
who looks out for himself. Frankly, I probably wouldn't trust
you if you didn't have some scheme in the works." He leaned
across the table. "I can tolerate many things, *mon ami,* but I
have no patience for stupidity.

"So, now that you know my position, perhaps we could
dispense with the pleasantries and put our cards on the
table—before someone meets an unfortunate end."

Nathan swallowed his bourbon and nodded. "All right, Mr.
Deschaines. But first," Zachary paused and looked pointedly
at Benny, "I don't make a habit of talking business in front of
the hired help. Especially a cheap hood like Benny."

Benny's face reddened with anger. He looked ready to explode. The level of tension in the room increased, and for a

moment, it looked like Benny was going to start shooting, regardless of the consequences.

Henri gave another wheezing chuckle. "You do like to live dangerously, don't you?" he said. "You should be careful . . . one of these days you might overplay your hand." He considered Nathan for a moment, then turned to Benny and added, "Benny, please wait outside."

"What?" Benny exploded. His hand rested on the butt of his gun. "Boss, *no one* gives me this kinda lip and gets away with it."

Henri flicked his wrist, and the tip of his cane rapped painfully against Benny's knuckles. "You're still new here, Benny," he thundered, "so you better get this through your head: You shoot when *I* tell you to shoot. Now get out of here."

Bertrand wasn't happy about the command either. "Papa! Maybe Benny's right—"

Deschaines waved him into silence. Benny walked to the door and exited without looking back. Nathan saw that the man's shoulders quaked with anger.

Good, he thought.

Nathan raised his glass to his host. "Here's to the possibility of a mutually beneficial business relationship."

"Ah, yes, business. That is the important thing, isn't it? Life without money can be tedious."

"I couldn't agree more. And I know that there's money to be had from this little venture of yours. Quite a setup, fixing the race."

The older Creole leaned forward sharply. "And what do you know about that?"

Zachary smiled and took another sip of his drink. "Don't worry—no one in your operation ratted you out. Like you, I'm not stupid. I listen; I watch."

Nathan stood and paced around the room. "You and I both know that my information, my contacts, and my guns, could be an asset in a number of ways. Especially for someone who has, shall we say, political aspirations."

Bertrand swore. "Father, don't trust this *cochon*—"

Henri silenced his son with a slashing gesture. "I appreciate your concern, *mon fils,*" he hissed, "but I'm quite capable of managing my own affairs."

He locked eyes with Nathan. "I would prefer that we confine our conversation to the race, Mr. Zachary. The other matter is not up for discussion."

Nathan nodded. "Very well. The way I figure it, you've got high-priced mercenaries flying as ringers, and you've used the qualifying rounds to control which locals make it into the race."

Deschaines nodded. "Go on."

"You stand to make a grand or so just in attendance fees," Zachary continued. "Not enough to cover the twenty-grand prize. Which means, you're conning the bookies. If I had to guess, I'd say you've leaked information that will make the odds long—so when your boys win, you'll clean up on bets."

"Very good, Mr. Zachary," Deschaines said.

"What I can't figure out is what you gain from cleaning out the bookies. Aside from some quick cash, that is."

"There's more to it than that, of course," Deschaines said. "A number of locals took out sizable loans—from my bank, of course—to bet on a 'sure thing.' "

"Ah, I get it. So, when they lose their shirts and can't repay the loan, you move in and foreclose."

"In essence, yes."

"Of course, this means you need me, Mr. Deschaines," Nathan said. "Tug stands a good chance of winning—and right now, my backing is the only thing that'll get him in the race."

Deschaines' poker face slipped into annoyance for a moment. "Boates is a nuisance," he said, "but against my men, he hasn't got a prayer." Henri painfully stood. "Come with me. I have something to show you, Mr. Zachary."

As Bertrand, Deschaines, and Zachary entered the hallway, Benny fell in step behind them. They walked out the door and toward the Packard. It seemed like a rather abrupt ending to the evening until Deschaines got in with them. He turned his head around slightly from the front seat to chat. "I think you'll find what I'm going to show you quite interesting, Mr. Zachary." With that, he turned back around and said, "Take us to the hangar, *s'il vous plaît.*"

The hangar was a few minutes' drive away from the house. It was a large building—big enough to house the eight M210 Ravens neatly lined up beneath its spacious dome. A handful of men worked in the hangar. They looked like typical mercenaries: grim jawed, hard eyed, and intensely focused.

The look inside the hangar was brief, but told Zachary what Deschaines had wanted him to know—the Ravens were in perfect condition and armed to the teeth—each plane now carried six .60-caliber cannons and a full load of rockets.

"As you can see, Mr. Zachary," Henri said, "we have more than enough firepower to handle one little swamp bandit."

Nathan smiled. "Maybe. But he's still a wild card. That means you're not wagering . . . you're *gambling.*"

Henri winced, and Nathan realized he'd hit a nerve. Henri Deschaines didn't just want to win—he *had* to win. The act of winning, by any means, was what mattered most to him.

Perfect.

"All right," Zachary said, "here's my proposition: I make sure Tug never flies in the race—and that he stays the hell away from Emmeline. Would that, and my silence about fixing the race, be worth twenty percent?"

Deschaines looked at Nathan thoughtfully, then shrugged. "I could assure your silence right now, sir," he said.

A chill crept up Nathan's spine. He had no doubt that Deschaines would order his death on the spot. If the appeal to his greed—the assurance of victory—didn't work . . .

"Still," Henri continued, "you make a good point about Tug and I suppose if you were to vanish into the swamp, I'd have to deal with that tiresome Cajun, Thibodeaux."

He made an exaggerated show of checking his pocket watch. *"Mon dieu,"* he exclaimed, "it must be later than I thought! What a thoughtless host I am. Pierre—you and Benny take Mr. Zachary back to town."

He clicked shut the pocket watch and placed it back in his

vest. "Mr. Zachary, it has been illuminating to get to know the man behind the mask, as it were. I need a little time to consider your proposition. Until then, I must ask that our conversation remain strictly between us."

With that, Benny escorted Deschaines into the house, then returned to the car and took his position in the backseat, next to Nathan.

As the Packard drove through the darkness, Nathan thought about the dinner and the conversation. It was difficult to gauge whether Deschaines believed him, or was just playing with him. One thing was clear from their conversation: Dealing with Deschaines was a chess game—played in blood.

At least he'd gotten inside the hangar, so he knew what kind of competition Tug would encounter in the race. That was worth something.

The car stopped in front of The Flyin' Horses. He opened the door and stepped out onto the street.

Zachary never saw the blow coming. He felt a sharp pain in the back of his head. His vision blurred; then everything went black.

His last conscious thought echoed in the darkness:
Damn it. Looks like Henri turned down my offer. . .

7: Family History

"**Z**achary . . . you are one lucky son of a bitch."

Nathan was only dimly aware of Thibodeaux's remark. Everything was black; for a fleeting moment, Zachary feared he had been blinded somehow. He struggled to remember what happened—it had to be a crash, or an accident, or—

". . . Or that little creep, Benny," he muttered. He could recall stepping from Deschaines' fancy Packard, and then *bang!* Someone turned out the lights. Zachary's head swam, but the darkness that clouded his mind began to recede. He risked opening his eyes. The light was too bright. Everything looked blurry, like an out-of-focus photograph: grainy and surreal.

He took a deep breath and shook his head to clear his blurred vision.

Big mistake. A wave of vertigo and nausea crashed into him like a freight train. He groaned.

"Right. Lucky." His stomach churned. "Just let me die, already."

Pain arced through his temples and then—like a miracle—began to subside. Something warm and soft rested gently on his forehead. Maybe he wasn't going to die after all.

Too bad, he thought. *Right now, death would be an improvement.*

"Hush now, the both of you." A woman's voice—surprisingly deep and soothing—washed over Nathan. "The boy needs to rest a spell."

Zachary risked opening his eyes again. The light was still too bright, but this time, no one jabbed knitting needles into his skull.

He was in a small dingy room. Boxes and crates were stacked in one corner. He lay on a small cot—too small, in fact. His feet hung off the end.

A woman sat next to the cot. Her appearance would have been intimidating and stern, were it not for the humor and wisdom in her sparkling black eyes. She was tall, with austere, regal features. Her skin was impossibly dark. Large gold hoops adorned her ears, and a heavy gold cross hung from a chain around her neck. She rested a maternal hand on his forehead.

She was older than Nathan, but—aside from a strand or two of gray hair and a fine network of lines at the corners of her eyes—her age was almost impossible to pin down.

"Where am I?" Nathan said, his voice hoarse.

"Back room of The Flyin' Horses," Thibodeaux said. The Cajuns' leader sat on a rickety chair in the small room, facing the cot. "This fine lady is *Maman* Léonie—she owns the joint."

"A pleasure, ma'am," Nathan said. He attempted to sit up.

Maman Léonie smiled and nodded slightly—then gently halted Nathan's attempt to right himself. "You just lie back, sweet. You have a nasty knot on dat pretty head."

"Most people who go inside chez Deschaines, they get a one-way trip into the swamp," Thibodeaux added. "Like I said—you pretty lucky, *mon ami*."

"The evening wasn't a total waste. Aside from a decent meal, I got a good look at Deschaines' place . . . and his men." Nathan closed his eyes as the throbbing in his head spiked. "They're an unpleasant bunch. Especially that creep, Benny."

" 'E's no local boy," Thibodeaux said. " 'E just popped up a few months back. S'posed to be some kind of mercenary."

"Figures. Deschaines' fliers are all hired guns, except for that cold-fish kid of his." Nathan rubbed the bump on the back of his head. It ached to the touch. "Plus, he's got a hangar full of Ravens—all armed to the teeth, naturally. That's a lot of firepower."

"So?"

"So, Deschaines is up to more than fixing a backwater air race." Nathan opened his eyes. The room wasn't spinning quite so fast now. He sat up. "He's using the race to fund something else . . . something big."

"Shh, *mon fils*, *soit tranquil*," *Maman* Léonie said, her voice calm and soothing. "You wan' to be careful. You fool 'bout too much, an' you'll end up regrettin' it, I think."

She reminded Nathan of his gran'mama, a Gypsy woman with a reputation for witchery. Though he'd left his heritage long behind him, he felt a chill run up his spine. Perhaps *Maman* Léonie was a *mamba*, a priestess of voodoo. They were not to be trifled with, these voodoo women.

"Eh, *Maman,* you worry too much. " Louis laughed. "This boy's got luck to spare."

The Creole woman gave Louis a cryptic smile and took Nathan's hand. She turned it over and ran her red-lacquered fingernail along his palm. Her brow furrowed as she looked at his hand and then into his green eyes. She folded his hand onto his chest and patted it gently. "Dis Gypsy boy . . . he make his own luck, and dat for certain."

Thibodeaux chuckled. "You got a pretty big clout on the 'ead, so I'm hopin' you haven't used up all your Gypsy luck. We gonna need it."

"This?" Nathan pointed at the lump on his skull. "This is nothing. Believe me, I've been through worse. But we've got work to do."

"You gonna be okay for now, Gypsy boy," *Maman* Léonie said. "But you an' Louis, you gettin' in deep wit' somethin' *très dangereuse*." She paused. "You both wash up an' come out front. I get you some coffee an' a little something to eat. There're t'in's you need to know 'bout Henri Deschaines."

She stood up and placed her hand on Zachary's head, as if in a brief benediction, and then left through the door to the kitchen. Nathan grimaced—the headache was bad enough. Another cup of chicory-laced coffee made his stomach churn.

He remembered the slip of paper that Emmeline had passed him during the dinner at Deschaines' estate. His flight jacket was tossed over one of the crates in the storeroom. He checked the pocket and was relieved to find the scrap still in his pocket.

He unfolded the paper. It read,

> MR. ZACHARY:
> PLEASE BE CAREFUL. THEY DON T TRUST YOU. SEND
> TOMMY MY LOVE.

"Now you tell me," he muttered.

Tug was a lucky man, all right. Emmeline was honest, kind, and brave as hell. It took some real grit to pass this note right in front of her guardian, her fiancé, and a pair of gunmen.

He put the note back in his pocket and made his way to the kitchen.

Once *Maman* Léonie was satisfied that Nathan and Louis had full cups and full plates, the proprietress of the speakeasy launched into her tale.

"Henri Deschaines claims to be from New Orleans—dat his family been in dese parts since forever." She scowled. "It's all a lie. He came to town years ago, broke an' tryin' to get a business off de ground, wit' no luck.

"But he's smart, Henri is, so he finds himself a local man—Guillaume Fonteneau. He's not so smart, Guillaume, but he's got some money, some political connections. Henri becomes his friend . . . an' soon, dey become partners.

"Henri ran de business—Guillaume was jus' a figurehead. Dey prospered. Soon, dey got nice cars, nice homes . . . an' nice wives.

"Henri, he married a girl, Virginia—from a good *famille*. She was a sweet girl, but weak. She passed away soon after Bertrand was born. Didn't matter none to Henri, though—he had a male heir, and dat's all dat mattered to him. Dat, an' money.

"Guillaume married, too. His wife was a nice local girl—an' soon enough, along came Miss Emmy.

"Guillaume busied himself wit' his new family, an' Henri, he stayed busy makin' money. And he always wants more: more power, more money, more prestige an' influence. Pretty soon, he's runnin' guns, stealin', blackmailin' . . . de works. All under de respectable front of de business.

"Guillaume figured it out, though. He threatened to end the partnership, an' to turn Henri in to de police. So, Henri arranged an 'accident.' Guillaume an' his wife died in a plane crash. Dere was never any proof—Henri paid off de judges an' de police—but mos' folks still think dat Deschaines sabotaged de plane."

"So, that's when Emmeline inherited her folks' money . . . and how she ended up under Deschaines' thumb," Nathan said.

She nodded. "Dis Henri, he's not a man. He's a demon wit' no heart. And de son, he no better dan his papa. Worse, even: he knows his papa is a bad man . . . an' he don' care."

Zachary studied the grounds in the bottom of his coffee cup, then set it down on the table. "All the more reason to take the bastards down a peg or two."

"Dis isn't jus' fun an' games," *Maman* Léonie said. "He

killed de girl's parents—an' he'll kill her, too. You go foolin' wit' Deschaines, you gonna need more dan Gypsy luck."

Maman Léonie grabbed Nathan's hand and turned the palm up. She pointed at his life line, her voice stern. "Dis ain't a guarantee, boy. If your luck runs out, Henri Deschaines' gonna kill *you*, too."

8: The Best Laid Schemes...

Nathan took a healthy slug of Louis' bourbon and leaned back in his chair. The back of his head still ached, but he felt a great deal better than he had in The Flyin' Horses. From outside, the muffled sounds of someone working on an airplane made his temples throb.

The trip back to the Cajuns' hideout had been without incident—nowhere near as harrowing as his first flight with Tug. Louis was a good pilot; unlike his young protégé, he didn't show off by pruning the treetops.

He looked at the clutter in Thibodeaux's makeshift office and grinned. "You ever considered hiring a maid?" he quipped. "It looks like a bomb went off in here."

Louis gave Zachary a sour look. "Very funny," he replied. "We can't all live in a zeppelin. Some of us still get our 'ands dirty."

Nathan chuckled and handed the bourbon bottle back to Louis. "Touché."

Thibodeaux snatched the bottle from Nathan's hand and set it down on his desk, hard enough to knock over a half-full coffee cup perched on top of a stack of navigational charts.

"Relax, Louis," Nathan said. "The way you're carrying on, you'd think *you* were the one who got clobbered by Deschaines' goons."

Thibodeaux paced around the tiny office, an uncharacteristic scowl on his face. "I ought to clobber you myself."

From outside, the metallic clanks and whirrs of airplane maintenance grew slightly louder. The pounding in his head aside, Nathan found the sounds familiar and comforting; the Cajuns' base might have been in the middle of a swamp, but the joint was always bustling.

"Next you'll try and tell me that gettin' smacked in the 'ead was all part of your 'big plan,'" Louis said.

"Well, not exactly," Nathan admitted.

"So now maybe you'll let me in on whatever this big scheme is?" Louis stood in front of Nathan, arms crossed. For a moment, he seemed distracted by more noise from outside—the clanging ring of metal hitting metal.

"I already told you the plan—the high points, leastways." Nathan sipped his bourbon.

"An' I still don' believe you, *mon ami*," Thibodeaux said. "You're always playin' some angle, an' I 'ave the feelin' you're playin' *me* for a sap." Thibodeaux started pacing again. "Now you've got ol' Henri on my back." He looked skyward, as if seeking strength from a higher power. " 'You'll get away clean, Louis,' you said. 'Don' worry,' you said—"

Nathan had to suppress a chuckle; Louis looked like he was about to have a heart attack. "Look," he said, "maybe I didn't tell you *every little detail* . . . but—"

Zachary was interrupted by a blast of noise. It sounded like a gunshot, loud enough to make both pirates jump.

"Mon Dieu!" Louis exclaimed. Nathan and Louis ran outside, and Thibodeaux grabbed the nearest Cajun—the big man with the obscene chest tattoo—by the arm. " 'Ey, Marcel," he demanded, "what the 'ell was that?"

The big pirate looked puzzled. "What're you talkin' about, boss?" he asked. "That old Doc fella's fixin' up the planes."

"What?" Louis exploded. "What 'ol' Doc fella'?"

Nathan cleared his throat. "He's talking about Doc Fassbiender, a friend of mine."

Louis rounded on Nathan. Zachary braced himself—Thibodeaux looked like he was going to take a swing at him. "Let me guess: another 'little detail' that you some'ow forgot to mention, *oui*?"

Nathan nodded.

"You know, *mon ami*," Louis seethed, "ever since you blew into town, my 'ideout's become Grand Central Station."

Before Nathan could respond, Louis wheeled around again to face Marcel. "An' you! Do we let jus' anyone wander in 'ere an' start foolin' wit' our birds?"

"Tug said it was okay—"

Louis shook his head in disgust. He waved Marcel away and scowled at Nathan. "Any other li'l surprises I should know about?"

"As a matter of fact, yes." Nathan clapped Louis on the shoulder. "Come take a look."

"I can 'ardly wait," Louis groused.

They walked across the pirate compound, toward the machine shop and repair hangar adjacent to the landing strip. Nathan felt a surge of excitement—his Devastator sat just outside the hangar.

The plane was painted a vibrant blood red, offset by curved black-and-white trim. Aside from the Fortune Hunters' insignia on the wings, the plane's sole decoration was nose art. Painted just below the cockpit was a scantily clad woman, nominally "dressed" as a fortune-teller. She gazed seductively from within a crystal ball. Beneath the picture were the words GYPSY MAGIC.

Nathan's wingman, Jack Mulligan, painted all of the Fortune Hunters' nose art. Most of the Fortune Hunters agreed that *Gypsy Magic* was Jack's best work. He had real talent, too; if Jack ever tired of piracy, he could make a mint as an artist. Once, after a skirmish with the Hollywood Knights, Jack was mortified to find a line of .30-caliber bullet holes had marred the fortune-teller's beauty.

"Nathan, you get her shot up again," Jack had griped, "and I'll sock you in the jaw."

Zachary's pleasure at the sight of his plane diminished as a second blast of noise erupted from the hangar—and blue-gray smoke puffed from his plane's exhaust. He smelled burning oil.

There was a torrent of German from beneath the plane, and

a thin, stooped figure stepped into view. He kicked the Devastator's front tire and cursed. "*Verdammt* piece of—"

"Hey, Doc," Nathan called out, "take it easy!"

Doc Fassbiender squinted through his soot-streaked goggles for a moment. His face brightened as he recognized Zachary. "Ah, Nathan, my boy," he exclaimed, delighted. "So good to see you!"

Fassbiender was older than Nathan—in his seventies, in fact. Despite his advancing age, he moved around with the vigor of a much younger man. He was thin, and a network of deep lines crisscrossed his face. An unruly shock of silver-gray hair formed a halo around Doc's head. Humor and mischief shone from his blue eyes.

Nathan had known Doc Fassbiender since the Great War. At sixteen, Zachary had lied about his age and joined the Escadrille Lafayette—pilots fighting the Kaiser in the Great War. What started out as youthful adventure ended in disaster after Nathan tangled with Heinrich Kisler—and lost. After Kisler shot Nathan's plane to pieces, the young pilot spent most of the war in a German prison camp.

Wilhelm Fassbiender was in that camp, too—the Kaiser took a dim view of the Doc's refusal to develop war machines for the military. Nathan, Doc, and a handful of Allies broke out of the camp and fled to Russia, then Europe, and finally to the States.

They'd lost touch with each other for several years, especially once Nathan had formed the Fortune Hunters and turned to piracy. A few months ago, the Fortune Hunters sprung the Doc—and his daughter, Ilse—from the Boeing "Special Projects Group." Doc and Ilse had perfected a new fuel-boost system that Boeing was wild about—and so were the Red Russians.

Everyone who knew about the engine—code-named the "Blue Streak"—was looking to abduct the Doc. Nathan and his gang got wind of the Fassbienders' predicament and rescued the old man and his daughter—and filched the nitro booster in the process. Doc had traveled with the Fortune Hunters ever since.

Nathan adored the old coot; sure, his crackpot "experiments" and "inventions" occasionally blew up, but he was a bona fide genius. Nathan could barely remember the man who had sired him; in many ways, Doc was the only father Nathan had ever known.

He gave the Doc a kindly pat on the arm. "So, how's my plane?"

Doc fiddled with his tool belt. "*Ach.* Temperamental, as always," he said, "but she should be ready soon."

"Good," Nathan replied.

He made introductions and was gratified that Louis seemed amused, even fascinated, by the wily old scientist. They traded pleasantries, and Thibodeaux finally relaxed a little.

For his part, Doc seemed pleased to show off his handiwork. He slid aside part of the Devastator's engine cowling and explained his nitro booster to Louis; the booster could increase the plane's top speed by as much as 150 miles per hour, in short bursts.

Louis looked skeptical. "You'll be lucky if the thin' doesn't explode, or jus' rip the wings off."

Fassbiender looked wounded. "It's not luck, my boy. It's *science.*"

"See, Louis?" Nathan interjected. "Nothing to worry about."

Louis snorted. "*Right.* Nothin' at all."

Damn. Thibodeaux still needed convincing . . . and without his help, this caper was sunk. "You win, Louis," Nathan said, "I'll tell you everything you want to know."

"And 'ow do I know you're tellin' the truth, *mon ami*?"

Nathan's face was a mask of innocence. "Hey, would *I* lie to you? Trust me."

Louis shook his head in exasperation but he led Nathan back to his office to talk.

Nathan did his best to ignore the roar of the engines and the noise of the crowd. Deschaines' big race was just under an hour away, but the racecourse was already filling with spectators, racers, and bookies.

Outside of Free Colorado pirate enclaves like Sky Haven and Boulder, Nathan had seldom encountered a more disreputable mob. Races in Manhattan or Los Angeles were generally cultured affairs; the spectators at Deschaines' race were more interested in bread and circuses.

Louis leaned close and pointed to the front of the vault building. "There's the big man himself," he said.

Henri Deschaines stood amid a contingent of his hired guns—including several cops. The gold tip of his cane reflected the thin, haze-dimmed sunlight.

"Let's go pay our respects," Nathan said. "Just remember to stick to the plan."

The pirates crossed the field. As they approached Deschaines, Nathan could see that the old man had a smile on his face. "Hello, Mr. Deschaines," he said.

The old man's smile faded at Nathan's greeting.

"Mr. Zachary." Deschaines nodded, his poker face firmly in place.

"It's almost post time," Nathan continued. "Have you considered my proposal?"

Deschaines expression darkened—he didn't like being confronted so directly, or so publicly. Nathan struggled to keep his own expression neutral; if Deschaines actually *agreed* to Nathan's "proposal," the whole plan was in jeopardy.

Finally, Henri favored Nathan with an alligator smile. "I have indeed," he said. "I regret that I must decline. Your reputation speaks for itself—you're a liar, a cheat, and a thief, if I might speak plainly. Assuming that my profits were intact at the end of the venture, I would then have to split them."

Nathan almost exhaled with relief, but caught himself in time. "I'm sorry to hear that." He reached inside his battered leather flight jacket and withdrew a wad of cash. "You've left me no choice but to back Tug—and to protect my investment, I'll be flying today, too."

Nathan studied Henri's face intently; this was a poker

game, and a good player always looked for his opponent's "tells"—physical tics that revealed much about the man behind the cards.

If Henri was surprised or upset by Nathan's decision to race, he kept it well hidden. Instead, he merely nodded and said, "Very well, sir."

Time to up the ante. Nathan handed over the cash.

Henri collected the stack of bills, and Nathan thought he caught a flicker of surprise in Deschaines' eyes. "You appear to have overpaid rather handsomely, Mr. Zachary," he said.

"Not exactly," Nathan replied. He pointed at Thibodeaux and added, "My friends will be flying, too."

This time, anger flashed across Deschaines' face—but only for a moment. He croaked with harsh, humorless laughter. "I am happy to accept your entry fees, gentlemen."

Deschaines counted the money, folded the bills, and then placed them in his pocket.

"Here are the race rules, Mr. Zachary," he said. "The winner is the pilot who completes five laps on the course in the shortest amount of time . . . either that, or he's the only one to cross the finish line. Is that clear, sir?"

"Crystal."

"Any racer whose plane is not ready to fly within five minutes of the starting gun forfeits his entry fee and is disqualified. Is that also clear, sir?"

"Yes," Nathan said.

"Then good luck to you, sir," Deschaines said. He turned to his men and added, "Come Sunday, I must remember to thank the good Lord for the heaven-sent parade of suckers he's seen fit to bless me with."

The gunmen laughed at their employer's joke—all except Benny, who stared at Nathan with blank, dead eyes.

It was time to prime the pump. Deschaines oozed confidence—now Nathan had to shake that confidence.

Zachary drew another stack of bills from his coat. "The only amateur I see here is you, Mr. Deschaines," he growled. "Perhaps you'd care to wager on the outcome of your little contest?"

"I'm always happy to part a fool from his money," he shot back.

"Very well. I've got five thousand francs that says Tug will cross the finish line before Bertrand."

"Five thousand francs," he said. "Done."

Perfect, Nathan thought. *He didn't even hesitate. Deschaines can't help himself—he* has *to take the bet.*

Deschaines opened his pocket watch. "By my reckoning, gentlemen, the race begins in forty-nine minutes. Good day." He clicked the watch shut, a clear dismissal.

As Nathan and Louis turned to leave, Benny stepped forward and blocked Nathan's path. "This time," he growled, "you're gonna get more than a tap on the head, Zachary."

9: The Starting Gun

Nathan tightened the shoulder harness and took a deep breath. He patted the plane's stained and worn instrument panel and tried to forget the butterflies in his stomach. It never failed: despite the countless tough spots he'd been in, he always got a case of nerves before flying into battle.

He nudged the throttle forward. The Devastator's engine growled in response, and the heavy fighter rolled into position on the starting line. He flexed his fingers, then resumed his light, steady grip on the control stick. Doc Fassbiender had worked his usual magic—the Devastator was in tip-top shape.

The big fighter, with its unusual biwing design, was far from state of the art; in fact, Hughes Aviation had stopped producing the Devastator years ago. Of course, the manufacturer hadn't counted on Doc Fassbiender either. Doc had gotten rid of the old Tornado engine in favor of a slick Rolls-Royce job. Even with the thick armor that Fassbiender had insisted on, Nathan's plane was surprisingly agile.

Of course, Nathan thought, a grim smile on his face, *that's not the only ace up this baby's sleeve.* He tapped a pressure gauge, bolted to the instrument panel just above the airspeed indicator. The needle twitched and then steadied. Doc's custom nitro booster was ready for action.

Zachary gave the instrument panel a final once-over, then—satisfied that everything was in order—looked over his right shoulder and surveyed the other racers awaiting the starting gun.

The Devastator sat near the center of the line of aircraft. Just off his starboard wing, Louis readied his green-and-purple Brigand for takeoff.

Nathan flicked on his radio and adjusted the frequency. "Hey Louis," he called out. "You think you could cook up a gaudier paint job for that bird?"

"Barbarian," Louis replied. "These are Mardi Gras colors . . . *lucky* colors."

"If you're lucky," Nathan chuckled, "no one'll shoot you just for flying something so hideous."

"Very funny. An' if you're lucky, I won' shoot you for talkin' me into this."

"Relax, Louis," Nathan said. "Think of the money."

"I am. I'm thinkin' I'm gonna 'ave the mos' expensive funeral in 'istory."

"Just stick to the plan, and everything'll be fine."

The midmorning sun burned away the mist and left the air moist and heavy. Though the last several days had been comparatively cool and rainy, today promised to be plenty warm. Nathan wiped a trickle of sweat from his forehead.

He turned his attention to the control tower. The tall, open-framed wooden structure marked the starting line position. Mounted on top of the tower were powerful speakers—the public-address system for the race's announcer.

In the distance, Nathan could see the bleachers, filled with cheering spectators. Unlike the previous day's visit, the stands were filled to capacity. He could faintly hear the roar of the crowd, despite the roar of aircraft engines.

"Two minutes! All racers, the race begins in two minutes!" The announcer's voice crackled through Nathan's radio headset. Ground crew mechanics finished last-second work on their planes and then sprinted off the field.

Zachary's unease faded away. In its place was a glacial calm. It didn't matter that he was about to fly against dozens of armed opponents. Now that he was once again behind the stick of his beloved Devastator, his fate was in his own hands.

The local fliers didn't look like much of a threat. Most of them were has-beens, with their best days long behind them—either that or rookies, desperate for a long-shot grab at the brass ring. When the shooting started, they'd do their best to stay the hell out of the way. Which left Nathan and the Cajuns against Deschaines' mercenaries.

That suited Nathan just fine.

A curse in static-shrouded French burst from the radio. "Nathan! I got a problem 'ere!"

Nathan twisted in his seat to look at Louis' Brigand. Smoke poured from the plane's engine cowling. There was a sudden grinding noise, and fire shot from Louis' engine.

Nathan keyed the radio. "Get out! Get out of there!" he yelled.

Louis threw open the canopy and struggled to loosen his shoulder straps. Fire and smoke billowed from the plane, followed by another metallic bang—this one much louder. A noxious black cloud swallowed Louis.

A dozen mechanics swarmed over the damaged Brigand. They doused the engine with fire extinguishers and pulled Louis from the cockpit. He was soot-streaked and filthy. From what Nathan could see, Louis was mad as hell, but unharmed.

The announcer's voice blared from the PA. "Ladies and gentlemen, we have a fire on the runway. There will be a short delay . . ."

Nathan slid back the canopy as Louis climbed on the Devastator's wing. "What the hell happened?" Zachary asked.

"You tell me," Louis said, his face grim. "Your Doc Fassbiender 'fixed up' my bird. Perhaps 'e's not the mechanic you think, *mon ami*."

"There isn't a machine on Earth the Doc can't fix," Nathan said. "This is something else. The only time I've seen an engine seize up like that is when I've hit it with a burst from my sixty cals."

"Which means?"

"Which means sabotage."

Louis met Nathan's stare. He threw his flight gloves on the ground in disgust. "Deschaines."

Nathan nodded. "Has to be. His guys are all over the place."

"Speak of the devil," Louis muttered, and nodded in the direction of the control tower.

Nathan followed Thibodeaux's gaze and spied Henri Deschaines. Deschaines cautiously picked his way across the field, accompanied by his assistant with the wire-rim glasses. As he approached Louis' Brigand he fanned away the smoke with his panama hat.

"Well, gentlemen," he said. "It would appear that Mr. Thibodeaux has been disqualified. I'll have my men tow this heap off the field . . . for a small fee, of course."

Louis jumped down from Nathan's plane and confronted Henri. "*Bonne chance* tryin' to collect that fee, Deschaines."

Henri held up his hands in a placating gesture. "Now, now, *mon ami*," he rasped. "You know the rules. If your plane isn't ready to fly when the race starts, you forfeit. It's out of my hands."

"The hell it is," Nathan snarled. "That plane was sabotaged."

A faint smile played across Deschaines' gaunt features. "*Sabotage* is such an ugly word, Mr. Zachary," he said, "and I'd hate to think that tone in your voice is directed at me, sir."

He turned and looked Louis up and down, and added, "I do not believe this was sabotage. More likely, it is the result of shoddy maintenance. Backwater hedge robbers are not known for being . . . fastidious." He shrugged. "In any event, Thibodeaux here is out of the race."

"Now just a minute—" Nathan growled. He reached to unfasten his shoulder harness.

"If you'd care to exit the cockpit and discuss this further, Mr. Zachary," Henri cut in, his eyes flat and hard, "I'll happily accept your forfeiture, as well."

A large flatbed truck trundled along the damp ground and took up position in front of the damaged Brigand. Mechanics chained the plane to the truck and began to tow it from the field. Louis gave his plane a forlorn look, then climbed back up on the Devastator's wing. "What do you think, *mon ami*? The race begins in a couple minutes."

"I think someone ought to knock that creep on his ass."

Louis chuckled and nodded. "*Oui*. But it'll 'urt 'im worse, I think, if someone takes 'is money, *non*?"

"You're right," Nathan sighed. He settled his flight goggles in place.

"You jus' be careful, Nathan," Louis said. "Ol' Henri's boys play rough."

"I'm always careful." Nathan gave Louis a lopsided grin. "But stick by the radio just in case."

Louis nodded. He latched the Devastator's canopy shut and dropped from the wing. He gave Nathan a jaunty salute and then jogged toward the bleachers.

The roar of the racers' engines deepened as race time neared. The noise was thunderous.

Seconds ticked by—then a checkered flag waved from the top of the control tower. The announcer's voice blared from the radio: "And they're off!"

Nathan jammed the throttle forward, and the Devastator leapt forward and climbed into the sky.

10: Aces or Better to Open

Thirty seconds into the first lap, everything went straight to Hell.

Like most air races, the race began once all the competitors were in the air; they flew in a circular pattern until the announcer called "Go." Nathan had a few moments to view the racecourse and the red balloons that marked the maximum allowed flight ceiling—about a thousand feet up. Anyone who strayed above the ceiling was instantly disqualified. It made Nathan feel like he was flying in a box.

The radio blared the "go" signal—and nearly every competitor opened fire.

Nathan sent the Devastator into a sharp portside turn as a rocket slashed at him from above. The rocket exploded in a deceptively delicate blossom of fire. He flinched as a piece of blackened, twisted metal embedded itself in the canopy beside his head.

He rolled out of the turn and pushed into an inverted dive. The ground rushed to greet him as the Devastator dropped like a stone. A scant few feet from the ground—he couldn't spare even a glance at the altimeter—he ruddered hard to starboard and righted the aircraft.

From above him, a trio of rockets splashed into the swamp and exploded. Mud sprayed across the Devastator's canopy. Nathan snarled and sent the Devastator into a wild corkscrew roll. The maneuver slowed him slightly, and the attacking fighter overshot. He hauled back on the stick and brought the Devastator's nose in line with the underside of the pursuing aircraft—an emerald-green F2 Bandit.

He fired a burst from his guns and laced the Bandit with .60-caliber magnesium rounds. The insidious bullets—coated with phosphorous—were soft enough to worm their way into a target's fuselage, and burned hot enough to melt through the metal for several minutes.

A moment later, he was rewarded by a puff of smoke and flame as the magnesium rounds found their mark—the Bandit's primary fuel line. The Bandit hit his flaps to shed speed. A moment later, the fighter slammed belly-down into the swamp in a plume of filthy, brackish water.

Nathan twisted around in his seat and searched for another target. The air was filled with fighters. Most of them were solo fliers—locals, from the looks of them. They hugged the terrain and struggled to reach the obstacles. Passing through an obstacle, rather than over it, shaved precious seconds off the racer's lap time.

The rest—the Cajuns, a handful of local fliers with more guts than sense, and Deschaines' squadron—dived into the twisting ballet of the dogfight. Cannon and rocket fire filled the air.

He switched the radio frequency and yelled: "Cajuns, form up on me! Tug, you're on my wing."

"Roger, Nathan," Tug acknowledged.

Tug's Fury slotted into position off Nathan's port wing. The rest of the Cajuns formed a V-formation, with Nathan's Devastator at the front.

"All right, Cajuns," Nathan barked, "ignore the other racers and concentrate on Deschaines' boys."

"Cajun Two to Lead: What if the other racers shoot at us?"

"Then break off and defend yourself, Two," Nathan replied. "All right, boys, let's get to work."

He spied Deschaines' squadron—they bore down on a string of local racers. The locals were low to the ground, approaching the makeshift merry-go-round—easy prey to an attack from above.

Nathan opened up the throttle, and his Devastator's Rolls-Royce engine roared. The Devastator swooped into position behind the trailing Raven. "Knock knock," he murmured, and squeezed the trigger.

His cannons blazed and spat a line of fire at the enemy fighter. The telltale sparks of bullet impacts pinged from the Raven's tail—but only for a moment.

The Raven's pilot was good, all right; the blue fighter rolled onto its port wing. Nathan's second burst missed; the streams of bullets passed the Raven on either side. Before Nathan could roll his own plane to bring his cannons in line with his target, the Raven pilot broke off. The blue fighter banked to starboard—and gave Nathan a peach of a shot at the Raven's spread-eagle profile.

He ruddered to the right to match the Raven's maneuver. His finger tightened on the trigger—

—until a burst of incoming fire riveted across his wing.

Directly ahead, the Raven's wingman screamed head-on at the Devastator. The wingman opened fire and bullets stitched a line across the Devastator's starboard wing.

Nathan cursed and again inverted the Devastator, just in time. The fighters skimmed past one another, belly to belly.

For a terrifying moment, Nathan was convinced that they'd trade paint—and auger into the swamp, locked in a twisted-steel embrace.

Deschaines' boys worked well as a team—that was for sure. The lead Raven had suckered him in and allowed his wingman to get into position. Which meant that, after narrowly escaping the wingman, the first Raven would be looking to finish Nathan off.

He rolled the Devastator, then kicked into a port climb. "Tug," he called out, "watch my back!"

Nathan craned his neck, looking for either Raven—and spotted them both, right on his tail. Another burst of cannon fire drummed along the Devastator's armor plating.

"Coming around to the right," he called out—then pulled his Devastator to the left.

The Raven jinked right as Nathan began the maneuver; the bastards were listening in to the Cajuns' frequency. "Nice try, pal."

He had begun the maneuver in a climbing left bank, and tightening the turn had shed even more speed. As the Ravens banked to regroup, Tug's Fury flashed into view and opened fire. The lead Raven slowed as smoke poured from a line of bullet holes in the engine cowling.

"Bull's-eye!" Tug crowed.

Nathan rolled the Devastator out of the climb and dived in on the second Raven. He fired a pair of rockets at his target.

The first rocket missed and exploded harmlessly in the swamp. The second caught the Raven just above the starboard wing. The explosion detonated a handful of the Raven's own rockets. The Raven tumbled into a sickening death spiral as the starboard wing sheared off.

Two down, Nathan thought. *Six to go.*

"Nice shootin', Nathan," Tug cheered.

"Thanks," Nathan replied. "Now, let's go find Bertrand."

"Don't worry, pirate," Bertrand's voice crackled from the radio. "I'll find you—once I settle accounts with your little buddy, Tug."

A trio of Ravens in a delta formation swooped after Tug's Fury, guns blazing.

"Okay, Cajuns," Nathan said, "kid gloves are off. Pick a target, and take it out."

The Ravens swarmed around Tug. Nathan grimaced; the kid's plane just didn't have the firepower to deal with three-on-one odds. The Fury had been designed as a zeppelin-based aircraft—it normally didn't even have landing gear, relying on a zeppelin docking hook for takeoffs and landings. Furies usually carried a single massive .70-caliber "Goliath" cannon, slung beneath the fuselage—more than enough to shred a Raven in short order.

Unfortunately, Tug had been forced to shed the Goliath and add landing gear, since the Cajuns didn't operate from a zeppelin. Tug's bird carried a pair of .40-caliber cannons and some flak rockets—pretty light arms given the hardware the other racers carried.

Nathan swooped in close to cover the kid's tail. He snapped off a quick shot at one of the trailing Ravens, rolled, fired again, and then dropped into a covering position. "Okay, Tug," he said, "let's get ready to—"

Without warning, the Devastator shuddered and a sharp metallic *clang* rattled his teeth. Something had just slammed into his fighter's fuselage.

He twisted in his seat and immediately saw the problem: a cylindrical piece of metal protruded from the port side of his Devastator. The end of the metal cylinder was offset by a quartet of fins—the tail of a rocket.

If it had been a high-explosive rocket, he would've already been dead . . . which meant that the weapon embedded in his fuselage was either a dud—or something more sinister. He felt a pang of dread and quickly dialed the frequency knob on the plane's radio.

A moment later, a droning, high-pitched tone beeped from the radio, a sound he recognized immediately.

It was a homing signal.

"Damn," he muttered. "A beeper rocket."

Since the early part of the decade, the "beeper-seeker" rocket had become a common enough weapon. Essentially, the system consisted of a pair of rockets: a "beeper," which embedded itself in a target and broadcast a short-term ultrasonic or radio signal; and a "seeker" rocket, which homed in on that signal. The beepers lasted only a short time—usually sixty seconds; but every seeker rocket fired within that time would home in on the target.

With a beeper in his hide, Deschaines' men would fire every seeker they carried and blow the Devastator right out of the sky.

Zachary looked around, desperate to find cover; the only chance he had was to find enough cover to block incoming seeker rockets. If he was lucky, he could last long enough for the beeper signal to cut out. If not . . .

He had a flash of inspiration. He quickly changed radio frequencies. The drone of the homing signal vanished in a squawk of static.

"Nathan! Nathan! Can you hear me? Are you okay?" Tug sounded like he was in a near-panic.

"I'm okay, Tug," he said. "Try to keep some of these creeps off my back. I'm going to pay Bertrand a visit."

He twisted the radio dial until the homing signal again filled the radio headset. With that, he sent the Devastator into a dizzying series of banks and rolls—right into the heart of the *Fauçons'* formation. Deschaines' men, startled by the reckless maneuver, scattered in all directions to avoid collision.

His eyes locked on to Bertrand's Raven as the Devastator inched closer . . . closer . . . closer . . .

The Devastator dropped into position, inches from the Raven's starboard wing. Before Bertrand could react, Nathan rolled the Devastator up onto its port wing and skimmed even closer to the Raven—suicidally close.

He hit the transmit button on the radio. "Tell your boys to blast away now, Bertrand," he whooped.

The planes were close enough that Nathan could see the look of surprise on Bertrand's face. He quickly regained his composure and tried to bank away from the Devastator—and was forced to stop. The Raven's wingspan was massive; if Bertrand tried to break off too quickly, the Raven's wing would collide with Nathan's smaller Devastator.

The Raven could drop altitude, however; Bertrand sent his

plane into a shallow dive. Nathan struggled to keep his plane in position as they fell lower and lower.

Nathan immediately spotted Bertrand's objective: the slowly spinning Ferris wheel . . . dead ahead.

The obstacle was too narrow for them to fly through together. Worse, it had started spinning. It would take a hell of a pilot to fly through the wheel—it would take a miracle for both of them to make it through.

If Nathan broke off, he'd be open to seeker rockets and cannon fire—he'd be dead in seconds. His only chance was to pull ahead of Bertrand's fighter and keep the Raven between his own plane and Bertrand's wingmates.

"All right, Bertrand," Nathan muttered to himself. "Let's see what you've got."

He firewalled the throttle, and the Devastator shot ahead. He ignored the tracers that burst from Bertrand's guns, and he lined up on the Ferris wheel. He took a deep breath, then hit a switch on the instrument panel.

A hissing noise from the engine turned into a high-pitched whine . . . and then a roar like thunder as Doc's nitro boost kicked in. Nathan was slammed back into the pilot's seat as the Devastator zoomed ahead at blinding speed.

A bead of sweat formed on Nathan's forehead as he hurtled at the wheel. If he'd made the slightest miscalculation, the Devastator would become his coffin. ·

The Devastator careered through the obstacle and shot out the other side, narrowly avoiding the steel support spokes inside the wheel. Nathan breathed a sigh of relief—then realized he had a new problem.

Doc's nitro boost fired in bursts—once the switch was thrown, the boost would continue until the pressure gauge dropped to zero. While the booster was in operation, the plane's handling turned sluggish. Anything other than gradual turns would tear the wings right off the plane.

Bertrand's Raven emerged on the far side of the Ferris wheel and opened fire. The Devastator—trailing fire from the booster exhaust—pulled away, but not fast enough.

Bullets chewed through the engine cowling. The needle on

the booster pressure gauge twitched and then dropped to zero. He was lucky the whole damn thing didn't explode.

The acceleration eased as the booster died away, and Nathan pulled into a loop—then he broke off. A seeker rocket arced right for him, locked on the beeper's homing signal. At the last second he dived, and the rocket skimmed past. The rocket began a lazy turn back toward the Devastator, relentless as a bloodhound.

Without warning, the homing signal died away—the incessant beeping on the radio replaced by static. He changed back to the primary frequency. Nathan swooped out of the seeker's path and breathed a sigh of relief.

"Tug, where's Bertrand?" he said. "I lost him."

"Cajun Two to Lead: I got him. He's all over Tug—on your three o'clock."

Nathan turned to the right, and a short distance away, he saw Bertrand's Raven open fire on Tug's Fury. The kid evaded the attack, and a pair of Cajuns covered him. Cannon fire forced Bertrand and his wingmen to back off.

"'Ey, *mon ami*," Louis' voice broke in, "I thought you were always careful."

"Well, maybe not *always*," Nathan admitted. "Is Henri there?"

"*Oui*."

Nathan's hand tightened on the stick, and he fought to keep the anger out of his voice. This race was serious, deadly business; the fact that Henri allowed his own son to compete meant that he either had one hell of an ace up his sleeve—or he just didn't care if he lost his own son.

"Put him on."

There was a burst of static. A moment later, Henri Deschaines' rasping voice broke through. "Well, Monsieur Zachary," he said, "a very exciting contest, wouldn't you say? I'm surprised you have time to talk to me—I would think you'd be more concerned with staying alive just now."

"Your concern is touching."

"What do you want?"

"I want to up the ante in our little wager," Nathan said.

"I've got another ten grand that says none of your men finish this race—regardless of who crosses the finish line first."

"And how do I know you've got another ten thousand francs?"

"Contact Don Giovanni DeCarlo in Chicago. He's holding the cash," Nathan said, "unless you'd rather concede now and save us a lot of trouble."

There was a brief pause. "I see," Henri said. "You've put some thought into this little contest of ours. I knew you were playing some angle."

"Enough patter. Are you going to take the bet, or not?"

"Why should I? I'm quite satisfied in the original conditions of our wager."

It was time for Nathan to play his trump card—a blow to Deschaines' vanity. "Because if you don't," he said, "regardless of what happens, you'll never know if you could beat me."

There was a static-drenched pause, then, "Very well, sir," Henri hissed. "You have a bet. An additional ten thousand francs."

11: Upping the Ante

Nathan flexed his hand and forced himself to relax his grip on the control stick. There was a brief respite as the racers struggled to regroup—a good dozen aircraft had been taken out of the race as lap two began.

The *Fauçons* stood off at a distance, playing it safe—uncharacteristic behavior for them. "Okay, Cajuns," he called out. "Looks like Henri is giving his pilots new orders. Let's hit 'em!"

The Cajuns formed up on Nathan, low to the ground. The Devastator swooped back and forth to avoid the stooped trees that rose from the swamp. Within seconds, the *Fauçons* were within range.

Nathan sent the plane into a climb and opened fire on the

tight formation of Ravens. The Cajuns followed hot on his heels, and rockets and tracer fire crisscrossed the sky.

He raked his guns across the trailing planes in the formation. Between the rain of cannon fire and the barrage of rockets, one of Deschaines' planes went down in flames.

The Cajuns accounted for a pair of Ravens, as well—but not without cost. "Cajun Two to Lead: I have to bail out! They shot my rudder to hell!"

"I read you. Climb as high as you can and get clear!" Zachary ordered. "Cajun Three, cover him."

There was a brief pause. "Three to Lead: If I climb too high, I'll be disqualified," the pilot cautioned. "You sure you want me out of the fight?"

Zachary's jaw was clenched. "Roger. Cover your wingman, and get to the ground."

"Aw, Zachary," a familiar voice cut in, "ain't that sweet. You're bringing a tear to my eye, it's so touching."

"Come a little closer, Benny," Nathan snarled, "and I'll show you tears, little man."

"First things first," Benny replied. A single Raven—undoubtedly Benny's—broke formation and dived for Tug's plane, guns chattering. Bullets punched into the Fury's fuselage, but Tug rolled his plane out of the way before he took too much fire.

"I could use a little help over here!" Tug shouted. "Somebody get this clown off me!"

Nathan risked a snap shot and sent a rocket streaking for Benny's Raven. No luck—the fighter banked out of the line of fire and rejoined the *Fauçons'* formation. The rocket exploded harmlessly in the distance.

"Tug, stick close to me," Nathan said. "Cajuns, take out the trailing Ravens, but leave Benny and Bertrand to me."

The Cajuns acknowledged and broke off. They slammed into the line of *Fauçons*.

It was a close fight. The Cajuns fought well, but Deschaines' men were good—too good. Neither side gave quarter, but Nathan could see that the Cajuns were taking too much fire. Smoke poured from several of the Cajuns' fighters. A number of the Ravens were in rough shape, too—but not enough.

Fortunately, most of the locals had figured out that getting between the Cajuns and the *Fauçons* was a bad idea. A dozen of them stayed low and skimmed through the obstacles.

The only way to shut down this fight was to take their leader out. In the confusion, the Cajuns would have enough time to press the attack. Nathan looped around and hunted for Bertrand.

The radio squawked for his attention. "Well, Mr. Zachary," Henri said, "you and your disreputable allies seem to be ac-quitting yourselves rather well. Would you be interested in in-creasing the stakes of our little wager, sir?"

"How much?"

"Two hundred fifty thousand francs says my men win this fight . . . and you personally will not make it through the race."

Nathan snapped the Devastator into a tight roll and fired a burst at Benny's plane. He cursed as the Raven danced out of his gun sights.

"That's a lot of cash. I may not be able to front it."

"I'll accept your collateral, Monsieur Zachary," Henri replied. "Your plane, for instance. Plus your zeppelin, the *Pandora*—and her crew, of course. By my calculations that's worth almost two hundred thousand francs. A high roller like yourself shouldn't have any trouble producing a mere fifty thousand."

Benny's Raven came around for another pass, and bullets pinged off the Devastator. Nathan triggered another burst and fired his last pair of rockets. They missed the Raven, but forced Benny to break off.

Nathan's mind raced. He was almost out of cash—and he had no time for subtlety. It took all his skills to concentrate on the dogfight in the sky and the deadly poker game on the ground. This was his chance to bury Deschaines, once and for all.

"Louis, you there?" he asked.

"*Oui,* Nathan," Thibodeaux replied. "What's it gonna be?"

"I need fifty thousand francs. I'm good for it."

"What?" Louis sputtered. "Are you out of your mind? It's bad enough I let you talk me into this mess. Now you wan' to borrow money from me?"

"There's no time for this, Louis. I have to keep my head in the fight, or I'm dead and so are your men. Fifty thousand— yes or no?"

There was a pause. For a moment, Nathan had the sinking feeling that Louis was going to turn him down.

"All right, damn you," Louis finally said. "But *if* you make it back to the ground in one piece, we're gon' have words, you and I."

"I'm afraid that's not good enough, Monsieur Zachary," Henri rasped. "Thibodeaux's word has no currency with me, and unless I see the fifty thousand in cash, I'm afraid I can't accept."

Damn.

"What'll it take, Deschaines?" Zachary growled. "It's not like I can run to the bank for a withdrawal."

"Aside from the *Pandora*, your plane, and the clothes on your back?" Henri chuckled. "Why, just Thibodeaux's marker—for the Rajin' Cajuns' liquor distillery and their planes. That would be acceptable collateral."

A torrent of French obscenities filled the airwaves. "*Non.* Impossible."

"Louis, there's no time for this. You *have* to trust me. It's my neck on the block, too."

"You better be right."

"I'm always right."

"Sure. Jus' like you're always careful." Louis sighed with resignation. "Done. Nathan, you'd better win. Otherwise, I'm gonna kill you."

"Take a number," Zachary muttered.

Nathan pointed his Devastator at the nearest *Fauçons* Raven and opened up the throttle. His fighter thundered through the sky and drew closer. There were fewer planes in the air now; many fighters had fallen prey to the rain of bullets that punctured the skies.

"Oh, just one other thing, Monsieur Zachary," Henri said. "Since there's some small danger of you and Thibodeaux attempting to skip out on your debts—following your inevitable loss, of course—I'm forced to call in a little insurance policy."

"Nathan, we've got a problem," Tug broke in. "One o'clock high!"

Zachary looked up and spotted Deschaines' "insurance policy." Dropping through the clouds was a zeppelin—armored and bristling with cannons and rocket tubes. Emblazoned on the zep's envelope was the insignia of the New Orleans Police.

The zep took up position at around two thousand feet. It hovered over the bleachers and turned its broadside guns toward the racecourse.

"Great," Nathan whispered. "Some insurance policy, Henri."

"What can I tell you?" Henri chortled. "The good mayor of our fair city saw fit to ensure that today's festivities would be safe."

Nathan snorted. "I'm sure he did . . . particularly when you threatened to make a certain set of photographs public if he didn't send in the troops."

"I'm sure I don't know what you mean," Henri replied. The false camaraderie in his voice was replaced by icy anger.

"You're so unoriginal, you're practically a vaudeville act," Nathan shot back, mocking Henri's tone, "but you've got ambition, I'll give you that. Slipping the chief a Mickey and photographing him in a compromising position isn't exactly the freshest scam. But pulling the same trick on the mayor? You've got moxie. No wonder the cops turn a blind eye to your operation."

"You seem to know a great deal about my business, Monsieur Zachary."

"I have friends in low places, Mr. Deschaines," Nathan said.

"I'll make sure to give them my regards . . . at your funeral." With that, the signal faded into static.

Nathan turned his full attention back to the dogfight. His comments to Henri had had the desired effect. In seconds, the remaining *Fauçons* dropped into a diamond formation and banked right for him.

12: Wild Card

"Cajun Four bailing out!"

Nathan watched helplessly as Bertrand's cannon fire chewed apart a Cajun Brigand. He was too far away from the scrap, and there was no way to get there in time. Doc's nitro boost had some kind of leak, thanks to Bertrand's guns— the gauge read a paltry 50 percent. He fired his cannons anyway.

Deschaines ignored the ineffectual fire and put a final burst through the Brigand's starboard wing.

The pirate managed to bail out in time—but he was dangerously low. Nathan cursed as white silk bloomed and then crumpled as, seconds later, the downed pilot splashed into the swamp.

Before Nathan could slot in behind Bertrand, another pair of Ravens swooped in and forced him to break off. Tug stuck close behind Nathan and covered his back, but the *Fauçons* superior teamwork was starting to take its toll.

There was only a handful of Cajun Brigands left—the rest had pulled out of the fight or been shot down. So far, Nathan hadn't received word of any fatalities, but the pilot who had just bailed out was guaranteed a long hospital stay. The fight was turning ugly.

"Nathan!" Tug shouted. "I've got Bertrand on my six!"

Without hesitation, Nathan snapped the Devastator into a loop. At the top of his arc, he flipped the plane over and pushed out into a dive. Sure enough, Bertrand and his wingman had latched on to Tug's tail.

He fired a burst, and Bertrand's wingman broke off to engage him. The radio crackled. "Let's see how funny you are now, comedian," Benny growled.

"The only joke here is you, clown," Nathan responded. "And here's the punch line." He triggered a second burst, but Benny was ready for the attack. The Raven banked and twisted, and evaded the stream of magnesium rounds that sizzled through the air.

Benny returned the favor and sent a hail of .60-caliber bullets slashing at the Devastator. A few punched through the starboard armor plating. Nathan pushed the stick forward and dived beneath the incoming fire. The two fighters circled one another, like wary, punch-drunk boxers near the end of a bare-knuckle bout.

Just ahead, he could see that Bertrand was still hot on Tug's tail. The kid was holding his own for now, but just barely.

Benny's Raven dived in for another pass—and Nathan saw his chance. He applied more power to the Devastator's engine and placed himself on a collision course for the oncoming Raven.

The Raven wobbled for a moment, then banked hard to the left—unprepared for Nathan's mad dash. Nathan grinned—he had a clear run at Bertrand.

Nathan hit the trigger and peppered Bertrand's Raven. Bertrand pulled up and spiraled away to the right; Tug dived to the left.

The Devastator was moving too fast—it sped past Tug's plane and almost collided with one of the local racers, low to the ground. Nathan hauled back on the stick with all his might and kicked the rudder hard to the left. He skimmed past the other plane, which careened out of the way and almost plowed into one of the taller trees.

Close. Too damn close.

Before Nathan could correct his course, bullets hammered the Devastator. Bertrand had taken advantage of Nathan's predicament and dropped right onto his tail.

Tug's Fury roared back into the battle. A pair of rockets streaked from the Fury and passed directly behind the

Devastator—for a split second, Nathan thought Tug was shooting at him.

The rockets exploded directly in front of Bertrand's Raven, starring the glass in the canopy.

"Nice shooting, kid," Nathan said. "You sure you can handle this clown?"

"No problem. You just keep Benny off my back," Tug replied.

"You got it."

Nathan kept an eye on Benny as Tug and Bertrand looped, rolled, and dived at one another. Every time Benny tried to move in and help his boss, Nathan swooped into the battle and chased him off with cannon fire—a stalemate.

Finally, Benny broke off and began to circle the course. Nathan turned his attention back to Tug's fight with Bertrand. He knew the kid had a score to settle, and that he'd be hopping mad if Nathan interfered. Nathan was stuck on the sidelines, as long as the kid didn't get into trouble.

With Bertrand and Benny held in check, the *Fauçons'* coordination faltered. Nathan grinned as the Cajuns' Brigands slammed the Ravens with rockets. Within moments, three more Ravens were out of the fight—but not before two more Cajun Brigands splashed into the swamp.

Nathan looked back and forth, and could just make out the tiny silhouettes of the other planes as they turned into the final lap. They were too far away to be an immediate threat.

The Devastator made another tight turn, and Nathan spied Tug's Fury. Tug cursed as Bertrand's Raven turned inside him. Tug frantically tried to correct his course, but Bertrand sent his plane into a perfect split-S. He locked on to the Fury's tail like a pit bull. Bullets knifed through the Fury's tail armor.

"Damn it," Nathan shouted, "break off! Break off!"

"No way," Tug replied. "I got the bastard right where I want him."

Suddenly, twin streaks of fire burst from the Fury's exhaust, and the battered plane shot forward like a rocket. The Fury pulled away from Bertrand's bird in seconds. "Thank you, Doc!" Tug cried.

The Raven wobbled for a moment and then turned into a clumsy bank; Bertrand had clearly been startled by Tug's sudden, unexpected burst of speed. Nathan saw his opportunity.

The Devastator dived like a hawk. Nathan fired his guns—not to hit the Raven, but to force Bertrand to turn back to the left.

The maneuver worked. As Bertrand struggled to shake Nathan off his tail, he turned ... right into the path of Tug's guns.

The Fury had looped back around and streaked for the Raven. There was a sustained burst of cannon fire—then smoke and fire, as Tug's shots shattered the Raven's engine.

The Raven's canopy popped open, and Bertrand bailed out. Tug sent the Fury into a victory roll.

"Nice shooting, kid," Nathan said.

"I hate to interrupt your victory celebration, *mon ami,*" Thibodeaux's nervous voice broke in, "but there's still one of Deschaines' men left in the race."

"I see him," Nathan growled.

Benny had pulled away as the racers entered the final lap. His Raven was well ahead, a speck in the distance.

The Devastator shot ahead as Nathan firewalled the throttle. He dropped low and shot through the makeshift merry-go-round, narrowly avoiding a fiery crash.

The Raven was bigger and slower, but Benny had a big lead. "*Mon ami,*" Thibodeaux warned, "you aren't gonna make it."

"The hell I'm not," Nathan snarled. He glanced at the nitro booster's pressure gauge—it read just shy of 60 percent. Bertrand's bullets had smashed up the main compressor—either that, or punctured the booster's feed line. If he hit the switch, there was a good chance that the whole plane would explode.

Tug's bird was too shot up to make it in time; plus, he'd just fired his own booster. It would be almost a minute before he could fire it again. There wasn't enough time.

"Okay, Louis," Nathan said, "hang on to your beret."

The racers had banked into the final lap. The course arced

back toward Nathan. He pushed the Devastator's engines as hard as they would go. The Devastator drew closer to the cluster of racers. They were now less than a mile from the finish line.

Nathan opened fire. The racers scattered and broke off as Nathan's fighter bore down on them. A handful decided they'd had enough and climbed above the flight ceiling.

"You missed him!" Tug yelled. "Benny got past you!"

Nathan pulled the Devastator into a loop and came around on Benny's tail. The finish line loomed just ahead.

"It would appear that you've lost, Monsieur Zachary." There was no mistaking the triumph in Henri's voice. "You're out of rockets, and you're out of time. . . . One of my men is going to finish the race. You lose, sir."

"Is that so?" Nathan replied. "You readin' this, Jack?"

"Loud and clear, boss."

"Ditch that piece of junk."

"With pleasure."

With that, Benny's Raven slowed and banked—away from the finish line. The Raven climbed above the flight ceiling, and the pilot bailed out.

Nathan chuckled as Louis' laughter crackled from the radio. "Hey, Louis, did I ever introduce you to Jack Mulligan . . . my wingman?"

"Not yet, *mon ami* . . . but I can' wait to meet 'im." Louis was delighted.

"Hey, Henri," Nathan added, "look on the bright side—now you'll always know you can't beat me."

". . . You'll pay for this, Zachary." The false *bonhomie* was gone. "If it's the last thing I do, I'll see you die."

The radio squawked; Deschaines had apparently switched off the radio—or changed frequency.

"'Eads up, Nathan," Louis cried. "Looks like Henri's a poor loser."

The police zeppelin began to move. It picked up speed and climbed. In moments, a squadron of police fighters dropped from the zep.

"Uh, Nathan?" Tug sounded nervous. "What's the plan?"

"Simple. I'll handle the cops. *You* cross the finish line. You've still got a race to win."

"What? Are you nuts? There's gotta be a dozen of 'em!"

"Don't argue, kid," Nathan said. "It's under control."

Tug's Fury pulled away as the police fighters drew closer. "Attention pirate fighter: surrender or be destroyed."

Nathan ignored them and circled around to put some distance between him and the approaching police zeppelin. The fighters drew closer . . .

Closer . . .

Nathan switched radio frequencies yet again. "All right," he said, "hit 'em."

Nathan heard the thunder of massive guns, despite the roar of his own engine. The police zeppelin reeled as a rain of cannon fire raked her side. Half of her port-side engine nacelles exploded like firecrackers. The airship listed and slowed.

A second zeppelin dropped from the cloud cover. She was shark white, with daggerlike, angular rudder fins. The Fortune Hunters insigne gleamed on her envelope. A single word—pandora—was stenciled in large block letters on the bridge gondola.

Pandora's broadside guns boomed a second time, and a barrage of cannon shells ripped through the police zeppelin's rudder. The crippled zeppelin began to drift in a wobbling, erratic spiral.

Nathan moved his Devastator closer to the formation of police planes. They had slowed their advance in the face of *Pandora*'s arrival. Their formation broke as the police zeppelin crumpled under the hail of cannon fire.

"Attention, constables," Nathan announced, "stand down. It's over."

"Like hell it is!" Henri howled. "There's only two of them, damn it! Kill them! Kill them!"

"There's not exactly two of us, Henri," Nathan chuckled. "Colonel? They're all yours."

At Nathan's words, several of the "local racers"—who had scattered as Nathan tangled with Benny—fell into a tight diamond formation. They screamed back into the race area and fired a series of warning bursts.

"Attention, New Orleans Police," a woman's voice announced. "This is Colonel Andrea Hawks of the Flaming Witch Company. Stand down, by order of the prime minister."

The police planes fell back in disarray. Finally, the lead police fighter dropped his landing gear. "Saint Leader to Colonel Hawks: We surrender."

Nathan breathed a deep sigh of relief. He watched in satisfaction as the police fell back to the landing field. The crippled zeppelin's envelope began to deflate as her captain struggled to put her down safely.

"That's one bag of hot air down," Nathan muttered, "and one to go."

Epilogue: Loose Ends, Last Call

Nathan climbed down from the cockpit and stripped off his flight goggles. He wiped his sweaty forehead with a grimy hand and looked around. The race area was crawling with armed men, most of them from the Foreign Legion garrison in New Orleans. Cops arrested cops and led them away in handcuffs. Race spectators and bookies were being lined up and herded into blimps—New Orleans' answer to the paddy-wagon.

Thibodeaux stood amid a cordon of men in uniforms, right in front of Deschaines' vault. There was an even dozen of them, all armed—a mix of Foreign Legion officers and local cops who hadn't been on Deschaines' payroll. Nathan spotted both the chief of police and mayor of New Orleans among the soldiers and police.

Henri and Bertrand Deschaines stood in the center of the knot of uniformed men. Bertrand had a bandage on his arm and a bruise above his right eye. Both of them looked furious.

One of the Legionnaires stepped forward. "Henri and Bertrand Deschaines, I'm placing you under arrest on the charges of racketeering, illegal gambling, and the blackmail of government officials."

"On what authority?" Henri spat. "This is local jurisdiction—the garrison has no business interfering here."

"Actually," Nathan spoke up, "he has all the authority he needs—directly from Prime Minster DuPre."

The Legionnaire officer gestured at the policemen—who slapped cuffs on the Deschaines.

The mayor scowled at the prisoners. "It's about time."

Henri glared at the mayor. "I'll ruin you," he vowed. "I promise you, your career is over."

The mayor paled at the threat. Zachary stepped forward and handed the mayor of New Orleans a brown envelope. "Mr. Mayor? This might help."

The portly official turned a dangerous shade of red when he viewed the contents of the envelope—a small, neat bundle of photographs. "The negatives are inside the envelope, as well, Mr. Mayor," Nathan added. "You needn't worry about them falling into the wrong hands."

Henri cursed as the policemen led him and his son to a waiting squad car. Nathan held open the door for him.

The mayor shook Zachary's hand. The bundle of photos was clutched tightly in his other hand. "How—how did you get these?"

Nathan grinned and said, "I had some help." He gestured at a line of stretchers nearby.

A dozen or so pilots—most of them Deschaines' mercenaries—received care for their wounds. A stocky, red-haired man sat on the nearest stretcher, propped up on his elbows as he flirted with one of the nurses.

Louis and Nathan walked over to the stretchers. "Get up, you old goldbrick," Nathan said. "Louis, this is my wingman— Jack Mulligan. You probably know him better as Benny, the cheap hood."

Jack gave Louis a jaunty wave. "Sorry for not getting up."

Nathan turned serious. "How bad are you hurt?"

Jack shrugged. "Not too bad. Busted my leg—so I'm gonna be laid up for a while. I guess we're even for that smack on the head I gave you."

"Kind of overdid it, didn't you?" Nathan groused. The knot on the back of his head had receded—but it still throbbed.

Jack chuckled. "I'm not sure which was worse—bustin' my leg, or wearing that damned 'bum' disguise. I'm gonna be itching for months."

"It had to be done, old buddy—your performance had to be convincing," Nathan said with an apologetic smile. "Deschaines can smell a con a mile away, so you had to look like the real thing."

Jack smirked. "With that disguise, I'm sure he could smell *me* a mile away."

Louis nodded appreciatively. "So, you sent Jack in undercover to 'ire on wit' Deschaines."

"Right." Nathan nodded. "So, when I had dinner at Henri's place, I made sure I got 'Benny' ticked off—and thrown out of the room. While I had my . . . chat with Henri, Jack rifled his safe and got back the photos and the negatives."

"So, what about that clout on the 'ead in front of The Flyin' 'orses?"

"Easy," Nathan explained. "Benny was still new to Henri's organization—they didn't quite trust him. Knocking me out cold made it easier for Deschaines to believe he was on the level—then, he just slipped me the photos while I was on the ground."

"And what about my planes—and my pilots?"

"Look around, Louis." Nathan couldn't resist a smug smile. "Aside from Tug, do you *see* any of your men?"

Thibodeaux looked over the men on stretchers—none of the Cajuns were there. His frown deepened. "So, where are my men?"

"Aboard the *Pandora*, manning the guns."

"What?" Louis exploded. "Then who was flyin' my planes?"

"*They* were." Nathan pointed to the landing field where several people clustered around one of the damaged Brigands.

The group—dressed in flight jackets—spotted Nathan pointing and walked over to join them. There were five of them, laughing and joking amongst themselves as they crossed the field.

"Louis," Nathan said. "Meet the Fortune Hunters." He pointed at the five of them in turn.

"This is Eddie Conroy—we call him Sparks. He usually mans the radio, but we got him up in the air for a change."

"Sir." Conroy nodded and shook Louis' hand. "A pleasure."

Nathan gestured at a lithe, curvy woman with long, curly honey-blond hair. A pearl-handled Colt revolver rode her hip. "This is 'Tex' Ryder."

"Hey, sugar," she said with a grin. "Sorry f'r messin' up y'r birds."

Nathan moved down the line to a tall black man. He was thickly muscled and stood nearly six feet tall, though his fearsome appearance was softened by the humor and warmth in his smile. "This is John Washington—we call him 'Big John.' "

"Can't imagine why," Louis muttered.

A sandy-haired man in his early twenties was next in line. He stepped forward and stuck out his hand. "Bob Deere, Mr. Thibodeaux. You can call me 'Buck.' Mos' everyone does."

Last in line was a petite young woman, just out of her teens. "How ya' doin'?" she chirped.

"This is the newest Fortune Hunter," Nathan explained. "Betty Charles—aka 'Brooklyn.' "

Louis' frown deepened. "So, you were playin' me, too, *mon ami*," he said. "You switched my pilots for yours. Why?"

"I didn't want your men to get hurt—this was my scam, after all." He paused, a sheepish look on his face. "It's also why I had Doc rig your plane—I needed you angry enough to back me when Henri raised the stakes."

Louis' expression darkened. "Go on."

"A few of your men filled out the rest of the flight, but I made sure that my guys took the lumps." He shrugged. "At least on the ground, no one was shooting at you."

This did not mollify the Cajun pirate. "So why not confide

in me? You think I couldn't pull off *le grand* con, eh? Monsieur Famous 'as to come down 'ere and show the locals 'ow to conduct their business?"

"Look on the bright side, Louis," Nathan said. "Not only do you get a share of the spoils—I'll fix your planes up out of my share. Fair enough?"

Nathan stuck his hand out. Louis hesitated, then shook. "I still think I should deck you."

Zachary laughed. "Yeah, you probably should."

They were interrupted by the growl of plane engines. "Looks like the Witches are leavin'," Jack said.

A lean woman crossed the field and waved to Nathan. She was attractive, if severe, and she walked with a compact, precise military bearing. She wore her hair short, and her temples were starting to show signs of gray.

"Colonel Hawks," Nathan said. "A pleasure to see you again."

Col. Andrea Hawks' stern expression broke into a sly grin. "Hey, Zachary. This has been fun. . . . Let's do it again sometime, okay?"

She gave Thibodeaux a friendly nod. "Monsieur Thibodeaux." She kissed the Cajun on both cheeks in the Continental style, which he didn't seem to mind at all.

"*Merci*, Colonel. The pleasure is indeed mine." He gave Nathan a nudge. "Although it would per'aps 'ave been better if I 'ad been included in the plan."

Hawks chuckled. "Don't blame Nathan for that! He was just acting on orders from Prime Minister DuPre."

"You're kiddin'." Louis rounded on Nathan. "You mean you've been workin' for the prime minister?"

Nathan nodded. "But that's not the best part, Louis. *You've* been working for the prime minister."

"But—but—'e's been tryin' to shut down the Cajuns for months." Louis was flabbergasted. "I mean, 'e put a *price on my 'ead*, Nathan."

"That's right," Nathan replied, "especially since you boosted that payroll shipment out of Baton Rouge. He's not real happy with you about that." Zachary grinned and punched the Cajun pirate lightly in the arm. "Deschaines was going to use the money he won here to finance his bid to win the next election."

"So, now the great Nathan Zachary's turned into a privateer?"

"For a while. DuPre's an old friend—we fought together in France during the Big One." He smiled. "Of course, he's not stupid—my letter of *marque* expires in one month. Guess he doesn't want us to wear out our welcome."

Colonel Hawks waved good-bye. "I'll leave you boys to sort this out between you. We're off." The two men watched as she ran to her plane and clambered up into the cockpit. With a final salute, she maneuvered her plane down the runway and led the squadron to a flawless takeoff.

"What do you say we finish this conversation somewhere more pleasant?" Zachary started to walk toward his Devastator.

At The Flyin' Horses, the celebration was in full swing. Nathan leaned back in his chair and surveyed the room full of pilots, friends, and even the garrison commander of the Legionnaires. Tug and Emmeline came over to his table; the kid was grinning from ear to ear, and the young girl was radiant.

"We can't thank you enough, Monsieur Zachary, for all of your help." Emmeline, who was snuggled close to Tug, reached her slim hand to Zachary, who took it between his and gave it a gentle squeeze.

"Don't thank me, Miss Emmy, thank your fiancé—he was the one who really stood up to Deschaines."

The young Texan pilot blushed as Emmeline turned his face to hers and gave him a passionate kiss. Nathan grinned; beneath her fragile southern belle exterior, Emmeline had a lot of fire . . . but Nathan had a feeling that Tug would find that out soon enough.

"What's your plan—after the wedding, that is?"

Emmy gave Nathan a conspiratorial smile. "Well, it appears that I will soon own quite a bit of property—including the house."

"An' the hangar an' the airstrip," Tug added. "I'm thinkin'

about maybe startin' a little flight school here, an' maybe a small private line."

"Sounds good, Tug. I'm happy to help you out where I can." Zachary had a moment of nostalgia as he thought about himself at that age. The kid had a lot going for him.

"Thanks, Mr. Zachary—I mean, Nathan. And listen, you an' the Fortune Hunters, you've always got a place to park when you're in this neck of the woods, okay?"

Zachary saluted the couple with a raised glass. "Thanks, kid."

The happy couple turned as one of the Cajuns called out Tug's name and waved a bottle at him. They rejoined the festivities as Nathan relaxed.

"So, *mon ami*. Boy gets girl, the bad guys go to jail, and 'ere we are." Thibodeaux plunked himself down across the table from Zachary. "So, what did *you* get?"

"Bruises, mostly."

Louis cocked an eyebrow and waited for Nathan to continue. Zachary sighed and admitted, "Under the letter of *marque*, I'm entitled to a percentage of Deschaines' seized assets . . . plus any and all gambling winnings. That's why Tug had to cross the finish line first. After fixing up our planes, we scored a little over a hundred grand."

He paused and took another sip of champagne. "Plus, I got to derail Deschaines' little election scheme."

"What do you care about that? You're not a politician."

"No . . . but I have to admit, Henri got my goat." He finished his champagne and set the glass down on the table. "At heart, he was just a penny-ante grifter with delusions of grandeur . . . a hustling rube. Someone had to take him down a peg. He gives honest con men like us a bad name."

"And of course, men like us mus' always keep busy, *non*? Otherwise, we lose our edge."

"Funny you should mention that." Nathan looked around the room briefly and then leaned toward Thibodeaux. "I hear there's a zeppelin casino that operates over the Gulf of Mexico that's just ripe for the taking."

Louis frowned. "*Non!* Impossible. The Cajuns 'ave been casin' the zep for months. If it's anybody's score, it's mine."

Nathan met Louis' gaze, his own face impassive. Though the pirates respected each other, Nathan knew full well that there was no honor among thieves. Finally, he said, "I can see there's only one way to solve this."

He reached into his jacket. Louis watched him like a hawk and dropped his hand to the butt of his gun. "Careful, *mon ami*," he warned.

Nathan slowly removed a small cardboard package from his coat. He opened it and removed its contents. "Like I said, Louis," he said, "there's really only one way to solve this:

"Pick a card."

Appendix: Crimson Skies Over North America
The Path to the "Modern Aero-Age"

There was no single warning sign that pointed to the breakup of the United States of America. The American Civil War in 1860 may have played a part, say some, while others blame the so-called Founding Fathers, who failed to predict the collapse of the nation. Regardless of the root cause, the result is the same: The United States of America, that great experiment in Democracy, crumbled in the late 1920s.

1920

The first signs of the coming collapse became apparent in 1920, in the aftermath of the postwar influenza epidemic. Many isolationist movements—whose supporters were already convinced of America's involvement in Europe's troubles—were only strengthened after so many citizens fell to a disease brought back by returning servicemen.

President Wilson's push to form the League of Nations drew increasing fire from U.S. citizens, allowing Warren G. Harding's "New Independence from Europe" campaign to gain momentum. Harding called for greater separation from the world in general, and the Regionalist party adopted it as part of their platform. Many Regionalists who won office in 1920 used their new power to push forward their own programs—most notably, Prohibition (which failed ratification as a Constitutional amendment that year).

1923

Prohibition consumed the political scene for the next three years, splitting its supporters and detractors across regional lines. Its political power undercut by the Regionalists,

Washington's indecisiveness forced politicians to support efforts to sign Prohibition into law, or to reject it, for their own states.

The death of President Harding in 1923 handed the Presidency to Calvin Coolidge, who refused to get behind the wavering Federal Prohibition Bill. Without Presidential support, the bill quickly died in committee.

The Prohibition issue that had polarized the country became a battle between regions that supported it, and those that did not. Checkpoints appeared on state borders as authorities tried to restrict the flow of alcohol into "dry" regions. Many states also used these checkpoints to levy unofficial—and highly illegal—tariffs.

1924

The election campaigns of 1924 illustrated the growing shift in power from Washington to the statehouses. States demanded more authority, and state governments seized greater power for themselves. Despite Federal efforts to reverse the tide, the states continued to appropriate more power. The result—stronger states and weak central government—is exemplified by the 1924 Bluefield Incident.

Kentucky and West Virginia began armed conflict with Virginia and North Carolina for control of the Appalachians (the source of a large percentage of illegal alcohol that was smuggled north). The Virginia National Guard captured a large Kentucky convoy outside the town of Bluefield, only to discover that their prize was a Kentucky guard unit running alcohol out of the Appalachians toward the West Virginia border. Though jurisdiction clearly belonged to Kentucky, the men were tried in Virginia on vague charges and jailed. Virginia refused Kentucky's request to transfer the men back to their home state, and later rejected a similar "suggestion" from Washington, D.C. Only under the threat of U.S. Army intervention did Virginia finally release the prisoners to Federal authorities, almost two years after their capture.

1927

Except for the Bluefield Incident (and a few other isolated flashpoints in the United States and Mexico), the period from 1924 to 1927 was among the best the United States had known. The elections were over, the Prohibition issue was largely settled—at least within individual states—and the country had a brief respite from the growing political unrest. Unemployment dropped dramatically as states employed their own people to maintain growing internal infrastructures (even as the national infrastructure began to show signs of strain). Per capita income increased, and more people began investing in the stock market—foolishly, in most cases.

The Federal government might have reclaimed its authority then, but chose to wait for the next major election year to increase its power base and avoid reawakening Regionalist opposition. Washington waited too long.

In 1927, a new and deadly strain of the influenza that ravaged the country in 1918 appeared, delivering a crippling blow to national morale. States—and even many cities—closed their borders and converted their liquor checkpoints into quarantine-enforcement sites. Necessary border crossings were made under armed supervision with strict controls. Smugglers and raiders began adopting the airplane as their primary method of border-jumping, avoiding the limitations of ground-based transport.

1928

The election of 1928 suffered from poor voter turnout, as most people avoided large groups (for fear of contracting influenza). Capitalizing on this, the Regionalists launched various "Strong State" platforms, effectively curtailing the Federal government's remaining power. Governors negotiated with their neighbors to establish interstate alliances, formalizing the segregated regions that had grown out of the preceding decade's isolationist policies. In many cases, these new alliances merely reinforced divisions that had existed from the United States' founding days.

In early 1929, Utah enacted the Smith Law, which made the Church of Jesus Christ of Latter Day Saints the state's official religion, with state government support. With the Federal government's impotence and Utah's isolation, cries to heed the traditional "separation of Church and State" were largely ignored. Fearing similar measures, strongly anti-Mormon states such as Pennsylvania and Massachusetts began to discriminate against the Mormons, driving many toward Utah.

In October of 1929, the stock market crash sounded the death knell for the United States. Regionalism had decimated the national economy and Washington, D.C.'s, call for financial assistance from state governments was roundly rejected. President Hoover called out the military to keep D.C. from slipping into lawlessness, further damaging the reputation of the central government.

1930

On January 1, 1930, Texas seceded from the United States, with California, the Carolinas, Utah, and New York following suit almost immediately afterward. Each formed a new nation, much as the Confederacy had done in the 1800s. Unable to mount the political and military campaign necessary to hold the United States together, Washington was now powerless.

This new period of extreme Regionalism created turmoil on a grand scale. Quebec broke away from Canada, as well. Mexico moved against Texas, and a minor shooting war erupted. In the ten months following Texas' secession, California, the Carolinas, Utah, and New York withdrew from the Union, forming independent nation-states.

North America's love of airplanes—once rooted in the exotic, adventurous mystique surrounding them—became deeply ingrained, as commerce between the new North American independent nations ground to a halt. Various brushfire wars demolished the intercontinental railway system at national borders, and the few large highway systems built or under construction quickly fell into disrepair or were sabotaged. The automobile, once thought destined to become the national shipping vehicle, gave way to gyrotaxis, aerobuses, and large cargo zeppelins that commanded the skylines and made trade possible between friendly nations.

The first "air pirates" began capturing the public eye during this period of chaos. Generally small, disorganized bands of thrill-seekers and publicity hounds, these pirates began crime sprees that would inspire others to follow in their footsteps in later years.

1931

As the Federal government in Washington, D.C., crumbled, a large segment of the nation's military began to desert. The soldiers' pay was slow in coming, and many were starving. Many returned to their home states, while others began selling their skills as mercenaries or bandits. A few thousand troops remained loyal, relocating to Washington, D.C., to defend the capital.

The political geography continued shifting throughout the year: The short-lived Outer Banks nation of Virginia and the Carolinas quickly folded itself into the rest of the Southern states, giving rise to the new Confederation of Dixie throughout the South. Samuel Morrow formed the People's Collective in the Midwest (abrogating all loans and mortgages among its citizens, a move that angered outside financial interests but kept the new nation from drowning in the Great Depression).

The formation of the People's Republic also led to one of the last major engagements of the Federalist armed forces; on Presidential orders, the Army moved to retake the People's Collective, but was roundly defeated.

Like dominos falling, various new nation-states began to form quickly; the Industrial States of America (formed around the industrial centers of the Great Lakes); Appalachia formed in the South; the Maritime Provinces and Atlantic Coalition declared independence in the Northeast.

The first serious pirate threat manifested in mid-1931. Jonathan "Genghis" Kahn—a former businessman from Chicago—formed the infamous Red Skull Legion. The Skulls moved into Utah (posing as People's Collective militia) and stole a military zeppelin, nearly starting a Utah-Collective war in the process. The age of the air pirate had begun.

1932

In early 1932, the Native American Navajo and Lakota tribes took up arms and seized a large portion of territory in the American West. With little Federal opposition, the Natives managed to secure a fairly broad section of territory before closing their borders to outsiders. Particularly scornful of bootleggers, the Navajo and Lakota—never the greatest of allies—still band together to fight off any incursion by pirates, outsider militia forces, or anything else deemed a threat to the tribes.

Free Colorado, in contrast, formed for entirely different reasons; today, it is becoming a haven for pirates, bootleggers, and the other, more anarchistic elements. In light of the lawless freehold's formation, President Coolidge ordered troops to seize the lands near Washington, D.C., (including parts of Maryland and Delaware) and declared a "state of emergency;" the nation of Columbia was born.

Louisiana seceded from Dixie soon afterward, requesting support from France for its independence. Ill-prepared to go it alone, the Midwestern states sank deep into the Depression and then resurrected themselves as a Christian Communist nation, the People's Collective. The relatively strong Lakota and Navajo Native American tribes founded their own nations as well, carving territory out of the nearly defunct Dakotas and the barren deserts and plateau country of the American southwest.

Even worse, as national borders continued to form, conflict became inevitable. The first serious conflict occurred near the end of 1932, as I.S.A. forces clashed with People's Collective militia. The source of the conflict is hazy; some claim it is a natural battle between capitalists and socialists, while others believe that the I.S.A. thought that their technological superiority would allow them to capture the territory—and therefore the natural resources—of the Collective. Whatever the case, through the rest of 1932 and into 1933, the conflict continued.

1933

The political destabilization and shifting of borders continued throughout 1933; small brushfire conflicts between ground and air militias forged new national boundaries, fueled by the continuing conflict between the I.S.A. and People's Collective. In light of the hostilities that seemed to be on the verge of blowing up into full-scale war, the Outer Banks nation (formerly the Carolinas and Virginia) formed an alliance with Dixie, becoming a Protectorate of the Confederacy, and fueling conflict between Appalachia, Dixie, and the Outer Banks.

1934-1935

The low-intensity border skirmishes between these new nations continued to flare up, and amidst the chaos, the bootleggers and pirates thrived. Scores of new militias—most determined to defend their hometown or state—formed to battle increasingly colorful and flamboyant raiders. The Redmann Gang, the Red Skull Legion, the Black Swans, and hosts of other pirate groups continued to raid across national boundaries (sparking additional conflicts as overzealous militia pilots strayed across borders into unfriendly territory in pursuit of the raiders).

1936

The borders and politics of the North American nation-states solidified in 1936. Combined Navajo and Utah forces allied long enough to fight off incursions by pirates based in Free Colorado; the Broadway Bombers (the premier Empire State militia) decimated the Hell's Henchmen pirate gang in the Alleghenies; I.S.A. and the Peoples' Collective conflict flared up yet again, though this time the Collective fared far better than in previous engagements, retaking small parcels of their territory.

1937

Sky pirates have prompted the rise of air militias to protect the shipping lanes. The pirates maintained an edge, however, and their early successes gave way to today's large and numerous pirate groups. Piracy got another boost when militias began raiding rival shipping, often receiving bonuses from their employers that reflected the value of the cargo taken or destroyed. As pirate and militia raids cut deeper into national economies, the various governments began subsidizing air wings.

Piracy actually lessened in the face of this organized response, though only briefly; the pirates adapted to the changing times by forming larger, better-armed gangs. From there, it was only a matter of time before nations began to subsidize pirates as well, handing out letters of marque in order to direct pirate activities away from their own zeppelin fleets and toward those of their enemies.

Today, North America is a hotbed of conflict: Rival militias prey on each other at will, striking in defense of their nations' interests; pirates and privateers battle the militias for control of the skies, and are too often victorious. The skies above North America are the new frontier, where a single individual with skill and nerve can make the difference between victory and defeat.

—Professor Warren Gilmont, Harvard University (1938)

Check out this official prequel to the
explosive Xbox™ game!

BRUTE FORCE™
Betrayals

by Dean Wesley Smith

At the dawn of the 24th century, the
Confederation of Allied Worlds maintains an
uneasy peace among the many races and
worlds of its fifty star systems. When trouble
erupts, the Confed's most effective weapons—
swift, savage, and totally secret—are small
teams of elite combat operatives who employ
brute force to eliminate potential threats.
Teams of deadly fighters like Tex,
Flint and Hawk.

They are the rare Operatives who have
survived countless covert operations in lethal
hellholes across Confed space. But when mysterious alien artifacts begin to turn up during
routine missions, they realize that the enemy
they fight may be more sinister, and closer to
home, than they imagined. . . .

This novel is based on a
Mature rated video game.

Published by Del Rey Books.
Available wherever books are sold.